THE QUIGLEY ALCHEMY

A DANNY QUIGLEY ACTION NOVEL

To Caroline
with best wishes
Russ.

E.J. RUSS MCDEVITT

The Quigley Alchemy:
A Danny Quigley Action Novel

ISBN-13: 978-0-9734902-2-0

DEDICATION

I WOULD LIKE TO DEDICATE THIS BOOK
TO NEDA WHO SHED HER BLOOD, AND
DIED FOR FREEDOM, ON THE ROCK-
STREWN STREETS OF TEHRAN. ALSO TO
MALALA, THE 15 YEAR OLD PAKISTANI
GIRL WHO WAS SHOT IN THE HEAD BY
THE TALIBAN FOR SPEAKING OUT ON
THE IMPORTANCE OF EDUCATION FOR
GIRLS.

THE HISTORY OF THE
SPECIAL FORCES

The British Special Air Service (SAS), has a history that goes back to long range reconnaissance, against Rommel's African Corps in the Second World War, and was founded by Major David Stirling. Since then it has become recognized as one of the world's best trained, and most professional Special Forces units, in all aspects of unconventional warfare.

The U.S. Delta Force was originally based upon the training tactics and methodology of the SAS. Officially set up in 1952, the history of the U.S. Special Forces goes back to the Second World War, to the O.S.S. (Office of Strategic Services), and the joint American/Canadian 1st Special Service Group, called The Devils Brigade. The O.S.S. was also the first American Intelligence Agency, and moved on with a number of its members to create the modern Central Intelligence Agency. Also created around the same time, were Navy's Sea-Air-Land teams (SEALS), and the Air Force's Air Commando units.

Strangely, the Special Forces were not very popular with the Services they were attached to – the Army, Navy, and Air Force, and were virtually at the bottom of the food chain in terms of the funding of equipment and training. In any operation, they had to beg, borrow or steal aircraft, vehicles and equipment to complete any task given to them. They were equally starved of the type of roles they could have fulfilled as Special Forces. Fortunately, President J.F. Kennedy took a great interest in the further development and support of Special Forces. That was because the C.I.A. had messed up at the Bay of Pigs in Cuba, and he was looking at other alternatives. He approved and dramatically increased the size of Special Forces, in all services. With the onset of Vietnam, they played a huge role in covert actions in that war.

A massively important event happened in 1987, in the U.S. Congress: the creation of a unified Command for Special Forces called S.O.C.O.M., based at McDill Air Force Base in Florida. That was to control all the special operational forces, currently under the three Services, Army, Navy and Air Force. It meant that Special Forces then had their own funding and unified command structure, in effect creating a 5th Service after the U.S. Marine Corps., which in itself was exempted from S.O.C.O.M. and kept control of its own Force Reconnaissance teams (Force Recon.). The reason for this was because the Marine Corps had already invested heavily in its own group in terms of funding, training, and equipment.

Massive investment and representation at the highest level then meant that Special Forces could truly start to train specialists for their teams. The training became tougher, the selection process more protracted, and the skills-set more diverse. The men tried to shake off their Rambo image, and strived to become known as "The Quiet Professionals". They worked on their language and problem-solving skills, and learned all they could about the cultures of the specific countries they were assigned to. As they formed into highly cohesive teams, they learned a whole host of complementary skills: defense and medical training in post-war situations; de-mining; evacuation of Embassies in trouble spots; the training of special police squads and body guards; engineering skills, and the capture of war criminals as had been done in Bosnia, Croatia and Kossovo. A lot of their training was carried out at Fort Bragg in North Carolina, with specialist training being run at other locations.

General Schwarzkopf in Desert Shield in 1990, resisted having Special Forces involved, but by the time Desert Storm had broken out in January 1991, they were playing major roles in his war plan. At the end of the war he gave credit to the various Special Forces units that had played crucial roles in the action. Their actions during the Iraq and Afghanistan wars are still being written.

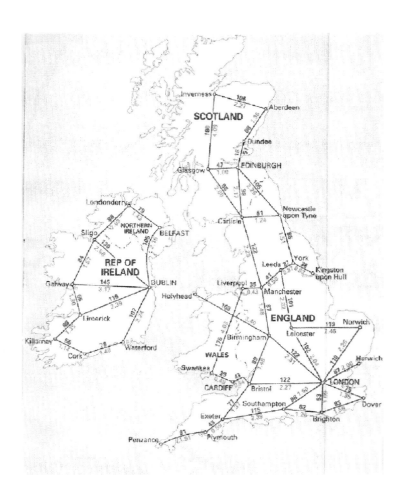

CHAPTER 1

Kandahar, Afghanistan

The armed Drone aircraft was like a hunting dog that had just sniffed its quarry. It banked sharply as it locked onto the lasered target below. Half a world away in the U.S. the hand of a human operator fired off the missiles.

Down on the ground Danny Quigley grunted in satisfaction as the target he had been tracking, a small group of Taliban planting IED's were vaporized in a massive explosion. Even a quarter of a mile away lying flat out on a hilltop ledge, he felt the blast in the air two seconds later. Danny eased his lean six foot frame off the ground to stretch the kinks out of his back and wiped off the sweat that had matted his dark hair on his forehead. Careful to keep under cover he lifted his binoculars and scanned the area where the explosion had taken place.

Nothing moved.

Focusing on the hard cratered territory below he wondered for the umpteenth time, like the rest of the team, the wisdom of him being there at all. They had been told that their purpose was to bring freedom and democracy to the Afghans. Too bad, he thought, that the Afghan people didn't appear to appreciate the efforts on their behalf!

His short wiry regiment mate, Scotty McGregor, sitting across from him, froze as his radio spurted out a brief message.

"Eagle six, this is Hawk. We're aborting your mission. Chopper on route, over."

"Roger that. You have an ETA yet, over?"

Scotty listened carefully and after a moment he lifted his head, a grin creasing his face.

"They're pulling us out. Chopper'll be here in figures ten," he shouted.

Danny's lean, tanned face snapped sideways, his interest aroused. He crouched down and moved cat-like across to him.

"Any idea why the mission is being called off?" he asked.

Scotty shrugged.

"No idea why the mission is being aborted but I like it."

Hunkered down in the bleak stony and dusty hills of Afghanistan, Danny and his mate Scotty McGregor were part of a 16 man SAS team which had been operating as scouting patrols in advance of regular British military excursions into hostile Taliban country. In the main, their job was reconnaissance and intelligence gathering with the specific task of locating IEDs which were wreaking such havoc on coalition patrols.

Their role required them to stay out of sight as long as possible so as to prolong their mission. When they had earlier witnessed a small group of Taliban planting IED's they had relayed the details back to base with grid and GPS references. Armed drones already patrolling the skies, materialized within twenty minutes, guided in by Danny's lasering system. The subsequent destruction of the enemy provided some satisfaction to the troopers although they would have preferred a more direct combat involvement. For the past few days the real enemy had been the searing heat of the merciless sun, they lay with minimum movement on the hard unyielding ridge. News of a return to base was one that made them both groan with relief.

Shortly after, a helicopter dropped down, and as soon as they jumped in, it rapidly took off again. The rest of the team were already on board and shared relieved grins as they all headed back to their unit. The chopper had a cooler full of soft drinks and were passed around to the parched troopers.

Within forty five minutes they were back at the base where the immediate priority was a shower and a slap-up meal in the canteen. Afterwards, as Danny was cleaning up his kit, Scotty dashed up in a state of high excitement.

"Hey Danny, I heard we're going to operate with a Delta team. Can you believe it?"

Danny looked up, his intense blue eyes sharing some of his mate's excitement.

"Yeah, Delta know their stuff. I'd be pleased to work with them anytime."

Scotty appraised the focused concentration on his team-mate's tanned face as he snapped an empty magazine into the M16 rifle.

"They have a reputation all right, but I doubt they could match you out there Danny. Man, you're as cold as ice when it starts to come down. That's why I like working alongside you."

Danny stopped what he was doing, suddenly embarrassed by the remark.

"Hey, what brought this on Scotty?"

He looked away avoiding his glance.

"I dunno Danny. I've just had a funny feeling since we got that call back there in the hills. Like someone walked on my grave."

Danny thumped his shoulder, jumping to his feet.

"God, I thought us Irish were weird but you Scots take the biscuit. Come on lets go check out this rumor about those Delta guys."

Scotty had always been an admirer of the US Special Forces and had inundated Danny and anyone who cared to listen with their history and culture. He had collected everything he could on their background and methods of operation.

Shortly afterwards they found themselves in a large briefing room with an Operation Detachment Alpha (O.D.A.), from the US Forces, more popularly known in the media as an 'A' team. As Scotty went round the room excitedly introducing himself to the US Delta team members, the ice seemed to break and other members of the SAS team crossed over and began chatting. There was a natural brotherhood among Special Forces, especially between their two groups as the Delta teams had originally been formed along the organizational structures and training of the SAS.

Danny stood up as a crew-cut, slim Delta team member came over grinning and stuck his hand out.

"Rory Hanlon," he said. "When we heard we might be doing an operation with the 'Sass' we couldn't wait. You guys are top of the pole as far as Delta teams are concerned."

Danny's taut face relaxed in a grin as he returned the strong grip, looking down at a rugged friendly features of the shorter American.

"Danny Quigley. Yeah, we kinda hold you guys in some awe too, the stories we hear."

Hanlon laughed dismissively, pulling a chair over and sitting down.

"The stories you heard about us are mostly hyped up by the media. We just do our job and move on. We're not interested in creating attention. Those young soldiers riding vehicles along roads out there that could have IED's buried in them are the real heroes."

Danny leaned back and peered keenly at him.

"Rory Hanlon! Now that's an Irish name isn't it?" he commented.

"Yeah, second generation. My parents were Irish, from Donegal. My Dad came over just in time to volunteer for the US army and saw action in mainland Europe on D-Day. Got a heap of medals too. It was his stories that got me to join up. I was airborne for six years, and then in Delta for the past five. What about yourself? Danny Quigley is about as Irish as it gets."

He nodded. "I was born in Waterford and my parents moved to Wales when I was eight years of age. That accounts for the lack of an Irish accent. Like you, I did time in the parachute regiment and went for selection in the 'Sass'. Luckily I got through."

"Luck had nothing to do with it, Danny. It's like a Delta qualification. If you get through the "Q" course you're in the top 5% and that says it all."

Hanlon leaned back thoughtfully.

"We've all heard of the exploits of the SAS guy, Paddy Mayne, from the second world war. He was some warrior!"

"The Ulsterman? Yeah, he was that! Won four DSO's and was the most decorated British soldier in the second world war. We have a lot to live up to, Rory."

Their conversation was cut short as three commissioned officers entered the room. One was a US captain, one a British captain, and the third a US major. There was no jumping to attention as would have happened in other regiments as Special Forces tended to be relaxed around officers. Many of them even enjoyed spending some of their off-duty time together.

The three commissioned officers sat at a table in the front of the room while the Special Forces teams reached for the nearest chairs and sat down.

The Major stood up, clearing his throat.

"Welcome to all of you and glad to see you've already started getting to know each other. I know the Sass team have spent the last five days down range and did some nice work out there on recon. I can attest to two highly effective air strikes they called in to us and the body count was impressive. The Delta team came back in a week ago after two weeks clearing out some caves along the Pakistani border and discovered weapons caches that would sooner or later have ended up against our coalition forces. They killed a number of Taliban, twenty in all I believe, and brought in two prisoners who are turning out to be interesting. I only mention these operations to emphasize that, while the job we're tasking you with could be dangerous, all of you here are seasoned veterans.

You know the country and the kind of challenges it can throw up."

He paused for a quick drink from a glass of water on the table in front of him while the roomful of men took a thoughtful look around.

Then he continued.

"The coalition forces have been working in the Shah Wali Kot district in Kandahar province, blocking the Taliban and Al Quaeda coming through from the mountainous border areas. It's tough going and isn't helped by the Taliban firing on them from villages behind women, children and friendlies. That's why it's so important that we win these villages over by demonstrating that their situation will improve in real terms when they decide to start cooperating with us and sharing information on Taliban movements. Once they see that we can build schools and community centers with basic training programs and medical clinics, install fresh water pumps and start giving them some hope for the future instead of relying on the poppy crop, they'll have no reluctance in informing on the Taliban.

Now the reason for this proposed mission which is approved by Southern Command is this. We have information that the headmen in a village, even further out in the mountains than we currently patrol, are willing to talk to us. This is in a way, a pivotal village as it sits at a crossroads from those border areas."

The US Captain turned on an overhead projector showing a map of the area in question. Danny and the other men in the room leaned forward, peering at the picture. One of the Delta team called out.

"That's pretty far in. How do we know it's not a trap? I mean they know how we operate by now. They know we'll come running when we get a sniff of some village turning against the Taliban."

"Good question and certainly one we asked ourselves and always have to ask before committing Forces to any plan. Yes, it could be a trap, but we believe we have to take the risk because it's too good to pass up. We all know there are some pretty committed Taliban and Al Qaeda fighters back in those mountains, but equally there are men who are intelligent and want something better for their children. Perhaps they've visited other villages and have seen what's happening there. Basic healthcare would be a miracle to some of those areas, or even running water. It's happening elsewhere in the country and we still have a massive task ahead of us, but you know there are signs that a change of attitude is starting to creep in and we have to keep up the momentum. This mission, if we pull it off, could be a big wedge against the hard-line Taliban and the terrorists, and could shorten our time here in these damned mountains. If we can win the hearts and minds of the village, establish a base there, we can eventually pass it over to the Afghan army and police who are starting to show their mettle. President Karzai believes we're making progress too and he's already talking to some of the border-line Taliban. There's no doubt that the Afghans make tough effective soldiers when given the training and the time to gain experience. Remember how long it took each of you, even after you finished basic military training, to start getting a handle on what being a soldier was all about? It's just going to take time guys, and we have to do the heavy lifting in the meantime."

The Major sat down and the British captain took over to start briefing on the specifics of the mission. They would have two days to prepare for it.

Two Chinook helicopters would fly them in, one with a Delta team of fourteen men, an Afghan interpreter, and two SAS troopers on board. One of the troopers would handle communications with the British Forces who were responsible for the area they would be flying over. Once on the ground that same trooper would be responsible for guarding the choppers and providing covering fire for evacuation if needed. The other SAS trooper would accompany and liaise with a Delta team member on perimeter defense, and could call in an air strike if required. The second chopper would carry the SAS troopers who would provide reconnaissance and a protection perimeter around the village. They would also provide a withdrawal screen for the ODA whose role was to enter the village and meet with their head men. This Delta team had a diversity of skills that they intended to use to front their meeting with the villagers: medical, training, engineering and teaching skills, construction and village defense. The SAS reconnaissance team would have direct contact with the Delta team in the village for evacuation at the slightest hint of anything going wrong. The choppers would be put down close to the village and immediately covered with camouflaged netting to reduce the chance of being spotted from the nearby hills and attracting mortar fire. The estimated maximum time on the ground was four hours. However the US Delta team officer could abort the mission at any time if he wasn't satisfied with the general tone of the meeting or had any suspicions that it might be a set-up.

Essentially that was the overview.

The two teams broke up to discuss the operational details and resources required for the proposed mission. Like all special ops forces, the members liked to work out a plan of action and then try to tear it apart. They liked to have alternatives and options should things go wrong, as they often did. In this case, both teams had to coordinate their efforts and that meant learning each other's methodology and processes. Call signs were allocated to specific team members.

Both captains were going with them. The US officer who would enter the village, while the British SAS officer Captain Paul Richardson would be in charge of perimeter reconnaissance.

It was decided that Danny and Scotty fly in on the Delta team chopper with Scotty in charge of communications with the British Forces, and also acting as a guard on the chopper once it landed. He wasn't happy with the role as he usually worked with Danny in the field.

Instead, Danny was teamed up with Rory Hanlon, whose call sign was 'Rattler,' on the perimeter reconnaissance and defense. He suspected that the American had asked for him.

Then it was time for weapons selection, and Danny was in the pole position as Rory was the weapons sergeant for the team.

CHAPTER 2

The light machine gun used by the Special Forces was the M249 5.56 mm squad automatic weapon. It could be mounted on the choppers, or fired either in the prone position or standing by using a shoulder strap. It could fire ammunition from belts or a thirty-round magazine. Equally, a gunner could feed the weapon from a 200-round plastic box magazine. There would be one of these weapons on each chopper with Scotty handling one and a Delta team member on the other.

While the M 16 combat rifle (M 16A2) was probably the most used weapon in the US military, Special Forces were responsible for a new carbine being designed and issued. The M4 A1 had a collapsible tube butt-stock, a shorter barrel and weighed only 5.65 lbs unloaded, using thirty round magazines, ideal for special operations. Most of the Delta team intended to carry this weapon with extra magazines.

Each ODA team also carried two M203 grenade launchers weighing only 3 lbs which could be clipped onto the barrel of the M4 A1 carbine. The Americans had agreed to take care of the required weaponry and they brought the SAS team in small groups to a large metal trailer in a secured compound to show them their selection options.

All Special Forces were weapons junkies and the Brits were soon drooling over the new AK 47 which was virtually indestructible and would never jam even if left in sand or water. The US team also had a greater variety of pistols and automatics, to the envy of the Brits, for ownership of all of these were now banned back in the UK.

Rory Hanlon showed Danny the M9 Baretta 9mm pistol, which was a general issue to US Special Forces. It was equipped with a fifteen round magazine, which Rory intended to carry. Danny suspected that he had already used it in combat by the way he handled it.

Danny pointed to a Heckler & Koch MP5 on the wall. The weapon was just over 26 inches in length, weighing 5.6 lbs, firing a 9mm caliber in a 15 round magazine or a 30 round box.

Rory nodded in approval.

"Nice weapon. We use it a lot in ops. Depends on the task really. In Iraq we might go for a heavier caliber as we have to cope with enemy vehicles, but out in the mountains here it's not as important, though you still run across those Toyota pick-up trucks that the Taliban move around in."

He hauled the weapon off the wall and passed it across.

"Is this the one you want, Danny?" he asked.

"Hmmn…beautiful weapon…I've used it a few times in action and it's never let me down."   He glanced at the American.

"Would you by any chance have the silenced version with the special laser sight?" he asked.

Rory laughed. "A connoisseur we have here it seems. Interesting choice. I'd probably have picked it for a night op where stealth was important and the ability to eliminate perimeter guards quietly, but yes, hang on a second………."

He walked over to a metal cabinet and extracted a second Heckler and Koch along with some packages, and passed the weapon to Danny.

"It's yours if you want it and these packages are your attachments….the silencer and laser sight. Now do you want to go for ammo magazines or the box?"

"I'll go for a bunch of magazines. Probably tape two together for fast reloading. Oh and what about grenades?" Danny asked tentatively.

He knew that two of the Delta team normally carried grenade attachments to their weapons.

"Sure, no problem there." Rory replied. "I'm one of the designated guys for grenades on this op and you and I'll be working together, so if I need extra, you'll be close. Here's hoping we don't need them at all. In and out smooth as silk, that's what I like."

He went across to another section and came back with a satchel, which he placed at Danny's feet.

"There's your M67 fragmentation grenades and I've shoved in a few colored units for signaling, just in case. You'll obviously have your rescue beacon too for extraction if anything goes wrong."

He pointed to another set of shelves.

"As you can see the ammo's stacked over there." He made a face. " Just help yourself but remember you have to carry all this shit!"

"Danny smiled. "Don't I know it! I'm always threatening to take only the bare minimum with me but you should see the bloody marks on my shoulders from those Bergens."

Hanlon's face crinkled.

"That's the pack you guys carry, I gather. Now we have a special backpack that you might like for a change. It allows one of those 3 liter hydration packs to fit in, that enables you to take fluids while on the move. Oh and some of the new performance enhancing nutrition bars would probably be a welcome addition as well."

Danny's head was reeling. They'd come over to choose the weaponry for the operation and now he was like a kid going on a hiking trip. The difference was that this trip could kill you.

"What about pistols Danny? Anything you like in particular?" Hanlon enquired.

"Hey, the one you carry is a beaut. That 9 mil Baretta. I'll stick to that if there's still one available."

"No problem there. Now what about body armor?"

Danny groaned. "It's so bloody heavy and hot in this heat, Rory. Do we have to wear it? After all this is mooted as being on the ground for a max of two hours."

"I know where you're coming from Danny. None of Special Forces like wearing it but it's a personal choice at the end of the day. We have a new lightweight Kevlar helmet and flak jacket system you might like. They're good and we've seen lives saved by them. I'd suggest you try them on anyway."

After inspecting them he decided to use a set on the forthcoming operation.

Hanlon steered him round the trailer showing him a variety of weaponry being tried out by the US Special Forces, some not even available on the open market as of yet. The gun companies were always trying to get a break-through in gun technology and were quick to place new systems with the people who carried out hands-on work in the field.

Danny's eyes lingered on an M24 sniper rifle and Rory caught his glance.

"My God, you're still looking at weapons! This isn't the Alamo we're flying into you know. I thought I was bad!"

"Yeah I know." Danny said ruefully. "Sounds like I'm insecure taking a whole armory with me. I did your marine sniping course last year, so in a way it's ingrained in me."

Rory whistled. "That's some course I understand. One of our weapons sergeants on another team did one and it blew his mind. They had some guest lecturers, vets from the Vietnam war who'd had over a hundred confirmed kills! Can you imagine that?"

Danny nodded. "Yeah I met them. They took the Viet Cong out at ranges even beyond one thousand yards. Now that's some shooting, Rory!"

Hanlon took the rifle down off the wall and slapped the stock into his palm.

"This one is only geared for hitting targets up to 500 yards so it wouldn't be used by full-time snipers like they have in the Marine Corps, engaged at times in taking out long range targets. Great for setting up on top of a building in Baghdad or Bazra, and taking those bastards out when they come riding in wearing masks and waving RPG's. It's based on the old Remington 700 sniper rifle and is equipped with a 10/24 Leopold M3 ultra scope and fires the M118 special ball round, which means more weight to carry."

He slapped the weapon into Danny's hand.

"It's yours and we can share the load on the extra ammo. I think you're crazy, but then again, I understand - hell we're both Irish!"

Danny grinned broadly and staggered out of the trailer to the cat calls of his SAS mates who were also loading up on the available toys.

Once Danny had gone back to his quarters they both sat down and cracked a beer together, sharing some operations they had done in various areas. Danny had been on operations in both Africa and South America, while Rory had been in Grenada and Panama. They had both been in operations in Iraq, Afghanistan and the Balkans. The time passed and finally Rory stood up.

"Well Danny, final briefing tonight and off at the crack of dawn tomorrow. How do you feel?"

He considered the question thoughtfully.

"Fine. I'm always an optimist anyway. Probably because I rely on my training which is superior to anything we normally come up against. Also on my mates or buddies as you call them, to back me up. No problems Rory...I'm ready for it."

He paused for a moment and the American was quick to spot it.

"But........."

Danny sighed. "I just wonder sometimes what the hell we're doing here. The Russians didn't have much luck trying to occupy this place, and from what I've seen, the people of Afghanistan certainly don't want us here either."

Rory regarded him thoughtfully. "Yeah, we wondered that in Iraq too but it's starting to pan out over there with the Iraqis taking responsibility for their own lives. Remember in Afghanistan, unlike the Russians, we're not here to occupy the place. Our team spent some time in Kabul and Kandahar and did a tour of schools where young girls can attend school for the first time, and health clinics are being run by women doctors and technicians. I've seen villages where they have running water for the first time ever. Believe me Danny we're making a difference here."

A flicker of interest crossed Danny's face.

"Okay Rory, I hear you. I guess there is an end game here and I should concentrate on that."

Rory nodded. "We all entertain doubts at times Danny. Look at your own Northern Ireland situation. I understand you guys did numerous operations there over the years and must have wondered many times what the hell you were doing there. But look at the place today - old enemies sitting down and running a prosperous country together. Now, I have one more thing to give you."

Danny raised his hands.

"More? You gotta be kidding. I'm not sure they'll even let me on the chopper in the morning."

"This won't take up much weight."

He reached up and took a braid from around his neck. Danny noticed that hanging from the end of it was an animals tooth. Rory carefully placed it over Danny's head and stepped back.

"An old Apache chief gave it to me out west. It's the tooth of a cougar he killed with his bare hands. Said it was for warriors to wear into battle. I was to pass it on when it felt right to do so. It feels right to give it to you, Danny."

He turned and left without a further word. Danny stood there for a long time. He felt a tingle run down through his body as the cougar tooth rested against his chest. At that moment he knew he was going into battle.

For some reason it reminded him of the number of times he battled in the small Welsh school ground as a youth. He had come across from Waterford in Ireland with his older sister Cathy, so that his father could get work. Normally friendly and outgoing, he'd gradually become more intense and introverted as he adjusted to the hostility of the locals. It became even worse when his parents divorced and his mother re-married a miner who turned out to be violent and abusive both to herself and to Danny. His sister was sponsored by an uncle in Ireland and went off to a top girls school in Cheltenham. On her occasional home visits their stepfather became a totally different person giving Danny and his mother a brief respite from his bullying. The whole situation came to a head when Danny arrived home one day at the age of sixteen to find his mother lying injured on the floor from a brutal assault by his stepfather who sat there smirking. Big for his age and having taken judo lessons for four years, Danny in a wild rage tore into his stepfather and left him unconscious on the cottage floor. He and his mother moved out the same day as his stepfather was carted off to hospital. His mother never really recovered and died two years later. He never saw his stepfather again. When Danny later joined the Forces, he took with him that edge of rage which was hard-wired into him.

CHAPTER 3

Afghanistan

They flew out at dawn.

The unmanned drone plane had flown over the target village a number of times prior to the Chinook helicopters sweeping in. The pictures it sent back showed it to be clear of enemy combatants. Now the two choppers dropped down speedily to avoid any possible missile or RPG attacks. Once on the ground the teams bailed out and ran for the nearest cover.

The dust had barely settled when Scotty and one of the team pulled a camouflage net over the chopper. The other team did the same. Should firing break out they would immediately pull off the nets. Scotty had taken just a moment to slap Danny and Rory on the back as they and rest of the team dived out and hit the ground. He didn't like being left behind and in particular didn't like seeing Danny heading off with someone else guarding his back. He immediately braced himself against the M249 machine gun on the chopper mounts and swiveled it round through the camouflage netting in the direction of the village.

After a few minutes of clinging to the ground, both Special Forces captains stood up and waved their individual teams forward. The British SAS team had already chosen from maps the positions that provided both the best cover and overall view of the surrounding area.

They quickly located their defense positions. The SAS captain Paul Richardson and his defensive team immediately started sweeping the surrounding areas with their field glasses, looking for signs of possible enemy presence. After a few minutes the scouts gave the thumbs up and the captain spoke into his helmet microphone giving the all clear.

The American Delta team went straight up over a rise. As they reached the top they were met by half a dozen locals who greeted them and pointed back down into the village. Slowly and still fully alert, they made their way behind the villagers, stopping at what appeared to be the proposed meeting place, a stone-built community house.

A number of the Delta team down in the village, raced to pre-arranged positions that gave them the best overview for defense in the event of an evacuation under hostile fire. The rest of the team went inside the building.

Back in his defensive position Danny had set up his tripod for the sniper rifle and the MP5 was still slung across his back. He opened the grenade satchel and pulled it around on his belt for easy access. Rory was a few feet away, already with his grenade pouch open and the breech-loading M203 clipped to his weapon ready to fire. They settled in to wait, the whole crew spread out, each sweeping the mountainous areas and ridges around them with their glasses. Richardson, the SAS captain, crept up to them and knelt down.

"All set lads?" he asked. Danny and Rory both nodded, still sweeping the areas around them. Just as Richardson was climbing back up onto his feet Danny caught his arm and handed him his field glasses.

"Have a look at that large cave just up behind the other side of the village. That didn't show up in the terrain pictures we looked at. We normally would have checked it out first before we sent in the Delta Team."

The captain looked carefully at the area for a minute, then sweeping around it. Finally he handed the glasses back to Danny.

"Hmm....hard to say just how big that cave is and if it could hide very many in there. You're right though, we should have checked it out as a matter of routine but we're committed now and things are quiet down there. Probably still at the tea drinking stage. Just keep an extra eye on that area and I'll pass your observation on to the lads."

With that he carefully inched his way along to the next two troopers.

"Good officer?" Rory asked.

"Yeah, knows his stuff and looks after his men," Danny replied.

"We have good people too. Hell they wouldn't last long if they weren't.........holy shit Danny! That fucking cave!"

Danny swiveled his glasses round and saw a number of armed men racing out of it and starting to inch down the steep gradient towards the center of the village below them. Rory was already screaming into his helmet mike.

"Snowbird this is rattler. Enemy hostiles coming down from behind you ... numbers unknown.....get the hell out now, over!"

Just then there was burst of fire from directly inside the village. Rory was still on the radio listening. He shouted to Danny.

"All hells broken loose. They just shot the interpreter and our lads are in a fire fight in the community center."

Danny was too busy to reply. He was already firing, carefully using the sniper rifle. He saw the first armed man drop and moved to the next. He started to count out loud.......
"one, two, three, four, five, six, seven...."

The men suddenly became aware that they were under fire and some tried to back up into the cave again. Danny moved the sights further down the gradient where a number of armed men were sliding down, and firing their weapons. He resumed counting, "eight...nine...ten...eleven...twelve..."

Bodies of the armed men he was shooting started tumbling down the slope as the Delta Team streamed out of the community house, now under fire from inside the village as well. Rory was blasting away on his right and had just fired the grenade launcher that blasted the roof off a house in the village, where enemy weapons had opened up. The rest of the team were firing away rapidly. Rory shouted at Danny.

"Keep firing at that cave, there's more pouring out."

For good measure he let loose a grenade that overshot the cave but caused some boulders to come tumbling down. He heard Danny counting again on his left.

"Thirteen, fourteen, fifteen, sixteen..." as more bodies fell down the gradient. At that moment something thumped into Danny's back and he fell forward.

"Shit, I think I'm hit Rory," he shouted.

Rory scuttled sideways taking a brief look.

"You're one lucky son of a gun Danny. It's buried in your pack somewhere, but that shot came from behind us."

They both looked around and saw a large group of armed men storming down from a mountain ridge a hundred yards away firing as they raced towards the American and British positions. Bullets started zipping around them as the whole team turned and re-directed their fire at the new enemy positions rapidly approaching. The second grenade launcher opened up from the team. This and Rory's fire power made some gaps in the approaching group of fighters. Danny began firing again, alternating between the approaching group and the enemy fighters still straggling from the cave. He'd got to 20 counting out loud and then stopped, his whole focus was to reduce down the number of bodies coming from both directions. It was obvious they wouldn't be able to hold them much longer as there appeared to be at least a hundred fighters still racing towards them. Enemy RPG rockets were starting to crash into the rocks nearby. Danny was aware that some of the SAS team were taking casualties. Rory listened to his mike and glanced sideways at him.

"The Delta team are out of the village and heading for the choppers. We're to withdraw a.s.a.p."

Just then Captain Richardson crawled past and slapped Danny on the back.

"We're withdrawing. Start heading back and keep up your fire as much as you can."

Rory crawled up to Danny.

"You heard the man, let's go."

Danny handed him the sniper rifle.

"Just run out of ammo…take it with you…don't want the bastards to get their hands on it. I'll cover you over that next rise and then I'll join you. Look, I'll take whichever is the nearest chopper, so don't wait for me…go!"

Rory looked uncertainly at him, then threw his satchel of grenades he still had left across to Danny.

"You might need these buddy," he shouted above the din, grabbed the sniper rifle and dashed for the rise thirty yards away that led down to where the choppers waited, the camouflage netting already removed, and started up their engines.

Enemy fighters were now running up from the village and firing as they came. Danny could see the bullets kicking up dust around Rory's feet as he ran. He lifted the MP5 Heckler and Koch MP5 with the silencer and special laser sight, switched to fully automatic and sent a burst of shots down into the advancing villagers, sending a number flying. Strangely, they didn't appear to notice his position because of the silencer and their focus was on the choppers engines starting up below the rise. He swiveled and began firing at the second group, now closer. Hearing bullets whine and zip around him, he looked up quickly and saw Rory's startled face peering over the top of the rise. Danny hurled two grenades in quick succession at the fighters rushing up from the village and saw several go sprawling. He waved to Rory to keep going.

Danny knew he wouldn't have a chance of surviving a dash to join him at that stage. He also knew his position would shortly be over-run by the second group which was nearing him. He peered over the top and cut down five of the group, then slithered off down a small cutting in the side of the hill, crawling into some brush twenty feet further down.

Within minutes he heard the enemy fighters race past above him, their focus on the two choppers with their potential prize of capturing or destroying a Special Forces team. Danny looked cautiously above and around him and, seeing no faces watching, started crawling towards some large boulders about fifty yards away. Almost immediately he could hear the sounds of the helicopters taking off, their on-board weapons coming into play. A massive explosion rocked the whole village. Danny didn't know it, but a missile had been fired from one of the choppers directly into the cave exploding and tearing the whole side of the mountain apart. It had obviously housed a considerable amount of explosives and ammunition. He took advantage of the confusion to crawl further away from the village and eventually made his way around the side of a small hillside about 500 yards away. He kept moving, trying to get as much distance as possible between himself and the Taliban fighters. He knew that if he was spotted a search would be launched for him and he would be quickly cornered. He also knew that the Special Forces team would come back for him. That was normal practice but the question was when?

With that in mind he took his pack off and checked his beacon with its signaling device to attract his rescue helicopter when it returned. It suddenly dawned on him that the bullet that had ploughed into his pack had also smashed his rescue beacon. He was stranded on his own in the hostile Afghan mountains, where the Taliban reigned supreme and would wreak a savage vengeance on him if they caught him.

As the choppers took off straight up into the sky Scotty grabbed Rory.

"Where the fuck is Danny?"

"I think he's on the other chopper. He said he'd take the nearest one. It got a bit hairy out there at the end. Last I saw he was hosing them down on both sides of him. He lobbed two grenades at the fighters coming up that should have cleared a gap for him. He waved me off and I thought he was right on my tail."

Scotty pushed his way up to the front of the aircraft and spoke to the pilot.

"Can you check if Danny Quigley's on the other chopper?"

The pilot never took his eyes off what he was doing.

"If you hadn't noticed I'm trying to reduce this poxy village to an ant hill right now and dodging lots of weapons firing up at us. CAS (Close air support) were diverted to help the Canadians, who are in a sticky situation right now."

Scotty paused holding back an angry reply and slowly made his way to the back of the craft. Rory looked at him enquiringly but he shrugged, saying nothing. Hanlon leaned forward and shouted above the noise.

"Quigley was incredible back there with that sniper rifle. He kept counting out loud as he killed them. When he got to twenty he just stopped counting but kept taking them down at the cave entrance and at the second group as well. The team wouldn't have got out of the village if Danny hadn't spotted that cave. Hell he pointed it out to your officer Richardson in the first place. He was a bloody killing machine. I've never seen anything like it!"

Scotty turned his face away, still silent. He knew that if he'd been with Danny on the ground he would be sitting beside him right now, dead or alive.

Back at base Scotty was first off the chopper and dashed across to the SAS team as they struggled from their helicopter.

"Danny Quigley? Where's Danny? Is he on board?"

The group stopped moving and stared in silence, their faces starting to register dismay. Captain Richardson looked up.

"We thought he was with your group. He came in with you. Hell, I told him myself to head for the chopper."

Scotty shook his head angrily.

"The Delta chap, Hanlon, said Danny waved at him to keep going and that he would get the nearest chopper….yours. Apparently it got a bit hairy right then with two groups of Taliban converging, but Hanlon still thought Danny was right behind him."

Richardson looked back at the distant mountains, hostile and bleak in the fading afternoon sun.

"Shit! Danny's back there in those bloody hills surrounded by Taliban. We can't make it back there tonight but at the crack of dawn I'll fly back in with a rescue team. We've got to get Danny out before they catch up to him, if they haven't killed or captured him already."

Scotty nodded grimly

"I'll be right there with you Captain. I'm sure the lads will be on the trip as well. I do know from experience that Danny is a tough man to kill, but that's some hard country to survive in, even without the Taliban!"

CHAPTER 4

Afghanistan

Danny spent the evening crouched down behind some large boulders overlooking the camp as the last of the light disappeared. He'd watched the Taliban gathering in their dead and carrying the wounded to the community center. They were in high rage, sporadically firing their weapons in the air. A number of women had emerged from the houses and their dirges and laments over the dead echoed up clearly to where he was hiding. He felt a flicker of fear in his stomach at the thought of being captured by the Taliban and instinctively found his hand clutching the cougar tooth hanging around his neck. Almost immediately he felt a sense of confidence as if the old Apache chief was sitting beside him.

After a couple of hours he could see that they were evacuating the village, probably in anticipation of a return in the morning by US forces to wreak revenge for the ambush. An air strike could equally be unleashed at any time, even at night. What did concern him was that the Taliban were setting up several anti-aircraft weapons positions around the outside perimeter of the village, presumably in the hope of catching some of the aircraft in a deadly crossfire when they returned. He still had two color grenades to attract the incoming choppers to his position but now he couldn't use them anywhere near the village. If he attempted to take out some of the Taliban in their ambush positions, he would give away his predicament and his capture would be imminent. The only decision he could make was to reluctantly leave the rescue aircraft to their own devices. He had to get as far away from the village as possible while it was still dark. The evacuating villagers were heading back in the direction of the Afghan/Pakistan border which suited him. His direction was back towards the city of Kandahar and the British Forces, hopefully on patrol in some of the outlying areas.

The Taliban traveled mainly in old pick-up trucks, or they used pack animals and camels to transport weapons and food. He felt that he could safely make his way down to the road in the darkness while staying alert for approaching vehicles. He tried to re-distribute his load by transferring Hanlon's grenades into his satchel and slung the MP5 over his shoulder. He brought he pistol forward out of its holster and stuck it in the front of his belt. The bullet that had slammed into his pack had also punctured his hydration insert. A small amount of liquid remained at the bottom of the container which he finished off eagerly before getting to the road. He hid the damaged hydration pack and the Kevlar armor under some rocks and chewed on half of one of the performance bars as he edged carefully out onto the road, which was more like a narrow track. His commando knife which he normally carried strapped to his leg, had a compass imbedded on the top of the hilt. Checking this he confirmed his direction and started walking. Though the track was narrow, there were sections that widened out to facilitate vehicles passing. In some cases these were huge natural breaks in the rocks and enclosures, where a half dozen vehicles could pull off and stay for the night if necessary. His plan was to hole up somewhere during the day and travel by night. He would have to stay alert to the sound of helicopters approaching and be ready to fire off one of the color grenades. One of his first priorities was to find water.

He walked most of the night, not coming across any other travelers on the road. With dawn starting to flick across the heavy skies he decided to take advantage of one of the breaks in the stone perimeter of the road, and turned wearily in towards the opening.

When he turned the corner around a large slab of rock everything changed in a moment. He was suddenly facing a small encampment containing four pack animals and three people….. two men and a woman.

The elder male who was carrying an AK 47 swung it into firing position, his finger searching for the trigger. Danny's automatic reaction with the 9mm Beratta, was faster and accurate. The shot hit the man straight in the chest and he slumped to the ground. He swung the pistol slightly to the right to take out the second man, a youth with a scraggly beard, already swinging his rifle up. Danny pulled the trigger only to hear a snick of a misfire or a jammed bullet. The look of fear disappeared from the youths face as he stepped forward grinning and shouting something. He then lifted the rifle deliberately pointing directly at Danny's chest, his finger tightening on the trigger.

Danny braced himself. After all the action he'd seen all over the world, to be finished by a misfire and killed by a youth! A shot rang out. Danny blinked and then watched in astonishment as the youth slid to the ground, the front of his head exploding.

A tall girl, wearing a hijab and carrying a smoking rifle, stepped out from behind the pack animals now swirling around in panic from the gunfire. Danny stared at her dumbly wondering if he was next. The girl lowered the weapon and stepped forward towards him.

"I prayed……..you came," she managed to say in broken English and then sagged down onto her knees sobbing.

Danny's surprise and shock at the turn of events was easing off as he tentatively went over and knelt down beside the girl gently taking the rifle from her shaking hands. He wasn't sure about the culture of putting his arm around a young Muslim girl but he carefully did so. She collapsed against him, crying out even louder. It was obviously the first time she had killed someone.

Her sobbing lasted several minutes. Just as suddenly she stopped and sat back on the rocky ground. He could make out part of her face now.......dark eyes and a firm jaw from which the hijab had fallen down. She must have been about sixteen years of age, perhaps a bit older he estimated, though he was no expert on the ages of young Muslim girls.

Danny looked closely at her and pointed to the dead youth.

"Why?" he whispered.

She struggled to her feet then and he helped her steady herself.

"Why?" he said again.

She nodded, understanding his question. She pointed to the older man on the ground and then the youth.

"Uncle and cousin. Pashtuns tribe in Pakistan. Taliban."

She pointed to herself.

"I live Afghanistan."

Danny nodded. "Taliban......right. Where are your parents?"

She looked down. He was afraid she was going to start crying again but she didn't.

"Father dead........mother die not long...."

She pointed to the dead men.

"Were to bring me Kandahar to mother's sister, but try to take me as woman."

She lifted the rifle from the floor where he had placed it. Danny tensed.

She went on. " I keep rifle close......they still try.....just before you came...they try again. I pray for helper. You came....you save my life.....thank you."

"What is your name? Mine is Danny," he said, pointing to himself. "Danny," he repeated.

"Da...ne." she spoke slowly, concentrating fiercely, with her face crinkled. "Like it......Da..ne.....I Jamila.....Jamila Mehsud," she replied, pointing to herself.

36

"What will you do in Kandahar ah….Jamila?" he asked, speaking very slowly.

She concentrated on his words again.

"I want to be doctor…help my people…mother's sister work in medical clinic….. Kandahar."

Already he was hearing an easier flow in her English. He looked in wonder at this young girl with such a driven purpose in life and so determined to achieve it.

He was suddenly aware of the increasing daylight and the threat of this to him.

"Can you please help me Jamila?" he asked, looking directly at her.

"How?" she asked.

"To get back to Kandahar…..escape Taliban and Al Qaeda."

She pondered for a moment looking closely at his attire.

"Take clothes off…change with him."

She pointed to the younger of the two dead men.

"No blood on clothes…..do quickly," she urged.

He immediately set about pulling the garments from the young dead male and struggling into them. Jamila had run across to one side and started gathering something from the ground. She hurried back to him. He saw that she had gathered a chunk of brown moist earth which she set down on a rock, at the same time retrieving a water container from the back of one of the pack animals. Danny grabbed the container and took a long swallow. It tasted better than any pint of Stella he'd ever drank. She smiled at his sounds of appreciation and then reached up to his face. He realized that she was trying to stain his face so that he'd look more like a native. To accommodate her he sat down.

She immediately started to work on his face, neck and visible shoulders, hands and arms, stepping back occasionally to examine her handiwork. She pointed to his white legs, making a face. The older male was wearing white faded trousers so he quickly changed into them. She still wasn't satisfied and pointed to his feet. He went and pulled the

Afghan boots off the older male as well and put them on. He felt relieved that they actually fit and covered his feet much better than the sandals worn by the dead youth. She then went across to the older dead male, took the turban off and spent a minute wrapping it around his head.

He pointed to his chin. "No beard.....not good?"

She struggled to understand, so he tried again. "No hair......no good," he said.

She nodded, already aware of the problem. She reached up and loosened a loop from the turban and pulled it over his chin, attaching it behind his neck. Then she stepped back examining him closely.

Finally she nodded. "You not speak on road." She pointed to his throat.

"I say you wounded .... fight ......lost voice...can't speak. If people speak to you...you just go Agggha......and point to wound...okay?"

"Okay Jamila. Thanks. Tell me, what's in the packs on the animals?" he asked.

She made a face. "You go look."

He strode over, un-strapped the first pack and looked inside. He stepped back, shocked.

"Holy shit!" he whispered.

He checked the next two animals as well. They were full of IED's. About six per animal, representing a whole lot of death and carnage if they had got as far as Kandahar province and its capital. The last pack animal carried what appeared to be food, cooking utensils and blankets. He whistled, thinking rapidly. He could destroy the IED's right there using some hand grenades, but there was a possibility that they might somehow be useful on the trip. He decided that they would take the animals and packs with them. It was in the last pack that he found a small satchel tucked down under the blankets. He unbuckled the top and looked inside. It was full of sapphires. He poured some into his palm and turned to her.

"Sapphires! Where are they from? What are they for?"

She could see his amazement.

"Yes, sapphires from the Himalayan mines..... across Pakistan... near India. For Taliban in Kandahar Pay for guns."

He was stunned at the discovery. He was no expert but the gems must be worth a few million dollars at least, probably a lot more. So this was how the Taliban were paying for their weapons. Most intelligence estimates suggested that either Bin Laden or the drug trade had been supplying the funding for this - or both.

He poured the sapphires back into the sack and turned, handing it to her.

"This will make you a doctor for your people. They're yours," he said, pressing it into her hands.

She looked at him in astonishment.

"You not keep for self?" she asked, amazement reflected on her face.

"No! No! They're yours Jamila. Hide them somewhere safe for the trip just in case we're searched."

He left her sorting out a hiding place as he started deciding on what to take with him in the way of armaments.

He took his grenades out of the obviously military satchels and stored them in the same pack as the IED's. He placed the 9 mm ammunition for the MP5 in there as well as the spare magazines which he buried deep. The pistol he reluctantly ditched, not just because it had jammed but it presented the problem of carrying it without a belt. The MP 5 he managed to sling under the roomy caftan in such a way that it was accessible in a second if they were challenged on the road. He stuck the commando knife into one of the seams of the animal packs which he intended to stay close to. Then he took all his military clothing and surplus items, carried them across to some large rocks and shoved them deep into a crevice before rolling some rocks over the top, and went back to Jamila.

She obviously had more on her mind as she stood directly in front of him.

"I think ....on road I go first...not Afghan way... man go first..... but I talk first if stopped........ walk with food and clothing packs in front... okay?"

He nodded.

She wasn't finished yet.

"I say you very sick...wound....no can talk.......you hang on animal as if sick...no look up...not good you have blue eyes so no look at people okay?"

Okay, so I avoid eye contact and sag on the animals back, he thought.

"Anything else?" he asked.

She nodded. "Yes, keep hands down...no Afghan...no work hands. Afghan's very smart...know people."

"Bloody hell!" he thought. "This isn't going to work."

He felt like a stage actor on opening night, only in his case he hadn't had even one rehearsal session. Within five minutes they were out on the road, Jamila in front with the lead pack animal, the next two following and Danny coming up in the rear with the fourth animal. For some reason Danny thought of Scotty and wondered what he would think of the situation he now found himself in, but right then he realized that Jamila was much more of an asset to him than the tough Scotsman.

CHAPTER 5

Afghanistan

The first five days went extremely well to the extent that Danny was starting to relax into the role. They had encountered a number of small groups on the trail going in both directions, some riding camels, others using pack mules, while others were in pickup trucks or on ancient motor bikes A few of the groups stopped briefly and spoke with Jamila. The topic of conversation seemed to be the attack on the village further back in the mountains. Afghans, despite their primitive lifestyle still had access to mobile phones with satellite connections. Especially the Al Qaeda, Taliban and opium drug smugglers.

Jamila appeared to handle the situation quite well with groups passing on swiftly without too much attention to Danny who felt that his "aaghs" were quite believable. In the evenings they pulled off the road and set up camp for the night. Danny was amazed at how swiftly Jamila's English was improving and she seemed to have a hunger to practice and welcomed being corrected.

On the sixth day a red Toyota pick-up truck tore up behind them with six fighters clinging to the back and two in the cab. He presumed they were Taliban, possibly from the village that had ambushed the Special Forces team.

The truck slowed down and paced them for a few yards, the fierce faces staring at them from the cab and the back of the pick up. Jamila waved to them. The men continued to stare at her without any acknowledgment, then the truck sped off up the road. After four hours of walking on that particular day, Jamila took advantage of a break in the stone rocks to pull over to the side and relieve the animals of their packs.

They wandered off chewing on the burnt grass. Jamila pointed to some flat boulders.

"Sit, we eat." she said, smiling at him.

She was more and more impressed after the past few days in his company at the way he fitted into the role and the quiet strength that emanated from him. In particular, the respect he showed her as a woman was something she had never encountered before. She was also confused at feeling attracted to him after her conditioned upbringing and the tribal hatred towards 'the infidel'.

"We not eat much ....don't want make fire. Taliban see smoke and come look."

Danny could see that she actually had a young woman's form under her flowing robes and upwardly revised her age to probably eighteen. In the end he couldn't resist asking her.

"I'm seventeen," she replied. "Had to help mother run home...three years...she was sick. Me, two brothers and three sisters."

"So you had to run the home pretty well yourself because your mother was sick?" he asked.

"Yes.....lot work....woman's work....I grow up fast."

"Where are you brothers and sisters now?" he prompted, his curiosity growing. In truth he loved the sound of her voice, which was gentle and had a tinkling quality to it.

She crinkled up her face the way she did when she was trying to find the words to answer him, and he liked the way she did that as well.

"Oh, two brothers in Pakistan. One seventeen, fight with Taliban. Other fifteen, live with cousin in Afghanistan. Work in poppy fields. Drugs. Sisters now live with aunt in Kandahar. How you say that? Aunt? Is good English?"

She impulsively reached out and touched his arm in embarrassment.

"Yes, very good Jamila. By the way, I thought young Afghan girls had to marry young, at fifteen we've heard. Why are you not married yet? Or are you?"

She arched backwards laughing.

"No, not married My mother want me get out of village….go Kandahar….not marry in mountains. She chase men away with stick."

Now Danny laughed. The impression of this young girl's mother chasing some fierce male mountain suitor from making approaches to her daughter was amusing.

She peered up at him. "Are you married Da..ne?"

He nodded. "Yes I am. I have one child, a girl. They live in London. I'm afraid I don't see them much."

"Do you miss them?" she asked tentatively.

"Oh yes indeed, but I'm a soldier. I'm used to being away from home. By the way how did you learn English Jamila? It's quite good you know."

She looked pleased.

"My mother had books…..English. She teach me. Say help me get away from village one day. Years ago American men come to village……work with Grandfather…kill Russians. My mother learn English from them."

He could see the connection now. The CIA had been in Afghanistan years before teaching the Taliban how to use shoulder-fired heat-seeking missiles to shoot down helicopters, and it had broken the back of the Russian invasion. Things had come full circle he thought. Now we're fighting these same people or at least their children, and they're using techniques taught to them by the CIA.

"Will the fighting ever stop?" he asked.

"Oh yes," she said brightly. "I read book from Government."

"A book?" he said. "What book?"

She went over to one of the packs and extracted what looked like a magazine from one of them, came back and sat down handing it to him. He opened it gingerly thinking that it looked very much like an English comic book, with simple pictures and illustrations. It wasn't written in English though.

He looked at her.

"I don't understand it. What does it say?"

"Oh what Government say........what will do for Afghan people. Human rights......rights for women......education too...a chance for people be better...have better life. I want this very much," she said fervently, her eyes shining.

"Wow," he thought. " Perhaps I've got this all wrong."

He spotted something written in English at the bottom of the last page: USAID/Canadian Provincial Reconstruction Team. So someone had finally got it right and were communicating a message to these people that they were buying into. At least the young ones like Jamila were. He knew that the old Taliban mountain men felt threatened by all this democracy and change. They wanted their ancient culture and way of life to stay the way it had always been. When the NATO Forces left, as they would some day, they would come back down from the mountains and undo all the changes that had been put in place. But despite his reservations, perhaps there was hope, at least for the next generation and for the fighting to stop. Could they walk away from this country one day with pride in what they'd accomplished?

He looked at her young face shaped by the jihab, so full of enthusiasm and determination, and felt a tremendous surge of admiration for her and her dream of becoming a doctor.

Impulsively he tapped her hand and then gave her a thumbs up sign.

She looked uncertainly at him.

"This means yes, Jamila." He showed her the thumbs up sign again. "You go for it. Become that doctor. I believe you'll do it."

A huge smile spread across her face. "You think so Da...ne?"

"I know so Jamila!" he said enthusiastically.

She jumped up and gave him the thumbs up sign. "I know too. Now, get packs on….back on road.

They ran into trouble that afternoon.

CHAPTER 6

Afghanistan

It was the same Toyota truck that had past them earlier, now returning. This time Danny could see that the back was carrying an additional load of small sacks leaving little room for the six men clinging to the sides. He surmised that the sacks contained a load of refined opium on the way to the market.

Previously the truck had slowed down and he had been conscious of hard fierce eyes regarding them as it passed. Now it pulled over in front of Jamila and her lead pack animal, blocking it. Two men in the cab of the truck got out. They sauntered slowly down the side of the truck making comments that set the Taliban in the back roaring with laughter and catcalls.

The two men were tall, probably in their mid-forties, and dressed in scruffy, dirty clothing. Their faces were long, thin, lined and burnt with the sun. They were also hard and cruel. They both carried rifles. Danny knew they were in trouble.

The leader strode up to Jamila and started shouting at her.

She stood defiantly looking up at him and pointed back at Danny, pointing to her throat.

Both men glanced momentarily at Danny, dismissing him, and moved closer to Jamila.

Suddenly the leader reached out and grasping the top of her clothing tore it down, exposing her breasts. Both men glanced at each other wolfishly and the men in the truck roared encouragement at them.

The leader started fumbling at his clothing as the second man pushed her back against the pack animal. Danny moved away from his pack animal, which he had been leaning against and started walking towards them. As he did so he dragged his right foot in a shambling gait and started roaring as if in agitation "Agggha," and shaking his head from side to side.

Both men stopped what they were doing and turned towards him, sneering at his walk and turned their attention back to the girl.

Jamila tried to cover herself and retreated alongside the pack animal.

Danny was ten feet away from them when he lobbed the grenade with a short fuse over their heads into the back of the truck. Almost mesmerized, the eyes of the two men started following the arc of the grenade. At that precise moment Danny shot them both through the chest with the MP5 under his clothing and kept moving past them, still aware of their shocked eyes as he dived for Jamila, bringing her to the ground just as the grenade blew up. The sound of the explosion was shocking that close up. The air was suddenly filled with flying pieces of metal, flesh and a powdery substance.

Danny lay there, his head spinning, and became conscious of something lying up against him. Opening his eyes he saw a dead pack animal lying alongside himself and Jamila. Fortunately for them it was the one carrying the food and blankets and not the IED's.

Struggling to recover his hearing Danny crawled to his feet still holding the MP5 and raced to the back of the truck, which was awash with mangled bloodied bodies.

A couple of the men were still alive and screaming. Danny dispatched them both with measured shots to the head. Then he turned to Jamila who was struggling to her feet covered in greyish powder. She was clutching at her ears, unaware that her whole chest was now totally uncovered. Danny could see blood welling from a cut in her shoulder from some flying object. A keening sound came from her throat as she looked dazedly around. He could see that shock was starting to set in.

He hurried over to the dead pack animal and grabbed a blanket, now exposed by the explosion and lying half out on the roadway. Gently he covered her with it, led her up the road about 50 yards and sat her down at the side of the roadway.

He had work to do and no idea how much time he had before more travelers came along. To the left of the track was a massive drop, hundreds of feet down with jagged rocks below. Amazingly the Toyota engine was still working when he turned the key. He juggled the wheel back and forward until the vehicle was facing over the precipice. He then stacked all the bodies on the truck and pushed it over the edge where it smashed onto the rocks below.

He gingerly unpacked the dead animal. Most of the food was no longer usable but he extracted what he could. He stuffed what was left of the food, along with the remaining blankets, into the packs of the other two animals. Thankfully they had been carrying some of the water.

It took a massive effort but he managed to drag the dead, mangled animal over behind some rocks and discovered a severed human leg lying there. Grimacing, he quickly disposed of it down over the edge of the road where the pick-up had gone, then turned to survey the scene.

Only then did he become aware that one of the pack animals had disappeared back down the road out of sight. Probably the explosion had frightened it. It could have been struck by part of the grenade or a flying object. That particular animal had 6 IED's strapped to it and some of his hand grenades. He debated whether to chase after it but he could see that Jamila needed his help and he couldn't leave her alone right then.

Decision made, he turned and collected the remaining mangled pieces of metal from the truck and threw them over the side as well. The road was still awash with fresh blood and would probably attract attention. The truck would be spotted but the evidence of the dead pack animal might suggest a traffic accident had occurred.

He caught the remaining two animals and hurried them up the road to Jamila's position. She didn't protest when he lifted her onto the back of one of them. He briefly checked her shoulder and tied a piece of torn blanket around it, stopping the bleeding. He had to find a place soon to check it more thoroughly and give her a chance to rest for the night.

In a much-reduced convoy they started up the road. Danny hoped that they wouldn't meet any more travelers as Jamila was no longer in any shape to converse with them.

CHAPTER 7

Afghanistan

A mile down the road Danny found another massive break in the granite and headed back into it on what looked like a well beaten track. It widened into an enclosure the size of a football field so he assumed it might be utilized as a stop by other travelers. For this reason he made his way further along a narrow trail that led off from the far corner of the enclosure treading carefully around large split rocks and boulders. When he couldn't go any further without endangering the animals, he spotted what looked like a large hole in the rocks.

He stopped and went over to examine it. He was delighted to find that the narrow entrance lead into a small cave which had room both for them and the animals.

Not wasting a moment he lead them up into the cave, helped Jamila dismount and led her inside. Having done so he laid out some blankets on the ground in a corner and helped her lie down. She smiled wanly at him without saying anything. He then went and pulled the animals inside. Grabbing the water container he tore another strip off a blanket and knelt beside her.

"You okay Jamila?" he asked as he gently tucked another folded blanket under her head.

"Yes……..okay…..see men get killed……bad men but….." He had to bend lower as her voice was faint.

He nodded. "Yes, I know. It can be a shock, and it happened quite suddenly. No time to warn you. Sorry."

She shook her head violently and made an effort to sit up. "No, they deserve punishment…..were going to take me right there."

"Yeah, I'm afraid I had no option Jamila. It was them or us out there." He pointed at her shoulder. "I need to look at that."

Without waiting for a reply he pulled back the blanket that he had wrapped around her on the road and carefully untied the rough bandage he had placed on her shoulder. The wound was superficial and had probably been sliced by a piece of flying metal. He was glad it wouldn't require stitching because he had no way of doing that. He had seen field medics do a rough job of stitching in emergency situations but they usually had the kits and equipment to carry it out. The wound had stopped bleeding so he gently dabbed the moist blood from her shoulder and tied the bandage on again. The adrenalin from the brief battle was still pumping in his veins.

Despite her frontal exposure, he found himself totally detached in ministering to her. He wasn't seeing her as a woman.

Their continued escape was contingent on getting Jamila back on her feet as soon as possible. Without meeting her eyes he clinically wiped the worst of the blood from her chest and other shoulder as well.

He was aware that she was watching him.

When he had finished he took the blanket from her shoulders and cut a hole in the center with his combat knife helping her put her head through it, providing her with a cape to cover her. He offered her the water container and supported her back as she drank a small amount, then helped her lie back on the blanket. Covering her up, he sat there watching as she closed her eyes. He reached over tentatively and gently held her hand.

He knew the process for treating shock and believed that a nice warm drink of tea was quite often recommended for starters. Lacking this facility as he sat holding her hand he was glad to feel a slight return response from her. After a while he felt that she was either asleep or resting deeply so he went, took the packs off the animals and led them outside to feed on some rough scrub between the rocks. Hunger would not likely cause them to wander back through the rough winding track. Growing thirst might however, and he had to address this problem soon.

Back inside the cave he went through the remaining supplies.

There were twelve IEDs left from the two pack animals and twenty hand grenades. Also remaining were two color grenades, to signal an extraction team if the opportunity presented itself, three double-taped ammo magazines with 15 rounds in each, some extra ammunition and his combat knife.

He sifted through the food and placed it separately on a rock off to one side. There was a hard piece of bread that he devoured greedily and slowly ate one of the 6 OOH AH energy bars that he had taken with him on the mission. He had a small sip of water as they only had one small bag left and took a quick look outside. The two animals were eating close by, seemingly content for the moment.

From habit, he dismantled the MP 5 and cleaned it thoroughly before setting it up where he could grasp it in a hurry.

A wave of fatigue started to sweep over him, a wave he recognized as post action relief. He tried to fight it off knowing the importance of staying alert. Sitting down with his back against a curved rock he watched Jamila as she rested.

He had just come face to face with the enemy and for the first time realized that people like Jamilla would never have a future as long as they were in control. Perhaps they had a real purpose in being in this country after all. His mind drifted off......

He woke suddenly and could see that it was getting dark outside. He must have slept for at least two hours. Jamila was already awake and had been watching him sleep. He could see that she was looking better. There was color back in her cheeks and that sparkle showed again in her eyes.

"I watch you sleep," she murmured. "You looked nice, resting."

He was distracted, suddenly thinking of the animals outside. He glanced down at her as he sprang to his feet.

"The animals! I need to see where they are."

He indicated the mouth of the cave and dashed outside. The animals were nowhere in sight. He groaned and started slowly back down the track, carefully trying to avoid the chunks of granite and rock strewn around. He caught up with them close to the large enclosure which had greeted him when they had left the main road. He managed to grab their halters and turn them around to head back to their location. Just then he became aware of strange noises coming from the enclosure - the sound of motors being revved and voices shouting. He steered the animals in the direction of the cave and gave them a whack on the rump to keep them moving. Then he crept back fifty yards, crouched carefully behind a large boulder and peered out.

He was suddenly wide awake and focused.

The enclosure was full of Taliban fighters and a number of pick-up trucks scattered around with two of them completely blocking the exit to the road. Some tents had already been erected and cooking fires were lit.

A number of AK 47's were stacked in bunches around the area. He couldn't see how many were inside the tents but estimated there were anywhere from 100 to 130 Taliban camped there.

They were trapped.

He wondered if the Taliban would investigate further back down the track at some time, when they had settled in? Danny and Jamila were also running out of water and had two thirsty animals with them.

CHAPTER 8

Afghanistan

Danny hurried the pack animals back along the track and into the cave entrance. When he came in Jamila sat up and seemed to sense that something was wrong.

"Something wrong Da-ne?" she asked.

He pointed. "Taliban or Al Qaeda in the enclosure out there. They're settling in for the night. Some tents are going up and they have the entrance blocked with two pickup trucks."

She climbed to her feet, coming over to him. He noticed that she seemed stronger after her rest.

Jamila suggested, "pack animals will get noisy….no water…better you tie something around noses."

Danny hadn't thought about that though he knew donkeys could bray pretty loudly when they started. That could certainly attract the attention of the fighters camped out front. Following her instruction he tore two strips from a blanket and wrapped them around their noses. They didn't like it very much and swung their heads from side to side as if trying to shake them off.

She touched his arm. "I want go see men," she announced.

He flinched. "That's not a good idea Jamila. They might see you for starters and we wouldn't have a chance back here.

You're also wounded and not very strong right now. Stay here and I'll keep an eye on them. Hopefully they'll be gone in the morning."

She shook her head. "No I must see. If Taliban, maybe they go back into mountains in morning. If Al Qaeda, maybe wait for supplies or guides. Stay longer. Could be days."

He could see from the determined look on her face that this was an argument he was going to lose so he just shrugged and pointed to the cave mouth.

"Okay lets go but I'll go in the lead just in case we run into something," he said.

Danny lead the way cautiously out of the cave followed by Jamila and started back down towards the fighter's encampment. He carried the MP 5 at the ready, alert to any sign of movement ahead. They could hear sounds coming from the encampment as they got closer - the babble of voices, the revving of trucks and the hammering of tent pegs.

When he reached the spot he had observed them from before, he knelt down and whispered to her.

"Keep your head down and stay very still when you look over this rock. A sudden movement is easy to spot if someone's looking this way."

She nodded and carefully inched her head up over the top of the boulder. Danny cautiously did the same. As far as he could see the camp was much the same with a couple of extra tents going up and some men working on the trucks. Fires had been started and food was being prepared. With only an hour to dusk it was obvious that the people in the camp were preparing to bed down for the night.

An idea was starting to form in his mind as he watched. He took careful note of the layout of several areas. It seemed that the majority of the fighters would be sleeping outdoors and the chosen few would be inside the three tents.

He felt Jamila slide back down the rock and he joined her. To his relief she pointed back down the track and they both quickly retreated to the cave and went inside.

He glanced at her without saying anything, his expression a question.

"Al Qaeda," she said matter of factly. "Probably be there one to two days."

He looked surprised. "All Al Quaeda? That's a large bunch for them. I thought they worked in smaller groups leading Taliban fighters."

"Yes, lots of them......not Taliban...I think go fight Americans."

He knew from his Iraq experience how ruthless the Al Qaeda could be in imposing their presence and rule on local militia and even supporters. Making a strong statement by beheading a number of them was common practice. He wondered if the NATO forces were aware of such a large force of pure Al Qaeda heading in their direction.

As if reading his mind she turned to him.

"You fight them, you get killed!" she said vehemently. "Better wait and they go sooner maybe."

Right then he had no intention of sharing the plan that had been germinating in his mind since he first saw the fighters. Since learning that they were an Al Qaeda force, probably on the way to create mayhem with the NATO troops, he was more determined than ever to attempt to put his plan into action. The possible danger of being discovered was certainly high but staying in the cave for two more days was also out of the question.

Smiling he turned to her. "No, not fight now. We eat and then sleep."

He found himself starting to speak pidgin English in responding to her. He carefully put some water in a small basin and gave a small portion to each of the animals who obviously wanted more, and then tied their noses up again.

The two of them ate some of the stale bread and sipped some water without any conversation. Then she went back and lay down on the blanket, her face away from him.

Danny leaned against the back of the cave feeling the cold start to seep into his bones. Jamila rolled over, looked at him and pointed to the spot beside her.

"Come. You keep warm here," she said gently.

He considered it for a moment then walked over and laid the MP5 on the ground beside her bed. Lying down he settled in, pulling some of the blanket she had released over his shoulders. She rolled partially back towards him and he could feel her shapely form through her clothes, her dark eyes only inches away from him. He could feel her warmth and see the need in her face to be held close. Perhaps the proximity of danger had brought this on.

He realized that he could take her right then with her full cooperation and that it would be a wonderful escape from the present situation. At the same time he felt an almost out of body experience in which he saw a thin and pregnant Jamila sitting in a crowded market in Kabul, wearing a bourka and begging for money. All her ambitions of becoming a doctor and helping her people shattered because of a liaison with a British trooper in an Afghan cave. Danny hugged her instead and settled down, placing his arm around her as she turned away. Right then he wanted to see her ambitions fulfilled more than he wanted his own personal gratification. Almost as if she read his thoughts, he felt her hand close over his.

CHAPTER 9

Afghanistan

Some three hours later Danny quietly slipped out of the bed, carefully covering her slight form with the blanket. He sat cross-legged down on the rocky surface of the cave and closed his eyes. He was mentally preparing for battle. Few people could crawl out of bed, go out and cold-bloodedly start killing people. Most warriors needed some sort of transition period or ritual to get the adrenalin going and to toughen up mentally.

Danny visualized the enemy outside getting ready to rally forth and kill NATO troops, his SAS friends, and abuse more young Afghan girls like Jamila. He saw himself as rock-hard and competent, moving into their camp and taking down as many as he needed to in order to accomplish his plan. He insulated his mind from any fears or doubts and saw all his training over the years leading to this moment - training that was far superior to any the Al Qaeda forces could have experienced. He relived a number of the highly challenging but successful operations he had taken part in since joining the regiment and saw himself using the same deadly skills against the enemy camped outside. Then he stood up and started to loosen his muscles by stretching, trying some silent strikes with his hands and feet. Noticing the pack animals beginning to stir, he retrieved his MP5, crept from the cave and made his way back down to the enemy camp, staying alert to any possible Al Qaeda sentries coming his way.

The camp was totally silent. He touched the cougar tooth that Rory Hanlon had given him as if for re-assurance. For 20 minutes he crouched down watching for any movement that would indicate that sentries were posted, but didn't spot anyone. The Al Qaeda forces obviously felt secure in the mountains and were not expecting any trouble. The night was overcast with occasional shafts of light coming through from the moon. He could see that small groups lay together around the dying embers of the cooking fires. Fortunately there were no dogs in the camp, which would have created a different challenge. He had decided to remove the cumbersome Arab clothing, which would make it easier for him to fight should the situation arise. He placed the MP5 on the ground, drew his combat knife and crawled towards the first group of fighters lying together twenty yards away.

His plan was to locate a cell phone on one of the Al Qaeda fighters, and if it had a GPS facility, try to contact Captain Wainwright back in the UK. The plan was fraught with danger as he would have to kill any terrorist first before searching him. Killing someone in the midst of his companions, without waking them was the challenge. The British Gurkha troops were past masters at that.

Slowly he moved up directly into the closest group of sleeping fighters and chose one who was sleeping off to the side. Any commando will tell you that killing a sentry silently means cutting their throat and holding their mouth at the same time to stop them from screaming. Danny also had the additional problem of preventing him from flopping and flailing around, when he was struck, which would have woken the fighters sleeping nearby. Carefully he lifted one of his feet across the still form until he stood astride him. Then he dropped straight down with his knees pinning the man's arms, his left hand clamping across his mouth and his right hand swiftly slicing across the exposed throat. The man's body trembled spontaneously and thrust upward, a moan coming from his clamped mouth. A geyser of blood splashed across Danny's body as the terrorist just as suddenly lay still. Danny maintained the hold on the man's mouth for a moment longer and then eased back, quickly running his hands down the slain man's clothing, looking for a cell phone.

Nothing!

Without thinking he proceeded to the next Al Qaeda member. Still nothing! When all six of the terrorists were dead he stood up. None of them had a cell phone.

He re-considered his options but there weren't any. Even more so he had to carry through with his plan because when the men woke up in the morning or sooner, they would know that an enemy had penetrated their camp and must be nearby. He realized that it had been presumptuous of him to believe that common file Al Qaeda members would carry cell phones.

He looked across at the three tents set up in the middle of the compound and decided that his best bet was in searching the top echelon Al Qaeda leaders sleeping in the tents. He started across, his body and undergarment soaked in blood, looking more like a demon from the abyss than an SAS trooper.

He skirted around various groups sprawled around the compound, crouching low, his every sense alert to any stirring or movement across the camp. Finally he reached the first tent and stood still again listening. The only sounds from inside were various levels of snoring. Parting the tent material he peered through and saw four sleeping forms stretched out on the floor, their heads resting on folded blankets. He crept inside and moved up directly over the four men, his eyes sweeping across them. When his gaze came across the fourth terrorist he froze. The man's face was one he had seen recently in a picture at a briefing prior to the mission.

The man was Mohammad Qureshi the top Al Qaeda leader in Afghanistan, wanted by NATO for many attacks against their forces and murderous assassinations against pro-government villagers. Danny made a decision to start with him and proceeded to do so.

He found his cell phone.

Standing up he looked at the other three sleeping forms. He didn't believe in killing for the sake of killing but if either of those three men woke up during the next phase of his plan it wouldn't work. Reluctantly he dispatched them as well.

Looking around the tent he spotted a document case lying on the ground near the head of Mohammad Qureshi. He snatched it up, crept to the tent door and carefully peered outside.

Still nothing stirred.

Stepping out he looked thoughtfully towards the other two tents, wondering if there were more Al Qaeda leaders sleeping there that he should take out. He decided not to stretch his luck and darted across the compound heading back down the track towards the cave. When he was far enough away from the camp where they couldn't hear his voice, he huddled in behind some rocks and took out the cell phone.

He dialed the Afghan exit code and a number back in the UK, hoping against hope that the phone was linked up to a satellite When the number started ringing he breathed a sigh of relief. He smiled when he heard the voice on the other end. He had dialed the man's home number: Captain Wainwright, his CO of the troop in Hereford.

"Hello?"

"Capt Wainwright, this is Danny Quigley."

There was silence at the other end, then finally "Who is this? Stop messing around!" the voice barked.

"It's Danny. I'm stuck out here in the mountains in Afghanistan and I need your help."

There was a gasp at the other end.

"Danny? But we thought you were …."

"Yeah dead. I know. Nearly was a number of times. Now I need you to listen. I haven't got much time."

Danny briefed him on his situation. There were more exclamations when he told of Mohammed Qureshi and the dispatching of the terrorists. Then he told Wainwright of his plan.

"I don't want you to cut off this phone when I've finished the call. I'm going to leave the line open and bring the cell phone back into the center of the camp. Obviously don't speak on the line again or it might alert them. What I want you to do is to get NATO to triangulate the cell phone and throw in an air strike a.s.a.p. There are 120 hard core Al Qaeda back there heading towards the American zone and they're up to no good. Now tell them to make their run parallel to the road and not back into the rocky part behind because I'm hiding there. Can you do that?"

Wainwright was struggling to assimilate the new train of events.

"Okay Danny, I've got it. Now I have to tell you there's no guarantee on how fast this can happen. If the Americans have assets up in the air already, an armed drone perhaps and can divert them, it could happen fast, but they may have to pull some planes off their carriers so that would take longer."

Danny listened impatiently. "Look Captain, if that camp wakes up I'm a dead duck back here. I still have a weapon and some grenades but I would run out of ammo pretty quick."

Wainwright could sense his tension.

"Okay, look, I better get on to it. Now assuming we can pull this off, how will we extract you afterwards, Danny?"

"You'll have my position from the triangulation and I'll be heading directly down the road from this location towards the British positions. I still have two color grenades I can set off if I spot a rescue chopper. Oh by the way, I have a case of documents I took from the leader's tent and I have a woman with me. I want her extracted as well."

"A woman! Danny, I don't know what to say."

"Say nothing. She saved my life a number of times. She comes out with me."

"Danny, I'm just thinking, going back into that camp is risky. Could you not just place the cell phone as close as possible to the area and let the air strike plaster the whole area?"

"I could but I'm not going to. Half the terrorists could possibly survive if the Americans were even slightly off target, or they could blast me back here. No, I'm heading back in and remember, be careful not to break this connection. Bye Captain."

"Bye, Danny," said Wainwright reluctantly.

CHAPTER 10

Afghanistan

Danny stood up. He was careful to keep his hand away from the buttons on the cell phone as he crept down the track towards the compound. Again he repeated the same procedure of listening and moving carefully back across the camp. He had decided to place the cell phone just outside the other two tents so as to increase the possibilities of killing the Al Qaeda leaders. The camp appeared to be still in a dead slumber until he rounded the corner of one of the tents and almost bumped into a man standing there relieving himself. They were almost eye to eye momentarily and as the man drew his breath in to scream Danny did two things automatically. He dropped the phone on the ground and reached up with his left hand, clamping it on the man's mouth. Then he plunged the combat knife in and up into the man's stomach. As he fell Danny went back down with him twisting the knife upwards and clamping harder with his left hand. A half moan came out of his throat as his body writhed. Danny held on grimly until the man's body was still. He lay there for a moment waiting to see if anyone had been alerted. Then with trepidation he searched around until his hand came into contact with the dropped cell phone. He lifted it up to his face and it was with relief that he saw it was still connected. That was far too close, he thought. The whole plan depended on the camp staying asleep and the cell phone connection staying open. He knew there was technology in existence that could track cell phones even when they were switched off but he wasn't exactly sure how it would work in the mountains or until the experts had triangulated it in the first place. He carefully placed the phone off to the side of the second tent behind some packs and stole away to the edge of the camp where he had previously discarded his clothing. Gingerly he put them back on feeling them stick to the congealed blood on his body. Turning, he went back to the cave.

When he was almost up to their location he became aware of a form dashing towards him and caught his arms. It was Jamila.

"I woke...you were gone." She felt the stickiness of his clothing and gasped. "You are hurt!"

"No, no, I.........." he started.

"You fight? You go fight Al Qaeda?"

"Yes I.........look the Americans may be coming."

She looked around. "Coming, from where?" she asked in obvious puzzlement.

"Air strike I hope. I try a signal. We need to get inside the cave."

Once inside she got some of the precious water and gently washed the blood off his face. His clothes were still a mess. The two pack animals started thrashing about smelling the water. Danny tried to explain what he had tried to set up using the cell phone. She didn't ask him how he had got blood all over him. Then they sat down together. Danny still couldn't relax after the action, aware that there was more to come.

It was over an hour later that the first explosion came and made them both jump at its suddenness. Several more followed, the last of which rattled the cave mouth and they heard boulders crashing outside. Then it was over. Danny waited for a few moments, grabbed the MP 5 and raced out of the cave back down the small track. It had changed considerably by the explosions with fresh boulders and rocks strewn all around. As he was nearing the end of the track two blackened fighters staggered around the corner in front of him, still clutching their rifles. He dispatched them swiftly with a short burst from the MP5 and continued racing into the camp wanting to catch any survivors while they were still shaken up by the attacks. He found several more, some unscathed, and just kept going, totally focused, moving on through the camp as he cut them down one at a time. Finally after finishing off about twelve terrorists he went over to where, approximately, the tents had been situated. There was nothing but burnt and blackened bodies strewn around and the whole camp looked like a charnel house with half naked lumps littering the compound. The exit was now clear with the pick-ups blown off to one side by the force of the explosions. He did a slower circuit of the compound checking for survivors. Finding none, he raced back down the track to the cave.

Jamila was waiting.

"They're all dead," he gasped, breathless after his sprint.

Her face changed. "All? All dead? How can this be?" she whispered.

He looked at her closely. "An air strike has terrible force, and in a contained space..... well..." He patted her arm. "Now the exit is open so we need to get out of here. Lets grab those animals Jamila."

They were back on the track within ten minutes. Danny tried to shield Jamila as they came through the devastated Al Qaeda camp. She still had the presence of mind to grab two water packs from one of the pickups that had previously blocked the camp exit as she went past.

CHAPTER 11

Afghanistan

They had barely gone a mile down the track when they heard a motor cycle coming from behind and in a moment they were overtaken by an Arab who skidded to a halt beside them. He was a large brutish man with fierce suspicious looking eyes as he got off his motorcycle, un-strapped his rifle and strode across to Danny and Jamila who at that point were standing together. He stopped in front of Danny and spoke something harshly to him.

Danny did his usual 'Agghh' and pointed to Jamila who spoke up. The man's eyes flicked briefly to her but came back to Danny. He took in his bloodied clothes, then suddenly reached up and tore the scarf from his face.

Recognition flashed on the man's face as he became aware of an English soldier standing directly in front of him.

He stepped back, starting to swing his rifle. Danny stepped forward striking the man's right shoulder behind with his left hand and the front of the left shoulder with his right, effectively swiveling him, and slipping him into a strangle hold. Danny dropped to his knee maintaining the hold and heard the neck snap.

Then he stood up. Jamila was standing there looking at him. He couldn't tell what she was thinking.

He sprang into action unloading the two pack animals and set them free. He dragged the remaining packs of IEDs across behind some rocks and retained two color grenades. Jamila moved too, surprising him by catching the dead Arab by his boots, tossing him over the edge of the road and sending his rifle after him.

Then Danny jumped on the motor cycle and started it up. Jamila stood there on the road looking at him, fear reflected in her eyes. He pointed to the back.

"Come on. Jump up."

A look of relief flashed across her face as she raced to the bike and hopped on.

CHAPTER 12

Afghanistan

After traveling for three hours and with dawn starting to streak across the sky Danny cocked his head listening and slowed the motor cycle to a halt. It was the swishing sound of an approaching chopper that had stopped him. In a moment he saw it sweeping along parallel to the strip of roadway. He extracted a color grenade and threw it on the road ahead of him. Within minutes a helicopter with US markings settled down before them. Danny switched off the bike and dismounted, helping Jamila do the same.

The first thing Danny noticed was a camera pointed at him from inside the helicopter. Two soldiers had stepped out of the chopper, weapons at the ready.

"Step away from the vehicle," one barked.

Danny shrugged bringing his arms to waist height.

"Look I'm Danny Quigley," he started.

"Step away from the vehicle." The voice was harder, more insistent. "The woman too."

Danny shook his head and nodded to Jamila who was standing there, confusion written all across her face.

They stepped away from the motor cycle.

"Now get those fucking A-rab clothes off," the soldier continued, his weapon steady on Danny.

Danny hesitated. "I spent several days in these mountains fighting Al Quaeda and the Taliban and now I have to fight you bastards as well......shit...so much for fucking allies."

He reached down and lifted the loose fitting blood-stained garment from his body flinging it to the ground, followed by the turban. He stood there bruised and soaked in dried blood on the hard dusty road, the MP5 on his shoulder.

The weapons of the two soldiers wavered and dropped.

"Shit," one of them gasped. "Will you look at that?"

A face stuck out of the chopper.

"Sorry about this Quigley. We had to be sure. I'm Major Blackburn, Intelligence. We need to talk."

Danny strode across to the chopper, ignoring the two soldiers, and shook the Major's hand. He handed him the document case he'd found in the Al Qaeda camp.

"Found this on the Al Qaeda leaders. Might be useful. Now what is it you need to talk to me about?"

The Major looked around nervously.

"We need to get out of here pronto. We're sitting ducks right now so let's get airborne."

"Fine, but she comes with me," he said pointing to Jamila who was standing there uncertainly. The Major was starting to help Danny into the chopper.

"Sorry we don't take women on board, especially Afghans. Regulations."

Danny extracted himself from his grasp stepping back.

"I arranged for this woman to be extracted with me. She risked her life to save mine and she wouldn't last five minutes on this road by herself."

"Sorry Quigley, but as I said......."

Danny strode over to the motor cycle pulling it straight and nodding to Jamila who jumped on.

"If she can't come then piss off. I was doing quite well without you," Danny shouted reaching for the key.

"Wait, wait, wait," the officer pleaded, jumping out of the chopper and coming over to him.

"Okay, I'm breaking all the rules but we need the intelligence you picked up out here and in particular we need to view the target area of the air strike and film it. We understand you identified and killed Mohammed Qureshi back there and some of his cohorts."

Danny nodded grudgingly as he climbed off the bike and helped Jamila do the same. Then he pushed it to the side of the road and, taking Jamila's hand, went over and climbed aboard the chopper with her.

The two soldiers avoided his gaze.

Danny and the Major joined the pilot and he directed them back up the track. When he got to the site where he had dumped the IEDs he pointed down. The chopper landed and the soldiers went and carefully recovered the explosive devices and the hand grenades.

"Better in our hands than running the risk of the Taliban getting them," the Major commented.

When they got to the enclosure it was exactly as they'd left it. The chopper had difficulty landing with the dead bodies strewn around. The crew stared in amazement at the killing ground.

"Jesus, it reminds me of the final scene in that film about General Custer and the battle of the Big Horn….all the bodies lying around," the Major said dazedly.

"Except this isn't a film and those aren't actors," Danny pointed out.

Jamila and the pilot stayed in the plane while the two soldiers grabbed their cameras and started going round the camp taking pictures.

Danny led him to the center of the compound where the tents had been originally.

"I killed Mohammed Qureshi in one of those…not sure which one now, with the air strike."

"How did you kill him?" the Major asked.

"I cut his throat," Danny replied.

The Major started examining the bodies. " There's others here with their throats cut too."

71

Danny shrugged. "I figured they must be big wigs as well, being in the same tent, so I took them out. There's another bunch over there," he pointed. "I had to deal with them when I first came into the camp. I was looking for a cell phone but none of them had one so I moved over to one of these tents."

The Major whistled. "My God you were busy Quigley."

Just then one of the soldiers called over.

"A number of these have been shot."

The Major turned to Danny. "How come?"

"After the air strike I came in here fast and found some survivors. There's more up that track. Naturally I finished them off " he said lamely.

"Ah…naturally….how many exactly? Do you recall?" the Major enquired tentatively.

"Probably a dozen or so. I wasn't counting. Some of them had weapons and were as mad as hell."

"I don't blame them Quigley. A whole group of Al Qaeda wiped out, and their leaders. Now show me where you were holed up prior to phoning in to your CO in the UK?"

It took a good half hour to wrap up with the Intelligence Officer's requirements and then they took off again. Despite the danger the Major insisted on back tracking to the pick up truck that Danny had rolled off the road with the dead terrorists. When they reached the location the terrain was too rough to land but the strewn bodies were lying around the crashed vehicle and the cameramen were busy again.

Just then Danny spotted the pack mule that had run off, after the pick up explosion and pointed it out. The Major peered down at it with his glasses.

"No room to land there but we can't leave six IEDs for the Taliban to find."

He nodded to the pilot who swung the chopper round parallel to the track. The Major spoke to the two soldiers who fired off a long series of bursts at the animal. Suddenly there was a massive explosion and the animal evaporated. A whole section of the road disappeared and collapsed over the edge into a ravine. Danny glanced at Jamila who avoided his eyes. He wondered if the animal had been part of her family.

The Major looked at Danny, chortling.

"Hey, look at that! Closed the road as well. That'll slow the bastards up. Come on lets go home. You know we counted a hundred and twenty dead Al Qaeda back in that compound, at least twenty two killed by you personally. There's another eight killed in that pick up back there. I understand from a debriefing of yours and our Delta team colleagues that you personally killed at least thirty Taliban in the village at the ambush site and saved the unit from being wiped out by allowing them to withdraw. That's one hell of a record for several days in the field."

Almost as an afterthought he asked "where did you get the motor cycle?"

Danny looked embarrassed. "Ah this Taliban stopped us…" he started to say.

"Dead too?" The Major glanced sideways at him.

"Ah…yes…actually he is," Danny added.

"What about those IEDs? Who did you get them from?" the Major enquired.

Danny's gaze flicked across to Jamila. He didn't want to get her involved.

"Well…..I took them from two Taliban. I'm afraid they're dead as well."

"Hmm…on top of your actions back in the village, the pick up truck you blasted and the air strike, you can take responsibility for taking out approximately a hundred and sixty Taliban and Al Qaeda with their leader Mohammed what's his name? Also removing a bunch of IEDs from their forces. That in itself will save many coalition lives."

He hefted the document case.

"This could be a gold mine too. Quigley, if I have anything to do with it you're going to get the highest decoration that America can give you, and that's on top of anything the Brits give you. Who knows, the Afghan government may honor you as well. Right now let me shake your hand and apologize for the way we greeted you when we first met you."

When they landed back in Kandahar, Danny was surprised to find the Delta team lined up on the tarmac and right in front of them Captain Wainwright. Everything seemed a blur after that.

Danny had pulled on the blood stained Arab clothing again as the chopper crew didn't have anything with them. There was a collective gasp from the waiting group as he sprang onto the tarmac. He turned and helped Jamila down and introduced her to Wainwright with a few terse words.

"Get her please to her Aunt's medical clinic here in the city Captain. Tell her I'll contact her a.s.a.p."

Wainwright nodded.

"The troops are out on a mission right now Danny. I flew over directly I got your call last night...special flight. It's ready to fly you back to RAF Lynehan when the people here are finished with you and I'll arrange for Fiona and your daughter to be there waiting for you.. Sorry but intelligence wants to do a de-brief here with you first and check you over. You know the routine. Catch you later mate."

He caught Jamila gently by the elbow and Danny gave her a quick hug as she turned away and disappeared with Wainwright into the crowd.

In a moment he was surrounded by the Delta team and other coalition forces who had been waiting. Danny was suddenly clasped by Rory Hanlon in a fierce grip.

"Danny, thank God you got out. I'm sorry I didn't wait to see you get clear. I thought you were right behind me."

Danny smiled easily.

"It was my choice Rory...I just waited too long after I waved you away. No fault of yours at all. Don't worry about it."

Two days later Danny finally got the clear from the medical check ups and debriefing and took a taxi to the clinic in the city. It was closed down. Through an interpreter he found out that the clinic had closed two days ago and the woman running it had moved to Kabul.

There had been a young woman with her when she left.

Not a man with ready tears, Danny felt himself choking up when he saw a large contingent from the regiment lined up to greet him when he climbed down the steps of the plane at RAF Lyneham back in the U.K. Out in front he spotted the red hair of his wife Fiona and a smaller form huddled beside her; His daughter Allison, who launched herself into the open space between them and hurled herself into his arms.

Her words struck him like an arrow in his heart.

"Please don't leave me again Daddy," she sobbed.

Fiona heard this plea as she came up alongside Danny.

"From the mouth of babes Danny. Allison echoes my sentiments exactly. I understand the regiment is giving you two weeks of compassionate leave. This gives us lots of time to discuss where this family is going."

CHAPTER 13

London, England

It wasn't so much a discussion as an ultimatum. Fiona told him, in no uncertain terms, to get out of the Forces, or else. He took it to mean divorce.

Afghanistan had been the last straw for her. She did not want herself or Allison, to ever go through that trauma again.

Danny had been in the Forces for most of his married life. That meant months away from home, and for Special Forces, the deployment could be to any trouble spot in the world: a phone call in the middle of the night, and he was gone, without any knowledge of where he was going, when he would return, or even if he would return.

Like most military wives, she lived in dread of a visit from the regiment Padre, signifying bad news. In order to survive emotionally she moved from their rented house outside the base in Hereford, to London, where she started studying interior decorating. As her career progressed she bought a small house, which meant that Danny, who now lived on the base, had to take a two hour drive on his weekend passes.

The thought of leaving the regiment was a shock to Danny. His whole identity, the core of who and what he was as an individual, was as a warrior in the SAS, a regiment in the British army. He excelled as a member of that elite group and was held in great respect by his fellow soldiers for his courage, competency and skills. His future career was assured, and his promotion to Sergeant was imminent.

He argued with her, reasoned with her, and finally pleaded with her, but to no avail. Allison had clung to him ever since he had returned, and in the end his decision came down to the words she'd greeted him with on the tarmac:

"Daddy, please don't ever leave me again."

Game over.

He took his discharge from the regiment…reluctantly, however, his challenges had only just begun. The top jobs for ex-special forces were in Iraq and Afghanistan, providing security for visiting politicians and re-construction crews. They were non-starters as far as Fiona was concerned, so he went hunting for a normal civilian job.

The next four months were a blur to Danny.

He got a job checking trucks into a construction site and lasted a week.

Employed in a frozen food plant, he was fired when he stuck up for an immigrant worker who was being verbally abused by a manager. The humiliation of the whole process!

He was telling Fiona about it one evening after Allison had gone to bed.

"There I was sitting across from a pimply-faced, twenty year-old clerk, in the job center, looking disdainfully down at my personal data, and he says:

'You don't really have the qualifications that most employers are looking for Mister Quigley.'

Can you imagine it? Having put my butt on the line for my country, time and time again, that nerd, who, at the time, was probably smoking pot outside his high school, tells me that I'm of no use to society!"

She looked searchingly across at him.

"You're finding this difficult aren't you Danny?"

"Difficult?" he exploded. "That's not the half of it. The questions I'm asked at an interview, when I get one, like

'What major skills have you developed, while you were in the Forces?'

I'm tempted to say, well I can kill someone with my bare hands in five seconds."

"How on earth do you answer it?" she asked.

"Oh, I say I'm very focused and efficient in carrying out designated tasks."

She chuckled for the first time.

"What other questions do you get?"

He sat forward, really warming to it.

"Well the other day, I was asked what one task I had handled really well in the army. Well, I thought of the time I took a five hundred yard shot with a sniper rifle in Iraq and brought down a terrorist, just as a sand storm started to sweep in."

Her interest piqued, she asked.

"You surely didn't tell him that. What on earth did you say Danny?"

He grinned.

"No, I said that I was given the task of terminating someone's employment, because they had been contravening safety regulations, and that I had concluded it to everyone's satisfaction."

His grin faded as he glanced across at her.

"You know Fiona, these last four months......."

"Yes," she cut in. "Yourself and Allison have grown as thick as thieves. You two are nuts about each other. Nearly makes me feel insecure."

"Well, yes, that's super, but it's me that's feeling insecure here. Fiona, you and I are living almost as brother and sister. We had more going for us, when I was home on a weekend pass. Now I feel like an intruder. Remember, you're the one who insisted that I get out of the regiment."

She shifted in her seat.

"Okay, fair comment. Here's the thing Danny. I've been running my own life for the past several years, and trying to make a career for myself. On weekend passes, you were here and gone, and my life went back to normal. Let's face it, you were really married to the regiment. Even when you were home with Allison and myself, you never stopped talking about your mates in the Sass, and the crack you had together. I could see your mood lifting, when you were packing to go back down to Hereford, after a weekend with Allison and myself."

"What exactly are you trying to tell me Fiona? I certainly wont apologize for the bond that existed between myself and my mates in the regiment. You're right, they were like family. We trusted each other totally. We had to! Hell, we'd saved each others lives, on many a mission."

She reached across and touched his hand.

"I'm sorry Danny. I'm saying all this wrong and I'm really trying to sort it out in my own head as I'm going along. I suppose it's having you home for the past four months, that's made me realize how little we have in common any more, apart from Allison, that is."

They fell silent. Awareness of what was happening, struck both of them.

Finally Danny stirred.

"One thing's for sure Fiona. Getting out of the regiment has helped me discover what an incredible daughter we have. She's just amazing and I love her to bits. If I'd carried on, I would have missed these years and I can now see how precious they are, so thanks for that anyway."

She made a face.

"It's very little to thank me for Danny. I feel that I've really messed up your life."

He shrugged.

"Water under the bridge at this stage. but in view of our little chat, would you mind if I moved into the spare room from now on? It's just that being near you and not able to ………"

Impulsively, she reached forward and gave him a hug.

"I'm so sorry Danny," she whispered.

Incredibly, the next day he was offered a job.

CHAPTER 14

Danny Quigley realized that he would have to master how to sell Life Insurance or go back to killing people. Possibly starting with the difficult prospect sitting in front of him who appeared to be an expert at coming up with objections.

"Why do I need life insurance?" he demanded, "I'm a young man and I've no intentions of dying soon anyway."

Danny blinked, his lean hawk-like face showing none of the frustration he was feeling inside. Right then he could think of a dozen ways to make him die soon and at that stage, he would make sure that it was a painful death as well!

The prospect, Jeremy Peters, a short stocky man with prematurely receding hair, smirked and cast a triumphant glance at his wife Debbie sitting across the table from him. She in turn, looked beseechingly at Danny. With two small children, a mortgage and a car loan, she had discovered the previous week that her husband had no life insurance and had contacted the branch. However, the husband didn't share his wife's concern and appeared to look on Danny's visit as an opportunity to demonstrate to her just how clever he was. The fact that he measured up pretty poorly against Danny's tall athletic appearance might have sparked the adversary role he'd adopted when he first called at the house. Danny realized that according to the way this meeting was going, he wasn't doing a very good job of providing for the particular family's security, or his own career for that matter.

Desperate, after four months without a job, he had leapt at the opportunity of a career in Financial Services. However the transition from being a macho trooper in the Special Forces, to making sales, was a lot more challenging than he had at first appreciated. Now sitting at a kitchen table with Jeremy Peters, his prospect, he was frantically trying to recall the training he'd had on his induction course on how to overcome objections.

"Well, ah, … Jeremy, you're a married man with a wife and two young children and they would be up the proverbial creek if anything happened to stop your income, such as death or terminal illness. This plan would kick in and pay off your mortgage and car loan and provide a basic income until the children were finished school. Statistics show that at your age there's a one in three chance that you could get hit with a terminal illness before you reach age 65. Can you see how valuable this plan could be in the event that might happen?"

His wife Debbie reached across the table and touched her husband's hand.

"Oh Jeremy, it sounds exactly what we need," she entreated.

He withdrew his hand, his face reddening.

"Look we can't afford to pay any insurance premiums right now. Anyway I'd want to shop around and compare rates. How do I know this guy isn't trying to rip us off?" He almost spat the words out.

Danny felt his leg muscles tense, as if they were ready to deliver a swift kick under the table at him. At that stage he was coming to the conclusion that he didn't even want the guy for a client, but conscious of Debbie's reliance on him, he decided to hang in there. He leaned forward and looked Jeremy directly in the eye.

"I appreciate where you're coming from Jeremy. I wouldn't dream of telling you how to run your financial affairs, but in fairness I'm sure it would be easier for you to come up with seventy five pounds a month for this program than for Debbie to find two thousand pounds a month to pay the ongoing bills if you died prematurely. Oh and by the way, I can provide you with the top five quotations from across the whole industry which I can show you right here on my laptop, so in effect you decide which one you want to invest in. Would you like me to do that?"

Jeremy looked from one to the other and stood up from the table.

"I feel I'm getting ganged-up on right now with you two. Anyway I'd like to think about it. Look, leave me your card and I can contact you at a later date."

Danny eyed him levelly. Yeah, much later, he thought. Reluctantly he stood up also, closing the front zipper on his laptop and flicking an apologetic glance at Debbie who was sitting with her head down. He didn't even bother leaving his card, and after a few muttered exchanges quickly left the house and went to where his car was parked. Sitting inside he ran his mind back over the visit that he'd just finished. It should have been an easy sale. He wasn't sure what else he could have done to salvage the situation.

Shrugging his shoulders he started the car and headed back towards the office, greeting Glenna the branch secretary, cheerfully.

She smiled sympathetically at him when he recounted how the call had gone. She had initially taken the telephone enquiry and stuck her neck out by convincing his manager Chris Ellison to pass it to him.

"You can't win them all Danny. The guys here who've been doing this for years say that sometimes it's like falling off a log, and at other times it's like pulling hens teeth. Even the real pros couldn't close those ones. Hey, it's par for the course. Don't let it get you down. Too bad old C.C. isn't here, he'd be glad to help you out."

Danny's face creased with interest.

"Old C.C. Who's he?"

She ignored his query and cut across him.

"Oh, by the way, Chris wants to see you when you get in."

Danny made a face. He wasn't looking forward to meeting his manager right then. Glenna was a pleasant-faced, slightly overweight woman who tended to play a motherly role with the sales consultants just like she did with her two teenage sons. There was something about Danny however that she had particularly taken to. Most women would have been attracted to his lean good looks, dark hair and relaxed confident manner but Glenna was struck by his ready smile, his intense blue eyes and courteous manner. Now she waved a thumbs-up to him as he went past her towards the manager's office. He waved back.

Anna, a curvy blonde drifted over.

"He's something else isn't he?" she commented.

Glenna glanced up.

"Yeah, he's real nice, is Danny."

"Nice isn't what I'm talking about Glenna. Though he has a nice butt I'll grant you. See how he walks? Like he's treading on eggshells. There's something almost dangerous about the guy."

Glenna took a half-hearted swipe at her.

"My God, you young ones! Is that all you ever think about?"

"What else is there Glenna? Tell me and I'll go there. It's certainly not calling my so-called prospects for the next two hours. Danny would be a nice distraction instead," she added, rolling her eyes.

"Oh for God's sake Anna, he's a married man," Glenna said reprovingly.

"Soon to be divorced Glenna. He's fair game. Wife gave him an ultimatum to get out of the Forces and then handed him divorce papers after four months. How's that for little apples?"

"Yes, so I hear." Glenna shook her head sadly. "That's a tough call for Danny, and him with an eight year-old daughter as well, cute little girl called Allison. She was in here one day with him and they obviously think the world of each other."

She nodded at the manager's office door.

"Struggling to make a go of it right now as well. Chris is having a chat with him."

Realization flooded Anna's face.

"Talking of butts. I better get off mine and make some calls or he'll be hauling me in next."

She hurried off to her desk leaving Glenna smiling.

Chris Dennison was a solidly built ex-rugby player, who had grown a successful career in financial planning over several years, with a methodical focused approach to the business. At this point he was running a team of fifteen consultants and still servicing his existing clients. Now his shrewd eyes looked up as his new recruit walked into his office.

"How did the call go Danny?"

Danny smiled ruefully as he recounted the events of the mornings disappointing call.

After finishing he looked askance at his manager.

"I blew it didn't I? I'll bet you could have sold him."

Chris leaned forward.

"Let me tell you Danny, I can blow it like the rest of them and just as fast. Now look, let's put this down to the learning curve. I'm not worried about you at all at this stage. You're a good looking presentable young man and you're pumping in the activity, sending out the letters, making the phone calls, seeing the people and so on. From my experience this inevitably leads to business."

"Yeah I know," Danny said obviously frustrated, "but I seem to be missing something in this whole process. It's just not working for me. In the meantime the company is advancing me money on a monthly basis, and it's not going to do that forever is it?"

Chris nodded, his face thoughtful.

"Okay, fair comment. In a months time, if you haven't written any business I'll be having a much more serious chat with you. Head office will want an account of your progress or lack of, but right now keep on doing what you've been doing. Perhaps you could ask some of the more established agents for some advice on closing sales, or accompany them on a call if they don't mind. Too bad old C.C. isn't here, you might have caught him at the coffee point and picked his brains. He was something else."

Danny sat up straight.

"Glenna just mentioned his name a moment ago. Who is this C.C. exactly?"

Chris chuckled.

"Who is he? Clive Courtney, known as C.C.. Who was he, you mean? Only the best life insurance salesperson in the whole country, possibly the whole world. Earned an average of over half a million sterling every year. Now he's disappeared - upped and quit and no one knows where he's gone. Apparently he consulted with head office and arranged for a dedicated team to service his business, but then he disappeared into thin air, period. Our regional manager is off sick as a result. You can imagine the hole in his figures this year!"

Danny looked puzzled.

"Does anyone here know how he got his level of business? Surely he worked with someone. What about his personal assistant, wouldn't she know?"

"She's quit too," Chris replied. "C.C. set her up with a fully funded pension which, because she's over 50 years of age, she can draw on right away. Apparently she's moved house and has let it be known that she wouldn't welcome people coming and trying to debrief her or reveal where C.C. has gone."

Danny expelled his breath noisily.

"I find this hard to take in. A guy walks away from a half a million a year income and no one knows how he did it or where he's gone. Sounds like a fairy tale to me."

Chris laughed.

"A fairy tale, yes, and probably a pot of gold for anyone who can locate him and gain his confidence. Yeah, wouldn't that be something?"

The meeting went on for another twenty minutes and when it was finished Danny went back out and sat down at Glenna's desk.

She smiled at him.

"Was Chris able to help you then? He's good - knows his stuff."

"Well, yes and no. I accept I need some seasoning in getting this job right Glenna, but I'm running out of time. I need to start cracking it real soon. I can't just keep spinning my wheels here until head office give me the boot."

"I'm not sure where this conversation is leading. Danny. Is there something you expect me to do for you? As I said, Chris would be the best guide to help you start driving your business forward."

He leaned forward and looked her directly in the face.

"C.C. Courtney, Glenna. Since I heard that name it's sort of resonated inside my head and I have a strong feeling that I need to find him and talk to him. Now I'll bet you have some contact with his old PA. Someone as friendly and outgoing as you would naturally be a confidante of hers. Aren't I right?"

She studied his face carefully.

"Whether you're right or not isn't the point. If Sonya didn't want to be found, and she didn't, and had confided in me, I certainly wouldn't betray a confidence. Seriously though, without trying to hurt your feelings, what makes you think that C.C. at his level in the business would even want to meet with a rookie like you?"

"Ah ha ... Sonya! So she has a name at least. That's a start. Why would he want to see me? I don't know the answer to that, but I do feel a strong pull to pursue this and if you don't help me I'll have to find some other way."

She sighed.

"Danny, Danny, you're a terribly nice young man and I'd love to help you and see you do well just as I do with all the consultants here, but you're going on the wrong track. Listen to Chris. There are no short cuts to this business and I've seen salespeople come and go over the years. Some of them think there has to be a better less painful way to make it in the business, and so they throw out all the techniques and concepts they learned on their training course and do their own thing, and guess what? Before you know it they're out the door, and working at McDonalds for a pittance. Had they been prepared to pay their dues and work the process designed by people who have succeeded in the business, they probably would have made it. I hate to say it Danny but that sounds just like what you're doing. My advice is to get your head down and work your way through this. Forget C.C. and whatever you thought he could do for you. The challenge for you is right here and now, and C.C. can't help you with that."

She reached forward and touched his arm.

"Sorry, I didn't mean to make a speech, but there it is. That's how I feel."

Danny smiled ruefully.

"I hear you Glenna and I appreciate your advice. I mean that."

He stood up and paced back and forth in front of her desk and then turned back to her.

"It's just that it goes deeper than that. For some reason I very strongly feel the need to find C.C. for reasons other than learning his secrets, though I confess that's my primary motivation and I don't really understand it myself. There has to be a way to locate him and I'm going to keep trying. In the meantime, you're right of course. I've been shown the blueprint and I just have to master it. Speaking of which, I'm off to make some phone calls. Thanks again Glenna."

Glenna watched him go into the open plan area of the office towards his desk. Then looking around her almost covertly, she picked up the phone and spoke quietly into it for a minute before hanging up.

CHAPTER 15

Danny was in the middle of his twentieth cold call on the telephone to potential clients, which was turning out just as disastrous as all the previous nineteen. He was using the standard script given to him on the head office training course.

"I have some ideas that I believe would be of benefit to yourself and your family and what I'd like is the opportunity to sit down with you sometime next week and go over these with you. The service is free and without obligation. Now are mornings or afternoons better for you?"

"I'm not interested."

The voice sounded aggressive in his ear.

"You're not interested! But I haven't even discussed some of these ideas with you yet. How can you say you're not interested in something you haven't even heard?"

The voice at the other end was even more aggressive and angry.

"You're not very good at listening are you? I said I'm not interested and that's final."

The phone was slammed down at the other end.

Finally in frustration Danny tidied up his desk and headed out to a local pub where he had a hot sandwich and a coke. Danny's gut feeling to locate C.C. gnawed at him more than ever. The trainers at head office had warned him about the difficulties of getting his business off the ground but he didn't think it would be this mind-numbing. There must be something he wasn't doing right.

On his way back to the branch he spotted Glenna crossing the road in front of him and ran to catch her up. Hearing his footsteps she glanced back.

"Oh it's you, and you're running. Why am I not surprised? Everyone in the branch comments on how fit you look."

They started chatting as they walked back together. Danny was keeping straight ahead when she caught his arm and pointed out a short-cut through an underground garage. Once inside it turned out to be a dark and dismal place full of parked cars. As his eyes adjusted to the dimmer light he spotted a bulky-looking beggar with unkempt hair and dirty, scruffy clothes. He was leaning up against a parked car and watching them approach. As they drew nearer he moved into their path and stuck his red face out aggressively, his breath smelling of booze.

"Come on me maties, how about a few coins for a meal?" he muttered, his eyes measuring them speculatively.

"Just ignore him," whispered Glenna, quickening her pace and brushing past him.

Danny had come to the same conclusion and hurried to catch her up, only to bump into her as she stopped suddenly.

"Oh God," she exclaimed.

Looking up Danny saw two more heavy-set, thuggish-looking men up ahead, emerging from behind some parked cars, and approaching them with hands clenched and mouthing obscenities. Looking back they saw the hulking beggar they had brushed past bearing down on them, a sneer on his mottled face.

"Ignore me, is that what you said missus?" he growled menacingly. At the same time he grabbed her arm and twisted her handbag savagely off her shoulder. Danny, out of his peripheral vision saw the first fist flying at him from one of the other two villains. Without thinking he dropped slightly lower and found himself automatically blocking the blow with his left hand and chopping down onto the thug's arm with his right. He heard the bone break and the man screamed, dropping to his knees. Danny's foot shot out as he swiftly kicked him in the stomach and the attacker sprawled backwards on the cement floor.

Somewhat blocked by his fallen mate the other man stumbled momentarily and Danny took advantage of this to turn to the one who had wrenched Glenna's handbag from her. Witnessing the quick dispatch of his partner, the beggar took a step back and produced a wicked looking cosh from his coat.. He rushed at Danny.

"Here, I'll fix your bloody face mate," he muttered, taking a massive swing at his head.

This time Danny didn't block but swayed sideways as the cosh swished past, and then kicked sharply at the shin bone in front of him. The man howled in pain and Danny carried through by chopping down savagely on the side of the man's neck.

Not even waiting to see him fall, Danny turned smoothly to face the opposite direction in time to see the third thug produce an open flick knife, coming at him with the look of someone who had some experience.

"Who the fuck are you mate?" he mouthed. "A cop I hope. I like gutting cops. If I'm going away I want it to be for something worthwhile."

He lunged at Danny who circled around him trying to keep Glenna, now petrified, from getting mixed up in the fray.

Danny grinned suddenly.

"You want to know who I am matey? I'll tell you. I'm you're worst bloody nightmare, and I don't like people who pull knives on me. I really don't. Now put it away and get you ass out of here before I really get annoyed."

At that his attacker moved closer, suddenly thrusting his knife straight at Danny's stomach. Glenna screamed. The thug was leaning forward on his right leg and Danny brought his own left leg around in an ankle sweep, unbalancing him. At the same time he elbowed him directly on the nose, smashing it. Grabbing the knife hand he moved in close and sent the man crashing to the cement floor with a hip throw. The knife flew off to one side. For good measure Danny dropped straight down on the thug's stomach hearing him scream in pain and then lie still. Danny leapt to his feet, turned and quickly surveyed the scene. The first assailant remained on the ground clutching his broken limb and moaning while the cosh man was still out cold.

"Mother of God Danny! What have you done to them?" breathed Glenna, a shocked look on her face.

"Nothing to what they would have done to us, given half a chance," Danny enjoined.

"I've come through here for the past two years and never a bother," she said in a shocked whisper.

"It was a set up. They were waiting for us. The first one was a decoy with the other two waiting in ambush ready to jump us. Those guys weren't looking for handouts. They were out to assault us. The average person wouldn't have had a chance."

She looked speculatively at the men lying on the ground.

"You're not just the average person though, are you Danny?"

He looked down at the three injured men, feeling somehow crestfallen at the incident. Still alert and watchful he turned to her.

"Do you have a mobile phone on you?"

She nodded still shaken. He caught her by the arm.

"Okay, it probably doesn't work in here but go outside and call the cops and tell them to get here a.s.a.p. and to bring an ambulance. You comfortable with that Glenna?"

She nodded again, starting to move uncertainly away.

"Will you be ok here Danny?" looking down at the three injured moaning men. Then, "oh … of course you will."

She walked off.

When she was away the first beggar attempted to get up, probably with the intention of fleeing until he saw the menace in Danny's face as he gestured that he should stay on the ground. Glenna came back in almost immediately and indicated that she had made the call. She stayed huddled back behind a pillar, hardly daring to look. It took exactly eight minutes before an ambulance and two police cars swept into the garage. Two beefy looking men emerged rapidly from the police car and came across to Danny. The first was a tough-looking middle-aged man who surveyed the scene quickly. He identified himself as D.I. White and his colleague, a younger man, as D.C. Cranwell.

Danny quickly filled them in on what had happened. The ambulance crew started to examine the injured men. Danny broke off from the two policemen and went over to them.

"That guy there has a broken arm and maybe a sore gut and this one has a damaged shin bone and a sore neck," he volunteered.

"What about him?" asked the medic, nodding to the third assailant.

"I wouldn't be surprised if he didn't have a broken nose and a very sore gut as well," said Danny with a slightly embarrassed look.

D.I. White moved up alongside them and carefully scrutinized the three thugs.

"You tangled with a bad lot here today, no doubt about it. We know these people. They all have records for various crimes including assaults, robberies and intimidation That one there was up for rape but beat it when the victim was threatened."

He looked closely at Danny.

"A bit hard on them weren't you?"

Danny shook his head in disbelief.

"Hey, these people weren't playing games! Oh, by the way there's a knife over there that one of them pulled on me."

He pointed in the direction that the knife had fallen.

D.I. White nodded to his colleague who went off to locate and bag it, then he touched Danny's arm.

" Just checking. The prosecutor will want to make sure you're not some gung-ho martial arts jockey getting some practice outside the dogo. Anyway, there's a second witness I believe?"

Danny pointed to Glenna and both policemen went over to speak with her.

After a few moments D.I. White came back.

"Looks good. Her story supports yours one hundred per cent. Shouldn't be any problem putting these blokes away for a long time. Oh by the way, she spoke about how totally in control you were the whole time. Even said you smiled and spoke to them at one time."

He nodded at the injured men, now handcuffed and being lifted into the ambulance.

"Very scientific! I heard you describing the injuries to the medics. Where did you learn to do that?"

"Oh, the parachute regiment," Danny volunteered off-handedly.

DI White's face puckered skeptically.

"I know the Paras are good and can handle themselves, but that stuff you did there, I didn't think they were that good."

"I'm not sure what you mean," said Danny.

"The last time I saw workmanship like that was when I was posted with the Special Branch in Northern Ireland during the early troubles and was in liaison with an SAS operation. Very surgical, those boys, when it came to taking people down."

He scrutinized Danny's face closely.

Danny spread his arms out as if baffled.

"I'm not sure where this is going D.I. White. All I know is that I defended myself and Glenna there against an unprovoked attack. My military record, you can access anytime you want and it shows that I spent the last eight years in the Paras. Now I'm back in civvy street and selling life insurance for a living."

D.I. White chuckled.

"Pull the other one Danny. You know damn well that if you were SAS your record is sealed. Anyway, I think you'd better take your friend Glenna back across to your office and get her a cup of tea. It looks like she's badly shaken. We can take the statements there."

After statements were taken Glenna was sent home in a taxi but not before she came over to Danny and thanked him.

"If you hadn't been there Danny I don't know what I'd have done," she said, kissing him softly on the cheek.

"I understand one of those thugs had been charged with rape at one time, so I may have had a very narrow escape."

As she said that he felt a slip of paper being pushed into his hand. When he looked at it later, it contained the full name and address of Sonya, C.C.'s P.A.

The next hour passed in a blur with Danny being the center of attention. He managed to get a quick call through to Fiona at her office and filled her in on what had happened.

He still slept at the house in the spare room pending the divorce. He also told her that he planned to make some more telephone calls to potential clients before heading home.

He never got the chance as a sudden commotion out in reception announced the arrival of a bunch of press and photographers demanding details of the story and an interview with Danny. Chris managed to slip him out the back door where he picked up his car in a side street and headed home.

CHAPTER 16

On his arrival, he discovered that Fiona herself had cut her day short and come home early as well. She was a tall beautiful woman, with chestnut red hair and a sensuous walk, which used to set Danny's heart thumping when they'd first met in her home town of Bath. The pending divorce however, had not helped their communication which was now virtually non-existent. For a change, her indifferent demeanor had melted somewhat and he even got a long hug.

"What the heck's going on Danny? I thought you'd left all that violence behind when you got out. It just seems to follow you like the plague."

He shrugged.

"Yeah, I know Fiona. This wasn't of my doing at all. It just came at me out of the blue. Lucky I was there because one of those thugs had been charged with rape a while ago and poor Glenna could have been in serious trouble."

She raised her eyebrows.

"So how come he's walking around out there free to harm other women then? Why isn't he locked up?"

"The cop told me he had the victim threatened and she withdrew the charges. Happens all the time apparently."

"Well in that case I'm glad you were there to look out for Glenna and teach those thugs a few lessons."

He made a face.

"I wish the policeman felt the same. DI White as much as accused me of going over the top with them, suggesting that I may have used too much force and quizzing me about my military background. He didn't seem to buy into my story about being in the Paras."

"What were you supposed to do for God's sake? Three thugs come at you with a cosh and a knife! I'd like a few words with this DI White and give him a piece of my mind!"

Just then the front door opened and Allison rushed in all agog with the normal days events at school, and they were swept up in her enthusiasm and excitement. Later, after supper when she was doing her homework, Danny filled Fiona in on the other aspect of his day – Clive Courtney. She listened as he recounted his conversations with Glenna and her initial reaction to his interest.

"I agree with Glenna," Fiona said " Where's the sense in chasing this mystery man when the challenge for you is right here. You've found a company that's willing to give you an opportunity to build a new career for yourself. You know Danny, you always were a dreamer just like your Dad. That's the Irish coming out in you."

He grinned.

"You used to like that in me at one time. I was different, you said, than the average Brit male trying to get you into the sack back then. What's changed between us Fiona?"

She sat back.

"Let's not go there Danny. We've been over this many times before and always end up having an argument. You know as well as I do that we're not compatible any more. I've been running my own life for far too long and you just don't fit back in."

Then, as if trying to change the subject,

"Show me the address of this Sonya that you intend to contact. When do you plan to see her anyway?"

"I was going to nip out after supper and just go knock on her door. Her phone number is on there as well but I've been discovering that it's too easy for someone to hang up on me, so I felt that a face to face would give me a better chance."

"A better chance if you had a female along. Like some company Danny?"

His jaw dropped.

"But you just told me … …"

He paused, his mind swirling.

"You're something else. I'd forgotten how impulsive you could be at times. Yes, absolutely. Do come along with me."

Forty minutes later they were standing on the doorstep of Sonya's address. Fiona rang the door bell. Sonya Wilcox wasn't used to hearing her doorbell ring at that time of the evening when she had settled in to watching her favorite TV program. She was a tall lean, horsey-looking lady with prematurely graying hair. She had beautiful piercing dark brown eyes which now reflected irritation at having her routine disturbed. She glanced through the curtain of her semi-detached house and saw a well-dressed couple standing on her door step. Mormons she thought. I'll get rid of them right quick. Sighing, she opened the door.

"Yes?"

"Sonya Wilcox?" asked Danny.

"Yes," she replied guardedly. "Who are you two?"

Danny handed her his calling card.

"I'm Danny Quigley, a new advisor at the office. Glenna gave me your address and said you might be willing to talk to me."

"Talk to you about what?" she asked.

"C.C."

"Clive … C.C. … Oh." Looking down at his card. "Well Danny Quigley, I never discussed C.C.'s affairs when he was here and I certainly don't intend to begin now. Glenna phoned me this afternoon and told me you were nosing around."

She started to close the door in their faces. Fiona leaned forward.

"Please Sonya. Glenna and Danny were attacked in the underground parking lot just outside the office this afternoon, by three thugs with weapons. That short-cut people take. Thankfully they came through it without getting hurt. Glenna only gave Danny your address because he'd saved her from a possible assault and rape. She had to go home early today in shock."

"Glenna, in shock?" she exclaimed.

She looked at Danny.

"Can this be true? Why, I've taken the same short-cut through there for years and I never had a problem."

He nodded.

"I'm afraid it's true Miss Wilcox. Of course you could call her and check if you like."

"Well, yes, I'll do that anyway to see how she is, poor thing. Come in won't you and I'll give Glenna a quick call. We were such good friends you know, over the years."

She shook her head.

"What's the world coming to when nice people like her can't go out to lunch in broad daylight without getting attacked?"

A moment later they were sitting in the living room listening to the murmur of Sonya's voice in the hallway. She finally put the phone down and joined them.

"Glenna didn't spare any details. You really saved her skin today, didn't you. Thank God you were there with her."

Danny shrugged.

"I was saving my own skin too, I can tell you."

She waved her hand dismissively.

"That's not what Glenna says. She said you tried to shield her as you were being attacked."

She looked at him speculatively.

"You look extremely fit and I noticed how light you were on your feet when you came in."

She nodded to some pictures of herself in a basketball uniform.

"I used to coach you see. I can spot these things."

Fiona cut in.

"Danny's fit, that's for sure, but it hasn't helped him get going in Financial Services. He's really struggling right now and he only has a month left to prove himself. He has a strong feeling that C.C. has some magic formula that will help him succeed."

Sonya leaned back smiling.

"Well, you're right, he had. 'The Sales Master' I called him. He made it all look so easy. The business just flowed to him."

Canting her head she looked at Danny directly.

"Tell me, is that the only reason you want to see Clive, to get his sales secrets, to make money?"

He paused before answering. Somehow he felt that the answer he gave was critical. He stood up gathering his thoughts. Why was it so urgent that he find C.C.? Was it just about money and success? He nodded more to himself than anyone else and turned to Sonya.

"No, it's not just about money, though obviously that is important. I know this sounds weird but I feel a kind of connection to him. His name has resonated in my head since I first heard it mentioned. I can't get it out of my mind, even with the other things that have happened today."

Sonya pursed her lips.

"I like you Danny, but being perfectly honest I don't believe C.C. would be willing for me to give you his new location. You admit yourself to being a rookie after all. Even if you did meet with him how could you relate to where he was in the business - right at the top?"

"I still believe that I have to meet with him Sonya," he said doggedly.

She sighed, looking from Danny to Fiona. Finally she lifted her hands.

"Okay, tell you what, I'll phone him from the other room and put it to him. Let him decide."

With that she left and soon they could hear the murmur of her voice next door. Fiona got up and wandered round the room, pausing occasionally as she examined paintings and magazines.

In a few moments Sonya was back and Danny could see the regret on her face.

"It's a no go isn't it?" he asked.

Sonya nodded.

"Sorry Danny, he doesn't see any point. If you were an experienced representative, who knows. Don't feel bad though, you're not the first to try and reach him and no doubt not the last. I'm sorry."

At that stage there was no point in lingering so they left quietly.

Danny's face was downcast as they sat there in the car.

"Well that's that then," he muttered despondently.

"Not quite," Fiona said grinning.

His head snapped up.

"What do you mean Fiona?"

"While you were sitting there moping, I was scouring around the room and guess what?"

"What, for Gods sake! Tell me," he demanded impatiently.

"I spotted a pile of mail and just happened to see one from your friend C.C. It had a return address on it that I didn't manage to memorize, but I did notice that it was from Sligo, in Ireland," she finished triumphantly.

"Ireland," he repeated dumbly. "C.C.'s in Ireland?"

She nodded.

"Without a doubt Danny, and for anyone with your training, finding him should not be a problem. Wouldn't you agree?"

A huge smile came to his face.

"You better believe it Fiona. C.C. is in for a visit whether he likes it or not."

CHAPTER 17

It was the ringing of the door bell that woke Danny at 7am the following morning. Standing in the doorway were D.I. White and his colleague.

"Can we come in Danny?" he asked

"Must be important to come here so early. Sure, come on in."

In a moment they were inside and sitting at the kitchen table. D.I. White didn't waste any time.

"Here, look at this," he said, spreading three of the morning papers out on the table.

Danny gasped. The headlines screamed back at him.

'Van Dam Quigley in underground garage attack' … … Beggars hammered by ex-para combat vet … … 10 seconds of destruction … martial arts expert demolishes thugs'.

All of the papers gave a rendition of the three thugs getting their come-uppance at the hands of Danny Quigley, ex-para, and now working as an insurance executive. The slant in all the papers was that Quigley, a trained combat expert, had gone over the top and used excessive force to subdue the three men who never even laid a glove on him. No mention of their records or that they had produced weapons during the attack. Danny did a double-take when he saw that two of the papers carried a picture of him. Not a very clear one, as it was obviously shot from the side as he entered the branch office after the attack.

"Where did they get this?" he demanded, looking up at DI White. "It had just happened a few moments before. How could anyone have been there with a camera? And the stories, in all three papers, have a common theme - tough ex-para using deadly force. Just what the hell is going on here?"

"I don't know Danny, but it's created one heck of a problem for us. These guys are all lawyered up already and laying counter charges against you for assault. They claim that they accosted you for some change and that you went beserk and started breaking bones. It looks like we'll have to release them this morning, as a judge has deemed it a possible infringement of their human rights."

Danny stood up and slammed the table.

"This is absolutely crazy! The paper makes it sound like I ran amok! What about Glenna? She was a witness as well. Surely that should be considered before these thugs are let out on the street again."

"I agree Danny, there's a lot here that I don't understand either. How did three beggars suddenly produce high price lawyers? None of them even made the usual phone call when admitted. Also we can't figure how all three papers have basically the same story. Okay, they refer to them as thugs, no one likes these lay-abouts anyway who hang around subway stations and intimidate people into giving them money. However the articles are written as if you used unnecessary force on them."

"But can they do this? Turn round and charge me with assault?"

D.I. White nodded.

"Yes, they can. Anything's possible in Britain today thanks to Blair's legacy. The bleeding hearts are running the show these days. Remember the farmer who shot the gypsy who was breaking into his house? The farmer was the one who got charged in the end. So yes, they could go after you on this, especially if they have some top lawyers on their side."

Just then Fiona came into the kitchen wearing a dressing gown, concern on her face. "What's wrong Danny? How come the police are here so early?"

He quickly summarized the situation and handed her the papers. After a few moments she glared accusingly at D.I. White.

"But this is slanted totally the wrong way! Glenna and Danny were attacked, and it was only when, in fear of their lives that Danny defended himself. Believe me, what he used was minimum force for him. He could just as easily have killed all three," she exclaimed angrily.

Danny gave her a warning look.

D.I. White appraised Danny closely.

"Hmm killed them eh? I was hinting at that when I quizzed you yesterday. If it turns out that you were ex Special Forces the prosecutor might hesitate at charging these thugs. If he drops the case you may be into a civil one."

"I don't believe what I'm hearing here," Fiona shouted in frustration. "Danny defends himself and Glenna from an attack by people with records as long as your arm, and he may be taken to court? He hasn't any money to hire lawyers. This will bury us right now!"

DI White shrugged.

"That's the law Mrs. Quigley. If I was Danny I'd start getting some legal advice today, and I hate to say it, but I'd keep a look out now that these three are back on the street. None of them are in any condition to do anything to you, but they may have friends," he finished lamely, standing up to go.

"Can you at least provide some protection for my family now that you admit that these people could be a threat?" Danny asked angrily.

DI White looked apologetic.

"We just don't have the manpower to provide round the clock protection for a threat that at this point is not real. Okay, if they do make a move against you, we would have to re-evaluate the risk. If the prosecutor decides to drop the case however, then you would no longer be a witness so we wouldn't be providing any level of protection. Oh, by the way, if you were planning to go to work today, I'd advise you not to. The press are already camped out at the front of the office."

With that they left leaving Danny and Fiona sitting at the dining room table staring at each other with concern.

"What's happening to us Danny?" she whispered. "This has got completely out of hand. I can't believe how much our life has changed since you went off to work yesterday morning. God, we could lose everything! The house is in my name, but that could go too as I'm still officially your wife."

Danny sat there saying nothing for a long time. Looking back on the previous day's events, he couldn't see how he could have done anything different. Hell, he'd actually been quite easy on those thugs as Fiona had, unfortunately, hinted at. The whole thing was turning into a nightmare.

He sighed tiredly.

"One thing is obvious. With those three out on the street, yourself and Allison are no longer safe here in this house. Okay, we don't know if they even know our address, but we can't count on D.I. White's crowd to provide us with any protection if we get a visit from them. We've got to get both of you out of here. Would your mother put you up for awhile until this clears up?"

She shot up in the chair.

"Now hold on a moment," she exclaimed.

This suggestion resulted in a long drawn out argument and discussion. Fiona's career and work was at a critical stage with an important new customer, and her colleagues were dependant on her to fulfill her commitment to the project. She initially wanted to move Allison and herself to a nearby friend's house for a few days. Eventually she saw that Allison would be very exposed and vulnerable if the situation deteriorated or if she was followed from her work. After a number of phone calls and rapid packing, Danny breathed a sigh of relief when he got them on a late morning national express bus to Bath, a city about two hours east of London. He felt a tug at his heart strings when he saw the appeal in Allison's eyes as the bus pulled out.

Fiona had left no doubt about her feelings before she left.

"If I lose my house and my career because of you I'll never forgive you," she whispered.

Fighting an unknown force on his own without the regiment and its resources to back him up was a new experience for him. Nevertheless, with his family out of the way he felt much happier in tackling any threat coming against him. He inwardly vowed to restore their security as soon as possible.

He turned the car round and headed home.

CHAPTER 18

Danny woke suddenly not knowing what had disturbed him. His training in the Forces had enabled him to wake at a moments notice and spring into action, but six months on civvy street had taken the edge off this ability. Twisting, he reached for the small luminous alarm clock. He groaned. 3 am! He always had difficulty in getting back to sleep again too. He didn't know what exactly had disturbed him or if he was having a dream. He reached for his dressing gown and froze. There it was again! Like the letter box rattling downstairs. Forgetting the dressing gown and just wearing shorts, he dashed out of his room onto the landing, flicked the light on and started down the stairs. There was definitely someone at the front door fiddling with the letter box. He started running down the stairs shouting at the top of his voice. There was that noise again, this time accompanied by a sloshing sound, like water running. Alarm bells started going off in his head. Suddenly he smelled petrol! At that precise moment the darkness in the hallway exploded in flames leaping out and consuming the telephone table and carpet. Danny's mind sprang into survival mode, his training falling into place. He dashed through the rising flames into the lounge where he had a couple of fire extinguishers that he had insisted buying for the house when he was on leave. Grabbing one, he pulled the pin and turned the hose of powder on the flames now licking the rose patterned wallpaper in the hallway. As he did so he heard the sounds of a car taking off outside, tires screaming

The flames were starting to recede somewhat when the extinguisher ran out. He smothered a curse, dashed into the kitchen for the second one and grabbed a fire-blanket that he had previously placed in a drawer near the stove. Coming back into the hallway he threw the fire blanket over the telephone where the phone books had now caught fire. He turned on the second appliance and directed it at the carpet and front door, still burning fiercely. The smoke was billowing back into the house causing him to choke and partially blinding him. He feared what would happen when the second appliance ran out.

Just then he became aware of shouting outside and someone calling his name. In the distance he heard the sound of sirens and hoped in his heart that they were heading his way. He continued to fight the fire which seemed to have a mind of it's own as the petrol-soaked carpet stubbornly resisted his efforts. He was aware of the siren stopping outside at the same time as the fire extinguisher dried up. He ran into the lounge slamming the door behind him and rushed to the window throwing it open. He clambered through rapidly, sprawling on the grass, his chest heaving as he fought for breath.

A fire fighter ran over, helping him to his feet while firing questions at him.

"Are you all right mate? Anyone else in there? Where's the fire concentrated?"

Danny struggled to speak.

"I'm okay. No one else in there." He pointed. "The front door. Petrol. Through the letterbox!" he rasped weakly.

The fireman caught both his arms and tried to support him as he collapsed on the ground with deep hacking coughs.

Before he knew it, he was being helped by someone he recognized as neighbor. Three firemen jumped through the lounge window pulling a hose behind them while another hose was directed on the front door which was crackling and burning.

Dimly he became aware of the neighbor speaking to him.

"A good job Mary got me up to feed the baby. I heard a car tearing away and looked out to see your front door in flames and called the fire department right away. A few moments more and the whole bloody street might have gone up. Where's Fiona and Allison by the way?"

Danny nodded his gratitude weakly still trying to get his breath. "Gone away for a few days, thank goodness."

He sat up suddenly feeling lightheaded. A moment later an ambulance pulled up and two paramedics helped him into the back of it, placing an oxygen mask over his face. Gratefully, he drew in the pure air as his coughing spasms lessened.

He went to pull it off but the medic restrained him.

"You may have some smoke damage to your lungs. Just keep the mask on for a few more minutes."

Danny lay back on the bed breathing in the pure oxygen gratefully as his mind tried to cope with what had just happened. Some people were definitely out to get him for whatever reason. He couldn't believe that a fight in an underground garage could result in someone trying to burn his house down with him and his family, possibly, inside. Danny sat up again just as the firefighters knocked the front door flat and the men who were inside started working their way out, still hosing the smoldering carpet as they did so. One of the fire fighters came across to him.

"Sorry, I don't know your name." he said.

"Danny Quigley."

"Well Mr. Quigley, you're lucky the whole building didn't go up. Petrol fires are like that, they just explode. Those little extinguishers aren't much good for petrol but you probably held it long enough to contain it to the hallway where our lads caught it. As it is, you're going to have quite a lot of smoke damage. We will have to tear up the hallway carpets and dump them outside as they're still smoldering from the petrol. The lounge is of course flooded and you'll need a new front door.

One of our investigators has to get a statement from you and your neighbor because it's obviously been deliberately caused. Your insurance company will need one too and I'd get on to them right away if I was you. We'll stick around for a while just to make sure the fire is fully out and to complete our investigation."

He looked closely at Danny.

"You're lucky Mr. Quigley. We had another fire on the north side a couple of hours ago and that unfortunate person didn't get out alive."

As he turned to move away he added. "We'll board up the front door for you before we go. I'd suggest you go with the ambulance crew and get checked out for any lung damage. Can't be too careful."

That was how Danny came to be sitting up in the casualty ward later when D.I. White appeared at his bedside, an embarrassed look on his face.

"Danny, I'm terribly sorry. I guess we got this one totally wrong. I'd never in a month of Sundays have thought it would come to this."

Danny glanced at him wearily.

"Seems to me you got a few things wrong since this whole thing started. Hell, I practically predicted something like this would happen, when you told me they were going to release those thugs."

He peered closely at D.I. White.

"They did release them didn't they?" Danny asked.

The policeman nodded.

"Unfortunately yes, after the newspapers came out depicting you as death wish five."

"I will be when I catch up with them next time," he volunteered.

D.I. White touched his arm.

"Danny, where were your wife and child? The firemen told me you were alone in the house."

"I sent them away yesterday to a safe place. A good job I did as it turns out."

"Well look, give me their location and I can now guarantee to provide protection for them under these new circumstances."

Danny thought quickly. The offer was tempting but he was still puzzled by the many unexplained patterns of events that were happening - his picture taken moments after the underground garage event; the exact pinpointing of their house which was listed in Fiona's name and not his; the thugs getting lawyered up with high price help right away. Something was wrong with this whole chain of events, and until he knew more he wasn't confiding where Fiona and Allison were hiding out. For all he knew the leaks were coming from the police themselves.

He looked skeptically at White.

"Thanks for the offer, but I'll look after them myself."

The policeman nodded understandingly.

"I appreciate where you're coming from on this Danny. As I say I'm sorry we weren't more proactive in the whole thing."

He looked at Danny measuring him carefully.

"Danny, there's something else you should know. That other fire tonight. It was your office colleague's place, Glenna's. She never made it out of the house. Burnt alive I'm afraid. Sorry to be the one to break the news to you. You can see my urgency in wanting to protect your family at this stage. This whole thing has now become a murder case and I'm worried that you might be next. Think on it. Here's my card if you change your mind."

He moved off leaving Danny sitting there dazedly clutching his card. Despite the protests of the ER staff, Danny pulled on a track suit and runners that his neighbor had loaned him and, still feeling light-headed, rapidly left the hospital.

CHAPTER 19

A few hours later Danny met, by arrangement, at a nearby pub with his manager Chris who, at that time, was fully apprised of the situation. Chris's face expressed his concern.

"Danny, I don't know what to say. I'm just stunned at the change in your situation in the last 24 hours - the attack on yourself and Glenna, now her murder, your family forced to flee, the tone of the newspapers practically blaming you for the whole situation, when I know differently. It's just unbelievable! It's obvious that you can't work at your job until this whole thing has blown over. Anyway, the good news is that the directors have agreed to continue to fund you beyond the normal time of your financing arrangement until you can resume your normal work pattern, even if this has to be at another branch. How does that sound?"

"Absolutely fantastic. I can't believe the company would support someone who just joined and is causing such a stir. Pass this on to them please, whoever they are, that I appreciate it very much and hope to repay them when this blows over."

"Well, they're not altruistic by nature, let me tell you Danny. This whole episode could reflect adversely on our recruiting methods and the company reputation as a whole. We have a stake in helping you clear your name so to speak."

Just then the barman turned up the sound on the television for some breaking news. Chris gasped. The announcer's voice cut through them like a knife.

"Police have just discovered the bodies, as the result of a anonymous tip, of the three men who had been involved in the recent underground garage assault. This follows the suspicious fire last night in which one of the victims of the assault, a female, was burned to death. The second victim, the so called death wish 5 ex forces veteran, narrowly escaped serious injury when his house was deliberately set on fire last night as well. Because of the nature of the men's deaths, they all had their necks broken, police are now searching for Danny Quigley who they wish to question in relation to their deaths. Quigley is suspected to be ex Special Forces, trained in the art of killing. Further news as it happens."

The pub exploded in discussion as Chris leaned forward.

"Danny, I don't know what's what any more but I still believe in you as a person and in your potential to clear up this mess and eventually do well in this business. I'll try and get the directors to still go along with their agreement despite this new setback. Look, you go and do what you have to do and stay in touch. I want to know what's going on."

He whipped out his card and scribbled on it.

"Here's my card with my home number and mobile phone number as well. Call me if I can help with anything, will you please?"

Danny nodded dumbly, his mind still reeling from the TV news program.

"I will Chris, if I can, and thank you again," he replied looking around and shaking his head.

"You know, all I wanted was a chance to make a life for myself outside the Forces. Now my wife is divorcing me, she and my daughter have had to flee London in fear of their lives, our house has been set on fire, and the authorities think I've killed those three thugs. Right now I wish to hell I'd stayed in the Forces!"

Chris leaned across squeezing his arm but saying nothing.

Danny sighed, standing.

"One thing for sure, Chris, is that I've got to get out of London right away or I'll be behind bars before the day's out. If I stay free I can at least start trying to unravel this mess. Something's weird about the whole thing and I intend to get to the bottom of it. When I do, there may very well be some bodies lying around that I'll claim responsibility for," he stated grimly.

Even in the warm pub Chris felt a chill run down his spine at those words and the deadly expression on Danny's face as he stalked out.

CHAPTER 20

Danny knew that the last place to go right then was home where he could pack some necessities. Fortunately, he had gone to his bank that morning and drawn the maximum in sterling that the account would allow. He knew he had to get out of London fast, and with the massive amount of CCTV cameras encasing the city, his margin of time was closing rapidly. He didn't know if the car he was driving, which was Fiona's, would immediately be connected to him, as he had sold his old Nissan banger to a mate in Hereford before he left. It still took him forty minutes to get out of the city and he tensed anytime a police car appeared or heard the sounds of distant sirens. At one time a police car came alongside him while he was stopped at a red light and he tried to stay calm, looking straight ahead. He breathed a sigh of relief when it shot off again as soon as the lights changed. That indicated, at least, that an all points bulletin had not gone out on him or that they hadn't twigged to Fiona's car. He knew it was only a matter of time.

Once on the M4 he started making good time all the while keeping an eye on his rear view mirror. At the Swindon exit he got off the motorway and waited to see if anyone followed him. No one did and he swung back on again until the Bath exit. He reached Bath by lunchtime and checked into a guest house near the river.

Danny nipped out and bought some items of clothing and toiletries then went back to take a shower. Still being careful, he went outside to a public telephone box and phoned Fiona at her mother's. Fortunately, she was in and they agreed to meet outside the old Roman Baths which were always crowded with tourists. She started to say something about the news on TV but he cautioned her to keep it until they met.

He was early and spent the time watching an amateur display of jugglers and fire-eaters in front of the Baths. Still alert he kept his eyes open as to anyone who was taking more than a normal interest in him. Then he spotted her coming round the corner of the old church. Seeing her he realized that the feelings he had held for her over the years had gone yet his heart still went out to her as she looked so vulnerable and on edge. When she saw him her face broke into a mixture of relief and a strained smile. Uncharacteristically, she threw her arms around him.

"Oh Danny, thank God you're safe! When I saw the picture of our blackened and boarded front door on television this morning I thought how lucky you were to have escaped. And then the news of those three thugs - I knew it wasn't you Danny. You're not like that. Oh, I know you've had to do some violent stuff in the regiment but that was against opposition and you were under orders."

He held her for a moment, patting her back reassuringly.

"Hey, thanks for the vote of confidence Fiona. I wish the cops were as discerning as you."

He was actually pleased that her mood had changed since heading off in the bus from London. At that time she'd made it clear that she blamed him for the whole mess. At least now she appreciated the wisdom of sending her and Allison away to her mother in Bath. She stepped back, her face brightening.

"I know a nice little cafe with delicious cakes and scones where we can have a chat. I'm not letting this whole mess stop you buying me a coffee," she declared.

Infected by her mood Danny grinned. Fiona was famous for her love of coffee shops and he wasn't surprised at her knowledge of the Bath scene as she was born and raised there. In a way he was glad that she was out and about, rather than staying indoors out of fear. She led him to a small hole-in-the-wall coffee shop which overlooked the weir in the river below. There they could see the river cruisers docked the other side of the bridge as they took on and discharged passengers. Still on the alert he approved the vantage point of the café, though the milling tourists made it difficult to stay focused and still talk to Fiona. They managed to get a small table in the corner and he felt himself relaxing. Examining her he could appreciate just how attractive she still was and how easily he had fallen in love with her when they first met. She still looked like a model.

Catching his intense gaze she said,

"What? What's going on in that head of yours Danny?" but he refused to be drawn right then. She glanced down at the menu.

"You know what? I'm feeling hungry all of a sudden. I wonder what that whole food sandwich would taste like?"

She spotted the waiter carrying a tray past their table.

"Hmnn, looks good. I think I'll try that as long as I can have my coffee and a cake to finish with. Is that okay?"

"Absolutely," he said, glad to be off the hook as he waved to a waitress in a Victorian costume who came over and took their order.

Somehow, despite the mess of their lives right then, Fiona felt secure for the first time in days. There was something about Danny that inspired confidence despite everything. She felt suddenly saddened that it was finally over between them. They had shared some great times together and they had a beautiful daughter. There was still a strong bond there between them.

The next hour was spent going over the company's agreement which hopefully they would still abide by, and his decision to get out of the UK until the dust settled. The police might crack the killings and the heat would then be off him. Danny had decided to fly over to Sligo in Ireland to escape from the UK and use the time as an opportunity to find CC. Despite everything that had happened in the past few days he was still strongly drawn to finding this enigma.

Fiona didn't like the idea of Danny going away right then but felt that living with her mother in Bath was a perfectly safe place for herself and Allison to stay. Danny discussed methods of keeping in touch so as to avoid the police from discovering where he had fled to, though he had no doubt that in time they would trace him.

After lunch they dropped in to a travel agent where he bought a ticket from Bristol airport to Dublin for the following day. Fiona wanted to see where he was staying for the night and was pleasantly surprised by the cleanliness of the quarters. Danny, too, was surprised when he saw that familiar look in her eyes, and even more surprised when she ended up in his arms kissing him passionately. Whether it was the uncertainty and danger of their situation, the need for comfort, or the different surroundings, they ended up in bed for the rest of the afternoon. There was no one more amazed than Danny who had been getting the cold shoulder for months.

The following morning she drove him to Bristol airport and as she dropped him leaned out the window.

"Yesterday afternoon doesn't change anything Danny. The divorce still goes through," she called out to him.

Without a word he spun on his heel and headed inside where he embarked for Ireland without any problems. His search for CC had now begun in earnest.

CHAPTER 21

Five years previously

Inexplicably Danny Quigley felt his gut tighten as he followed Scotty inside the small highland cabin and saw the man sitting there. They had just dropped their climbing gear on the ground outside after a day on the mountain and were looking forward over the next five days to tackling the other side of it.

It was Scotty's cousin Vinnie who ran the lodge down below.

Now he tilted his head towards them, his bearded weather-beaten face serious.

"Sorry lads. Telephone call came into the lodge for you a half hour ago. It was from your unit. They want you back at camp right away. That was the message ... nothing else."

He raised his arms as if in apology.

"I came up right away and will run you down to the train station. There's an evening train out in forty minutes so you better move your butts if you want to make it."

They threw a shocked look at each other and suddenly galvanized into action, throwing their gear haphazardly into their duffle bags. Within seven minutes they were in Vinnie's truck racing down the side of the mountain. They made the train by five minutes and slumped back in relief in a compartment that was still empty. Scotty looked across at him.

"What the hell could this be about Danny? Pulled off leave just like that."

He shrugged.

"Who knows. This is the s*ass* after all. Anything could be going down and you wouldn't read about it in the papers my friend."

Scotty snorted.

"Probably just another bloody course they want to send us on. I'd just as soon finish our five days on that mountain."

"Unlikely to be a course with this short notice Scotty. I have a feeling we're about to see some action."

Scotty sat upright.

"Man I'm ready for that! I've had so much training it's spilling out my ears. I sure hope you're right Danny."

With that he turned, put his head down and was asleep in minutes.

It was the first of four different trains they caught including one that broke down, before they lurched into Hereford the following morning. Scotty spent the entire journey sleeping and had to be woken up each time they had to change trains. Danny stayed awake and spent the time looking back on the last year and his selection for the SAS (Special Air Service), the UK's Special Forces. Most of the recruits to the SAS, referred to as *sass*, came from the parachute regiment including Danny, though not exclusively. He had just completed three years in the parachute regiment and had been one of over a hundred men going for selection. At the end of the process, he and 14 others made it through. They had all felt shattered physically and emotionally after the brutal de-selection process in the Welsh Black Mountains and the Brecon Beacons around Hereford. After induction into the 22nd SAS regiment which is a unit in the British army, their real Special Forces training began.

A further 14 weeks of advanced weapons training, demolition work, unarmed combat, map reading, working with small boats, use of communication equipment and coordination with other elements of the UK and NATO armed forces, not to mention Close Quarter Combat(CQB) in the famous Killing House at Hereford. Danny was also lucky in being selected for a months long snipers course with the U.S. Marine Corps.

One of the prime roles of the SAS was Counter Revolutionary Warfare (CRV), which was essentially counter terrorism. Danny already had his wings from the parachute brigade but now he had to jump out at higher altitudes and learn to glide stealthily in over targets. He demonstrated an extraordinary ability in unarmed combat where he displayed almost a sixth sense in anticipating an opponent's attack. It was as if he had a separate incredibly fast mental computer that down-loaded his opponents' moves before they even thought of them.

Just under six feet, Danny was lean and hard muscled. There was a coiled energy and alertness in his hawk-like face and intense blue eyes that warned men and attracted certain types of women. The fact that he had undergone four years judo training as a teenager had helped him considerably in mastering unarmed combat skills. Even the hard-eyed, unarmed, combat instructor commented to the regiment C.O.

"Quigley's a fucking natural. The guy's deadly with his hands."

The SAS unarmed combat training was a long way from the Bruce Lee type of martial arts. Its focus was in subduing an opponent as fast as possible, quite often silently, with maximum destructive force using elbows, knees, head or whatever weapon was available to get the job done. The training alone resulted in many casualties but the final result was finely tuned fighting machines who could explode into deadly action when the situation required it.

The SAS training points out that violence is only used when all else fails. They were past masters of the art of winning hearts and minds in areas of the world where local rebellion and uprisings threaten the status quo. When this fails only then do the SAS become the *Ultimo Ratio Regis,* the *Kings Last Argument* and wreak sudden and deadly havoc on the enemy.

One of the people selected with him was a short lean Scotsman named Scotty MacGregor, who had been brought up in England. Danny and he grew pretty close during the selection process and subsequent training. Scotty was five foot seven, lean like whipcord, with a round head that he used in fights with devastating effect. Danny and Scotty were laughingly referred to as *Little & Large* due to the disparity in their height.

After their first year in the SAS Danny had gone up to Scotland with Scotty to stay with a cousin on his first leave. Members of the regiment were not allowed to disclose their status even to their families and used the parachute brigade as their cover. However Scotty's cousin who was ex-forces gave them a knowing look when they were discussing some of their advanced training. Members of the regiment were fixated on fitness challenges especially during leave periods and Danny and Scotty were no exception. Most of their leave was spent climbing the challenging Scottish mountains during the day and nursing pints of Stella at the local pub in the evenings. Danny's real Dad, a widower, lived in Wales and Danny called him to bring him up to date on how his Forces career was going. He had never contacted his step-father since leaving home.

Their leave still had five days to go when they received the cryptic telephone message delivered by Vinnie to return to the regiment in Hereford at once. Wilting from their trip they reported in to the admin section and were immediately directed to the C.O.'s office. With some trepidation they went, presented themselves and stood to attention.

The normal conventions of rank were not highly observed in the regiment and the C.O., a Major, told them brusquely

"At ease Troopers."

Glancing at each other uneasily they did so. Major Wainwright looked at them closely for a long moment and then nodded to the chairs.

"Okay, sit down lads."

When they had done so he enquired about their leave in Scotland and how they felt now that their advanced training with the regiment was completed. Still not sure why they had been called back early to Hereford, their answers were short and cautious. Finally, the C.O. leaned forward.

"I guess you're wondering what this is all about. Well, as you know from your training, the regiment is occasionally called upon by the Government to help out in certain situations where our skills could be essential in achieving certain outcomes - a siege situation, plane hijacks threats to oil platforms and so forth. Occasionally, foreign governments ask for our help too. You've been told all this already of course but I want you up to speed when a Colonel Crawford of MI5 briefs you two this afternoon on a job they want to discuss with you. He's ex military but a lot of these blokes likes to be addressed using their old rank."

"Why us two sir? Hell, we're practically raw recruits in the sass There must be dozens of guys in the regiment who could be utilized for whatever job they have for us," queried Danny.

The C.O. nodded.

"Quite true under normal circumstances, Trooper Quigley. As you say, we have some highly competent and experienced people here. Some you met on your training, so you know who I'm talking about. We've worked closely with MI5 in Northern Ireland over the years so we have a well formed relationship with them. In this case they're looking for something specific. I'll let Colonel Crawford tell you himself. I'll be the only one in the unit who will know of this mission and you must tell no one else. Is that clear?"

He chuckled at their dumbstruck expressions.

"Oh don't worry, the lads in camp won't comment one way or the other when you play dumb with them. It's part and parcel of what we do here - covert operations, so security is paramount."

He stood up.

"Now lads, off you go and get some breakfast for yourselves and be back here at noon."

They straggled off to the cookhouse which accommodated members at inconvenient hours.

"What was all that about Danny?" whispered Scotty.

"No idea. Find out soon. Sounds like action though and I'm ready for that even if we are still virgins at it."

Scotty grinned hugely.

"Right on mate. Me too. They've got some cop-on putting us two together. What a great bloody team we'll make!" he exclaimed giving him a high five.

They were hardly aware of what they ate as they feverishly discussed and speculated who this mysterious Colonel Crawford was and what was going to be required of them.

Colonel Crawford was a hard compact ex-officer, approximately 40 years of age and dressed in civilian clothes. Over average height with crow-black hair his sharp features reflected an almost savage impatience as he kept them at attention while he studied their records. Their C.O. sat to one side having obviously deferred the meeting to his visitor. Finally the Colonel looked up at them.

"At ease troopers," he said.

They were both startled at the raspy almost hoarse whisper of his voice. His eyes appeared hard and almost cruel as he surveyed them speculatively.

"So, you're the two I've been reading about here," he nodded to the records before continuing.

"I'll cut to the quick. I need to infiltrate the IRA in Northern Ireland. We have been doing this for years and garnered some quality information from some of our deep cover agents and people we've turned. The peace process is well under way with the Protestants and Gerry Adams crowd sitting down together and running the North. However there's still a lot of distrust on both sides. The deal was for the PIRA

(Provisional IRA) to hand in their arms caches and that was done as we all know under Clinton's George Mitchell."

He stopped, as if considering his next words.

"It's our suspicion that a splinter group PIRA have held on to a residue of weapons and explosives. They still want to pursue an all Ireland solution, we need to make sure they don't access this material. We still see sporadic attacks on the police and military by these dissidents. The Prime Minister, wants to put this to bed as soon as possible. All it needs is for one more Canary Wharf type explosion to go off on the mainland of Britain and the hard-line Protestants will abandon the peace process. Then their units will start up and bobs your uncle, we're back to the old days again."

"But Sir, what I don't understand is …"

Catching the warning look from his C.O. Danny froze in mid sentence.

"Kindly be quiet, Quigley until I finish this briefing and give you permission to speak," Crawford commanded tersely.

Danny said nothing, his face impassive.

"As I was saying, we can't let that happen. Her Majesty's government have invested too much time and resources already in the so called six counties. As your C.O. has told you, we have operated extremely effectively with the *sass* over there but unfortunately a number of the regiment's more experienced people have left to take up lucrative security work, becoming body guards to pop stars, or providing protection for politicians in danger zones. Most of them are pissed off at repeated trips to Iraq which have wound down now but there's still Afghanistan and other areas of operations. A lot of it is family pressure of course."

He sniffed derisively.

"Some of your regiment people have had too much exposure in Northern Ireland and may be known to the IRA who have the best intelligence system in the world, barring the Mossad in Israel. So we don't underestimate them. We need some fresh faces for this job and we picked you particularly, Quigley, because you were born in Ireland. Now we know that your biological father moved you over to Wales when you were eight years of age. That's tenuous at best but could be a start. A lot of the Irish who moved to Britain became even more pro Irish in their attitudes and behavior. You've seen them in the Irish pubs, teaching their kids Irish dancing and so on, hanging on to the old traditions, and here's the important thing - becoming decidedly anti Brit in their views. Does that make sense?"

Danny nodded, not daring to make a comment.

Crawford continued.

"One of the reasons I selected you Quigley was because no one in your adopted town in Wales, so far as we are aware, knows that you joined the Forces, nor indeed in Waterford where you were born. We needed that because the IRA will most certainly check your background if they start to see you as someone they can use."

He looked pointedly at Danny.

"This serves our purpose of course but I'm curious Quigley, why don't your mates in Wales know that you joined the Forces?"

Danny shrugged.

"Hell, coming from Ireland to Wales at eight years of age with my older sister Cathy, I was an outcast from day one. Didn't really make friends. Went to Bristol for work after high school and then London working as a mechanic. Joined up in London and never went back to Wales. My dad would come to London occasionally so we kept in touch that way." he finished lamely.

Crawford nodded.

"Of course we know everything about you, every job you ever had. That was part of your security clearance. Anyone Irish gets an even more thorough going over I can tell you."

Crawford studied the file in front of him.

"Now, your dad still resides in Wales. Any problem getting him to play mum if he is approached, which hopefully he will be, if this operation is to succeed."

"I wouldn't think so sir. How much can I tell him?"

"Absolutely nothing Quigley," Crawford snapped. "Just let him know that any loose talk could put you in danger, got that?"

Danny nodded.

"Now, what about your step father?"

"What about him?" Danny replied stonily.

"What about him *Sir*? Crawford snapped testily.

"Yes *Sir*!" Danny barked, then, more quietly, "haven't seen him since I left home. My mother had passed away when I was a teenager so I had no reason to go back. I've no idea where he is or even if he knows I'm in the Forces."

Crawford surveyed him closely for a long moment before making a note.

"What about your sister Quigley?"

He shrugged.

"Finished teacher training college and went off to one of those South American countries to teach English. She's never stayed in touch. Had no friends in Wales anyway. She might have kept in touch with some of her Irish school friends."

"Hmm. Could be a loose end there," he remarked, glancing at the Major.

He then turned his attention to Scotty.

"MacGregor, you're not Irish, of course we know that. We couldn't find anyone else with an Irish background but in discussing it with your C.O. here he raised the idea of yourself going in on this with Quigley. It's known in your home community that you are in the Forces so we'll have to create a new identity that you have to familiarize yourself with. We would want you to play the role of a Scotsman with nationalist and strong anti-British views to work with Danny in trying to infiltrate the IRA. You two have apparently already formed a relationship of trust together and that's important when working undercover."

He looked over at the C.O.

"Anything to add, Major?"

He shook his head.

"No Colonel but I think it may make more sense to my lads when you tell them how you plan to infiltrate them into the lion's den as it were. They will also receive some additional and vital training from MI5 before they start the mission. They should know that MI5 have no powers of arrest in the UK and that obviously includes Northern Ireland. We liaise with Special Branch for that when it's needed."

"Quite so. I was coming to that. Here's the game plan, and I can't stress the importance of not breathing a word of this mission outside this room: not to your girl friends, your family, or even your priest, if you have one. Is that clear?"

They nodded in unison, their faces now eager to hear the rest of the plan.

"All right, here it is." Crawford looked closely at their faces for reactions as he started.

"We have a trucking company called Brennans, who've agreed to take you both on as truck drivers going across to Northern Ireland on a regular basis to Belfast and other cities. On your trips over there, you keep your heads down and frequent certain pubs on your overnights. Not the hard-core republican pubs initially, that would be too obvious for two Brits suddenly to appear in their midst. But gradually you make your presence known. Move on to some of the pubs with Irish music and we'll point you towards the IRA hangouts eventually. Easy does it. Oh, and don't drink Stella. Chris Ryan, who is ex SAS and writes excellent books about the regiment, always has the lads cracking a pack of Stella when they're chilling out. You'll be watched closely by the Nationalists so don't go asking any specific questions that would alert them. You'd be picked up by them in a flash and interrogated. You wouldn't want that, believe me. You'd both end up in a bog somewhere!"

He paused, measuring their reactions before continuing.

"You get to know the locals and let slip your Irish background and Scotty, your nationalist views. If they bite they'll come to you, but not until they check your backgrounds through Brennans initially, where we'll have dummied up a background for you both, or a *legend,* as we call it. More on that later and on getting accepted by the enemy. The mother lode will be if they try to recruit you for moving stuff over to the UK. That may never happen but if it does we'll let the stuff through on the first few runs, after checking that it's not a major national security risk, of course. You'll be briefed on contact codes and you'll have a dedicated team keeping you loosely under watch initially and ramping it up later if they take the bait. If things go wrong their job will be to extract you from the situation."

The C.O. coughed.

"Don't underestimate the danger here, lads. If they even suspect that you're part of the British establishment, as Colonel Crawford has said, you'll be lifted off the streets in a flash and interrogated, as some of our people have been."

"Quite right, Major. They need to be appraised of the downside here as well. Our extraction team are good but things can sometimes go wrong. Once in there, you'll be completely on your own, apart from relying on each other. Your C.O. is right, this could be a very dangerous mission. Our goal is to locate those weapons caches, if they exist, but any additional intelligence you pick up could be useful. My question now is this. Will you take on the mission? No one will blame you if you don't. It's early in your career in the regiment and if you say no we'll understand. It won't even go on your record."

Scotty and Danny exchanged glances and, without saying a word, indicated that they were on for the mission.

"We're okay with the mission sir. Can you tell us when and where the training with MI5 will take place and the duration?"

"It starts right now and will go on for the next six weeks, possibly longer. The location is outside London. You don't need to know any more than that, but," here he looked at them closely, "there is one small problem."

There was a long moment of silence in the room.

"Tell them, Colonel," the C.O. said.

The Colonel coughed.

"Brennans trucking have a small requirement from us first. You see, they're experiencing a number of their trucks being robbed, some of them burnt out in the process. They suspect a rival firm has some inside help but despite their best efforts and police involvement, the robberies continue. They only agreed to cooperate with us by hiring you both as truckers on the Northern Ireland run, if we could solve their little problem for them. So, your first job, on completion of your MI5 training, is to volunteer for a trucking job in the UK doing some safe standard runs initially. Then Brennans will slot you two in on their most dangerous routes which carry their most highly valued cargos. Our team will shadow you on this job as well and they'll sanitize any situation that you two create in solving these truck robberies. Are you still comfortable with this?"

Danny whistled.

"Comfortable, sir? It's a lot to take in just off the top like that, and no power of arrest either!"

Danny glanced at Scotty.

"Sure, I'm okay with it, and I can tell Scotty is too."

He peered closely at Colonel Crawford. " Tell me sir, will we be armed on this UK job?"

"Unfortunately not. You know the penalty for carrying a weapon in the UK. All we need is for some provincial policeman to find a firearm on you and it could cause problems if we have to bail you out and start explaining what we were up to. In Northern Ireland, of course, you can't carry a gun because that's the first thing the IRA would spot. Off duty SAS have, in the past, carried weapons either on them or in their vehicles and have successfully fought their way out of IRA illegal road checks. One of the things that attracted us to you two is that Danny is, apparently, a whiz at unarmed combat and Scotty extremely competent as well. Your C.O. has a lot of faith in you both, which is why he stuck his neck out to get you this mission. Any more questions?"

Danny and Scotty looked at each other and shook their heads.

"Okay," the Colonel responded. "Grab your gear and lets get moving."

A last handshake with the C.O. and they dashed to their quarters to retrieve their gear which they hadn't even unpacked, ignoring questions thrown at them by their mates. They were in the back of the Colonel's car in ten minutes heading for London. They even forgot to ask the C.O. if they could re-apply for the few days leave that they'd lost in Scotland.

CHAPTER 22

Ireland
Present time

On landing in Dublin Danny booked a connecting flight to Sligo with Ryan Air. As they approached their destination the plane came in low over Strandhill Airport and Danny felt a jolt of anticipation at seeing the rolling waves of the sea below contoured by some unusually shaped mountains. Already forgetting the two hour wait at Dublin airport he leaned forward for a better view of the scene below. A healthy tanned young man in the window seat turned and grinned at him.

"They hold world championship surfing at Strandhill you know. The waves are awesome when the wind gets up," he volunteered.

Danny noticed the Australian twang.

"Been here before then?" he enquired.

"You bet mate! I work at a bar in London and save every penny to come back over. Hey, the bars here are pretty good too and the Shielas are something else!"

He looked at Danny.

"Good looking guy like you should do pretty well."

"I'll remember that. Thanks," Danny responded, smiling at the compliment.

He reflected that their individual reasons for being there couldn't have been more different. When he had seen the green countryside prior to landing in Dublin he had felt some sort of mystical tug in his spirit. Something was definitely drawing him back. Ireland was not exactly an unknown country because he had been posted to Northern Ireland with his parachute unit prior to transferring to the SAS. Like many of the British soldiers he had come south to Dublin for R&R and at one time had Fiona meet him there for a long weekend. Yet something was different this trip and he wasn't quite sure what it was.

The two men chatted for a few moments as the plane taxied up to the terminal building. The Australian introduced himself as Josh from Perth in Western Australia. As they grabbed their bags he shouted.

"Hey, I may see you in some of the bars mate. It's a small town."

When he got outside Josh was already gone so Danny grabbed a yellow beat-up looking taxi standing outside. The wiry, ginger-haired, middle-aged driver threw his bags in the back and jumped in.

"Sligo is it then?" he asked.

Danny nodded, taking a last look at the pounding waves.

"Yes please. Somewhere central."

The driver lit up a cigarette and tore out of the village as if his life depended on it. An incredible greenness sprang at them from the fields and hedges, as they hurtled along. Through some low flying clouds he spotted an unusually shaped mountain in the distance that he'd noticed as the plane was coming in to land.

"God, that's a strange looking mountain over there," exclaimed Danny pointing.

The driver turned his head.

"Aye, Ben Bulben. It does take a bit of beating. Not a place I'd go near myself mind you."

He lifted the cigarette meaningfully.

"I'm not fit enough to climb it anyway."

He paused taking a drag.

"And? …" Danny encouraged.

The driver made a face.

"There's something about that mountain - something ancient. It's the setting of many Celtic legends, supposed to be the dwelling of 'The Fianna', a band of warriors who lived in the third century. You hear stories you know," he finished lamely.

"What sort of stories?"

The driver threw the cigarette out the window.

"Ah, just old wives tales, you know. Nothing to them but they keep the children awake at Halloween."

Cursing under his breath, he slowed down and slewed over to the side to let a tractor and trailer pass as it came towards him, its wide load of straw sticking out. Pulling back onto the road again he glanced at Danny.

"What are you over here for anyway? I'd say it's the golf or the shooting, looking at you. You look disgustingly fit, if I may say so."

"Well thanks, but I'm not a golfer. I'm actually looking for someone who's visiting here himself. A man known as C.C. You wouldn't know where I can find him, would you?"

The taxi swerved and a look of reverence came over the man's face.

"The Big Fellow himself, is it?"

Danny looked perplexed.

"The Big Fellow?"

"Have you seen the movie Michael Collins?" the driver asked.

"No. Can't say I have."

"Ah, you should see it. Anyway, Michael Collins was known as The Big Fellow and was played by our own Liam Neeson from Belfast. Courtney just happens to look like an older version of Neeson, only with a pony tail. The lads, when they spotted it, started slagging him with the name *The Big Fellow* and it stuck. Maybe the town was waiting for the right label for the man."

"I gather you approve of him then," murmured Danny.

"Approve of him? That's putting it mildly. My teenage daughter, Deirdre, needed an urgent operation and would have had to wait eight months for it. A matter of life or death. She was in desperate pain and I couldn't afford to go private. I got three thousand Euros stuffed in my letter box one night. No note or anything. As luck would have it, the day driver had come to collect me for the evening shift and was just sitting there waiting. He spotted the Big Fellow nip up to the door and shove something in the box. Seemed like he didn't want to be seen coz he darted away, quick like. I spotted the envelope when I was getting my jacket in the hall and nearly fell over myself when I saw what was in it. I dashed back and showed it to my wife. Well you should have seen her!"

"I can imagine," said Danny listening with fascination.

"No you can't. It was mind-blowing, the relief. Anyway I came out to the taxi, and Liam, the driver, asked -so what did The Big Fellow put in your letter box?"

Danny was sitting there shaking his head.

"So you knew who'd done it. What I don't understand is why Courtney didn't spot a taxi sitting there. After all it sounds like he didn't want anyone to know who'd given you the money."

"Ah, that's easy. Liam always parked up the road a bit so the messages on the taxi radio wouldn't disturb our smallest child Nuala, whose room is just over the street. The street light where he was parked had been broken for the previous four months so the taxi would have been sitting in the shadow."

"So your daughter got the operation then?"

"Over and done with and not a bother on her," he replied.

"What about Courtney, The Big Fellow, as you call him? Did you ever approach him and say thanks?" asked Danny, his curiosity aroused.

The taxi driver nodded.

"That was indeed my first reaction. I wanted to go and thank him face to face. Then I thought, if the man doesn't want it known, why should I be the one to muddy it up? Maybe there's others he'll help, if it's not commonly known what he does. The nearest I came to saying thanks was when I bought him a pint at McGlynn's pub one evening. He asked me what it was for and I just smiled. He looked a bit disconcerted for a moment but he raised his glass and looked at me, really looked at me. I felt he was reading the very center of my soul and somewhere back in those eyes, a long way back, I saw an answering smile. Just for a moment, but it was there."

They drove along in silence for a while. It was Danny who finally spoke.

"I'm looking for somewhere to stay for a couple of weeks - something inexpensive like a B&B or a Guest House."

The driver laughed.

"The town's full of B&B signs. They're a plague. The Sligo festival's pull in the crowds and of course they need somewhere to stay. Most of them are reasonable, though some are better than others as you might imagine. There's one on this road, just short of town, that's been built onto. Now it's more like a mini hotel, but with B&B prices. I've had relatives stay there when they came across from Boston and they loved it. Mind you, it's a fifteen minute walk from town."

Danny liked the sound of it so they pulled in shortly to a long L-shaped building. He told the driver to wait, got out and rang the door bell.

A trim, pleasant-faced lady of about forty years of age opened the door almost immediately and smiled at him. Danny took to her right away.

"The taxi driver recommended you. Have you a single room free right now, possibly for a couple of weeks or less."

"You're in luck," she answered. "We had a man who was here for the horse riding but he had to go back to Germany because his mother had a heart attack. He's probably going back on the same plane you came in on. Would you like to have a look at the room?"

"No, I'm sure it's fine," he replied. "I'll just get my bags and pay the driver."

He gave the driver a good tip.

"Thanks for the information on Courtney. By the way, where would one contact him in town?" he asked.

"McGlynn's pub any evening after 10 pm," the driver answered before waving to the lady standing in the doorway and speeding off.

The lady in question, a Mrs. McKeever, showed him his room and then laid on a snack of sandwiches and home-made cakes, which he unashamedly proceeded to stuff himself with. Mrs. McKeever whose first name he discovered was Anne, joined him as he finished up. She was an extremely attractive woman, probably in her late forties, who carried herself with that un-definable air of someone who has a great inner strength and confidence. Her features were nicely planed and she obviously took the time to look after herself and her appearance. She smiled gently, approving of his appetite and filled his cup for the second time.

They chatted for a few minutes with Danny supplying sparse details of his family in England. He mentioned his reason for coming to Sligo. Her eyebrows raised in surprise.

"Mr. Courtney, now that's a co-incidence you staying here!"

He paused, the cup half raised to his lips.

"Co-incidence, why is that?" he enquired.

"Well, he stayed here when they were renovating that place he bought a few years ago," she replied.

"It was probably due to the taxi driver. He's a regular PR man for you and your B&B," Danny pointed out.

She shook her head. "On the contrary, he arrived here on foot one night. Walked all the way from the train station and must have passed a dozen B&B's, all with vacancies."

She stopped, her eyes flicking sideways as if recollecting events.

"I bless the day he walked into this house," she whispered.

Danny carefully put the cup down.

"I gather he helped you somehow?" he ventured tentatively.

Tears glistened in her eyes as she averted her face. He waited for a moment but couldn't contain himself.

"How did Courtney help you?" he asked.

She took a deep breath as if clearing her emotions.

"It all came back to me for a fleeting moment. All the pain and trauma. My husband Pauric was dying you see - terminal cancer. A simple check up and there it was. The worst kind. Prognosis? Two months at best to live. Pauric took it real bad."

She paused shaking her head.

"A church-goer all his life, he got angry with God and just stopped going to church. The anger and the bitterness that came out of that man. I wouldn't have believed it!"

She sat there silently for a long moment as he waited, hardly daring to breathe.

"We needed to talk you see, as two people with a short time to look forward to. Things needed to be said on both sides - and the children too. He wouldn't hear it. It was too final. I had the priest call and he practically threw him out. Oh, it was a terrible time. I very nearly closed the business down but realized that it was all that was saving my sanity. I was virtually at the end of my tether when Mr. Courtney came looking for accommodation."

She paused before whispering.

"It came with him."

Her eyes flicked sideways again as if viewing an internal film. Reluctant to break the silence Danny coughed and quietly asked "What came with him?"

She looked at him with puzzlement in her eyes.

"The peace of course. It was on him and all around him like an aura. Almost tangible. It's hard to explain. You'd have to experience it to understand."

She went on to tell of the events that transpired following Courtney's arrival. She hadn't discussed Pauric's illness with Courtney at all but one day she heard voices in her husband's sick room and, opening the door, she found Courtney talking to him. She was about to tackle him for his uninvited intrusion when she noticed the look on her husband's face. All the hard lines and bitterness had softened and he had a rapt attentive look on his face. Courtney had been holding his hand when she entered the room. Over the course of the week the visits continued and Anne and her husband started to talk about life and death and those things that needed to be talked about. The children called too and went away with contented looks on their faces. The priest called one afternoon at Pauric's request and left with barely concealed tears in his eyes. Previously, Pauric had refused to be transferred into a hospice when his pain had reached a level that required regular monitoring of his medication. Now, he readily agreed and was moved into the hospice on a Friday afternoon.

Courtney moved out the same day.

The following Wednesday he came back to visit her. She paused, tears coming again.

"Look, if this is too much for you," Danny interjected.

She reached for his arm,

"No it's all right. I feel I have to tell you this for some reason. I'll be okay in a moment."

She paused again as if marshalling her thoughts.

"What's your first name?" she asked gently.

"Danny," he answered.

"Danny," she said as if savoring it. "That's a nice Irish name, so it is. You have to realize, Danny, that back then a virtual miracle had taken place. Pauric and I said all the things we needed to say, and the children too. He had come back to the church and had the last sacraments, which meant a lot to myself and his mother as well. I was still full of fear and trepidation about carrying on. I was mentally struggling with whether to sell the house with all it's memories and give up the B& B, but mostly, I feared the future without Pauric by my side. When Courtney came back we sat in the kitchen and he reached out and took my hand. All the guests had gone out and I had a girl out back doing the bedrooms.

Mr. Courtney asked me a question then. Do you trust me Anne? Oh yes! I replied with feeling. Most definitely. He asked me another question that I thought was peculiar at the time - do you believe you have a Spirit Guide? I told him I didn't know as that was not part of the Catholic tradition. Then he blew my mind completely - I want you to meet your Spirit Guide he said quite matter of factly. Somehow I didn't question it, willing at that stage to anything he proposed. Still holding my hand he told me to relax and suggested that I breathe in and out very deeply and relax each muscle as I did so. He directed me in that and I felt myself relax all over. The noises of the traffic going by outside just faded away as I felt myself drifting deeper and deeper. He told me to imagine that I was walking in a beautiful forest with flowers and the smells and sounds of summer all around - to feel the soft breeze and sunshine caressing my skin, the sounds of a bubbling stream and the bumblebees, to feel the moist green grass under my bare feet. Then he told me that I had come to a clearing in the forest and in the clearing were some fallen logs that made up a comfortable seat. I was to rest there with my eyes closed, emptying my mind of everything and just let the peace and ambience of the scene seep into my whole being. I seemed to let go and drop down into some sort of new dimension, like I was drifting, drifting, and circles of light seemed to ripple up my being. Then he told me to invite my Spirit Guide to join me and reach out in love to it. I was instructed not to have any pre-conceived form or shape in my mind. It could be anything from a beam of light to an animal. He told me to open my spirit eyes, still staying in the dream-like state. I couldn't believe what I was seeing! A tiny fawn standing there beside me with the softest eyes you could ever imagine and such love reflected in them for me. I told Mr. Courtney this and he instructed me to put my hands on the fawn and let all my pain, confusion and sadness soak into it's beautiful colored coat. He told me that it had endless capacity to absorb all my hurt and fear of the future, without any effect on itself. I did that and felt all that stuff flow from me almost like an old skin falling off. The eyes of the fawn understood and seemed to love me all the more. I felt a great joy suffuse my whole being like I'd never felt in my life before. Old hurts, disappointments and past baggage seemed to fall away. I felt life past, present and future and how Pauric had made a contribution in sharing my life and I in his before he went on to higher things. I saw myself living on and fulfilling my purpose in life. In my mind, I heard the fawn telling me that I could return to that special place as often as I wanted to and that it would be there to greet and comfort me. That it would always be watching over me. I just can't describe how wonderful it was. I didn't want to leave there but I understood it was time, and gradually I became aware that I was back in my kitchen sitting at the table. I was alone."

"Alone?" echoed Danny who had been sitting mesmerized by the story.

She nodded. "Completely. He must have crept out. I never heard him, I was so wrapped up in it all. My husband died the following day quite peacefully and myself and the family were all there. It was so beautiful ... and I grieved for him for a long time and still miss him, always will, but I wake up every day with a wonderful sense of - not just peace, but something closer to tranquility. I can't explain it any more than that," she exclaimed feelingly.

"Do you still see Mr. Courtney?" he asked.

"Not from that day to this, Danny. Oh, he's still in town, I know, and I could probably contact him if I wanted to. There's no need to though and he's probably doing his work elsewhere with someone else in need."

She examined him closely.

"I haven't talked about this with anyone, and then you called and I just felt that I had tell you my story. I don't understand it!"

They both sat there thinking their own thoughts for a long time.

Finally Danny stirred.

"So Courtney's a religious man then?" he probed.

She laughed.

"Religious? Whatever made you think that! If that's religion, I'd like to see more of it. It's the most potent religion I've ever encountered."

She looked intently at him.

"He knows you're coming doesn't he?"

Danny looked surprised.

" How did you …?"

"I didn't. I just heard myself saying it right then. It happens. I don't need to know why but it's a confirmation for you."

His head still spinning, he went to his room where he lay down, falling into a deep, dreamless sleep right away.

CHAPTER 23

When he woke up, Danny, for the first time started to have doubts about his presence in Ireland. Certainly the story back in the U.K. about the amazing Clive Courtney had sparked his interest in meeting with him. However, the attempted assault in the underground garage in London and the events that followed had blurred the issue of trying to locate Courtney. Now his mind was racing with anxiety about his family and the mess he was in with the authorities. Was this the time to be off chasing a dream, as Fiona would say, or should he call DC White and return to London? Admittedly, there was something else urging him on in his search for the man, something he didn't quite understand. Now he was bombarded with information from all sides which painted a completely different picture of Courtney. He thought he was chasing a whiz at financial services but it seemed that the man was also a combination of Mother Teresa and a mind-bending Guru!

Danny was not a spiritual person. His grandmother had dragged him to church in Ireland up to age eight at which time he moved to Wales. The only good thing about church then was when it finished and his Granny bought him a treat. In Wales there was no more church because his parents never went. The stories he'd heard since landing in Sligo were completely alien territory to him.

They say there are no atheists in a foxhole and Danny had been a member of groups of men going into action where individuals had openly prayed for protection. Most relied on their training, their skills and their mates to bring them safely through the action. Many of them secretly hoped the prayers for protection covered them as well. He'd actually heard the story of an artillery officer in the second world war who recited Psalm 91 every morning with his men and they had all come through the war unscathed.

Now, his mind had been completely blitzed with an overload of information, which was totally outside his mindset and ability to comprehend. He felt the need of some action himself and decided to have a workout in his room, which was quite spacious. Changing into shorts and a tee-shirt which he'd picked up at Dublin airport, he proceeded to work through a punishing schedule of exercises and martial arts moves until all the stiffness had gone and his mind was clear. By that time he was bathed in perspiration so he had a quick shower and changed. He decided he owed it to himself, having come so far, to at least meet with Courtney, before making any decision to return home. First, he walked into town and had some fish and chips in a small café.

It was 9pm when he walked into McGlynn's pub, which happened to be across from the police station. The place was noisy and full of locals with a good measure of tourists he judged as well. He discovered a separate lounge at the back where the music was played and this was more popular with the visitors, away from the bar where the serious drinkers congregated. Danny installed himself in the lounge and managed to grab a pint of lager from the busy barman. Vast quantities of Guinness were stacked up on the counter top as the bar staff attempted to satisfy demand. Danny himself had never liked the drink as it tended to make him feel bloated. Back in the regiment it was usually packs of Stella that they demolished in their off duty hours. It was hard to slough off the layers of his time and disciplines in the Forces. He still found himself alert and watchful, almost as if he was on a mission. The Irish voices swirling around him reminded him of his postings to Northern Ireland, just across the border from where he now sat.

Danny took another swallow from his glass and began to relax as the music group started up again. They appeared to be very popular and obviously had a following as evidenced by the number of requests for specific songs coming from the room. He had a momentary stab of regret thinking of Fiona and Allison in Bath, away from their regular routines in London. Fiona would have loved the *craic* in McGlynn's pub, he knew.

Glancing at his watch, he was surprised to find that it was already after 10 pm. He decided to check in the outside bar to see if Courtney or *The Big Fellow* as he was now known, had turned up. It would be easy to spot a pony tail, he figured.

The outside bar wasn't as busy as before so he ordered another drink. A burly red-headed man was just turning away from the bar with two pints of foaming Guinness in his hands, his attention on keeping the glasses steady. The man failed to spot Danny and bumped into him, the tops of the two glasses sloshing out on the floor. Suddenly the room went totally silent. The red haired man reared back, his face suffused with anger and alcohol.

"You stupid git!" he roared. "Just where the fuck do you think you're goin?"

Danny spread his hands apologetically.

"Hey, sorry mate. It was a pure accident. Let me get you a couple of fresh pints," he offered.

The redhead's eyes narrowed.

"Mate is it? A bloody Englishman we have here, knocking pints out of my hand. You probably did that on purpose just to prove how bloody clever you are eh?" he demanded.

Danny sighed.

"Look, I said I'm sorry and I meant it. I'm quite happy to replace those two pints. Lets just leave it at that, shall we?"

The redhead looked around him at the watching expectant audience, turned and placed the two glasses on the bar. Then he faced Danny who casually changed his stance.

"A bloody Englishman we have here going round knocking the glasses out of a man's hand who was minding his own business. I think I'm going to teach him a wee lesson."

With that, he drew his right hand back. Suddenly, a large form materialized between them and Danny saw the man's arms being held, as if by a friendly bear.

"Ah Paccy, that was amazing how you did that!" said the man as he gazed with animation full in the face of the red-head who blinked rapidly in confusion.

"Wha - wha," he stuttered, "How do you mean?"

"How you did that. I can't believe it. It was incredible!" said the stranger.

The other man looked sideways in bewilderment at Danny and back at the large friendly bear holding him.

"Sorry. I – ah – whadya mean?" he asked.

"The transformation, I mean lad. One minute you were there having never met this man and next minute you're ready to tear his head off. Tell me was it a picture you saw in your head first?" the big man enthused.

Paccy was more confused than ever trying vainly to extricate himself from the firm grasp.

"I don't know. Ah, it was - ah," he spluttered.

"I see. Probably something you heard in your head then. A sound or a word - perhaps a voice saying I'm going to kill him. Was that it?"

With that he released him and patted him on the elbow.

Paccy staggered back a step his face puzzled.

"Jasus! I don't even know what you're on about," he started.

"Ah," said the large man thoughtfully. "It was probably a feeling then. A strong feeling in your gut that you just wanted to smash him into the floor. Was that it, Paccy? Concentrate now. There you were with two fresh pints, looking forward to taking them back to your table and sharing them with your friend, and suddenly you bump into this man. Was that when it hit you? Just a sudden feeling in your gut?"

Paccy was sobering up quite fast as his mind tried to grapple with what was going on. His eyes moved down right as if trying to recall something.

"A feeling in my gut, you say? Yeah, it was. Just suddenly hit me. Wanted to smash his face in," he said lamely. "What's so fucking amazing about that?" he asked, curiosity in his voice.

The large man laughed, patting him on both arms.

"Oh, it's just a study of the brain I'm doing and how it works, and I've never seen anyone move through the emotional loop as fast as yourself Paccy. That was something to see. You're exceptional. You really are."

Turning to Danny he said.

"What do you think Danny? You were in the line of fire and yet it must have been amazing to watch."

As baffled as the red-head, Danny muttered some acknowledgement, his confusion mingled with curiosity as to how the man knew his name.

Paccy was still standing there his aggressive demeanor totally changed as the stranger guided him back to the bar and threw a handful of Euros down.

"Here Sean, keep Paccy in drinks until this is gone."

Turning to the redhead,

"That brain of yours! Paccy, what a loop - just amazing!"

It was only then that Danny spotted the pony tail.

CHAPTER 24

Courtney drove them up to Jury's hotel at the top of the Dublin road and ordered a large pot of tea for both of them. Danny hadn't said much since his rescue from a potential fight at McGlynn's pub. He'd spent the interim studying the man. He certainly was tall with large burly shoulders, which he carried in a relaxed manner like a nine year old walking to school without a care in the world. Probably in his late forties, he could have been mistaken for a much younger man. His face exuded a sort of glow. Of what? Danny wondered just as the man turned and looked directly at him. That's when he realized that the most striking aspect to Courtney, were his eyes. Dark and piercing green, they seemed to probe the very marrow of your bones when they looked at you, and yet he seemed at the same time to be listening to a distant drum beat. He was here and yet he wasn't.

Courtney held his gaze for what seemed an eternity, nodding slightly as he did so.

"Hmn. It's you I should have been talking to back there not that poor Paccy that you were just about to disembowel," Courtney offered, smiling.

"He was just about to knock my block off. What was I supposed to do?" Danny protested.

"A little compassion perhaps. After all you are a trained fighter. I saw the way you shifted your stance there in the pub. Tell me, would he have had much chance?"

Danny grimaced.

"None whatsoever," he answered.

C.C. nodded thoughtfully.

"I figured as much. By the way, if you had known that Paccy had brought up his disabled sister all by himself since both parents were killed in a car crash ten years ago, how would you feel? Waits on her hand and foot and only gets out one night a week for a few drinks. Yes, tonight as it happens. You wouldn't have made any friends for yourself around here by thumping him, I can tell you. The business in the North is pretty much settled, no more explosions or killings at least. What I was leading up to is that someone seeing you in action might have made a connection between you and the British Forces up there. They still have long memories around here and there's still some hard men around. Not a soft target like Paccy, who might just decide to take an interest in you. Could have ruined any plans I might have had for you as well."

"I had no idea, but still -" Danny started to defend himself.

"But still," said Courtney, squinting at him, "a little humor might have defused the situation Danny. After all you're now supposed to be in the communication business aren't you. Remember your head office training? Step into the client's shoes and try to understand their map of reality. Anyway, enough said, enjoy your tea."

Danny welcomed the silence as they both put sugar and milk in their cups and had their first taste.

"That's good, though I'm not much of a tea drinker. Tell me, how did you know I'd come over and what I looked like?"

The smooth skin creased into a grin.

"I'd love to tell you that I have these extraordinary powers and indeed some of the locals swear I have. As you know Sonya called me and described you and I decided to put you to the test and see just how determined you were to find me. You passed the test Danny."

There was a long moment of silence. Courtney reached sideways and picked something up.

"This helped too," he added. "the UK paper," handing it to Danny who felt himself grow pale.

The headlines screamed at him - Vigilante sought. Ex Forces veteran doles out rough justice. His picture, a more zeroed-in version taken in front of the branch office was featured square in the main body of the article.

"My God!" gasped Danny. "The police really do believe I killed them. I suspected they might initially, but I hoped they would find the real killers quick enough. I just didn't want to end up stuck in jail while they sorted it out," he volunteered.

Courtney regarded him closely.

"So you didn't kill them then?"

"Good God no! Hell I didn't even know where they were living - and executing them like that? I've seen enough action to know that you don't get three men to sit still while you break their necks one at a time. No, there had to be more than one person involved to get that result."

He paused looking appealingly at Courtney.

"I'm no vigilante Mr. Courtney."

"Well no, I can see that from your reaction sitting here right now, however …"

"However what?" demanded Danny.

"I have to say I detected a strong spirit of violence in you back there in the pub when Paccy got you going. Very close to the surface too."

Courtney's comments smarted Danny but intrigued him as well.

"I'm not sure what you mean. Okay, the paper makes it clear I was in the Forces, the Paras, and violence goes with the territory."

Courtney drank his tea silently, all the time observing him from under bushy lashes. A look of sympathy flickered across his face. Finally he stirred and sighed.

"I'm not talking about your Forces training Danny. You have what I've detected as a spirit of violence in you."

"A spirit of violence?" Consternation rippled on Danny's face. "For crying out loud I've just completed eight years in the British Forces. I'd be dead many times over, or seriously maimed and some of my mates too if I hadn't had the ability to react violently! Come on C.C. I'm not buying this!"

Courtney observed him quietly, then leaned forward and touched his arm.

"Danny, I hear you and I accept where you're coming from. Of course you needed your skills to survive and you were quite justified in doing so under orders in legitimate areas of conflict. The spirit of violence I'm talking about, goes back a long way in your past and it's something you are going to have to address if you want to progress beyond pounding people into the ground when they look sideways at you. The British Forces is simply the vehicle you chose to express that violence," he explained patiently.

"But look -" Danny started to protest.

"No, you look, young Danny. Would it be useful in the future when dealing with situations like McGlynns pub as a God given opportunity to hone your skills of communication? When you think about it, it's surprising how similar all human beings are. We don't really want very much; Food, shelter, clothing, some people who love us and sometimes just a little space and tolerance when we go off track a bit."

"Like Paccy, you mean?" Danny ventured.

"Exactly, Danny. You know the Chinese have a custom where two men who have a conflict, sit down in the square in front of the whole village and argue their views out - over a period of days if necessary. The one who loses his temper is the one judged to have lost the argument."

They sat quietly drinking their tea.

Finally, Danny interrupted the silence.

"What was all that about with Paccy, by the way? - did you see a picture etc.? You lost me completely. Actually I thought you were deranged for a moment there - you know, the effects of years of Guinness on the brain cells or something like that."

Courtney chuckled.

"Well it may come to that yet. Some people think I'm there already. Nooooo. What I did with Paccy was carrying out an intervention that effectively changed his mental and emotional state. It's called NLP, Neuro Linguistic Programming. It's an actual science and the European Union recognizes it as an established therapy. People take in information through their five senses - visual, auditory, kinesthetic, taste and smell. They're called representational systems. In the west we tend to primarily use visual, auditory and kinesthetic and while we use all of these, people tend to major in one.

A visual might indicate this for example by using visual words like *I see what you mean* or *that paints a clear picture.*

The auditory might say *that rings a bell* or *that sounds good*

while the kinesthetic might use words like *I feel that's right* or *I can't quite grasp that.*"

Danny's face was growing more confused and he was about to ask a question but Courtney stopped him with a hand gesture before continuing.

"I know exactly where you're coming from Danny. It is a load to get your head around. Just be patient with me for a moment longer. Oh and by the way, to confuse you a bit more, you can tell which representational system a person is using by their eye movements too. Now, I didn't learn NLP to stop bar fights, though you saw the results, but can you see the benefit of being able to change your potential client's mindset simply by asking some targeted questions based on whether they are visual, auditory or kinesthetic?"

Danny nodded, his face showing mounting interest.

"Hell yes! This must be one of the reasons you're such a whiz at sales C.C."

Suddenly Danny's face clouded.

"God, I just realized that Fiona, back in Bath, has seen this paper and will be going out of her mind. It's probably on TV by now as well!"

His voice had risen and he started to get up but Courtney pulled him back down.

"Hey, easy does it. Don't start attracting any attention to yourself right now where someone might remember you. The

UK police will discover your flight over here soon enough and alert the Gardai, who'll be on the lookout for you. They might not pick up your connecting flight and just concentrate on the Dublin area for the moment. That might give you a little time. Now, is there any way you can contact your good lady without giving away your location. Since 9/11, nothings private, even in the UK," he commented bitterly.

Danny was thinking fast. Prior to leaving Bath they had marked out three different telephone boxes and he had recorded their numbers. He had outlined a very simple method of maintaining contact with Fiona. If he called her mother's house, where she was staying, and she had to arrange this with her mother, to let it ring. Two rings would mean she should go immediately to a certain phone box, three rings to another, and so on. All were within a ten-minute walk from her house and Danny would call the number in exactly fifteen minutes. The only weakness in the plan was that the particular telephone box might be occupied by someone making a call. Hopefully not some teenager talking to friends. He explained the arrangement to Courtney who nodded his approval.

Danny looked at his watch. It was 10:30 pm. He made a face.

"A bit late getting her out but if she's seen the news she certainly won't be in bed. I'll give it a go anyway," he said, getting up.

Courtney extracted a card from his wallet.

"Here, use my BT international phone card. Save you churning coins into the phone."

Rising, Courtney escorted him out into the lounge where the public telephones were and showed him how to use the card and make the connection.

Danny returned a minute later.

"She's probably heading out right now and I'm going to call her at the kiosk as arranged."

They chatted for the next few minutes about the events leading up to him joining the branch and his struggle to make it work. Then the events following where he faced off the three thugs and the attempt to burn down his house. He explained how he had managed to get his family out of harms way and down to Bath. Danny glanced at his watch again.

"I'd better get up there and make the call, it's just about time."

It only had to ring once and the phone was picked up immediately. He heard Fiona's concerned voice.

"Danny, are you all right? Your picture was on the 6:00 o'clock news. They're practically accusing you of murdering those three thugs! Of course I know you didn't do it. My Mom's looking at me rather strangely though. What will you do?"

"I'm glad you know I'm not a murderer, Fiona. I know I've done some stuff in the military, but that was under orders and with clearly defined outcomes."

"Yes, of course I know that Danny. It's just that the media tend to twist things around so that it sounds like you're some sort of mad dog that needs to be put down. I nearly called that detective, D.I. White, to put him straight today when I read the paper."

"You mustn't even think of doing anything like that Fee. They would have traced you in an instant and pulled you in. I would have had to give myself up then, and right now I'm still free and with Mr Courtney. I don't know how, but I have a feeling that he may help me somehow."

Her voice sounded uncertain.

"Help you ... but how? You're not still chasing that guru Danny? Quite frankly, all that sounds totally insignificant in the light of developments. Surely, you can arrange some legal support over here and then come back and try to clear this up? We can't just go on like this ignoring it. Sooner or later they'll catch up with you and bring you back in handcuffs. That would look really bad and most certainly blow any future career you might have had. Wouldn't you agree?"

He nodded, forgetting that she couldn't see.

"I do agree, Fiona. All I'm asking for is a couple more days and I'll do something along those lines. Somehow, I feel that there are some answers over here as well. Not quite sure how but just trust me for the moment and give Allison a big hug for me. I'll contact you again soon. Promise."

He'd stayed longer than he meant to on the call. He knew that the British Government had a massive electronic listening post at Cheltenham that could be utilized by the police on request. Even public telephone boxes were not secure, as he had learned from his MI5 training.

He returned to the table and apprised Courtney of the call. They decided to leave prior to the 11:00 o'clock news coming on shortly. He'd told Courtney where he was staying but he made no comment on hearing the name of the guest house.

Heading out into the lounge again he spotted a familiar face. The man nodded to him.

"Hi there mate. How's it going?"

Danny remembered the Australian he'd flown in with that morning.

"Oh hello ... ah ... Josh. How was the surf then? Worth coming over for?"

Josh grinned expansively.

"Just beaut mate. Just beaut. The Shielas aren't bad either."

He nodded to the receptionist who was smiling at him. Danny mumbled something else and hurried after Courtney, who had kept moving.

Out in the car park he caught up with him and explained the Aussie. Courtney frowned.

"If he's just a surf bum over for a few days you might be okay. If he's hanging round bars and watching the news, he'll soon pick up on you and the Gardai will know toot sweet and that will lead to me," he grimaced. "I'm easy to describe, unfortunately."

They drove in silence down through town and out onto the Strandhill Road. Danny's mind raced with questions but he refrained from asking them. At the guest house Courtney told him he would pick him up the following morning and he could move in with him for the balance of whatever time he had left in Sligo or until the police came knocking on his door.

CHAPTER 25

MI5 Training House, North London
Five years previously

It was a tough slog up the M4 and M25 link road before they wearily arrived at their destination north east of the city of Cambridge. Colonel Crawford didn't make any effort to speak to them on the journey so both he and Scotty, like all soldiers, took advantage of that and managed to get some broken sleep in between the roar of the traffic. They pulled up at the entrance to what appeared to be a walled estate with a solid imposing spiked gate with a guard post. A man in a security uniform came out and spoke briefly to Crawford. The gate swung open and they proceeded up a long tree-lined drive to a sprawling complex of buildings and a large country style house.

They crawled out stiffly and Crawford spoke curtly through the lowered car window.

"They're expecting you inside. Tommy will settle you in and brief you. Your training starts at dawn tomorrow. I'll be apprised of your progress and will be back during your time here for part of it. This will be a very compacted course so we're throwing a lot at you in a short time. Remember, lives could depend on this including your own, so stay alert and focused. Got that?"

Without waiting for an answer the car spun around and disappeared down the driveway. As they proceeded up the steps the front door opened and a middle aged trim looking man stood there, a smile of welcome on his face.

"Come on in lads, come on in. Welcome. I'm Tommy. You must be knackered coming up the bloody motorway this time of night. We've got some grub ready and a nice cup of tea, or coffee if you prefer."

Danny and Scotty looked relieved after the coldness of Colonel Crawford, to find a warm reception upon arrival. Tommy, who later informed them that he was an ex member of the armored corps, showed them to their room which had twin beds and a large en suite bathroom. The cupboards contained a half dozen sets of civilian clothing, two complete sets of army clothing including battle dress, track suits, boots, civilian shoes and runners. Both sets were the correct sizes for the men, which indicated to them that some planning had already gone into the assignment.

After a quick shower they changed into clean track suits and dashed downstairs to be met by a giant meal of roast beef, potatoes, choice of vegetables, followed by apple pie. It reminded them of the regiment at Hereford, which always prided itself on providing the best of fare. Probably to make up for all the times they were stuck with cold packaged meals in many God forgotten places world wide.

They nodded their appreciation to Tommy who hovered around them as they ate everything he had put in front of them. Finally when they sat back satisfied he cleared his throat.

"Well, nothing wrong with your appetites lads. Glad to see that. I'll be looking after the catering while you're here and the people who run this place believe in providing good fare. We have a cook, who happens to be my wife. She comes in and also does the shopping locally for the house. Now, I'm not part of your field training crew, but my job is to fill in some of the gaps, see you provided with a full belly in the mornings. Tomorrow morning you are expected next door," he pointed to their right "at 6 am sharp. This establishment is run by MI5

156

who, as you know are civilians, so apart from weapons training out in the field, dress informally, but otherwise treat this as a continuation of your military training in terms of being at a certain place at a certain time, safety standards with the use of weapons etc. The one difference here is that no one's rank is mentioned, though you can assume that some of your trainers are in fact serving members. As part of your training you'll be leaving the base on specific assignments, and there's bags of civilian clothes upstairs in your room as you've seen. We're talking here about trips to London for example to learn surveillance techniques; how to follow people without getting detected, setting up dead drops for communication purposes without getting lumbered; how to use a car like a stunt man if suddenly you have to escape a trap."

He noticed Scotty's large grin. "I see we have one convert already," Tommy said, sharing his grin, before continuing with his briefing.

"As you've been told, the next few weeks will be much like force-feeding turkeys for Christmas so don't expect any nights off in the pub lads. If you get one, sure enjoy it but stay sober and alert and don't draw attention to yourself. And most of all, as has been emphasized, no mention to anyone, where you are or what you're doing here, understood?"

The grin had left Scotty's face.

"Telling an SAS trooper to take a night off and stay sober ... ooof!"

"Yes, I know. But if you can hold your drink this could be a distinct advantage if you have to hang out in pubs as part of your cover. I don't know your mission and I don't want to. Oh and a word to the wise - don't show off - even if you're exceptional at something, keep it buttoned and you might learn something. They'll have seen your records anyway so they'll know your back-ground and your skills-set.

Any questions? No. Okay, alarm clocks are in the room. Get yourselves up - civilian clothes as mentioned. A hot breakfast will be laid out on the table. I won't be here but Mable my wife will have laid everything out for you. You usually have lunch with the training staff in the canteen and I pick you up for the evening meal. We also supply you with a packaged lunch on occasion, as needed. Don't worry, all will be explained to you in good time."

With that he left them and Danny and Scotty went up to their rooms where they continued their speculation as to the training and the mission that followed directly from it.

They couldn't wait to get started.

The six weeks passed like a blur. From day one their feet hardly touched the ground. The team of twelve people who were responsible for their training were effectively in their faces day and night. Even meals were used as opportunities to inculcate more information - understanding the mentality of the IRA and the sensitive politics that presently existed in Northern Ireland. How blowing the mission could virtually blow the present negotiations going on. Some years prior to this, two Brits appearing in their midst would have resulted in both being lifted by the IRA and interrogated. However things had moved on from there with active IRA units standing down and the H-Block prison emptied. Still there existed a hard-core splinter group who wanted to go all the way for a united Ireland. This unit, given the opportunity, would have hived off some assets in terms of weapons and explosives for some future action; this, despite Gerry Adams' reassurances that all weapons had been destroyed, and that the IRA now spoke as one voice and accepted the inevitability of continued British rule in the North.

MI5 informants suggested otherwise. Their mission was to attempt to make contact with this group over a period of time and try to establish a relationship with them. It would take time and patience and the risks of discovery were high. An extraction team, as mentioned, would be close by at all times should they get in trouble. Their biggest initial challenge was to shed the characteristics of trained soldiers, so they were instructed to stop having haircuts and develop a civilian walk and slouch.

Their chief instructor, a lean sharp-featured man called Jack Patton who walked with a limp, was continually challenging them as to possible scenarios where they could give themselves away.

"So there you are in a pub and someone goes out of their way to pick a fight with you, what do you do?"

Danny and Scotty looked at each other. Finally Scotty volunteered.

"Well, we're supposed to be a pair of hard-ass truck drivers. We wouldn't let someone just walk all over us, would we?"

Danny murmured support.

Patton nodded.

"Just what I'd expect you to say Scotty. Now here's the thing. If they do suspect you as being undercover they may very well set this up to see how you handle yourselves. It would be pretty obvious right away that you were both trained in unarmed combat and you'd soon end up in the back of a van heading towards some interrogation center. Okay, the team might manage to rescue you, but the mission would be aborted. Can you see that lads?"

They both nodded.

"So, we may be hard-nosed truckies, but if we have to fight we make it look like we're enthusiastic amateurs, right?" volunteered Danny.

Patton nodded.

"Couldn't have put it better myself. Now here's another scenario and this is a worst case one. You get lifted by this splinter group and they start interrogating you. How do you handle yourselves?"

"Well, we're trained to take it. We don't tell them anything, period." Danny volunteered.

Patton made a face.

"Yes and no. Bear in mind they've lifted our people before who stood up to the interrogation methods. You may recall reading about that young Captain some years back. They killed him eventually, but they can tell by the way you resist questioning that you're reacting like a trained operative. Don't underestimate these people. We've been up against them for over 30 years now and they've learned a lot about our methods. So. How would you now handle an interrogation? Any thoughts?"

"Well firstly," said Scotty, "as we have a lot to learn about working undercover, we have a lot of unlearning to do first so that we can react like a couple of normal truck drivers and scream like bloody kids if they torture us - without giving away the mission of course!"

Patton smiled.

"Good, I see you're getting the picture. Now let's move on."

And move on they did. Days spent in learning the field craft of an agent: how to open locks and disarm alarm systems; hot-wiring cars using small cameras when the opportunity to record information presented itself; maintaining regular contact with their team and how to call in immediate help if they needed it; using non-military weapons, if and when necessary; taking out an enemy if called upon to do so by making it look like an accident so as not to alarm their associates; refining their knowledge of the use of targeted explosive devices.

Danny found the unarmed combat training particularly absorbing when they brought in an elderly Korean who showed them how to disable an opponent just by using slight pressure on nerve centers. This opened up a whole new window in his martial arts expertise. Scottie didn't put very much store in that methodology as he tended to rely on a savage double head butt that he'd learned on the streets of Glasgow as a boy.

They spent days in London learning surveillance techniques and how to spot and lose surveillance when it's directed against them. It was emphasized however, that if the enemy had the resources and personnel, they could stay on their tail regardless; for example a fleet of cars in front and back and on parallel streets. MI5 took over and sealed off an adventure park for a day and practiced escape and evasion tactics using vehicles. Scotty was in his element.

A great deal of time was spent rehearsing and role playing their proposed role as genuine truck drivers - the paper work and customs procedures, their routes and reporting procedures and a myriad of other details. The manager and owner of Brennan Trucking spent an afternoon going over the basics of the trucking role with them and all the details and routines that they would have to master. If, as they suspected, someone high up at Brennan Trucking was leaking information, they had to come on board as two new genuine drivers. It was the valuable cargoes in the UK that were being hijacked, however it wouldn't look right for these loads to be immediately funneled into Danny's and Scotty's route. It had to appear as if these were being equally shared with the different drivers across the country. They would be informed though when they were carrying the high-end loads. Back-up teams would shadow them on these runs. Backgrounds for both of them had to be established and they spent two days practicing driving the big rigs on the highways around the MI5 training grounds, down to the M25 motorway and back.

Scotty had to take on a completely new identity. MI5 had prepared a paper trail to support it, but, they were warned that one slip or hesitation in a conversation could torpedo the whole thing.

Danny had to memorize a background that excluded his military experience, and they pieced together his past as a barman, trainee mechanic, which was actually true, and invented time spent as crew on board cruise ships. Again, this identity would be set in place with the right people and the proper documentation if someone checked up on them. They also had to get licensed in driving the large haulage trucks and show previous experience on their employee applications.

During the six weeks of training the two men, despite the demand on their time both day and night, still managed to maintain a good level of fitness with early morning jogging and exercise.

Colonel Crawford appeared again during the final three days and having relentlessly grilled them on their preparations, provided the final details on their mission against the IRA. They realized however that it might have all been for nothing if they couldn't first crack the hijackings at Brennan Trucking.

They were given the weekend off and were told to report on Monday to Brennan Trucking at an industrial site in Luton, just north of their present location.

CHAPTER 26

Sligo

Danny could see small fluffy clouds clinging to the top of Ben Bulben as he sat in the breakfast room. It was an awesome looking mountain, like some pre-historic monster crouching there, just waiting for the right moment to spring into life and devour the countryside.

A party of people over from Germany for the horse riding, created a clamorous environment at breakfast as the group talked loudly across the tables. They swooned over the delicious Irish bacon and Danny decided to include this in his order too. It was a good-natured free for all and the Germans appeared softened by the relaxed Irish attitude. A different lady was serving breakfast and he didn't have a chance to talk to Mrs. McKeever until he was checking out. He was starting to apologize for leaving just after a day when Courtney arrived, drawing Anne into a side room where Danny could see them having a conversation. In a few moments they came back out.

Mrs. McKeever smiled at him.

"Sorry you won't be staying longer Danny. I understand Mr. Courtney will be looking after you for a few days."

She hesitated, looking at C.C.

"Oh and I'm not keeping a record of your stay in case anyone's looking for you."

Danny was counting out some notes, which he handed over to her.

"Thanks Mrs. McKeever ... Anne. I really enjoyed a great nights sleep. The place is more like a small hotel than a B&B. Great breakfast too, by the way."

It must have been the right thing to say as she beamed again, thanking him.

Courtney was gazing at the mountain with a strange luminescence in his eyes as he absently remarked,

"She's known for her breakfasts Danny. Just read the visitors book."

He fell silent again as if drawn to the mountain. Danny glanced at both of them uncertainly.

"Well, must get going then, eh C.C.?"

"Yes my boy, we have a lot to do today so lets get moving."

He drew Anne into a quick embrace and they left in a hail of good wishes from her.

They headed North out of Sligo on the Bundoran road, with the sea on the left and the massive Ben Bulben mountain on the right, now towering tall and majestic in the early morning sunlight. Neither of them spoke, but it was a comfortable silence as they admired the sensory experience of the lush Sligo countryside. Courtney pulled into the parking lot of a pub in a small village called Drumcliffe, and having parked, crossed the road into a cemetery. Danny followed with some puzzlement.

Courtney stopped at a particular grave-stone and pointed to the name. Leaning forward Danny read aloud,

"William Butler Yeats."

"Heard of him?" Courtney asked.

"Actually, yes, but I never connected him with this place. A captain in our company was very much into poetry and one summer came across the border to some sort of school on Yeats."

"The summer school. Yes it attracts people from all over the world. The Japanese love him believe it or not. Did you read the headstone?"

He pointed to the inscription. Danny leaned closer –

Cast a cold eye on life on death horseman pass by.

He read it musingly.

"What does it mean I wonder?" he asked.

"Indeed! What does it mean precisely? Some might interpret it as hoping that the grim reaper might not notice them or that we accept the inevitability of death and then get on with our lives. Ever thought about it Danny?"

"Dying you mean? Not really. Well you know when we're going into action, most men do reflect on that possibility, even the toughest ones. Some would write final letters. Others would go to the Padre, talk to him, perhaps get a prayer. Others would just sit quietly and you respected that and left them alone."

Courtney's face reflected curiosity.

"So what sustained you during those times?" he asked.

"I have to say C.C. that once you were in it, your training took over and you just focused on the mission and protecting your mates. That was the primary driving force - not letting your mates down and not doing anything to endanger their lives. In a way, they were family and their perception and opinion of you was paramount. I mean, you'd jump in front of them and take a bullet meant for them if you had to!"

Danny's voice had taken on a new intensity. Courtney studied his face for a brief moment.

"You know Danny, what you just described right there, was a form of love - throwing yourself in front of a bullet to protect them. You may be closer to the truth than you imagine. You miss them don't you?" Courtney asked gently.

He nodded.

"Strangely, I haven't thought about it very much in the past six months since I got out. Perhaps it's been brought on by the threat against myself and my family, but here I am totally exposed without any back-up as it were."

"Hopefully, not totally alone, Danny."

"Sorry C.C., I was thinking of the UK mess when I said that. I kinda connect you to the financial services business and what I'd hoped to gain from this trip."

Courtney searched his face.

"Tell me, Danny seeing as how we're on the topic of dying, have you ever thought what people might say about you at your wake? Or better still, what would you like them to say about you, your friends, your family, possibly, your clients?"

"God C.C., you bring me out into the middle of a graveyard to ask me that? I really haven't a clue to be completely honest."

C.C. laughed.

"Yeah, I guess I did kind of sneak up on your left flank with that one. Tell you what, lets go over to that pub where we parked the car, have a pint and one of their terrific sandwiches and while you're sitting down, I want you to write your obituary for me. Just humor me on this for the moment Danny, and lets see what happens."

So that's what they did.

Danny was embarrassed at first when CC produced a pen and paper that he borrowed from the bar staff, but gradually he became engrossed in the task. C.C. got the drinks and sandwiches and munched his way happily through them. Then he ate Danny's, as he was still full from the big breakfast he'd had earlier. Finally, Danny put the pen back and took a large quaff from the glass. Thoughtfully, he picked up the piece of paper and read through it again.

"Want to share what you wrote down?" asked Courtney.

Danny grimaced.

"I suppose so C.C. You know, I started this just to humor you as you asked me to, but somewhere in the process something happened. I realized very clearly that I wouldn't want anyone giving me accolades about how good I was at killing people or blowing them up. Hopefully my mates from the Forces, if they were there, would talk of the good friend I was and about how I never let them down. That would be nice to hear. Also Allison, my daughter would say that I was a good father. Well at least from now on I intend to be, given half a chance."

He looked up.

"It kinda got more vague after that. Though, at the head office course when they asked about our future goals, I liked the thought that I could help people plan their future and provide them with a better quality of life. Does any of this make sense C.C.?"

"Actually, you're spot on and I'm delighted, Danny. In a way, you remind me of myself. I'm hoping that when I die, a whole load of people will stand up and give testimonies to the effect that I guided them in protecting their families and their businesses. And, despite the financial mess the world is now recovering from, that I helped them save and invest money carefully, and set up secure retirement packages. Basically just that I held their hand and encouraged them through their lives, to stick with the plans and enjoy the benefits, and you know what?"

"No, what?"

"Tell me any other business I could get involved in where I could leave a legacy like that after I've passed on." He paused, "you can't can you?" he asked feelingly.

Danny sat there nodding.

Finally, realization creased his features.

"This is one of your secrets C.C. isn't it? The thing that drives you. Your belief in what you're doing?" said Danny. "I felt almost embarrassed when I was talking to prospects. I was thinking of the commission I would earn. Somehow, I hadn't picked up the sense of responsibility I should have to actually help these people, but that sort of conviction shines out of you so that people just couldn't help but buy from you. Isn't that right?"

Courtney's eyes expressed approval.

"Danny, you catch on fast. However, in a way it's more than that. It's unreservedly and without consideration of your own needs for commission, or whatever, above being willing to help people get what they want. There's a strange law in operation here. As you reach out and help people, success appears to reach out to you. Forget about selling things to people and making money. You should get so totally involved in your clients' needs that your primary motivation is to help them. You don't have to sell to them. They quite simply buy from you. Can you see that?"

"Yes I do," said Danny his excitement rising, "and I think I'm picking up another secret here. Am I right? Focus on helping people and the sales automatically come."

He suddenly slapped his forehead.

"I just realized why I blew the last call I made with that jerk Jeremy a few days ago."

"Jerk?" C.C. echoed.

He quickly filled Courtney in on the prospect he'd tried to sell to.

Courtney just smiled and said "I have to say to you, Danny, if that is how you feel about a prospective client, referring to him as a jerk, you haven't a hope in hell of selling anything to him. How do you know he didn't have a run in with his boss before he left work or one of his kids is ill. He may genuinely be concerned about providing his family with protection but doesn't think he can afford it. You just made him feel guilty and he reacted by fighting back. Now tell me, just how much rapport did you establish with him before you hit him with the figures?"

Danny blinked rapidly.

"Very little, really. Bear in mind, I got the call from his wife and assumed that they were hot to trot."

"You assumed? There's a saying in NLP that goes, *If you ain't got rapport, you ain't got nothing.* That's the starting point, showing an interest in the client and stepping into his or her shoes. I'm not telling you anything here that you haven't been taught in your initial training at head office. Am I making sense?"

Danny shook his head wearily.

"Glenna warned me about dumping all the stuff I'd been taught instead of sticking to the successful blueprint. Establishing rapport was part of it. In hindsight, I was only trying to help myself really - to make a sale and justify my existence to Chris my manager. I could have spent some more time getting to know Jeremy and his situation and perhaps could have shown him how he could afford it or even come up with a lesser premium that would have provided some protection for his family. The penny just dropped, C.C. I really blew it!"

"Don't be too hard on yourself Danny. You're describing myself ten years ago, so, there's hope for you yet and I'll show you a few shortcuts to ensure you avoid some of the pitfalls people fall into. There's a lot more I could go into right now but William Butler Yeats has served us well so far this morning. We'll leave it at that for the moment."

Finishing the remnants of their glasses they went outside and stood beside the car.

Danny could see scudding clouds forming over the distant Ben Bulben, and he marveled at the incredible changing moods of the mountain while the sound of the nearby Drumcliffe River murmured in the background.

Courtney swept his arms out embracing the whole scene.

"Good God man, look at it! Yeats had talent, creativity and adulation, and look where he ended up - in the ground! We're all terminal from the moment of birth. We just don't know the time nor the place, so enjoy the present moment, it's all we've got. It's the only guarantee we've got right now. Listen to the sounds of the river over there. Let it wash over you. Feel the soft touch of the breeze coming off Ben Bulben. Listen to the birds foraging and feel our connection to it all. Open your eyes, Danny and look at that mountain - really look at it. It's stood there for millions of years and now it's looking down pitifully on the pair of us trying to act as if we can really impact on the universe beyond our puny existence here on earth."

He paused, as if embarrassed by his own words.

Danny nodded.

"Kinda gets it into perspective C.C. Though I like your idea that we can somehow leave some sort of legacy behind in the planning we've done for our clients."

No more was said as they took one last look around, climbed into the car and headed back towards Sligo. Strangely, in the midst of all the trouble hanging over him, somewhere deep inside, Danny felt a peace start to creep into his being.

CHAPTER 27

Brennan's Trucking, Luton

After the first three weeks Danny and his mate Scotty felt they were old hands at the trucking business. Three weeks during which they had been continuously driving up and down the motorways from Birmingham to Carlyle to Edinburgh and other points along the south coast: Brighton, Bournemouth, Portsmouth and further west, to the tip of Cornwall. It was bone wearying work, even with two drivers, as they drove the big rigs across the UK. Traffic was a killer with bottlenecks still at Birmingham and accidents sabotaging their tight time schedules. With CCTV cameras everywhere in Britain now, there wasn't even an opportunity to make up time by speeding. They'd heard of one Dutch driver who had come to work for Brennans and lost his license on just one run up to Nottingham and back; an experienced driver who had survived years of hammering down the autobahns in Germany to and from the Swiss border without ever being stopped. Both Danny and Scotty found the job boring as hell compared to the action packed life they'd had at the MI5 training ground and their prior SAS training.

There had been one hijacking during those three weeks that involved another set of drivers who were running a high-tech load up to Aberdeen. Both men had been badly beaten in the robbery and were still recovering in hospital. This may have been why Danny and Scotty had pulled the two injured men's next haulage contract, picking up a high-value load in Plymouth on the south Cornwall coast and running it up to York.

It was 7 pm when they finally got loaded and started up the M5 planning to cut across just south of Birmingham, on the M42 towards the link road to the M1. There, they would head north on the back end of the run before swinging off east towards their destination. With the valuable cargo on board, this was the first trip where they were being tracked by their M15 protection team. As most large trucks in the UK now carried GPS tracking devices so their company could monitor them, the team didn't see any reason to plant a secondary device on board. Danny and Scotty though, had high tech cell phones programmed directly into the protection group traveling behind.

Danny took the wheel for the first part of the run as they ploughed on up the M5 motorway. Both were comfortable in each others company as the time passed. They chatted about the regiment and listened to some Bee Gees and Beatles tapes as the big rig moved northwards.

After three and a half hours they pulled over into a service station, used the toilet quickly and switched drivers. The weather was in their favor and the traffic had thinned out getting on towards midnight. Because of the nature of the trip they remained alert to vehicles showing an interest in them. None of the previous trucks that had been robbed had been pulled over by the hijackers, nor had there been any staged accidents set up to stop the trucks. All had been attacked when parked in a lay-by or at a truck restaurant.

Danny and Scotty discussed strategy time and time again in typical SAS rehearsal fashion prior to action. They knew from previous hijackings that their enemy was a large group of men in balaclavas, armed with iron bars, clubs and brass knuckles. No firearms or knives had been spotted. Both men had no illusions about how dangerous the confrontation would be. However, the object of the trip was to tempt the group to have a go at them. They had no desire to be slogging around the UK clogged motorways for the next three months.

The drivers back at base had shared the best places for them to pull into for rest stops, which usually included lots of parking space and good grub. They had passed this information on to the protection team and had indicated their proposed stop off areas.

Scotty glanced over.

"Just about there. Want to let them know behind?"

Danny grunted and picked up his cell phone He flicked on a small pencil torch to turn it on and activated the number. A voice came through immediately.

Danny cleared his throat.

"Pulling off now at designated spot."

"Roger."

The voice sounded faint in his ear. Scotty snorted. "Not great conversationalists, are they?"

Danny shrugged.

"Who gives a toss as long as they're there when we need them."

Within a few short minutes they had pulled into the 24 hour restaurant truck stop and cruised down to the far end which was virtually empty, though the lighting was still good. Again, they placed the truck in an inviting position that might flush out the hijackers. None of the previous trucks had been broken into. The attackers had simply waited for the drivers to return from their break and relieved them of their keys, using excessive and unnecessary violence.

They were ready for their stop-off and really tucked into a feed of bacon and eggs, which woke them up and reenergized them after the hours of inactivity. After a visit to the toilet and buying a few Yorkie bars, they strolled out of the restaurant down to their truck. Though alert and ready for possible action it was still a distinct shock to their systems when they rounded the side of the truck to be confronted by a gang of eight men wearing balaclavas and holding a variety of wicked looking clubs. Their spokesman was a huge bear of a man in a leather jacket who pointed a threatening finger at them.

"All we want lads are the fucking keys. It's the load we want so don't do anything bloody stupid. Both of yous can walk away unharmed."

"Yeah, like the last truck you hit," Scotty hurled back.

The hijackers were gathered loosely around their spokesman with Danny on the left flank and Scotty positioned to his right. Danny knew the advantage of a pre-emptive strike. He moved suddenly and swiftly with the Korean instructors single hand claw stroke on the carotid arteries of the throat of the first thug who held an iron bar. Danny was already moving past him before he dropped like a stone. Scotty delivered a savage down-stroke head butt to his first opponent, a tall mean looking thug holding brass knuckles who collapsed holding a smashed mouth and nose. Danny was already driving his boot straight into the knee joint of a second thug who screamed and fell to the ground. He was aware of something skidding off his shoulders and turned just in time to block another vicious blow directed at his head by a solid attacker holding a cosh. Without thinking, Danny went with the flow of the attacker and flipped him over onto the ground, dropping with his knee simultaneously on the thug's rib cage, which crunched under the pile driver. The man let loose an unearthly scream. Scotty had driven his toe-cap painfully against the shin bone of the next gang member who fell forward on his face moaning and clutching his leg. At that point he was grabbed from behind by someone who had wrapped his arms around him in a bear-like embrace. Scotty immediately swiveled and struck backwards with his clenched fist, feeling the impact as it connected solidly with the crotch of the thug. The man howled and, loosening his hold, flew backwards. He was still screaming as Danny, off to one side started to rise. Then everything took an unexpected turn.

As their sudden attack on the gang had erupted, the leaders eyes widened with alarm. In virtually seconds his tough crew were being demolished right in front of him, and by just two guys! His worst case scenario was actually happening, but he wasn't totally unprepared.

Danny froze as he looked up into the muzzle of a nine millimeter Browning pistol and he knew he was only seconds from death. Scotty's attention was suddenly riveted on Danny's predicament. His hand flashed backwards for the knife tucked away in his neck scabbard. Danny heard a zipping sound go past his ear and a knife was suddenly embedded in the gunman's right shoulder. He cried out as the pistol sagged in his hand. Danny was on his feet again moving forward and snatched the weapon as it dangled from his hand. The remaining gang member turned to run and Danny fired twice in the air, screaming at him to stop. He halted abruptly and Danny quickly had him spread-eagled on the ground.

He then looked around him. His three opponents were still down and Scotty had obviously taken out three more before he came to Danny's help with his well-timed knife throw. The leader was on his knees moaning, his hand vainly trying to extract the knife. Scotty stepped forward and swiftly pulled it free, the man screaming in agony as he did so. He then wiped it on the man's shoulder before it disappeared into a scabbard slung behind his neck. By pre-arrangement, Scotty opened the truck and grabbed a box of plastic handcuffs, quickly cuffing the man that Danny had stopped from running away, as well as the other casualties, both semi-conscious.

Only then did he pull out the cell phone and hit the programmed number.

"Contact made ... in control ... come in now."

The two SAS men started to relax though they knew that the adrenalin of the action would be pumping in their bodies for hours. In what seemed like only minutes, two large vans tore into the truck stop and six MI5 men jumped out with two liaison detectives from Special Branch.

The leader of the MI5 team was Patton, from the training school. He looked around at the parking lot strewn with moaning and screaming bodies.

"What the hell happened here? This is like a fucking war zone!"

Danny and Scotty looked at each other and shrugged, grinning now that the violence of the moment had passed and they were both unhurt.

"We gave them the opportunity to surrender but they just didn't see the sense in it somehow." Danny replied innocently.

Patton snorted.

"Yeah, sure you did. Poor bastards didn't know what hit them Looks like you ran them over with a tank!"

The rest of the squad were milling around shaking their heads and the Special Branch people were using their phones. Some truckers and staff from the restaurant, attracted by the shots were drifting towards their corner of the parking lot and Patton quickly placed two of his people to cordon off the scene.

Danny handed Patton the gun he'd taken from the gang leader and explained how Scotty had saved the day. Patton scratched his head. "Colonel Crawford didn't feel that any serious weaponry would be used by the gang. They hadn't used any on the other jobs."

Danny looked at him grimly.

"A good job Scotty doesn't put much store in the opinion of ex-commissioned bloody officers! He literally, saved my bacon tonight!"

Patton grinned.

"I'm an ex Sergeant Major Danny, so I tend to share his views on that topic. I won't share his views with Crawford though."

At that moment four ambulances and two police cars raced into the parking lot so the MI5 officials and Special Branch were busy issuing instructions for some time.

Finally, Patton came back to Danny.

"The so-called leader, the man who pulled the gun on you, is already talking and we have the leak at Brennans. It was actually his son, believe it or not, feeding his drug habit. Colonel Crawford sends his congratulations and wants you back at the MI5 school for a debrief, so one of our cars will take you both there."

"What about the truck?" asked Scotty.

"To hell with the truck," said Patton. Let Brennans worry about that. You two are on your way to Northern Ireland. Lets go!"

CHAPTER 28

Sligo

Courtney took a right hand turn just before the town of Sligo and drove several miles to the seaside village of Rosses Point. They stopped at a small pub with fishing nets on the wall and a group of cattle dealers in the corner who were trying to deplete the Guinness reserves of the North West in one sitting.

Danny was ready for lunch by then and decided to try their fish pie with a coke. Courtney, always ready for food, ordered the haddock and chips, and a glass of water. They settled back, increasingly comfortable with each other as they turned a corner in their developing relationship. Danny looked at the big man across from him and decided to ask the question that had been burning him up with curiosity.

"So tell me C.C., why did you decide to leave the UK?"

As soon as he had asked the question he realized from Courtney's expression, that he probably transgressed onto ground that was difficult for him. "Hey, sorry. I didn't mean …". Danny started.

Courtney spread his hands wide in an all embracing gesture as if trying to draw answers from the air.

"No, it's okay, Danny. You had to ask the question sooner or later. It's just … the reason is so personal, you see. It's hard to put into words so that someone else can understand."

Danny stayed silent as Courtney sat there trying to gather his thoughts.

Just then their meals arrived but they still sat there. Both stayed silent. Then almost by agreement, they picked up their knives and forks and started eating quietly.

It was Courtney who finally broke the silence.

" Discovering my Irish background, visiting Sligo was a huge milestone in my life. My grandparents were Irish, from County Down, and went across to England each year to pick the potato crop. They moved over there eventually. I felt the connection when I got here. I felt their voices calling me. Oh, you could say that I have a great imagination and you'd be right, but something happened. A sort of lightness in my spirit."

Danny's face was showing increasing confusion.

"But what is happening to your business C.C., back in the UK? What about your philosophy of helping people manage their financial affairs and holding their hands? Now you're deserting these same clients who came to trust you. Surely your business will start to suffer if you're not there, even if head office are servicing them at present?"

"That's why you're here Danny. I drew you here," he said quietly, watching for his reaction.

Danny dropped his knife and fork noisily on the table causing some of the other drinkers to look over at them.

"Come on C.C. Pull the other one. Drew me here? For crying out loud!"

"The same way that I attract clients, which may or may not interest you my boy."

He'd certainly got Danny's interest now as he pushed his plate away and sat up straighter.

"Attracting clients? This I got to hear C.C.!"

Courtney smiled smugly.

"I thought that one might pique your interest. Anyway it's quite simple really. Every Monday morning early before anyone got to the office, Sonya my PA and I, would sit down, hold hands, summon my spirit guide and mentally visualize loads and loads of people streaming towards me who needed my services. I would explain my intention to my guide of helping these people and the great benefits that would accrue to them as a result. I would explain the type of clients I wanted to work with and see these people filling up the space around me - hundreds of them, thousands! I would also ask my spirit guide to screen out and block any time-wasters and deadheads who might be drawn in. When I was satisfied with the numbers, I thanked my guide and dismissed him, who incidentally was an ancient Indian chief, and then dismissed the crowd of potential clients, and guess what? The phone never stopped hopping off the hook. People came looking for me asking for my services."

Danny looked flabbergasted.

"And this is how you made a half million a year? Come on there's got to be more to it than that C.C.!"

Courtney nodded.

"You mentioned your difficulty on the phone when you called them for an appointment. Well I would visualize a solid laser beam of love going from myself to my prospects prior to my telephone call. I'd mentally state the many benefits of doing business with me, and guess what? You'd be surprised at how many of those people greeted me as if they were expecting my call. Of course I bombed out on a number of them but my attitude was not that I was cold calling but contacting a friend who would welcome my call."

He peered at Danny.

"Can you see what a difference this can make?" he asked.

Danny whistled.

" A laser beam of love! We use lasers in the military for a completely different reason; to call in an air-strike and kill anyone in the vicinity. I'd have to try your application first before voicing an opinion, but yes, I can certainly see how it would alter my attitude when picking up that phone!"

He shook his head almost dazedly.

"A laser beam of love!"

Courtney shrugged modestly.

"Well, of course I'm good at what I do as well. Clients, you know, are asking themselves three questions when they first come to you:

Can I trust you?

Do you know your stuff?

Are you thinking of me?

In other words, Danny, I'd sum it up as -

Likeability; do they like you?

Believability; are you really on their side or trying to make a buck at their expense?

Credibility; your professionalism and knowledge, with trust being a key factor."

Courtney was amused at the confusion reflected on Danny's face and sat back looking at him.

Danny stirred as if thinking of something.

"What was Sonya doing sitting there holding your hands? Why was she involved at all?" he enquired.

"Good question. Well the bible clearly states, where two or three are gathered in my name, there I am in the midst of them. I'm wise enough at this stage of my life to harness the power of the creator of the universe to help run both my life and my business."

"I'm struggling with that one, C.C. Look, in the military we're trained to act, quickly and competently, and sometimes with deadly force in a certain set of circumstances. That's our bible, and to operate on any other basis would be to get ourselves killed or captured. Now you're introducing a whole new mindset here that, I have to tell you, is completely alien to me - attracting clients. Sending them a beam of love!"

Danny shook his head again in disbelief.

Courtney looked unperturbed.

"It worked with you, Danny. Once I made my mind up to leave the UK, Sonya and I, sat down one morning and started magnetizing you. Someone of integrity, who would share the same values as myself and look after my clients, and here you are," he finished triumphantly.

"Well why did Sonya give me the run around when I asked her how to contact you?" Danny asked pointedly.

"That's simple. For two reasons. One, is that quite a number of the branch agents and successful agents from other branches approached her, wanting to take over my client bank, or, in some cases, to buy out the business. She turned them all down and that was her initial reaction when you approached her too. She also felt that, as a virtual rookie in the business, you couldn't operate at the same level as myself with high net-worth clients. In a way she was right, but nothing that some training and initial guidance wouldn't redress. Then, of course, you and Glenna got caught in that trouble in the underground garage and the rest is history. Here you are Danny."

"Yes here I am, C.C. I'm still shell shocked with what you just said - attracted me. I was drawn to finding you that's for sure and I couldn't fully understand my feelings at the time. Still can't if the truth is known. There I was right in the middle of that mess and I still left my wife and child and hopped on a plane to find you!"

Pausing for a moment.

"But you know, C.C., I'm a long way from sharing your values which. you pointed out, were part of your criteria for handing over your business."

Courtney sat back and regarded him carefully.

"A long way Danny? I think not. You're a lot closer than you realize, he said standing up.

"Come on, I want to take you somewhere really special."

CHAPTER 29

Northern Ireland

After the quick result in the UK for Brennan Trucking, the initial runs across to the north of Ireland were pretty mundane. They had several un-eventful runs, before starting to relax into the role. Brennan's had two depots in the North, one in Belfast and the other in Portadown, a couple of hours drive away into the province. As the IRA hangouts in Belfast were a long way from Brennan's depot it wouldn't have been realistic for their drivers to be frequenting those. That left the Portadown depot, which was right in the heart of a number of pubs and clubs frequented by various pro-IRA elements - some hard men who had spent time in the Long Kesh prison, hangers on who got a thrill associating with them, and other vocal anti-Brit types, who talked a good fight. In the main though, the violence was becoming a distant memory. The political parties, Gerry Adams, Martin Mc Guiness and the unionist party were working together and making progress. Now the sounds of the guns and explosives in the streets were replaced with maudlin songs in the pubs of *the troubles* as they were called. And no one wanted to go back to the old ways. No one that is but the nationalist die-hards who would never give up their dream of a United Ireland.

As the night wore on in the pubs and the Guinness flowed, the songs became more maudlin and the stories more exaggerated. Colonel Crawford had warned them about the round system in Irish pubs where everybody in a group, sitting together would buy drinks for each other. At the approach of closing time a rush to the bar would occur as people attempted to complete their obligatory round. The result was tables spilling over with pints that had to be drunk up in a short space of time. Some of the pubs had adopted the new, more flexible, UK pub opening laws, but a surprising number stayed with the old routines. The problem of staffing and coping with even more drunken customers being too much to handle. Crawford's concern was that if anyone had a suspicion about them, they might draw them into the group and pour the pints into them to loosen their tongues. Scotty didn't seem at all bothered by the round system. Danny didn't like Guinness and preferred to nurse a pint of beer at his own speed. He didn't have Scotty's capacity to drink, though he could hold his end up if he had to. Crawford had also warned them about any contact by the police. Under no circumstances were they to confide in them or ask for help as M15 were doing this outside the normal jurisdiction of the Northern Ireland police, and there would be hell to pay if their attempted penetration of dissident republican factions outside the pale was discovered.

They had already made various contacts in the pubs since they started driving across for Brennans, mostly barmen and casual chats at the bar about their favorite soccer teams, or the occasional top level games that the whole pub watched as one. They weren't aware of any particular groups eying them up, nor had anyone made an effort to engage them in deeper conversation. They had, however, in talking to barmen, dropped in their occupation as truck drivers and their regular runs into the North from the UK. They rotated between three particular bars on Major Crawford's suggestion; Caseys, had been a hard-core IRA pub at one time, but the clientele was now a mixture of visiting fishermen and tourists, plus some republicans and a hodge-podge of sympathizers. The

Shamrock, was a pub with Irish music on Thursdays and Saturday nights, and was a great attraction to all and sundry, while The Lion's Tail was a large dark hall with various small booths scattered around where smaller more serious and quieter drinkers seemed to congregate. Two snooker tables were set up at the far end and appeared to have a regular following. Crawford had suggested that some off duty police might occasionally hang out there.

Danny had taken to the Shamrock straight away and, being musically inclined, was soon singing along with the Irish music group. Scotty raised his glass to him across the table, during one of the band's breaks.

"You're getting more like a bleeding Paddy every day Danny."

Danny laughed outright.

"I'm surprising myself. I'd forgotten that my Dad used to sing all these years ago. Had a good voice too. Strange how it's all come back after a few visits. I never looked back after we left Ireland. I was only eight and I guess a good age to fall under the influence of becoming a little Welsh lad; You know, rugby, soccer, comics and so on. I loved it. Had a tough time initially at school, in Wales, when I went there but I was always big for my age so I made out."

Scotty leaned over to Danny's ear and whispered.

"The Welsh are Celts at the end of the day and that makes a difference. Bloody good soldiers too as you may recall!"

Danny was about to remind him about the subject of military training which Colonel Crawford had warned him was totally taboo, when he spotted a ginger-haired middle aged man push up to their table. He was of medium height, with a long bony face which right then had a warm grin covering it. He plonked two pints of Guinness down on the table in front of them.

"You'll join me lads? Saw you sitting over here all alone and when I heard yer man there," he nodded at Danny "singing his heart out, I said I'd have to join yees. Mick Conlon, lads."

Startled, they both stood up shaking his outstretched hand in turn.

"I'm Danny and this is Scotty."

The man drew back.

"Jasus - a fucking pair of Brits is it?"

Danny laughed and made a face.

"For what it's worth, I was born in Waterford. Went to Wales as a kid. That's why I had a go at those songs. My Dad used to sing them. I dunno, they just came back to me."

The man scrutinized his face.

"Aye, I can see the Irish in you so I can, and even after all these years away. Welcome back."

He nodded to the barman who was approaching with a third pint. Conlon pointed up at him.

"Paddy worked in London for years didn't you?"

The man stood tall and blocky with massive arms and a brooding stare. Danny remembered ordering from him on one occasion when he'd come into the pub.

Paddy's eyes flicked from Danny's to Scotty's.

"Couldn't stand the place. Fucking Brits let you know where your place was. Glad to be back here amongst me own kind," he muttered his eyes darting angrily between them.

Mick clapped him on the back.

"Made your money over there though, Paddy, didn't you?" Looking back at them. "He came back here and bought this place. A run down pub it was then, and look at it now - standing room only on Saturday nights. Isn't that right Paddy?"

The man ignored the remark, shot them a hard look and disappeared back behind the bar.

Mick cocked his head.

"Doesn't like Brits very much. Sorry about that. I say let bygones be bygones at this stage. Water under the bridge and all that. Why, peace and prosperity are practically here now for all us Northern Irish, if Downing Street's to be believed. What d'you say lads?"

Danny shrugged.

"I haven't a clue, Mick, to be honest. Politics aren't my thing really. Too busy just trying to make a living. Scotty and I drive trucks over from the UK for Brennans Trucking. Been there a couple of years but we've only been on this run for the past seven weeks. Just starting to get the hang of it,"

Looking around, Danny went on.

"We sure like the pubs though, and this Irish music. Wow!"

"What did you say your name was?" Conlon asked. "I picked up the Danny."

"Danny Quigley," he replied.

"From Waterford originally, you say?"

"Yeah. My father moved to Wales when I was eight, to get work."

Mick nodded, a sad look crossing his face.

"Ah yes, the curse of the Irish, always tilling another man's field, eh Danny? What was your fathers first name then? I knew some Quigleys down there at one time?"

" Paul T. T for Thomas."

"Ah, I see. So where did you end up in Wales? A big shock for a young fellow I'd imagine."

"We ended up in Cardiff Mick, and you're right. I was just talking to Scotty about it a moment ago.

Mick made a face.

"You don't need to talk to us Northern Irish about the Welsh. We had their fusiliers posted here over the years. Nasty lot. We thought we shared a Celtic heritage with them but that didn't make any difference. I hear where you're coming from, Danny." Turning to Scotty. "So what's your story then?"

Scotty glowered at him.

"Didn't know I had to have one mate. I'm grateful for the pint but I'm here to enjoy the music and I don't want to be answering a lot of questions. No offence, Mick. That's just the way I am."

The band was beginning to tweak their instruments and the first strands of music started up. Mick leaned forward.

"No offence meant, Scotty. The Irish are always asking questions - it's the way we are. In a way it's our way of welcoming people."

He stood up.

"Enjoy the pints, lads. May see you again eh?"

They lifted their glasses in a salute to him as the music flowed over them, then looking at each other, Scotty raised an eyebrow. Was that, they wondered, an opening gambit in their mission or just a normal Irish welcome mat? Whatever, they would just have to keep burning up the rubber and playing out the hand they'd been dealt.

CHAPTER 30
Sligo

Courtney seemed to know the side roads like the back of his hand as he cut across country. They chatted as they went, or rather Danny did at Courtney's instigation.

"The stuff you did when you were in the Forces even though you were under orders, does some of it still bother you, Danny? By the way, I'm not sitting in judgment here by any means," Courtney remarked, glancing across at him.

"I don't even have to think C.C. There's quite a bit of stuff, as you call it, in my past. Bear in mind that training is designed to change you so you can survive in quite challenging situations where you work as a team and follow orders. I never questioned that. It just couldn't work otherwise, if everyone had free will to do their own thing. I mentioned once before of the bond you have with your mates and they with you, to look out for each other. However …"

"Go on Danny, this is interesting."

"Be that as it may, what I was going to say is that there are situations I was involved in that still haunt me to this day."

He fell silent.

"Aha," prompted Courtney.

Danny stirred.

"Well, for example, in one situation we were staked out, my team and I, around a make-shift camp in one of the African countries waiting to hit them at dawn. I was up to my chest in brackish water and getting bitten by swarms of flies even at that hour of the morning. We were trying to rescue some oil workers who'd been kidnapped, and the SAS had been invited in by the government on the instigation of the oil company. As usual the whole operation had been rehearsed time and again, and it was no different than the many mock exercises we had done, except in real life there isn't always a nice Hollywood ending. Anyway my role with six others was to cover the back end of the rebels' camp and prevent them from escaping. As well as the rescue, the African Government wanted them totally eradicated or captured if possible as they were stopping any further oil exploration in their country. In effect, we set up a kill zone .The rebels had been drugged up and full of booze as usual the previous evening and would wake up meaner than snakes. No one in the troop expected any of them to surrender.

Anyway, the rescue attempt was started by some of the troop when they crept into the camp. The rebels had no sentries and had fallen into a drunken sleep. Our lads quietly entered the huts where we'd spotted the kidnapped men being held at sunset the night before. Almost immediately the team emerged from the hut with the oil workers. They started for the perimeter spot as arranged and were half way across the rebel camp when a dog ran at them. He was a big ugly mutt, and fastened his teeth on the thigh of one of the people being rescued. Then three things happened: the man screamed, one of the troopers shot the dog, which howled, and the whole camp woke up.

Now those rebels were used to coming wide awake fast, grabbing their weapons and blazing away. Suddenly, bullets were flying in all directions. The rescue group reached the side of the campsite and hurled themselves down behind a large mound of clay. That made it a free fire range for the SAS team and they laid down a ferocious field of fire decimating large numbers of the rebel group. As instructed we held our fire and the rebels broke in our direction thinking the swamp ground was not covered by us, and was therefore an escape route. It wasn't for long. Once they were partly into the swamp we hit them, and I don't know if you have any idea the firepower that six soldiers can lay down, plus of course the rest of our team still catching them from behind.

Well, it was over quickly as you can imagine, and then the awful stillness fell as we stopped firing, our ears still ringing. We all emerged cautiously checking the fallen rebels, and it was then that it hit me. Most of the rebels lying there on the ground were just children. I'm no great judge of age but I'd say they were no more than 8,.9,.up to 12 or 13 years old. Some of them young girls too, clutching rifles and machetes in their dead hands.

Okay, the mission was a total success and the adrenalin was running high. We had no casualties either, apart from that dog bite to the oil worker. Afterwards, we heard that the rebel commanders had a policy of raiding villages, kidnapping those kids and press-ganging them into fighting. That kind of got to me and some of the lads afterwards, especially that captain I mentioned who regularly read the bible. He left the regiment shortly after that. I've no idea what happened to him," he finished lamely.

Courtney glanced across at him again.

"Still bothers you doesn't it?"

"You could say that, especially when I wake up at night sometimes. I still see their dead faces. Yeah, it still haunts me."

They drove along in silence for some time, both lost in their thoughts.

Courtney finally stirred.

"You know, Danny, training and indoctrination are designed to override a man's basic instincts. You're right, you have no option. You have to change in order to play a certain designated role and survive - in your case joining the military. That's what basic training in the military is all about. They break down your individuality as a person and rebuild it with a new group identity. All that marching in time, heels hitting the pavement in sequence, a great euphoric feeling of oneness. Those stupid and seemingly senseless orders, all designed to suspend your normal judgment, until you'd walk into hell rather than disobey a command. But you know Danny, deep down, the psyche of man is totally alien to that. I said before about man being a spiritual being, having a human experience, and that's so true. An iceberg has seven eighths of its surface under the water and just one eighth above it. Your spiritual being is the massive seven eighths under the surface while the physical is the one eighth. Yet most people spend all their time catering to the minute physical segment. You know, Danny, once you start to sense God's spirit in all the people you meet, your life will change forever. Irrevocably!"

"How does that apply to me C.C.?" asked Danny.

"You just told me that you're still haunted by some of the experiences you had. That's your spiritual being prompting you that there are parts of your past life you have to put right and you can Danny. You can!"

"Whoa, C.C., just a minute there. You've lost me. Okay I accept that I did things in the past that I'm not proud of - under orders mind you, and that has to be said. Yes, in retrospect. I ponder over some of those and do carry a certain amount of guilt, I'll admit that. If there was a way to come to terms with the past and have some peace of mind about it, I'd be open to it. I'm not quite sure where you're coming from though. What do I have to do to get to that peace, that acceptance? You know - join a church, read the bible through. It's just so complicated, the whole picture."

At that particular moment with dusk falling, they pulled up at a deserted parking spot out in the countryside. Courtney got out gesturing to him and they both walked forward towards some flickering lights through the trees.

"This is known as The Holy Well. For hundreds of years we Brits tried to smother the religion of the Irish by hunting down priests and demolishing churches. The Irish Catholics were very good at hanging on to their faith - for over 600 years! They used to meet in secret, at places like this, for Mass and the sacraments at the risk of their own lives. This is one of those sites." He pointed. "See up there, the outline of the altar with the lighted candles burning. There's a well there, with water, which is blessed and reputed to have resulted in cures and healings for those who drank it."

"Who lit the candles up there?" asked Danny, looking around at the deserted spot.

"Oh, people come here all the time, after work or dropping the kids off to school. It's never deserted for long I can tell you. They still have Masses here on special days. Can you feel the peace Danny?"

He could. It seemed to waft out at them with soft arms and encircle them. Almost calling to them. Even the birds were silent. Danny felt a tightness in his chest as if something inside him was trying to emerge.

"Let's go over and drink some of that holy water. It's a tonic, I can tell you. Come on."

Danny followed him. C.C. picked up a metal cup resting on a rock, dipped it into the well and handed it to him. After a moment of hesitation he drank it.

"Hmm, that's refreshing!" He savored the moment. "There's certainly something about it C.C. I'm not sure what it is."

Courtney took the cup from him and helped himself to a long drink "There is something here, isn't there?"

They stood there for some time absorbing the moment, and listening to the small stream of water that spilled over from the well and ran down hill towards the road.

Finally Courtney stirred.

"It's probably no coincidence that the place is deserted right now. This moment could be just for you. An opportunity to let go of all that stuff from the past that's blocking you from enjoying a fuller life. Accept that there's a greater power in charge of the universe. Call it what you want: God, universal mind, creator, and right now, just ask for release in those areas of your life that needs healing. See what happens."

Danny sighed, looking up at Courtney.

"Even people like me C.C.? With all I've done - the killings and everything - all wiped clean off my slate? If only I could believe it. I'd be crazy not to grab it with both hands!"

"Grab it Danny! Just grab it right now."

Danny looked up at him and nodded.

"So what do I have to do?"

C.C. took a deep breath.

"Okay. I'm going to go and sit in the car and all you have to do is to say out loud that you want to release your past with all it's mistakes and violence to a greater power for healing. You can reflect on individual events and situations if you wish and just let them go. I'm not disputing that you were under orders most of the time, but unfortunately violence, however justified, quite often leads to more violence. It feeds on itself. You may or may not be prompted to ask forgiveness from some people - those child soldiers you and your team cut down for example, on that mission. Ask for a new beginning in your life and the power and wisdom to fulfill your true destiny."

Courtney stood up and walked away leaving Danny alone.

He sat there silently for a while absorbing what Courtney had said to him, and the silence of the glade. He straightened and started speaking out the words that C.C. had suggested, feeling self conscious at first, but the words tumbling out of him as he went on. It was as if he had a screen inside his head and he could see all the compacted killing and savagery of his past life and the pain he had inflicted on other human beings. He also saw clearly the damage he had caused to himself, layered in and covered over, but still an open wound in his subconscious. Suddenly, he felt tears flowing down his face and sobs ripped through him. This went on for what seemed a long time. Finally, he stilled and as he did so felt as if a ripple of light was going up and down his body taking all his heaviness away. He felt a blackness lift from him and somehow he knew he was different. Something amazing had happened but he just couldn't grasp it. He didn't know what it meant but he wouldn't have reversed what had happened to him on that particular evening at the Holy Well. He knew that life for him would never be the same.

CHAPTER 31

Northern Ireland

Danny and Scotty fell into a practiced routine on their runs into the North. They would pick up a load at the depot in Luton and head for the ferry to Belfast. Truck drivers being a pretty chummy lot, they got to know a number of the drivers from others companies, especially on the boring ferry journeys. Scotty was the one who could drink or play cards into the late hours with the other drivers and still be as bright as a button in the morning when they had to roll. Danny would excuse himself and go down to the cabin where he spent time exercising and going through martial arts moves until the perspiration poured off him. The sedentary life style of the truck driver didn't suit him - hours sitting behind the wheel, large meals and no exercise. Scotty didn't seem to add an ounce to his weight, even with all the abuse to his system.

Their contact with Mick Conlon and the barman Paddy had been passed on to the team who now had both men under loose surveillance. No one really expected any useful intelligence to result, but they had nothing else to go on. Danny wondered how long M15 could afford to keep up the operation, what with all the home grown Muslim terrorists emerging in the UK.

They had been back in the Shamrock Bar on three other occasions and spotted Mick Conlon with a group on one of these visits. Conlon had waved to them briefly.

Danny had struck up a friendly acquaintance with Theresa, the sister of Paddy, the owner, and she worked behind the bar on busy nights. He approached her now.

"Got time for a drink, Theresa?" he asked, smiling.

She looked around the pub and shrugged.

"Sure, why not? Not too busy just yet. Paddy can handle it for the moment."

In a minute they were both back at the table. Theresa had spoken to Scotty before so they picked up a quick banter. Danny joined in and they chatted amiably for a half hour when Paddy suddenly materialized at the table shouting down at his sister.

"What the fuck are you doing sitting here with these Brit fuckers? I'm paying you to help out at the bar, not sit on your ass here while I'm working!"

A stillness fell over the room. Theresa looked startled, her jaw dropping.

"Jasus Paddy. All you had to do was ask and ..." she started.

He reached forward grabbing her arm and hauled her roughly to her feet. She cried out, her face paling.

Danny stood up suddenly, his face creased with anger.

"Let her go you moron. Can't you see you just hurt her?" he barked.

Paddy abruptly let her go and turned on Danny.

"Who do you think you're calling a moron you fucking limey?" he shouted, pushing Danny back a few paces.

Danny, his back to the table pushed him backwards to get some room and also to show his anger. He heard Scotty's voice off to his side, warningly

"Hey, Danny, take it easy there."

It was too late. A powerful right hand thrown by Paddy caught him square on the jaw and flung him across the table smashing it. Danny groggily got to his feet and started to move towards Paddy, gearing up to throw a roundhouse of his own. He was caught by four or five jabs in the face by Paddy and another massive right that sent him to the floor again. As he struggled to his feet Paddy was on top of him but Danny suddenly drove his right into his stomach and heard him gasp. He closed on him his fists wind-milling but Paddy blocked them and drove him back.

Suddenly, Mick Conlon was between them restraining them both. He spoke mainly to Paddy, thrusting his face into his.

"Calm down for Christ's sake. You're running a bloody pub here not a boxing arena! Beating up on your customers isn't the way you bring in business, and you're a fucking moron if you think you can. Go on, outa that with you," he finished, pushing the big man off in the direction of the bar.

Danny was aware that a number of men from Mick Conlon's table had grasped Scotty's arms preventing him from getting involved in the fight. At that point they let him go and went back to their table.

Conlon came over and put his arm round Danny's shoulder.

"Danny, Danny, I'm so sorry. That wasn't supposed to happen. Hey. we all come here for a good time and to have fun. I don't know what came over the guy. He boxed semi-pro in London for a few years you know. He may be a bit punch drunk. Tell you what, I'm going to get him to replace those two pints he smashed up."

Danny waved him off.

"Look, I'm in no mood for drinking after getting hit in the mouth by that idiot. Can you imagine, treating his own sister like that? I could see he hurt her right there. I tell you what, any man would have called him on that, and you know what, I was planning on inviting her out tomorrow night. That madman would probably kill me if he found that out."

Theresa, who was dabbing some blood off his cut eyebrow, stopped and looked at him.

"Were you really? God, I'll kill that Paddy myself."

She looked up at him.

"I would have said yes, you know. Hell we still can, if you still want to," she volunteered.

He looked sideways at Scotty and then across at Mick Hanlon. They were both grinning at him. He sighed. If that's what it took to get a date with Theresa, then it was worth it.

"Don't expect me to kiss you though cause one of my lips has been split as well."

She took a pretend swipe at him and then looked round at the bar.

"I'm not working here any more tonight that's for sure, until that idiot brother apologizes to me for his actions so we can actually have that date tonight if you're still up to it and if we can give these two the slip. What do you say, Danny?"

Within three minutes they walked out of the bar together. Outside she took his hand.

"Come on, I'll show you a nicer side of Portadown. I promise you, no one will attempt to knock your head off."

She had a car in the pub parking lot and shortly they drove towards the edge of town. Danny was expecting a nice hotel or restaurant and was surprised when she pulled into an up market town house on it's own extensive property. When she stopped, he looked at her in askance. She grinned impishly.

"This is my parents' house and they're away in Dublin for the entire weekend, so, despite what happened earlier, you could say that this is your lucky night Danny boy. I hope your friend Scotty won't be waiting up for you, because even with that split lip I still have some plans of my own for you this night. Come on let's see what you young Brits are capable of."

"What about my cut lip?" he teased.

"Nothing wrong with mine," she answered, making a suggestive move with her mouth. I've got enough for both of us."

She was as good as her word.

As soon as they got into the house she took his hand and led him to a well laid out, extremely tidy room with a large double bed planted right in the middle. She was already undressing him as the door closed, her lips working hungrily down his chest as she unbuttoned his shirt. He gasped at the shock of it, pulling at her clothes as she undid his zipper and fastened her lips on him, his trousers falling down around his ankles. He could only take a minute of it and pushed her off, stepping out of his trousers and lifting her up, her clothes falling from her. He carried her over to the bed and disrobing the rest of her, thrust into her mindlessly, her moans and small cries driving him to a frenzy. She finally cried out louder and lifted herself against him and he felt release as his power poured into her.

They lay still for a long time until she moved under him groaning.

"All that muscle. You weigh a ton Danny."

He rolled off her onto his back putting his arm around her neck.

"You are something else Theresa. Wow! Sitting at the bar you look like butter wouldn't even melt in your mouth. Hey I like this you a lot better," he said fervently.

She looked at him smugly.

"I'm only a good little girl when I'm back in Ireland. I wouldn't do this with any of the locals. My mother warned me it would ruin my marriage potential. I did let my hair down though when I lived in England. Kinda miss the freedom to do what I want without everyone pointing the finger."

She tilted her head back, smiling lazily at him.

"I wanted to do that with you Danny, the first night you spoke to me at the bar."

He sat up. "God, why the hell didn't you say so. I'd have been delighted to accommodate you, Theresa."

"Not a girl's place Danny, but speaking of accommodating, do I notice another stirring of interest?"

She was spot on. This time they were in no rush, and this time it was Danny who did all the exploring with his tongue all over her body until she finally grasped him and guided him into her desperately. Time stood still as they molded together, each on their own individual journey of fulfillment, yet aware of every movement and touch. Somewhere in those moments, both forgot Danny's cut lip and blood mixed with kisses as she drew him even further. When it seemed their bodies could no longer take the hammering, Danny felt her legs tighten around his back as she gave a last compulsive thrust and grunted throatily, her body collapsing. Danny came a second later, his head snapping back, and finally easing forward on her neck, which he kissed gently.

"Danny, Danny," she whispered, running her hands through his hair. "God, I didn't know it could be so good. That body of yours!"

He sat back still on top of her, his lungs pumping, shaking his head from side to side, his face euphoric.

"Me too, Theresa. Me too! I thought I knew the score, but this ..." He wasn't kidding.

She sat up.

" I need a smoke."

He looked at her in surprise.

"I thought you'd given up last year. I remember you told me when we chatted on my last trip," he added.

"I did but I need to savor the moment Danny. It's just too good to rush."

That set the tone for the night.

She got up after awhile and threw together a feed of steak and chips, which he devoured, helped along by a chilled bottle of white wine. They sat listening to some quiet music for a while, not feeling any need for conversation. Finally, she raised her eyebrows at him.

"I think we both need a shower Danny, don't you?"

Fortunately, it was a good sized shower. Danny had never seen one used so imaginatively before, but being a good soldier he never complained and at one point a small distant voice reminded him that he was doing this for Queen and country. The voice never came back as the night progressed and when the light of dawn started creeping through the curtains he was glad he wasn't driving a truck that day.

201

He dressed quietly as Theresa lay asleep, her left breast exposed. He found a pen and paper in the kitchen and scribbled her a note, which he left propped up on the table. Outside, it was a dry crisp morning with no traffic as yet. He started running and was back at the hotel in half an hour.

When he crept into the room he shared with Scotty he found two men from the team waiting, with Scotty wide awake and sitting on the bed.

"Lover boy returns," Scotty threw at him.

Patton stood up and patted him on the shoulder. The other man, Paul Walsh, smiled at him too.

"Well Danny, we've got us a mission finally. They took the bait last night, goading you into a fight. Paul was in there and saw it all. You did really well Danny. I bet you wanted to punch that Paddy into the middle of next week. We know what you're capable of. Now, we want you to look at these photos, our team took of people leaving the bar last night."

He spread a series of pictures out on the bed.

"What we're interested in are the chaps at that table with Mick Conlon. They were the players in what happened last night. They held Scotty, for starters."

He pointed to some of the shots.

"Scotty and Paul have already picked them out."

Danny nodded.

"Yeah, I can identify three of them anyway. I wasn't making the connection right then as the evening was just panning out the same as usual, apart from Theresa coming over, that is."

"Yeah, how did that happen anyway Danny? Did you invite her over or was she sent to create that scene?" Patton asked.

Danny nodded miserably.

"Yes, I invited her but I've been mulling over was whether she was part of that whole thing or not."

Scotty snorted.

"Of course the bitch was involved!"

Danny shook his head.

"I don't know about that. I'm not really sure. Did you see her face go pale when that bastard Paddy grabbed her?"

"He was just making it look good Danny, believe it." replied Scotty.

Patton held up his hands.

"Hey look, it's immaterial. The thing is that the people at the table are figures in this IRA splinter group. Some have been in jail and others have sheets as long as your arm. So they were there last night to eyeball you, hopefully before they make an approach. With that performance by you last night, they can't possibly think that you're a trained soldier - Scotty too, for that matter. It must have been hard for him to stand by and watch you get thumped."

Scotty made a face.

"You better believe it! Danny and I have been mates for a while. I very nearly blew it when those men grabbed me. They don't know how lucky they are."

Patton nodded.

"The next move is up to them and I wouldn't be surprised if it happens tonight as they know you head off to the UK on Sunday as usual and may not be back for a week or two."

Danny slapped his forehead.

"God, I left a note to Theresa, telling her I'd meet her at the Lions Tail tonight. I wasn't going to go back into the other place right away."

"No, that's actually perfect. It's the natural thing one would do, to go to another pub after what happened."

He looked keenly at Danny.

"We'll soon know if your girl friend is involved, if someone contacts you there to night."

Danny nodded morosely.

"I'm not sure I want to know," he said quietly.

The three men looked at each other. It was Patton who spoke finally.

"Look Danny, part of their hold on you will be the honey pot as we call it - Theresa. If they believe you're really smitten, it'll encourage them to make contact, and from where I'm sitting Danny, you sure look smitten. Am I right?"

Danny nodded, looking away briefly.

"What about her parents, are they involved somehow?" he enquired.

Paul Walsh answered.

"We followed you, of course, last night as arranged. We did a check on the address and assumed it belonged to her parents. Now we're running their names through the system and will let you know what we get. Bear in mind that Paddy, their son, is involved, and, more than likely, Theresa too. Sorry, Danny."

After pausing for a moment he went on.

"Republicanism definitely runs in families over here. We've pulled in some reliable Special Branch resources to start surveillance on that group of six at the table last night. We'll probably do the same with your girl friend's parents too, when they return. In the meantime, I'd suggest you freshen up, have some breakfast and get ready for this evening. The mission is full steam ahead now lads so stay alert."

After chatting for a few more minutes the MI5 men slipped carefully out of their room at the hotel. Danny and Scotty, lulled into a false sense of security over the weeks, suddenly realized that they had to raise their level of alertness back up to action level. They were no longer just truck drivers.

CHAPTER 32

Sligo

They parked at Glencar Lake, a beautiful blue diamond expanse of water reflecting small white clouds scudding along overhead. A fisherman was working along the shore of the lake in waders and waved to them. Danny put his pack on and then helped C.C. with his as he was struggling with the straps, before starting up the side of Ben Bulben. At first they could hear the sounds of waves lapping against the shore, but gradually that faded as the noise of their labored breathing increased. Danny's training kicked in after twenty minutes and he started to revel in the physical activity, which he had missed.

Around them were the myriad sounds of summer: the startled birds darting from the green bushes with indignant cries; the bees feeding in the plethora of wild flowers and gorse, and alongside the path, a small fast-running brook was funneling brown water from the bog above, down the mountain side.

They hardly spoke at all, focused, they moved upwards. Courtney appeared at ease walking ahead of him with a smooth, regular stride. Finally, after an hour, they started to reach the lower peak of the mountain. As the terrain leveled off it got easier to move and they walked alongside each other for approximately another mile.

Courtney stopped and threw off his pack.

"This will do nicely," he said.

Danny copied him and stood there awestruck at the panorama spread out before him. The mountain appeared to stretch for miles with its sculpted green and stone top, looking like a gigantic carpet. It towered over the surrounding countryside, making the white washed cottages in the distance look like tiny dolls houses. Further along he could see the blue-green of the sea, which Courtney pointed out, was just off the Bundoran road. Tiny white clouds drifted by and the long shiny grass rippled in the gentle warm breeze. Permeating it all was the incredible aroma of plant life. The heather and turf from some sections of the bog made him feel dizzy and almost detached from his body.

He smelled smoke and, turning, saw Courtney nursing a small turf fire into flames with the sods stacked in a pyramid shape. He grunted, in satisfaction, as the flames caught properly, the blue smoke whipping in the wind. Quickly, the packs were emptied and a small wind-break materialized, which prevented smoke from smarting their eyes. A blackened pot was filled at a nearby stream and placed on the fire. C.C. lit up a pipe and they sat there in silence. In a short while, the pot started hissing and then came to a boil. C.C. stirred the boiling water and threw a handful of loose tea into it.

"Best cup of tea in Sligo," he commented, a few moments later as he filled two large mugs and set them on the ground in front of them. Danny was about to reach for his when C.C. delved into his pack and triumphantly produced a small bottle of Powers whiskey, which he splashed liberally into each cup. He then passed along a bottle of milk and a jam jar full of sugar and a spoon which Danny used as well.

With some hesitation he then raised it to his mouth and tasted it.

"Hey, this is really something!" he said enthusiastically. "I've never tasted tea like this before."

Courtney looked pleased.

"It's a combination of the mountain water, the turf fire and just all of this," he said, waving his arms He took another large sup. "The Powers helps too," he added somewhat ruefully.

Danny laughed.

"It never occurred to me that whiskey could do this for tea," he remarked, taking another swallow.

They sat in comfortable silence for some time, settling back into the rushes and fern for back support. Some strange birds dive-bombed their site noisily, before flying off down the broad expanse of the mountain. Overhead, gulls lazily glided in the balmy air, bright eyes searching for food, before, they too, headed off towards the distant shoreline.

Courtney asked him about his background - his family. He filled him in on the details of how he'd met his wife, Fiona and their present situation. He touched on the recent part of his life in the Forces and his too-late effort to save his marriage. Danny's face lit up when he described his daughter, Allison, and his relationship with her. Courtney listened, nodding and encouraging him as he recounted his past life. Occasionally, he asked a question for clarification. Finally, Danny fell silent.

Courtney took advantage of that to share some Irish soda bread and smoked salmon. After every scrap was gone they both leaned back and fell silent.

Some time later Danny stirred and sat up straight.

"CC, I've been meaning to ask you about what you meant by *the spirit of violence* that you said you detected in me. Is it all gone from me now after the experience I had at the Holy Well yesterday evening?"

"Hmn. You're jumping the gun on that one a trifle. I wasn't going to bring it up just yet, but then, it's not my timing, it's His."

He pointed skywards before continuing.

"Okay, here's the thing. None of us have perfect upbringings. Our parents did the best they could with what they had at the time. It may take some years before one realizes that. Perhaps when we have children ourselves for example, but, we all carry baggage of sorts with us from growing up. A lot of it we come to terms with, as we go out into the world and mature. However, some experiences, the traumatic ones, can stick and come back to haunt us in later life. Usually, it's in regards to parents, siblings, something a teacher said and so on. For example, later in life, one could be reliving in our minds to our detriment, a time when we got fired or were made redundant. The bitterness of divorce and, of course abortion, can be biggies too. In a way, clinging to it like a dog with a bone. Make sense so far?"

Danny nodded, his interest quickening.

Courtney continued.

"If these traumatic experiences keep coming up time and again, we have to face up to them. Come to terms with what we call baggage and where necessary, forgive people and move on."

Danny shook his head violently.

"Some things you can't forgive C.C. Personally I couldn't let go and just move on as if nothing happened," he exploded fiercely.

Courtney looked at him with compassion.

"Look, Danny, un-forgiveness in your heart hurts you a lot more than the other person. It's like a golf ball of hate that just keeps gnawing away at your innards and eventually seeps out into your every day life and relationships. Believe me when I say this. And this is what I sensed in you when we met. I knew you would have to face up to it if you wanted to move on. At the Holy Well you started the process. Now you have to create a clean vehicle in yourself that God can really top up with His spirit. Once you experience that, you'll never look back. The good news is that your subconscious wouldn't have prompted you to bring this up if you weren't strong enough to carry it through right now."

He paused, watching his face closely.

Danny sat there nodding his head.

"Okay C.C., if you say so. Go ahead. I trust you."

Courtney hunkered down beside him.

"Okay, Danny, just sit back, close your eyes and relax. Breath in deeply several times. That's right. Now visualize a TV screen in front of you and on it is displayed today's date. It's a special kind of screen, because right now it's going to show dates flashing backwards into your past, and here's the thing. Your unconscious will guide you to the particular date or dates it wants you to deal with. Go all the way back. That's right. Just nod when you're there Danny. Take your time. There's no hurry."

There was silence for a few minutes and Courtney, who was watching him closely, saw him suddenly jerk upright.

"Tell me what's going on Danny?" he asked urgently.

Danny's face was screwed up as if he was in pain.

"Him! It's him!" His voice was labored and high pitched.

"Who Danny? Who?"

"Stepfather!" he managed to stammer out.

"How old are you." asked Courtney.

Danny's face slewed both ways, his eyes still closed.

"About twelve, I think. God that hurts," he moaned.

"Tell me what your stepfather is doing Danny?"

"J..just si..sitting there slapping my face, in my room … just slapping. A cruel look on his face as if he's enjoying it. I can hear the slaps. Not terribly hard slaps. Just going on and on …"

"Okay Danny we won't dwell on that too long. What happens next?"

Danny's head swiveled round again, his eyes still closed.

"My mother comes into the room, I can see tears in her eyes. She says nothing. Just takes the hand that's slapping me and pulls it away. Still holding my stepfather's hand she starts to lead him from the room. I open my eyes and see a look of triumph on his face. A while later I hear them across in their bedroom. Sounds like he's hurting her now. God how I hate him!"

He paused for a long moment.

"Once I dashed into the bathroom without knocking. My mother must have forgotten to lock it. She had her back to me and I saw lots of bruising on her lower back. She said she'd fallen against a table, but I knew. Christ, I hate that bastard!"

His voice dropped to a whisper.

"Okay Danny, you're doing fine. Can you work a little more with me on this? Good. Now fill me in on the rest of it," he said.

Danny nodded.

"Okay, the next few years are a blur, in a way. I was growing up, a teenager and quite big for my years. I came home one day when I was sixteen and my mother was slumped on the floor at the bottom of the stairs, a dazed look on her face. She tried to get up when she saw me but couldn't, and you know what? My stepfather was just sitting there drinking a beer at the table, that sneering, cruel look on his face. I remember going towards him. He must have seen something in my eyes because he jumped up, a look of anticipation on his face. Well, I just let loose a blow I never knew I had. It caught him on the nose and it was spouting blood. He screamed like an animal and fell over onto the floor. I just kept hitting him. He begged me to stop but I couldn't. When I finally did stop he was like a bloodied rag doll. I called an ambulance and the police. And then it was over. We never lived in that house again. We were in some refuge for a while. Then my real father, who my mother had divorced a couple of years after moving to Wales, took us back in. He waited on her hand and foot but she died a year later. I believe till this day that it was the treatment my stepfather doled out to her over the years that caused her premature death."

Tears were in his eyes, and his chest was heaving. Courtney put a hand on his shoulder squeezing it and held it there.

"Could you forgive him now, Danny?" he asked tentatively.

"Never. No, never in a thousand years. That bastard killed her - my mother, for crying out loud!" he spat out hoarsely.

Courtney squeezed the shoulder again, longer this time.

"Here's the thing, Danny. As I mentioned before, this un-forgiveness that you're holding onto is insidiously, whether you accept this or not, coloring every aspect of your life. You can't move on until you resolve it, d'you understand?"

Danny shook his head violently, his eyes looking desperate, shot open for a moment.

"I just can't C.C. … it's too much …" he rasped.

"Okay, here's the thing. Lets assume that you're willing to at least try to start to forgive, to start the process, say. Just nod if that's possible."

After a long pause, Danny nodded reluctantly.

"Good man. You're doing just fine. Now think about this for a moment. If you were willing to start to forgive your stepfather, and I hear you when you say that it's not possible, lets just suppose that you're willing to consider this. Now tell me what resource you would need in order for you to start this healing process. By resource, I mean understanding, tolerance, compassion, flexibility, wisdom, acceptance, even maturity. Any one, or all of these Danny. What would be a useful resource do you think?"

Danny's head swung from side to side.

"Well … if I was willing, which I'm not, probably understanding and maturity."

Courtney squinted at his stricken face.

"Hmm … good choice. Okay, here's what you do now. As that twelve year old, ask the future you, the Danny sitting here on this mountain, the experienced, trained, mature person you are, to send this resource, this gift of maturity and understanding, back down through the years like a laser beam, to the younger Danny. Now as him, accept this resource of maturity and understanding into your heart. Right now sitting there, extend your arms outwards and just embrace this gift from the future. Into the very core of your being. Accept it and thank the older Danny for this gift. Take a moment to complete this."

Courtney sat there for a long moment observing the changes in Danny's body language as he did so. Finally, he spoke to him again.

"Now, I want you to imagine that you're joined at this campfire by your stepfather sitting across from you, and you have a choice to have your mother there too, if you wish. Just nod when you've done that."

Danny's body twitched for a moment and he even tried to slide backwards. Finally he nodded.

"Good, Danny. Now tell me this, who's sitting here across the fire with us?"

"Just my stepfather, C.C." he whispered.

"Right. Good. You're doing very well here. Now I want you to turn to your stepfather and tell him of all the pain and suffering he caused to you and your mother, and how it affected your life, not only then, but right up to this present moment. Just let it all out, then listen to what he has to say. You can speak out loud or you can have a mental conversation. Then allow him to reply. Got that? Nod when you've finished."

Danny chose to use a mental conversation but Courtney could see from his body language and head gestures that he was having a genuine one way conversation. Finally, after a long time, he nodded. C.C. leaned forward.

"Tell me what he said, Danny."

"It was quite amazing C.C.! He told me how sorry he was and that he didn't realize the effect his abuse was having on myself and my mother. I could see he meant it too. The cruel look was gone from his face. He even asked me to forgive him. Can you believe that?"

C.C. nodded even though Danny's eyes were still closed.

"Now, this is important Danny and it's not going to be easy. For a moment I want you to step into your stepfather's shoes and see what his life was like during those years. He probably had his own problems - inadequacies, anxieties and pressures, that no one ever knew about. Do that now and nod when you're finished," he instructed.

Time seemed to pass slowly for the next few minutes. Some tears squeezed out from Danny's eyes. His head shook a few times. He moaned once. Finally he nodded.

C.C. leaned forward and squeezed his shoulder.

"Okay, Danny. Tell me what you discovered?"

"Amazing! Amazing C.C.! He was just a socially inept person and had no friends at work. He was never prepared for taking on the responsibility of a wife and two children, myself and my sister Cathy. He was scared of losing his job at the pit as well. He just couldn't handle the emotion of it all, came home and took it out on us. God, if I'd only known ..."

Courtney nodded even though Danny couldn't see him.

"Right, Danny, here's the two final things that you need to do to put this behind you. Are you ready for number one?"

He nodded.

Courtney sighed.

"Nearly there, Danny. Now look at your stepfather and repeat the following words to him after me ... out loud. Ready?"

Danny nodded again.

Courtney started

"What you did back then was not acceptable behavior in any way, shape, or form. The pain you caused to myself and my mother, you will have to account for to a higher authority one day, but as for me, I am now willing to forgive you and release you from my hatred and anger. In the main, because I now know this hatred is poisoning my life and would destroy any chance of happiness I might ever have. I now release you and I wish you well."

Danny was choking up as he repeated the words, but he carried on, gasping out the text after Courtney. Finally there was silence. Then some birds dive-bombed their site again.

"How d'you feel now, Danny?"

"Okay I guess," he replied, his voice stronger.

"Good. Now the final thing. Take the worst picture of your step-father that you have in your mind from your youth, when he was a real large forbidding figure to you."

Courtney paused for a long moment.

"Got that? Now start to reduce that figure of your stepfather down, down, down, until he's as small as your hand. That's right. Take that tiny figure and send him off out there onto the horizon. Take a moment to do that. Observe him for a moment and then push him even further away, completely out of sight. That image is gone forever."

Courtney fell silent, observing Danny's body language. Finally satisfied that he had completed the exercise he spoke again.

"Effectively you have now reduced the significance of your stepfather's influence in your life as far as your subconscious is concerned. It only needs to take a minute. It's incredibly powerful."

C.C. reached forward and touched his shoulder.

"Open your eyes," he said gently.

There was a long silence. Finally Danny stirred and sat up. He looked around dazedly and in wonder.

C.C. smiled at him.

"How do you feel now, Danny?"

"Wow! Incredible! Like a strong light has just immersed me and melted me somehow. A sort of peace. A sense of letting go - of burdens falling away. I can't describe it C.C.. It's a strange feeling, yet a good one at the same time, and my stepfather's cruel image has somehow drifted away somewhere. Does that make sense?"

"It most certainly does. Excellent work."

He looked at him speculatively.

"Something's still there bothering you, Danny. Okay lets have it."

He looked sheepishly at C.C.

"I'm a mess, aren't I? Okay, here's the thing. When I came across from Ireland at age eight, my eleven year old sister, Cathy, came with me. She was sponsored by an uncle in Ireland to a top girls school in Cheltenham. She came home for holidays and the occasional weekend. My stepfather was nice as pie when she was home - no bullying or violence. Perhaps he thought she would let something slip back at the school. So I always resented that I was carrying the can completely when my mother was being abused."

"And was she completely in the dark or did she just pretend to be? That's how some people cope, you know. Especially if they can't do anything about a situation. Did you ever try to tell her Danny?"

He nodded.

"Oh, I thought about it many times but my mother begged me not to tell her. It would destroy any chance she had of getting a proper education, she said. I did tell her on the evening of her graduation and the way she looked at me made me wonder if she had suspected something all along. She stayed silent and didn't comment. She then went into teachers training college and did some course on teaching English abroad and the last I heard she was off working in some South American country. I must confess that I still resent the fact that she got off so easy, when I got the brunt of the responsibility and the violence from my stepfather."

C.C. thought about it for a long moment.

"Okay, Danny. You actually now have the tools to work through this one yourself, in your own time. You have to decide what relationship you want with your sister, if any, and then install that. You may have to find her address and write her a letter outlining your feelings. It's up to you, how you want to pursue this.

Now I want you to close your eyes again. Take this gift, this feeling of peace, this new you and sweep it like a white light up through you're your past life, right up to the present moment. As you do so, allow this gift to change and heal all the hard edges in your life. All the violence, all the pain inflicted on you and your mother, and the pain you caused to others in your military career, which really was a knock-on effect from the violence you were exposed to as a child. It's all gone now. All forgiven. Imagine you're filling some balloons with the residue of the old you. Write the names on those balloons - hatred, fear, insecurity, and so on, and tie the tops of the balloons. Do one with your sister's name on it, if you like. Tie the tops and let them fly off into the heavens. Just release them ... that's right. All gone now, sitting here on the mountain top where you can open your eyes again and where everything will look different to you. Open your eyes Danny," he instructed.

He did so, sitting up straight and finally standing up and looking around, his face expressing astonishment.

"God, I feel so light. In fact, even the light looks different too, like some sort of scale has fallen from my eyes. Beyond that I'm not at all fully aware of what's happened to me, C.C. It's like I'm walking on air. Is this the normal reaction of people who do this?"

Courtney chuckled.

"You've been zapped Danny, that's for sure. I could see that watching your body movements. Everyone has a different experience in how they come through it. I'll tell you this for what it's worth. The experience isn't complete yet. It will be filtrating through your system for the next 24 hours or longer. You may find yourself suddenly laughing or crying, but don't worry, you're not going crazy. Just give it time. The new Danny will amaze and delight you."

Danny was about to reply when Courtney noticed the dark clouds descending and the increased volume of the wind.

"Hey, let's get out of here," he shouted, emptying the contents of the tea container on the fire.

They got to the brow of the mountain, as a sudden storm swept in, covering Ben Bulben completely.

CHAPTER 33

Bath, UK

Fiona had never thought of herself as sexy even though Danny was always telling her that she was. At least when he was home and not off with the unit somewhere. He had always liked the dainty way she pointed her feet when she walked. She was reminded of this as she moved through the crowded streets of Bath where she noticed several male heads turning. Half of her wished that it was Danny who was there admiring her, but the other half had accepted that he was no longer a meaningful factor in her life. She still replayed the last afternoon together in the guest house when they had made love passionately, even desperately. In a way she accepted that it was really goodbye, but she still longed for the comfort of his strong masculine presence, especially now that she was cut off from all her London friends and work schedules.

Today she was being dragged through numerous shops by Allison, who needed some new clothes. Allison had her own ideas on what she should wear and was very fussy as to what she finally purchased. Nevertheless, she was in a good mood as they dashed from shop to shop. They had just exited one large brand name store, when Allison said she needed the toilet. Somewhat miffed that she hadn't thought of that while inside the shop, Fiona turned back again.

Just then a blocky middle-aged man came swinging through the doors, almost colliding with her. He appeared to be startled at seeing Fiona facing him.

"Ooops ... sorry Mrs., how clumsy of me."

He held the door for them as they slipped passed

She spent the next few minutes locating the washroom. Back outside, she paused again thinking. Herself and Allison had a habit of enjoying a small snack upstairs in one of the arcade cafes when they successfully completed a shopping trip. Allison loved the ritual and even objected at Danny coming along on one occasion, as she saw this as her time with Mom.

When they got to the café, they discovered that there were no decent seats free downstairs so they went upstairs to see what seating was available. It was chock-a-block with people on their lunch break and tourists.

Fiona turned, sighing.

"Sorry Allison, it looks like it's downstairs and sharing a table for us today, or we can go back and try the place opposite the Roman Baths if you like."

Allison pulled on her hand.

"Let's go downstairs Mummy. There's still some seats and I like the cakes here much better."

Fiona ruffled her hair, smiling.

"You and your cakes Allison! If I let you eat all the cakes you wanted, you'd be like a little porker, wouldn't you?"

Allison giggled tugging at her hand again.

"Come on, Mummy, you know you like them too! I get my sweet tooth from you not Daddy, you know."

Fiona was beaten and she knew it. Turning, she started back down the stairs holding Allison's hand and being careful on the twisting stairs. She was relieved to see that a downstairs table had come free by the door but anxiously glanced at a figure starting to come through from the street, who might grab it. They made it in time and Fiona glanced up half apologetically at the person who had just come in.

The man spotted her at that moment and spun round and exited the café. Fiona's mind reeled. Despite the rapid exit of the man, she was in no doubt that it was the same man she had nearly bumped into at the shop earlier. She was being followed!

Danny had warned her to be careful and watchful, but didn't believe that anyone would know where she had fled to. She was suddenly acutely aware that she had no way of contacting Danny to let him know of this new development. Fiona had no option but to wait until he contacted her. The question in her mind was - who was following her? Was it the police or some other group? Perhaps criminal acquaintances of the murdered thugs from London?

Suddenly, she felt very vulnerable, sitting there with Allison who was chattering away, completely oblivious of the situation. She went through the ordering and subsequent snack mechanically, occasionally glancing at the door. Allison looked up as if sensing her change in mood.

"Are you all right Mummy?" she asked.

Fiona nodded smiling and reached across to touch her hand.

"Of course darling. I'm always fine when I'm with you. I was just thinking it was time we were getting back. Remember I promised my Mum that I'd do the evening meal, so I have some preparation to do for that. You can help if you like."

"Oh yes please, I'd love to. I always love the little dips I get of the food as we're doing it, especially the dessert."

Despite herself, Fiona laughed as they stood up and exited the café.

Up the street, the blocky man was huddled out of sight in a doorway, speaking into his mobile phone.

"She's twigged me! Just plain bad luck. Get someone round here to replace me. It's a routine shopping trip with the girl and I imagine they're going straight home in a few minutes time."

Fiona kept glancing casually behind them on their way home but didn't spot anyone following her.

"Danny," she thought desperately. "Please call me soon."

CHAPTER 34

Northern Ireland

That evening Danny and Scotty arrived early at the Lions Tail and spent some time playing pool towards the back end of the pub. Gradually the numbers in the bar increased until a pleasant buzz filled the air. Some football fans were crouched in front of the TV catching the Saturday scores. Scotty was quaffing his usual pint but Danny was sticking to coke, as he wanted his mind clear for the evening.

Finally, Theresa entered and a few whistles went up as she strode consciously across to both of them. The first thing she did was to put her arms around Danny's neck and planted a long kiss on his lips. More whistles from the pub patrons.

"Last night was fantastic," she whispered in his ear.

He glanced almost apologetically at Scotty, before responding.

"For me too. Hey, you're something else Theresa," he said with feeling.

Scotty slapped his cue down noisily on the velvet.

"Well, I guess that screws up the game then. I was just about to kick his ass Theresa!" said Scotty.

Her laughter tinkled.

"You guys carry on. I need to dash up to The Shamrock and collect some salary my brother owes me, and perhaps an apology too from that big ape for his stupid behavior last night. Catch you two shortly. Bye!"

With that she swept out to the sound of more catcalls. Scotty winked at Danny.

"Nothing like enjoying your work boyo. I'll grant you, she's a looker. Think she's in with them then?"

Danny shrugged his shoulders.

"God I hope not! If she is, she's one hell of an actor I'll say that for her."

"Maybe she just enjoys her work, ever think of that? Nothing saying a woman don't want it as much as us men and you do seem to appeal to the weaker sex Danny from what I've witnessed since we teamed up," Scotty interjected, a look of envy in his eyes.

Danny made a face.

"She's no little innocent colleen, that's for sure, but yeah, I did sort of fall for her and I thought she liked me too. Time will tell, but I really hope she isn't involved with this splinter group," he said fervently.

They didn't have to wait too long. Shortly after, she came back into the pub, followed by Mick Conlon, who wore a big grin on his face. Theresa avoided his eyes as Conlon indicated a table back from the snooker table and nodded to her to leave them alone. He turned to them.

"She's organizing some drinks for us but I wanted to talk to you lads before she gets back. Now look here, I know trucking is a tough way to make a living. You wont get rich doing it, isn't that right?"

"You're right there mate," Scotty said.

Danny mumbled agreement.

Conlon looked closely at both of them.

"So here's the thing lads. Me and my business colleagues were wondering if you would consider taking some extra loads with you over to the UK and back, and we'd see you right with some kick backs? Be worth your while I'm telling you."

Danny reared back.

"Now wait a minute. We can't risk our jobs here sticking our necks out like this. Apart from the cops getting onto it, we could, very well, end up in jail! Christ Mick, I don't know what you're thinking about here. What sort of stuff are you suggesting we carry anyway?"

Conlon held his arms up.

"Oh just some basic consumer goods. You know, things we picked up at outdoor markets from liquidators and so on. Legitimate stuff, really. We're talking about computers, stereo equipment, DVD's, CD's and so forth. The thing is, that if we have to pay for transport as well it cuts the profit way down. So this is why we thought you lads might be interested in making a few sheckles tax free, as it were, with no one the wiser. After all, you're practically one of us anyway, what with you and Theresa. You know," he grinned salaciously.

Danny groaned inwardly. So, it was a set-up. What an idiot he'd been. He looked up at Conlon.

"I really don't think ...".

Scotty put his hand on his arm.

"Wait a minute Danny."

Turning to Conlon.

"Just how much money are we talking about? As for me I'd like to buy a little farm back in Scotland one day and as you say, truck driving isn't going to do it."

Conlon smiled, looking at both of them.

"Seems like we might have a meeting of the minds here lads. Look, it's going to be a simple process. We put the stuff on board after you've finished loading up at the transport depot. Once you get to the UK, you pull over at a pre-arranged spot and we take it off and you lads get paid in cash. We've done it before and it works as smooth as silk."

"Some of our loads are sealed, Mick, how would you handle that?" Danny asked.

"Not your problem. Trust me, we can handle that. We have contacts everywhere."

Danny looked concerned.

"Who are *we*, Mick? I don't want to get involved in some sort of republican thing. I may be Irish originally but I'm a Brit as far as anything like that's concerned. I wouldn't do anything to hurt my country and, quite frankly, I have no sympathy for people who blow up innocent civilians."

Conlon threw his hands up again.

"Whoa there! Christ, where did you get that idea? That's all finished, done with, dusted off and practically sealed. It's in the politicians' hands now and we're all just getting on with life and trying to catch up and make a few quid. What's wrong with that Danny?"

Scotty touched his arm.

"He's right Danny. All that IRA nonsense is put to bed now. It's all systems go again so what's wrong with pulling in some extra cash, as long as we're not hurting anyone? I say lets go for it."

Danny looked reflectively at him.

"Well, when you put it like that. I've no problem with a commercial venture on a small scale but not on every run. Why push our luck, Scotty?"

Mick slapped him on the back.

"That's the ticket Danny! Look on it this way. You're no longer truck drivers but budding entrepreneurs."

Just then Theresa came back with a round of drinks and thrust them onto the table. She looked around at them.

"So business over then? Good, that's what I like, men who know what they want. Speaking of which, Danny knows what he wants too, don't you Danny?" she said, smiling wickedly at him.

He quickly downed the pint and left the pub leaving Scotty and Conlon engaged in animated conversation. He now knew her involvement with the group established without a doubt. Despite that, when they got back to the house, he was unable to hold himself back from Theresa's love making which was more passionate and imaginative that ever.

On the Sunday morning even the truck seemed to drag itself along up the highway in the Belfast direction. Danny didn't notice. He was asleep while Scotty drove, occasionally looking across at him and shaking his head. They had no illegal cargo on board but they were promised one for the next trip.

CHAPTER 35

Sligo

They eased away from the small quay in Sligo town. Courtney pulled the throttle as the boat shot forward in the clear water heading up river towards Lough Gill. They passed many semi detached houses with people working in their gardens, and one pub, still closed and with staff supervising the unloading of numerous beer kegs.

Danny had let it slip the previous evening that he was an avid fisherman and Courtney had agreed to an early start and a morning on the famous Lough Gill where the mayfly was rising. This was a massive stretch of water with many lagoons and islands. They had hired a small but strong boat with a reliable motor and C.C. had more than enough tackle for both of them. It was an incredibly beautiful morning with light patches of fog clinging to the lake as the boat cut through the deep, clear water. Birds of all varieties scattered the water along the shoreline as they dived and foraged for food. They could already feel some warmth from the early rays of the sun.

"A bit bright today for it," grumbled Courtney, nodding at the sky.

"It's so beautiful out here, it hardly seems to matter about the fishing," answered Danny.

Courtney nodded.

"I know what you mean. This used to be my first port of call when I flew over from the UK. All the stress would just fall away. There's dozens of lakes within easy striking distance of here, like Lough Melvin up towards Donegal, where you need to hire a professional gillie to find the good spots. You also have the smaller lakes further up where you wade along the shoreline and come home with a bagful of the sweetest pinkest pan-sized trout you could ever imagine. Then there's Lough Conn in Ballina and the famous Moy river where the salmon pools are the best in the world, if the poachers haven't got there first. Or, you can go to Lough Corrib near Galway and have a couple of days fishing that you'll never forget."

He shook his head as if remembering.

Danny smiled. "You really have taken to this place C.C., haven't you? How did you face up to going back to your work in the UK before you left for good?"

Courtney moved sideways carefully trying to maintain the boat's balance and to make himself more comfortable. His brow wrinkled as he considered the question.

"Well, I then had a a all consuming purpose if you like. Work became a means to an end to fund a permanent move to Ireland, as soon as possible."

"Can you be more specific C.C.?"

Courtney looked a trifle embarrassed.

"I don't mean to sound like some sort of Mother Theresa here. I came across some situations where the people involved were doing amazing work, caring for people but were desperately trying to stay afloat financially. One of them was a hospice, and I've taken on responsibility for partial funding of it. In fact, you might like to hear of a specific situation where *magnetizing clients* helped the hospice stay afloat."

Danny sat up straight, his face alight with interest.

"That I would like to hear about," he said.

"I thought you would! Anyway, the hospice got hit with unexpected expenses. It failed an inspection because of dampness in the structure. In effect it really needed tearing down, re-building and extending its capacity. It had out grown itself ages ago. They were turning people away for Gods sake! Well, I agreed to come over and look at the situation and I have to say Danny, I had no idea how I could help right then. I was pretty over-extended myself. So before my flight over, I really spent the waiting time at the airport magnetizing some big clients so as to generate lots of commission. On the flight I found myself sitting next to a catholic Bishop from England who was going to Knock. This is a Marian shrine in Mayo and he was on a retreat with some of his parishioners. We talked about what I did and my knowledge of the investment field. He was be-moaning the loss of freedom in the UK since 9/11, when the Blair government used that as an excuse to bring in slews of legislation, virtually doing away with an individual's freedom. Not a murmur of protest from the British people, and we brought in the Magna Carta, for Gods sake, guaranteeing man's inherent rights. The patriot act in the US, according to the priest, is a pussy cat compared to what's happened in the UK. I agreed with him totally and we had a real meeting of the minds during our flight. When we said goodbye at Dublin airport, with him off on a connecting flight to Knock, I left my contact number with him. He'd said he might drive up to Sligo from Knock and I offered to show him around. That's exactly what he did. He came up and spent two days with me and we got along famously. You know what happened? He had a responsibility for the finances of all the parishes in the west midlands and he switched them over to one of our portfolios, which was much more appropriate for their needs. Six million pounds, Danny! Six million! Can you imagine?"

Danny whistled.

"Six million? My God! That must have given you ...?"

Courtney waved the question away.

"More than enough to finish the hospice project I can tell you, with a wee bit left over."

Danny sat there stupefied. The boat was still cleaving it's way up the center of Lough Gill as Courtney, grinning at his astonishment, was fixing some rods up.

Finally, Danny shook himself and took the rod Courtney passed across to him.

"You know C.C., it sounds like you really have left the UK physically as well as emotionally. Once you realized where your heart was, could you not have advertised prior to this to get someone to come in and run your business? You know, someone who would service your clients, keep the income flowing as well as promoting and growing your business? I know you talked about magnetizing me over here but lets be realistic, I'm a complete rookie in the business. It would be years before I could operate at your level. You need someone who can hit the ground running and that's not me."

Courtney looked piercingly at him.

"The timing wasn't quite right before and something happened that forced my hand. I'll fill you in on that later. As regards your lack of experience, it's what's inside that counts Danny," touching his chest lightly, "and I can see that your heart's in the right place. The rest is simply training and we can arrange that. Now, enough of this chat. We came here to fish," he said, cutting off the motor and firing his line out the side of the boat.

Danny hurriedly cast his spinner out the opposite side and almost at the same time Courtney got a strike, which he nursed in carefully. Danny whistled at the sight of a nine pound salmon flipping around in the bottom of the boat and started casting with renewed enthusiasm. Two hours later and a bagful of fish better off, Courtney headed the boat towards a set of imposing buildings on the shoreline. They had the appearance of a large spread out college. When Danny asked where they were going he just grunted about getting something to eat. They anchored the boat on a small dock and made their way up through some gardens towards the back of the buildings. They hadn't even got close to the door when it was thrown open by a smiling, slim, dark-haired, young woman of about 30 years of age, wearing a nurses uniform. Danny immediately noticed that her face seemed to glow with what appeared to be some sort of inner beauty or tranquility and felt immediately drawn to her. Impulsively she threw her arms around Courtney and hugged him. He shrugged sheepishly at the demonstration and made a face at Danny.

"You see, Danny, these man-starved nurses, how they react when any old fisherman wanders up to their door."

She stepped back laughing.

"Any old fisherman, indeed! Why, I wouldn't even be here if it wasn't for you, you old devil. I spotted you arriving and we have some soup and sandwiches coming up." Looking at Danny, she asked, "did he stop talking long enough to catch some fish?"

"Oh will you whisht your gob woman!" said Courtney, surprising Danny with his use of the Irish vernacular, as he fired the bag of fish at her.

"There's some supper for the ladies," he added.

She caught it deftly and then looked at the catch.

"Wow, you have been busy, haven't you? I'm surprised you've done so well. There hasn't been much caught over the past few days. A bit too bright I'm told."

Looking at Danny, she asked, "so who's this fine looking young fellow then Clive? He doesn't look like your usual stray."

Her finely-boned face was tilted as she inspected him with growing interest.

"Danny Quigley and sorry to say Siobhan, only another Englishman at that, but an Irish background, if that helps."

She struck Courtney's arm.

"What do you mean, only an Englishman! Sure, aren't you an Englishman yourself? You know very well I love the English after nursing over in London for nine years. Wasn't I trained over there too? Get on with you!" she railed thumping his shoulder again.

Courtney backed off in fake alarm.

"Whoa, I'm warning you now, Danny, she's a real hussy with a temper to boot. Don't get too close to that left hook of hers."

She took another swipe at him before turning to Danny and taking his arm.

"He'll corrupt you, this fellow, Danny. Come with me. At least I'll feed you anyway. He can tag along if he wants to," she said dismissively.

Danny gathered from Courtney's benign expression that it was par for the course when the two of them met. He did enjoy having this attractive female escort him into the building, all the time chattering away with him and asking him questions. It didn't take her too long to discover that he was in the throes of a divorce and had a child.

They ended up in a small annex room that was laid out with a buffet lunch set for three people. Some bottles of drink were arranged on a side-table, which Siobhan poured once she ascertained their preferences. They chatted amiably for a few minutes and then an older lady came in carrying some bowls of hot soup on a tray. They got busy on that, aided by some freshly baked rolls and then started on the buffet.

Danny looked across at Siobhan who had joined them for the meal.

"So what's the purpose behind this building then?" he asked.

"He hasn't told you? He's a great one, isn't he?" she said with annoyance.

Danny looked at Courtney and back again.

"What's he supposed to have told me then?"

She glared at Courtney who looked away embarrassed.

"That man! I'll strike him dead some day, see if I wont," she said fiercely.

Pausing for a moment, as if collecting her thoughts, she continued.

" I came across from Ireland and finished my training as a nurse. However, I changed hospitals to further my career and found myself rostered for duty at the abortion clinic to cover for a nurse who had the flu.. On my first morning everything seemed normal and people were very nice to me. One nurse said she enjoyed working there. Then we went into the surgery and I found myself part of a team killed babies!

"Sorry. You see, it hadn't quite penetrated that the babies were quite healthy. In the past I've seen us fight to save premature babies just like them."

Courtney picked it up from there.

"I was advising people in the National Health Service on financial planning and as it happens, I had made an appointment with Siobhan to update her program. They say there are no co-incidences in life, just God's incidences and that portrays my meeting with her. I was confronted with a very distressed young woman and I can tell you, we never got around to discussing finances."

"Distressed!" Siobhain whispered. "You can say that again! Another hour and I would have killed myself. I had the tablets right there in front of me. I'd completely forgotten that Clive was coming round."

She looked across at Courtney.

"I thank God every day that you did."

Courtney looked at Danny.

"I did some work with her, not unlike what we did on the top of Ben Bulben. Oh, her healing didn't happen right away. I arranged for her to move back to Sligo and work in the hospice for a while."

She looked across at him with something close to adoration in her eyes.

"You saved my sanity and my life Clive, and for that I'll be eternally grateful!"

Impulsively she went round the table and gave him a hug.

Danny took advantage of the moment to pour another cup of tea. Looking at Courtney he enquired.

"So, what is this place then CC?"

His eyes flickered sideways, reflectively.

"Well, lets see. I was involved in the hospice by then. Siobhan's experience shook me and I discovered from some research that quite a few Irish girls were going across to England for abortions. I couldn't really affect the UK situation.

Here, in Ireland, it wasn't allowed unless the courts decide to allow it in extreme cases. I decided that with Siobhan's input, if there was a facility available that was pleasant and isolated, a percentage of those girls might be encouraged to have their babies here and place them for adoption. As it happens, a number of the new mothers did keep their babies after they were born anyway. We help them there, too, with initial costs and a support system when needed, but we've found that families are often terrific when they're confronted with the situation."

Siobhan leaned forward.

"This place came on the market. Clive bought it and installed me as chief cook and bottle washer, isn't that right, Clive?"

As if in silent answer, Courtney walked across to the window overlooking the gardens. A number of young ladies in various stages of pregnancy were emerging into the sunshine and the tinkling of distant laughter reached them. Danny walked over, looking out, in amazement, at the activity below.

"So how many have you got here at any one time?" he asked Siobhan, who had joined them.

"Oh, anywhere from seventy five to a hundred and ten, which we have at the moment, and we've been doing this for five years now," she answered, her eyes sparkling.

Courtney nodded soberly.

"It's a drop in the ocean really, when you think about what's going on, but at least we're doing something," he said matter of factly.

Danny whistled.

"Wow, that's some contribution to humanity! When I think of my own personal goals, you know, the car and the holiday in Greece, they all pale into insignificance compared to this."

Courtney put his hand on his shoulder looking directly at him. "So now you know why you had to come over here Danny."

Danny threw up his hands.

"Hey, this is coming at me far too fast, and I still want to know your role in everything you've set up. I mean you're still in the picture here with your finger on the pulse, as it were. Isn't that right CC?"

He looked at Siobhan at the same time but she avoided his gaze.

Courtney pursed his lips.

"It's time," he said vaguely.

Whatever his intentions, he never got the opportunity to state what they were.

Danny was turning from the window when, suddenly, the door crashed inwards and they found themselves confronted by four men, two carrying handguns and the other two with, what appeared to be, makeshift coshes. The first one in the door, a hulking black man, was roughly holding the woman who had brought in the bowls of soup for them and was holding a gun to her head.

"Don't nobody make a move or she gets it," he shouted.

The other three quickly followed in and manhandled Courtney, Siobhan and Danny into chairs which they then lined up against the wall, all the time shouting and using profanities.

Danny experienced a strange sense of the familiar in those first few split seconds. So many potential situations had been role played, time and again along similar lines in his SAS training that he found it difficult at first to accept the reality of the situation. Courtney wasn't under any such illusion.

"Just what the hell are you playing at, barging in here and frightening the staff. We don't have anything worth stealing. Now take that weapon from Mrs. Duffy's head and let her go for Gods sake. She has a heart condition man!"

The black man's head shot round.

"An Englishman, from the accent, and probably the man I've been looking forward to meeting. Courtney, isn't it?"

Danny didn't know why he did it, but leaned forward and said.

"I'm Courtney and I don't believe I've had the pleasure of meeting you before."

The man cackled.

"Pleasure, is it? I don't think so," and smashed him across the temple with a pistol, sending him and the chair crashing to the floor.

Courtney interrupted.

"Look, he's not …".

As he started, Siobhan gripped his arm, and shook her head warningly. His face tightened as he watched the other men drag Danny to his feet and shove him back into the chair.

The gang leader sneered.

"Not so big now are we Courtney? No, we didn't have the pleasure of meeting, lucky for you. But you've heard of me all right - Pierre Bonat."

Courtney's face paled.

"The pimp from London and Manchester. The devil incarnate, leading all those girls straight to hell," he breathed.

"Your right, where you lot is concerned, I am the devil incarnate, and I'm going to introduce Courtney here to his own private version of hell within the next few hours. I can't wait to watch you die."

Bonat back-handed Danny across the face and this time the henchmen prevented him from falling. He could feel his mouth filling with blood and a tooth had come loose. He shook his head to try to clear it. He wanted to distract attention away from Courtney.

"Ah, Pierre Bonehead, you said. The name sounds appropriate all right," Danny mouthed with difficulty.

The man's face twisted as he leaned forward and delivered two cutting blows with the gun-sight, starting a fresh rivulet of blood streaming down his face.

Courtney began to say something but Siobhan squeezed his arm warningly again.

Bonat was shouting in Danny's face, spittle flying.

"You've taken something that belongs to me Courtney, and nobody gets away with that. Nobody! Now it's pay back time baby. I've come to claim my property and make an example of you that will keep your people off my patch in future."

He placed the gun against Siobhan's forehead.

"Now down to business. I want my ten girls that you brought over two weeks ago, here and ready to travel in five minutes or I start arranging corpses around this room, beginning with this pretty one here. Now snap to it," he barked.

Courtney stared at him.

"You can't get away with this. Not from Sligo you can't. Why there's only three roads out of here and the police would have them blocked off in a flash. Why d'you think I chose ... ah ... he chose this isolated place?" he said, nodding at Danny.

Bonat missed the near slip.

"Thought you'd be safe tucked away in this inaccessible place did you? Well the girls won't be as keen to run away when they hear that Pierre's hand stretches as far as they run and brings them back. No escape for those whores," he grinned evily, "and when I've taught your ten little runaways a lesson back in the UK, they won't be listening to any bleeding hearts talking to them about making a fresh start. There's only one way out from Pierre's happy little family and that's when they can't pull a trick any more."

He cuffed Danny across the face with his free hand.

"They're tarts man. Nothing but tarts. They won't reform. They'll be back at it as soon as you let them out of here."

"I don't know what you're talking about." Danny sputtered through his bloodied lips.

Courtney turned to Danny, speaking meaningfully to him.

"Look C.C., it's no good trying to bluff Bonat here. He knows we encouraged those prostitutes, who were pregnant, to come over here and have their babies. Can we help it if they also make a decision while they're here to leave their immoral trade and make a fresh start?"

Danny suddenly realized what was going on and was glad he hadn't said any more. He didn't know why he had stepped in and assumed Courtney's identity, but he felt that the man had a much better chance of surviving if his identity was kept hidden. Danny was also amazed that despite the assault on him he didn't have any rage in his heart towards Bonat nor any desire to destroy the man as he normally would have. He was already regretting his conversion from violence and didn't know how the new Danny would react in the situation. He was keenly aware that he stood in the presence of unadulterated evil and that his life was in extreme danger. He wondered if this was the reason he had been drawn to this place - to ensure the survival of Courtney? Did it all end here for him?

Bonat was rambling on again.

"Don't come the little innocent with me, Courtney. You know bloody well that your organization is trawling the streets of London and Manchester trying to get my girls to leave the trade. Maybe it started with the abortions, but your people are now actively encouraging my girls to break away and I won't stand for that. Not after all my training and investment in them. Well, they won't be so keen to listen when they hear what's happened to the high and mighty Courtney!"

He dragged Siobhan forward pressing the gun closer to her head.

"Send the old bitch there and two of my men to collect my girls - weapons out of sight of course. Don't alarm the tarts. Just tell them it's a nice little surprise bus trip for them as newcomers and get them on the bus outside. Now do it," he commanded.

Mrs Duffy looked at Siobhan, who nodded and the three left the room.

Courtney looked at Bonat, his voice bitter.

"You talk about your investment in those poor girls. Half of them were hooked on cocaine so as to keep them in your filthy business. Anyway, as I've said, you'll have a devil of a job getting them out of Ireland unless you have your own helicopter to spirit them away. Englishmen get rough treatment in Irish jails, so I'm told."

Bonat glanced at him momentarily, then turned and whispered something in the ear of the remaining thug, a large rough looking man with a bullet shaped head, who nodded and left.

He turned to Courtney.

"Do I come across as stupid to you? I found you didn't I? Oh yes, one of your little girls who left here, squealed on your location. We simply withheld her juice for 24 hours and she told us everything we needed to know. You can't trust a tart, you see."

Just then they heard the sound of wood being smashed down by the lake shore. Bonat nodded with satisfaction.

"There goes the boat gentlemen. Don't want any heroes dashing back to Sligo while we make our way across the border, now do we?"

Danny and Courtney exchanged glances. They both knew the proximity of the border from Sligo, whether it was down the Manorhamilton road to Belcoo or up the Bundoran road to the crossing at Beleek. From their present position at the lakeside, they would come upon the Manorhamilton road fairly quickly, which was less traveled. Equally, they could skirt around the northern end of Sligo town and be on the Bundoran road quite rapidly. They would still have to maintain a fast pace to Bundoran and through Ballyshannon, to get to Beleek. The group could be out of the Republic of Ireland in under one and a half hours.

Courtney glanced at Danny and shrugged his shoulders.

Bonat's attention had been on Siobhan and his eyes flickered over her figure appreciatively. He now looked over at Danny whose face was covered in blood.

"You're coming with me Courtney. That's just a taste of what I'm going to give you later before I feed you to the fishes."

He hooked his hand around Siobhan, his long fingers fondling her breast. "Nice little bit o' stuff you got there. I'm taking her as insurance. I may even train her to do some tricks for me on the trip. Fairs fair after all. You take from me, I take from you. Might even have her out on the streets working her little butt off for me. They'll do anything once we get them hooked on the habit, you know."

Danny had to grab Courtney as he lunged forward to reach Siobhan. Bonat jumped backwards, his grip tightening, as he leveled his weapon at both of them. Danny suddenly felt CC's big shoulders relax.

Courtney angled his face around and looked meaningfully at Danny.

"Well, on your little bus trip C.C., Siobhan's just going to have to tell you about Christ and the money changers in the temple."

Danny looked puzzled but just then the bullet-headed man came back into the room and nodded.

Bonat grinned slyly.

"Right, that's it then. That old one has the girls outside in the bus right now. Your four cars have been demobilized so no one will be dashing off for help. All your phones are ripped out and the boys have confiscated any mobile phones they could locate. By now, of course, the rest of your little group knows that all is not well."

He nodded to Courtney and the old woman.

"We're going to lock you both in a small cloakroom but I should warn you, if you do manage to raise the alarm and I'm cornered, they wont take me alive, and I promise you I'll take the lot of them with me," he snarled.

No one there doubted him.

Bonat ushered them out into the hallway where bullet-head was already opening a small cloakroom door. He pushed Courtney and the old woman inside and Danny could see the desperate look of appeal on his face, directed at him, before the door slammed shut. Bonat held the gun against Siobhan's head as he ushered them both along the corridor. Once outside they found the other two thugs standing guard over a fifteen passenger bus with blackened inside windows in which the ten women were now seated. When they spotted Bonat, a wail went up from the bus and some women tried to get off. They were clubbed back brutally by the two men. Bonat chuckled and stuck his head around the door.

"Well well, lookie here. My little girls all set for a bus ride. Shall I tell you where you're going my dears? Right back to old Blighty where the only ride you lot will be getting will be from your horny customers. There's a little thing called punishment first when we get back. You won't run again, I promise you. And we're bringing your savior, Courtney, with us and this pretty thing as well, for my company on the trip, my dears."

Another wail went up from the passengers and with that he shoved Danny and Siobhan up the steps into the bus. When Danny recovered his step he looked up into the puzzled faces of the women and Siobhan, unobtrusively, lifted her finger to her lips. Some of the girls obviously got the message and whispered to each other.

Bonat suddenly fired the weapon in the air bringing instant silence.

"Now listen up," he snarled. "Like any good tour guide I'm giving you safety instructions. Disobey and it costs you your life. Got your attention? On the trip sit quietly and don't try to attract attention or the next shot will be in your skull. Got that?"

The girls looked at each other, their eyes sick with despair. Bullet-head produced a set of cuffs which he used to cuff Danny and Siobhan together, and then shoved them onto the back seat of the bus. He then took the wheel with Bonat in the passenger seat. One of the other thugs climbed aboard, sitting sideways so as to watch the prisoners. Danny could see the other thug, further up the driveway, put on a helmet and climb aboard a motor cycle. Bonat tested a walkie-talkie and the motor cyclist responded. Danny's heart sank. These men were highly organized and had done their planning well. The chances of them slipping up now were pretty slim.

The bus moved out and their guard reached up to pull a curtain across, cutting off the view to the front. It also prevented anyone glancing inside the bus. The despondency and despair in the bus could have been cut with a knife as it pulled out onto the main road. For the women, it was the start of a journey bringing them back to a life of slavery. For Danny, now masquerading as Courtney, the trip promised nothing but torture and certain death.

CHAPTER 36
Northern Ireland

It was two weeks later on a Friday evening, that Danny and Scotty rolled back into Portadown and dropped their trailer off at Brennans. They were hooked up immediately with their return load as they were catching the ferry back to the UK on the Saturday night. The accommodation for them alternated between a guest house used by truckers and two lower grade hotels, one which had parking that accommodated trucks. This was the one they swung into for their late Saturday evening take-off to Belfast.

They were both tired from the trip and Danny had a quick shower while Scotty flopped on to the bed and skimmed the TV channels. When he emerged from the bathroom Danny spotted a white sheet of paper which had obviously been slipped under the door since they had arrived.

"When did that come?" he asked Scotty, going over and picking the note up.

Scotty blinked, looking away from the TV.

"Haven't a clue mate. Been busy looking for some football. Never heard a thing either," he volunteered.

Danny opened the note. It was addressed to him.

Danny, we need to meet as soon as you get in. Something important has come up. Will be waiting at The Lions Tail. Please come alone. Theresa.

He showed the note to Scotty who whistled.

"Well, she's really got the hots for you or some news on our little agreement with Mick. In any event, we know she's certainly in with them. I don't like the *please come alone* bit though. Why would they want that if we're both in agreement with their little plan?" he asked.

Danny shrugged.

"I've no idea, but obviously they've got spotters watching for our arrival. That note was shoved under the door in the last few minutes while I was in the shower. I haven't any option at this stage Scotty but to head up there, and alone."

"I don't like the feel of this at all, Danny. Why don't I follow you and keep you under surveillance?"

"Too dicey, Scotty. They'd spot you a mile off and twig that we're not truckers. No, I have to run with this and see where it takes me."

Scotty sat up straighter.

"Okay, but how about I wander up there, say in an hour, as if by pre-arrangement, and in the meantime slip out and alert the team as to this new development. They normally start coverage on us when we head out, as per our routine, for a meal and then a few drinks afterwards."

Danny thought about it.

"That should do it. Perhaps we're panicking too soon. Maybe she just wants an early start in the pit, knowing we're not staying Saturday night this time."

Scotty relaxed and grinned.

"You lucky devil Danny! How come I'm living a pure life while you have a lovely colleen to warm your bed?"

"Yeah, a colleen with some dangerous acquaintances Scotty. Never forget that," he replied grimly.

He dressed quickly and slipped out the door leaving Scotty sitting up pulling on his boots.

Danny exited the hotel and turned right in the direction of the Lions Tail. It was just getting dusk as he strode along the nearly empty streets. As he passed an alleyway on his left he heard his name called.

"Danny, over here."

Looking over, he spotted Theresa, a few feet inside the alleyway gesturing to him. He stopped and went over to her and she reached out and caught his arm.

"Danny, you're in terrible danger. I had to warn you somehow. Quick, get out of sight," she said, pulling him further into the alley.

As he did so, two men materialized on both sides of him, with pistols placed against the side of his and Theresa's head.

She collapsed in tears.

"I didn't have any choice Danny. They made me do it. I'm sorry!"

Danny heard a familiar voice from one of the men.

Mick Conlon.

"Just take it easy Danny and no harm will come to you or your little love bird there. We're disappointed in her you know as we thought she'd go along with this. But no, it seems she's fallen for you. Too bad really. Now we're going for a little ride me boyo. Any resistance will just confirm our suspicions and I'll have to put a bullet in your head. Perhaps Theresa's too if she becomes a problem."

Danny's mind raced. All his training had taught him that the best time to escape a capture was right at the start before the enemy consolidated their hold on you. Even with two pistols it wasn't an impossible task, but having Theresa there presented an additional challenge. Was she really a reluctant participant or a good actress to make him come along easier with them? Research had shown that the person holding the gun had to react to your action and this sometimes provided an opportunity to deflect the shot and overpower them. The gun at Theresa's head created the real problem. He wondered if this event spelled the finish of the MI5 operation or just a hitch in the plan. Mick Conlon had mentioned his suspicions. Did that mean they hadn't any real proof that himself and Scotty were not what they appeared to be?

He sighed, making a mental decision to stay in role.

"God Mick, you scared the shit out of me! What's the guns for? I was heading up to the Lions Tail. You could have talked to me there for crying out loud! What's going on?" he asked wildly.

Conlon didn't answer him but waved his free arm and a van that had been parked further down the alley reversed back up to them. One more man jumped out of the driver's seat who he recognized as Paddy, and quickly snapped a set of cuffs on him. Then Conlon flung him forward into the back of the van and pulled him around so that he faced him. He lifted a camera up and said

"Lift those cuffs up Danny and smile for the camera."

The flash blinded him momentarily and when his sight had cleared somewhat he saw Conlon looking with satisfaction at the polaroid picture in his hand.

"Excellent. You're very photogenic Danny. Did you know that? Probably why our Theresa fell for you in the first place. Her parents will be very disappointed in her. They thought *the cause* was more important than some bloody Englishman."

He pushed Theresa into the back of the van and one of the men also climbed in producing a weapon which he covered him with.

The van moved off as Danny tried to analyze his situation. The unknown factor was whether the IRA gang had twigged to his real identity. Why had they snatched him and what was the purpose of the polaroid snapshot? He suspected that he was completely on his own as the protection team wouldn't be in place yet. He was now cuffed and being taken to an unknown destination and, if they knew who he was, it was going to be a one way trip.

CHAPTER 37

Sligo

The day that had started for Danny with the pleasant expectation of fishing on Lough Gill, had now changed to one where there was a distinct possibility that he would never see the sun rise again. The road round Lough Gill was an extremely circuitous and bumpy one with many sharp bends. Being small, the bus didn't have the long base to make the journey in any way comfortable, and with the curtain across, the passengers weren't able to anticipate the curves and bends in the road. Danny thought the driver was pushing the vehicle as fast as possible, but probably being careful not to risk going off the road. That would most certainly torpedo their plans. Once or twice they pulled over, probably to let oncoming cars pass on the narrow road. The women started to whisper to one another tentatively and fearfully. The hatchet-faced thug in front was sitting with his eyes closed, apparently ignoring their whispers. Encouraged somewhat, the women started to speak in quiet tones, still glancing anxiously, towards the entrance of the bus. The shadow of Bonat was outlined through the curtain. Danny didn't understand the apparent laxity in his strategy following the snatch. In a similar operation in the Forces, prisoners would be blindfolded and forced to travel in strict silence. Perhaps this was his way of relaxing them in case the bus was stopped by police for a routine check.

Handcuffed to Siobhan, he was aware of her eyes watching him and her perfume as she now leaned across and whispered.

"Why did you do that back there?"

Danny made a face.

"I don't really know. It was a spur of the moment thing. He's the indispensable one after all, isn't he?" he volunteered.

Her eyes warmed.

"It was a brave thing to do Danny, but, "she gestured around the bus "there isn't a happy ending here for any of us, is there?" she asked.

He examined her face carefully trying to read her perception of just how difficult the situation really was. He had no doubt that it was a one-way trip for himself posing as Courtney, and that Siobhan would be drugged and forced into prostitution once back in the UK.

Remembering Courtney's words when Bonat was distracted momentarily back in the building, Danny leaned forward again and asked.

"What do you think C.C. meant back there about the money changers and Jesus in the temple?"

She glanced again up at the front, where the man was still ignoring them but must surely be aware of their whispering.

"What area of your life was Clive working on with you since you came over?" she enquired.

"Helping me get rid of a spirit of violence," he replied quietly.

Awareness flooded into her eyes.

"Aha. Well he may have been trying to tell you that even Jesus used violence at one time, when filled with a righteous anger. He used physical force to eject those people from defiling his father's house." She looked at him closely. "Does that help you?"

He nodded, sitting there deep in thought. Aware that he had not answered her question he cocked his head and glanced at her.

"Possibly. Let me think about it," he answered.

The thug looked up then, his face sullen.

"Shut it back there or I'll come back and shut it for you," he shouted.

Bonat stuck his head through the curtain.

"We're cutting through part of town in a minute. I don't want another word out of you until we're back on the main road again," he snarled.

Silence fell on the bus and the thug at the front swung sideways again, his face glowering with threat. Danny looked across at Siobhan and shrugged as she sat back in the seat pulling his handcuffed hand with her.

Suddenly something dawned on her. The probable implication of Courtney's words to both of them. Would Danny have understood them? she wondered.

Conscious of the ban on conversation she looked around her in frustration. She noticed that the girl in front of her, Bridie, had her handbag on her shoulder and tapped her gently. When she glanced around, Siobhan pointed to her purse. Bridie was quick-witted and rapidly slipped her purse around the corner to her. Siobhan opened it and started searching through as Danny, now alert, looked in the purse through the corner of his eye. He kept the other eye on the thug at the front. Suddenly, she grunted as she spotted a small diary with a miniature pencil slotted into it. She opened it and flicked through a few pages, realizing, as she did so, that it had never even been used. Probably one of those useless presents one gets at Christmas, she thought.

She pulled out the pencil and looked meaningfully at Danny. Then she started to write on a blank page.

C.C. was telling you that fighting back is sometimes justified when confronting evil.

She passed him the diary and watched him read it. He looked at it for a long time. Then he nodded and, looking into her eyes, smiled ever so slightly. Somehow she felt a burden lift from her and started to close the purse, but she felt his hand restrain her. He nodded at the purse and she passed it to him, watching as his fingers flitted through the various items cluttered inside the bag. His fingers stilled suddenly and he turned his head catching her eye. She noticed that his smile had widened considerably.

CHAPTER 38

Courtney had his ear glued to the doorframe of the room that he and the older lady had been locked in. As soon as he heard the distant sound of the bus pulling out of the driveway, he turned to the older woman.

"Look Kathleen, I need to get out of here and try to stop them. The only way I see that happening is for me to lift you up to that small window and try to attract the attention of the girls out in the garden who must have heard those shots. Lets give it a go, shall we?"

She nodded agreement and he quickly leaned forward and, sitting her on his shoulder, stood and lifted her up to the window ledge. Kathleen reached forward, got a grip on the window latch and struggled with it for a few minutes.

"It's too stiff Clive - probably hasn't been open in years. If I had an old cloth or something I could get a better grip and might be able to shift it."

He put her down and looked around the small cloakroom, which had some light summer raincoats hanging up. It was something on a hook in the corner that attracted his attention - an old scarf, probably left over from the winter, which he quickly retrieved and handed to her. He hoisted her back up and she reached forward again straining to turn the window handle. There was a sudden scraping sound and Kathleen nearly fell off his shoulder.

"Got it," she cried as she pulled the window open. "Now watch your ears." She proceeded to shout down into the garden.

In a few moments they heard a voice below.

"What's wrong? Who's that shouting?"

"It's Kathleen. We're locked in the cloakroom. Run round here right away and unlock this door. Get the spare key from the key cupboard," she shouted.

There were some more questions starting to fly up at her but she cut them short.

"Don't ask any more questions, just get around her quick. This is extremely urgent."

Courtney let her down as they heard the voices disappearing.

"Well done, Kathleen," he said. "That was good thinking about the spare key."

In a few moments some of the girls looking very agitated arrived and had the door open quickly.

Courtney turned to Kathleen.

"Kathleen, is that jet ski we bought still stored in the old boathouse d'you know?"

She nodded.

"It certainly is, Clive, but don't ask me if it's still running. It hasn't been used this summer yet."

Courtney pushed through the small group of women who were throwing questions at them and dashed out of the building and round to the left where the dilapidated old boathouse stood. Once inside he spotted the maroon and yellow jet ski sitting on a trolley in the corner. He checked the level of fuel and was pleased to see that it was three quarters full. Reaching down, he turned the key and wasn't surprised that it didn't start immediately. He tried it another half dozen times and was delighted when it finally burst into life. He pushed open the boathouse door and was pushing the jet ski on the trolley towards the lake when Kathleen rushed up.

"Clive we found a mobile phone across in maternity. I suppose you'll be wanting to contact the police?" she said breathlessly.

He stopped and thought hard.

"This may sound crazy Kathleen but no, I don't want to contact the police. I want to try to sort this out myself and perhaps with the help of young Danny, who knows. Once I involve the police, the anonymity of this place is blown and probably it's effectiveness. Tell you what though, you keep the phone and I'll take the number with me and that way I can stay in touch."

It took another dash into the house to get a pencil and paper and he tucked the note in his pocket. She looked pleadingly at him.

"Those poor girls, you know, back on the streets, Clive. Are you sure you shouldn't contact the police?"

"I may regret this Kathleen, but that's the way I want to play it. If I decide to involve the police then I'll do it. Your job right now is to calm those girls down and try to get them back into their routines. Keep your fingers crossed."

With this last remark he pushed the jet ski off the trolley which he had run down the loading ramp, into the water. He turned the key and, jumping on roared off up the lake, startling birds along the shoreline. Kathleen turned sighing and headed back into the house.

When Courtney ploughed ashore where they'd rented the boat, he shouted to Pauric, the boat man, to take care of the jet ski and dashed for his car.

Pauric looked after him with puzzlement on his face.

"Hey, where's the boat, Big Fellow?" he shouted.

Courtney waved dismissively and, jumping in the car, headed off into town.

Sligo was a major bottleneck for traffic coming from the Dublin direction and the locals were used to inching their cars through town. Courtney took a chance and made an illegal right turn across a one way bridge against blaring horns for about a hundred yards. Then he quickly made a left turn down to the Bundoran road and swung right heading north. He took numerous chances, passing cars and trucks and a couple of slow moving tractors. He tried to tune into Siobhan's presence by sending beams of light love and reassurance to her until he felt her presence strongly. Strangely, after a few miles, that feeling started to fade and he decided to pull over and stop.

Something's not quite right here, he thought. Quite often he could feel Siobhan's presence, like a soul mate, when going to visit her and vice versa. He re-played the conversation with Bonat back at the women's home and asked for wisdom and guidance from his higher self. Bonat's voice came into his mind with one sentence.

"I'm going to feed you to the fishes," he'd said.

Courtney tensed. A busy ferry wasn't exactly the ideal place to throw someone overboard, he thought. Suddenly he smacked his forehead. Bonat wasn't going towards the border or a coastal ferry at all. He'd very nicely laid a false trail in case the authorities got involved, with only one slip. "He's heading for Mullaghmore!" he said out loud. "He's got a boat there waiting for crying out loud."

Mullaghmore was a small fishing village on the coast which had gained notoriety for being the place where Lord Mountbatten had been blown up in a boat, years previously. Courtney's conviction was that Bonat had come in by boat and planned to slip out the same way, thus avoiding any possible involvement with police either in the Republic of Ireland or in the North. A very clever plan and one that he probably could pull off.

Courtney swung the car round and started back down the Sligo road. After a couple of miles he came to a sign for Mullaghmore and spun right, keeping his foot on the gas pedal. He focused on Siobhan again and could feel her presence more strongly. He was convinced that she was somewhere ahead and that he was gaining on them.

CHAPTER 39

The bus appeared to be driven carefully as it proceeded through what they presumed was the edge of Sligo town. Bonat stuck his head round the curtain a number of times and the other thug sat alertly watching them closely. Then the bus sped up again on what appeared to be a straight road. Bonat's head came round the curtain again and his face looked more relaxed as he chatted with his accomplice. Danny caught a glimpse of Ben Bulben on his right as the curtain flipped back and realized they were on the Bundoran road. Unless Courtney could somehow break out and raise the alarm, they would be over the border within 30 minutes. No wonder Bonat looked so pleased. Danny was suddenly confused when the bus made a pronounced left turn and looked questioningly at Siobhan. She shrugged her shoulders. Bonat stuck his head round the curtain again giving the thumbs up to his colleague. He glanced back down the bus.

"Fancy a little sea voyage then girls? Just what you need to whet your appetite for the lads back home."

Pointing at Siobhan, he made an obscene gesture with his handgun.

"Me and you will have a chance to get acquainted, missy, on the trip. I find a cruise does things to me," he gloated.

Both men laughed uproariously and Danny felt Siobhan shudder beside him while the girls were looking back at her with pity reflected on their faces.

Danny closed his eyes and tried to re-collect the shape of the coast line from his tour of duty in Northern Ireland, with the parachute regiment. A sea voyage? he wondered. Where could Bonat have a large boat waiting along this coast? Then it came to him like a bolt out of the blue. Mullaghmore, famous for Lord Mountbatten's assassination and so obvious now as an escape embarkation point.

What a fiendishly clever plan! he thought.

Bonat had planned this like a professional. He tried to recreate those media pictures that were flashed round the world and recalled a safe harbor surrounded by high quay walls with easy access to the sea and fishing boats anchored nearby. The village had a couple of pubs, some shops and a sparse population. Danny immediately wrote off any chance of rescue at that point. Shortly, Bonat and his crew would be ploughing around the northern coast and heading for a UK port, probably some small place on the Scottish coast. Once there, Danny had no doubt that the same meticulous planning was set up to spirit them away.

Just then Bonat pushed back the curtain, a curl of satisfaction on his lips as he shouted down the bus.

"Now listen up good, ye hear? We're coming to this little harbor, where we're going to pull up directly beside a fishing trawler. When I tell you to, starting with my little treasure in the back and my mate, Courtney. Bill here will hustle your little asses off this bus one at a time. As you get off you'll wait in a tight little group beside the bus until everyone is off. Then on my instruction you will, one at a time, climb down a metal ladder on the harbor wall, down to the boat. It's about 20 feet but you'll have no problems getting down it. Now I want complete silence during the change-over. Anyone who has any clever ideas about crying out or making a run for it, believe me, I'm quite prepared to use this."

He hefted the gun menacingly in the air.

"There's only a few shopkeepers and some pub full of dossers here and probably some lobster fishermen. No one is going to help you. My other mate, on the motor bike, is 20 yards away, equally armed and is between you and the village, and Bill here, and the driver, will use their clubs if necessary. I'll personally make your life hell when I get back to Blighty if anyone screws up, unless I've already put a bullet in you."

CHAPTER 40

The vehicle eased to a halt and Bonat stepped down off the bus as soon as the door swung open. Through the front window Danny could see a stretch of the harbor and the rigging of a boat moored below the quay.

Bonat shouted.

"Okay Bill, send the first two in handcuffs out and then the rest. Stay alert and no mercy to anyone who tries to stall. Do it now!"

Bill came shuffling to the back of the bus. Waving his cosh he gestured to Danny and Siobhan.

"Let's go you two. Wouldn't want to miss what old Pierre has in store for you," he chuckled.

He prodded Danny painfully in the stomach who hunched over pretending to be hurt. This was to conceal the fact that he had already removed his cuffs with a hair clip from Bridie's handbag. Straightening, Danny brought his clawed hand upward in a savage chop to Bill's carotid arteries. He was instantly unconscious. Danny eased his still form to the floor stepping over him and indicated that Siobhan link up with him again as if still cuffed. The darkened windows hid any of this from Bonat standing outside. The girls in the bus watched, some gasping from the suddenness of his attack as Siobhan and he proceeded along the bus. Reaching the front she climbed down onto the ground first, with him close up to her, his free hand covering the unlinked cuff.

As Danny's foot touched the ground, they heard the sound of a horn blaring loudly and continuously. All three swung their heads around and spotted a car being driven along the quay in their direction fifty yards away. It was being driven at extreme speed, a man's face pressed to the windscreen.

Siobhan shouted.

"By God, it's Courtney."

That's when all hell broke loose. Bonat's head shot back to look at Danny, who just as quickly shed the loose cuff. The gun hand came round and Danny moved like lightning with a double chop to the outside wrist and the gun barrel which went flying off into the sea. While it was still in the air, Danny struck Bonat on the breast bone with a tremendous burst of power from the heel of his hand. Bonat fell backwards, his feet catching on some old lobster pots, and he went flying over the wall to the hard deck below. He was still in the air when Danny, without apparently looking, gave a back knuckle blow to the nose of the driver who had started to scramble across from behind the wheel. The man collapsed moaning and spouting blood.

Courtney, in the speeding car, and not with any particular plan in mind, had seen Siobhan and Danny descending from the bus and pressed the horn in desperation. At the same time on his left, he spotted a motorcyclist who was turning towards him, a weapon his hand. Without thinking Courtney swung the car sideways catching the man and the bike and sweeping them off the quay, out into the sea where they landed with an almighty splash. The car came to a screaming halt with the front wheels right on the edge of the quay wall. Then, Courtney jumped out and ran towards the bus.

Danny took two steps forward and looked down. On the deck of what appeared to be a fishing trawler, Bonat was sprawled out with his neck twisted at an unnatural angle. A rough looking fisherman was standing a few feet away staring at the fallen Bonat in consternation. From his peripheral vision Danny saw the motorcyclist swimming towards the vessel. A warning shout came from Siobhan.

"Look out, Danny."

He wheeled quickly catching a glimpse of the bloodied driver, on his feet and swinging a cosh at Danny's head. Just then there was a clatter of feet and Danny was brushed aside as Courtney, still running, lashed out at the driver catching him full on his damaged nose and sending him flying backwards into some nets where he lay still.

Danny stared at Courtney in amazement.

"What about love and peace on earth to men of good will?" he exclaimed.

Courtney, breathless, glanced at him.

"Sometimes I take time out for special occasions," he volunteered, a glint in his eye.

Suddenly, Courtney turned and bounded over the quay wall, moving down the ladder at incredible speed. Danny realized what had galvanized him into action. He had spotted that the captain of the fishing boat had sent a member of the crew to cast off the lines, obviously preparing to leave port in a hurry. Danny removed the single cuff from Siobhan's arm, dragged the still unconscious Bill out of the bus and handcuffed him to the bus driver, also unconscious. Then he climbed down the ladder and roughly shoved the deck hand away from the ropes.

Courtney looked fearsome, his large form quivering with rage. He grabbed the Captain and hauled him by the shoulders out of the sight of some curious individuals, who had emerged from the pub across the other side of the harbor.

Courtney nodded to Bonat's still form.

"Get that out of sight Danny," he instructed.

Danny got hold of Bonat's, now lifeless, body and dragged it behind some bales, covering it with fishing gear.

The captain was a rough looking man who had the marks of being an ex-prize fighter, but was like a doll in Courtney's massive hands. The man's eyes were wild with fear.

Courtney asked him,

"Where were you planning on landing this lot then?"

The man's eyes flickered around as if hoping someone would come to his rescue.

Finally glowering, "Okay, we were heading for Greenock," he said

"Is that a standard motor you've got there?" Courtney probed.

The man's eyes flickered.

"Ah ..there's some extra power," he offered reluctantly.

Courtney bent him backwards and glared at him.

"Come on, quite stalling man. I know boats and I can have a look."

"All right, it's a powered up job," he offered, resignedly.

Courtney looked at Danny.

"That makes sense then. A quick dash round the top of Ireland with a power engine, mix in with the other fishing boats and slide into Greenock while the search is going on across the border for them, and it almost worked."

Danny strolled over to the side of the craft where the hand of a wet motor cyclist had just appeared, grasping the edge. Danny grabbed the mans arm, hauling him up in one swift, powerful movement, while at the same time delivering a powerhouse blow with his elbow to the man's jaw. He slumped to the deck.

The Captains eyes widened further. Courtney reached out and grasped the man's shoulders.

"Now I'm giving you some new instructions. Take this lot back to Greenock with my compliments, and if I ever hear of you within a mile of these shores I'm going to let some of my friends in Her Majesty's Customs know about that souped up motor of yours that I'm certain is being used for many little illegal runs, apart from this attempted kidnapping today. Is that crystal clear?"

Hope sprang into the man's eyes.

"You're letting me go then, no police?"

"Lets just say I want to avoid the attention I would attract, if I did involve the police. However, I can always lay charges again if I want to. I have a whole bus load of witnesses after all and some may just want some compensation at a later date for the stress involved."

He pointed to where Bonat lay

"And take that load of garbage with you."

The man paled.

"God, I can't take a dead body with me back to the UK," he protested. Courtney grinned at Danny.

"He catches on quick. I wouldn't take a dead body back to the UK either."

Danny responded.

"Bonat said he liked the sea. I heard him say that myself. Likes to swim with the fish, he said."

The Captain looked from one to the other.

"You can't mean … I know he was a right bastard, but at least he deserves a funeral."

Courtney patted his cheek.

"You're the Captain my boy with all the authority that gives you for conducting funerals on the high sea. Oh and don't bother saying too many prayers for Bonat. It'll be a complete waste of time. His place is already reserved for him and I suspect has been for a very long time."

He pointed to the unconscious motorcyclist.

"I'd suggest you tie him up until you reach British waters, just in case he has any ideas of coming back here."

Turning to Danny.

"Can you pass those other two characters down gently to me?" He looked meaningfully at him, " then we'll cast off his lines and get him on his way."

Danny darted up the ladder and quickly hauled the handcuffed men to the edge of the quay dropping them over onto some bales on the deck. Then he started casting off the lines with the deck hand as the Captain, wasting no time, was already turning the motors over.

Courtney came up the ladder fast and caught Danny's arm.

"On the bus and out of here. Whatever you do, don't stop to give explanations to those people who are coming this way. Just go straight through them."

Turning to Siobhan,

"Go with Danny and take him to Ryans at Rosses Point. We'll book the girls in there tonight to help them get over this. Now go!"

CHAPTER 41

Danny started up the motor within seconds. After some backwards and forwards manoeuvering he managed to turn the bus around and started back along the quay. A dozen people were coming towards him, some waving their arms to make him stop. He pushed his foot down, pressed the horn and tore straight through them as they scattered to the right and left, shouting angrily at him. In the rear view mirror he spotted Courtney in his car, hot on his tail, who also dashed through them without reducing speed. A great cheer of relief went up from the passengers.

Siobhan leaned forward and hugged him.

"Hey, don't tell C.C. about that, he'll kill me," he teased.

"Don't talk about killing, Danny, you came pretty close back there, to getting killed yourself. Bonat wasn't going to let you go and he had plans for me too." She shuddered. "And thanks, by the way, for taking Clive's place. That was a brave thing to do, Danny."

"Hey, you like the guy don't you Siobhan?"

She glanced at him.

"Yes, but not in the way you think. We're soul mates at a spiritual level, which is why I delight in his presence. Hard perhaps for you to understand at this point, but it's not a physical relationship, which is what you were asking, isn't it?"

"Yeah, probably. He's quite a guy, whatever way you look at him."

"You're quite a guy yourself, Danny," she whispered, reaching forward and holding his hand.

On that note they headed back towards Sligo and on her instruction after several miles, he swung right towards Rosses Point. When they got there, C.C., who had passed them on the trip, had already managed to secure rooms for them at the hotel. He had also contacted the home base where Kathleen and the residents were on tenterhooks about the situation.

Courtney had Danny take the bus back to the Bundoran road where they abandoned it. Documents in the glove compartment showed that the vehicle had been rented in Belfast the previous day. Courtney, who had followed him in the car, said he intended to make an anonymous phone call to the car rental people telling them where the bus was, in the hope of avoiding any local police interest. They then drove back to the hotel.

On the way, Danny quizzed Courtney on what events had led up to the kidnapping.

"Reading between the lines, I gather that your contacts in the UK were treading on Bonat's toes by enticing the girls away to have their babies, rather than aborting them. Did you not have an inkling that he would strike back at some time?"

"Certainly not. Bonat's solution to pregnancy was a quick abortion and get them back on the streets fast, earning money, so we offered the girls a clean option. We were also getting referrals from here in Ireland, to girls who would normally go to England for an abortion. Then the Irish communities in England heard about us and started funneling girls back to us as well. A lot of young naïve Irish girls who went across to England, were targeted initially by men who introduced them to sex and then would trick them or intimidate them into prostitution. Quite often they hooked them on drugs just to lock them into the vicious cycle. I have to say that a percentage of the girls did go back on the streets after delivery and adoption. Unfortunately, we don't have a detox center here. Would be useful if we had, but at least we do what we can to reduce the abortion rate, however small our effort. We did have success by getting some of the women into training programs and subsequent employment, but it's never enough. Naively perhaps, we never expected any aggressive reaction from those evil pimps and madames who exploit them. After all, as far as we were concerned, we were in a different country and tucked away on the edge of Lough Gill."

"Does that mean you have to re-think the whole endeavor you've set up here, C.C.?" Danny explored tentatively.

"Re-think, yes. Probably by providing proper security for the complex on Lough Gill for starters. No one should be able to just drive straight in there and kidnap them as easily as they did today. Close down the whole support system? Absolutely not! If anything, I may even extend it to other cities, Nottingham, Glasgow, perhaps. The need is everywhere, I'm afraid. The thing is that we were starting to hurt people like Bonat and I find that encouraging," he finished. "Thank you for your inspired switch with me back there. I wondered how much I'd dented your effectiveness for invoking violence, with the work we'd done on top of Ben Bulben. I hoped that Siobhan would somehow make sense of what I was trying to tell you Danny. I was selfishly regretting the de-programming I'd done with you."

Danny frowned.

"It was a good test as to whether I'd changed or not. I was confused at first, I don't mind admitting. When Bonat was slamming me round the head I felt amazed that I didn't actually hate him and want to demolish him right there on the spot. I certainly would have in the old days. Nonetheless, I got the message about Jesus in the temple using righteous anger and at the same time accepted that I have been given a gift in the way of being able to handle myself. Also, it would be perfectly acceptable to use my gift to prevent bad things happening to good people. The penny kinda dropped and I'm okay with what I had to do back there. I still have some stuff to work through in my head C.C."

"Perfectly understandable too, Danny and we can work together on that. I had planned to help you nurture the spiritual dimension under the iceberg - that seven eights that we had talked about, but I thank you for what you did do back there. My mad dash would have just resulted in me getting my butt shot off if you hadn't been there and reacted the way you did."

Danny clapped him on the shoulder in silent acceptance as they drove back after abandoning the bus, to the hotel in Rosses Point.

Danny had a quick shower when they got back to the hotel. He then decided to give Fiona a call as they hadn't been in touch for a couple of days. He felt bad about that but the events of going fishing on Lough Gill had totally consumed his attention and any opportunity to make contact.

He set up the initial call to her and waited the agreed ten minutes for her to get to the delegated phone box.

After the call he stood there, stunned at Fiona's news.

She and Allison were being followed in Bath by unknown people. On the phone he had asked her numerous questions as to who these people could be and if she had spotted any surveillance since then. Fiona had no further information but she did say that the media had stopped running his picture as well as articles on the events in London. She was in a state of great anxiety which had now been picked up by Allison.

Danny's mind was in a whirl and he hung up intending to discuss it with Courtney and possibly travel back to the UK to be with Fiona and his daughter. He was hurrying back into the lounge to fill Courtney in on the situation when he glimpsed him sitting in the corner with Siobhan and the girls, all chattering together and looking happy. Danny turned away. He couldn't interfere with their relief and celebration by bringing up his problems at that point. He decided to go outside and walk down by the dunes to clear his head in the evening air.

CHAPTER 42

It was dark outside as he made his way through a large parking lot used for the hordes of tourists during the day, and through it to the beach. He strode out letting the sound of the waves wash over him as he tried to grapple with the turn of events in Bath. Was it time to go back to the UK and attempt to clear his name, he wondered? Had the police investigation moved in another direction? Perhaps they had new suspects in mind for the killing of those three thugs. Was it the police who were watching Fiona and hoping she would lead them to Danny? In frustration, he threw some fast punches in the air as his mind examined the options. One thing was for sure - he had to get Fiona and Allison out of there to some other location. Getting back into the UK would be the problem, with the alert that was out for him at all ports.

Still in deep thought he started back to the hotel, climbing the sand dunes and returning to the large parking lot, which was no longer deserted. Under one of the lights, there he saw a van parked with the figure of a man squatting by the rear tire as if checking it. When he came up to the van the man looked up and he realized that he knew him.

"Hey, you're Josh, the Aussie surfer," said Danny, stopping. Josh stood up.

"Oh, Gooday mate. Danny, isn't it?"

"Yes, it is but what are you doing out here all alone at this time of night?" Danny asked.

"Just checking out the location for tomorrow. Me and some of me mates are coming over early for some surfing."

He pointed to the rear tire, stepping to Danny's side as he did so.

"Thought I felt a wobble coming in from Sligo, but they look okay."

Danny peered at the tire. Then, suddenly, Josh wrapped both his arms around Danny and shouted. "Got him!"

The doors of the van exploded open and three men leaped out, one swinging a lead cosh. Danny's last conscious memory was of hands grabbing him. The men threw him into the back of the van and handcuffed him with plastic cuffs. Two of the men sat behind with Josh and the driver in front. Josh looked back at Danny's still form.

"He wasn't so hard to take after all. I thought he was supposed to be so tough, the best of the best, so I'd been told, the original Rambo! Hell, I could have taken him myself," he said contemptuously.

The driver looked sideways at him.

"Element of surprise - not expecting any trouble. Hey, maybe that friendly accent mate," one of the men in the back interjected. "His reactions were zilch all right, but that's what civvy street does to you. Makes you wonder, though, what chance he'll have with this job for Crawford, if he's lost his edge."

They drove for nearly an hour down the Manorhamilton road towards the border crossing which now had a stripped down presence. The custom's man on the Irish side waved them through, but they were stopped on the British side by a British soldier. Josh rolled down his window, flashed a card and was waved through. A few moments later they entered a fortified police station and parked around the back in an underground garage.

The driver pursed his lips musingly.

"Reminds me of the old days when we dragged those poor bastards in every night and squeezed them for information. No bloody oversight or regulations like we're starting to get now from these youngsters coming in with their pieces of paper from Oxford and Cambridge," he said with disgust in his voice.

Josh grinned.

"Hey, you guys have had your turn back then. It's my chance to do some squeezing, as you call it. Quigley's mine!"

Inside, Danny started to regain consciousness and groaned audibly, his head pounding. His first coherent thought was that he was cuffed and hooded and seated in a chair. He heard a voice coming from a direction in front of him.

"You disappoint me, Danny. My boys tell me you were like a friendly little puppy dog. They were a trifle disappointed, especially Josh there, after you're little display back in the underground parking lot in London."

Danny heard his own sharp intake of breath.

CHAPTER 43

"Colonel Crawford! I recognize that raspy voice. Just what the hell is going on? Why am I here?" he demanded.

"All in good time Danny and by the way, belated thanks for the people you killed for me in the past."

There was muffled laughter from the group.

"You could thank me a lot more Colonel, by taking this hood and these cuffs off me right now and start giving me some explanations. You mentioned the underground garage, for example. I knew something was twisted about that whole episode and now it makes some sense, if your filthy hands were involved. And just to remind you, I'm a civilian now, which you've seemed to ignore."

Crawford chuckled good humouredly.

"You know the drill Danny. Heck you've done this often enough to some other miserable sods – blindfold, frighten, disorientate, strip them naked, threaten, torture, using different methods and a few invented by yourself and your mates in the regiment."

"Colonel, get a grip on yourself. You have just kidnapped a civilian and you have no authority whatsoever to hold me here!"

He sniffed the air thoughtfully.

"I recognize the smells Crawford - gun oil, bacon and butties. We're across the border aren't we?"

The Colonel nodded to Josh who grinned and walked across to Danny smashing him across the face, sending him and the chair crashing to the floor. Both were manhandled back up again. Colonel Crawford continued as if nothing had happened.

"Good, you haven't lost it entirely trooper, sensing where you are, and you're right. We are across the border and as you know from past experience, I'm God here as far as you're concerned. Another little clue, as long as this mission lasts, you address me as Colonel Crawford, is that clear?"

Danny straightened up, his hooded head pointed forward.

"Fuck you Crawford. You're just a bloody civilian like me and a pathetic excuse for an ex-officer in Her Majesties service. So don't go throwing your ex military rank at me," he shouted.

With that he felt more blows to his face but the chair held as the other men held it steady.

After what seemed an eternity Crawford sighed.

"You know you disappoint me, Danny. You disappointed me when you got out of the regiment, just when I'd trained you to perfection. Now I'm stuck with sheep-chasing colonials, like Josh here, who has his uses but can't do the kind of work you used to do for me."

Danny heard a muffled curse from Josh and suffered another blow to his face. He felt the blood trickling down under the hood. Crawford continued.

"I really didn't think you'd last on civvy street. Not with your refined talents, and selling financial services! Come on, Danny, don't make me laugh. Anyway, civilian or not we have a need for your talents once more, and we had to get your attention, which we did. Call it a going away present if you like. We want you to kill someone for us."

Danny's voice hissed.

"So it was you setting me up all the way along. Those thugs, their murders, the fire in my house. But how did you know I'd go through that underground garage that day?" he asked, straining forward.

"Good Danny, excellent. You're putting it together. Glenna of course. An appeal to her along the lines of national security and so on. You know how convincing we can be."

Danny's head was nodding.

"That's why she was burnt to death, wasn't it?" he said bitterly. "She would have started to put things together wouldn't she? And what about my house? What was that all about?"

"Run rabbit run, Danny. Remember? Get the hare running and shook up and before you know it they're in such a mess that we have no problem turning them. You surprised us Danny, especially when you ran all the way to Sligo. Surprised and delighted us really because Strabane our target area, is just a few hours drive up the road and fits in nicely with our plans."

Josh cut in.

"Yeah, I thought I'd have to shake your letter box all night until you woke up. You disappointed me then, Danny. I kept hearing what a switched on rambo you were - sleep with one eye open and all that crap. Hell I could have gone in to your house and cut your throat," he laughed cynically.

"You're a right murdering bastard Josh just like your psychotic friend here, Crawford," Danny spat out.

He was expecting the next blow and wasn't disappointed. This time the chair went with him. As he was being straightened up, some signal must have been given because the hood was removed from his head. A quick look around the room showed four other men including Josh. Danny was conscious of Crawford's hooded eyes watching him closely. Danny looked up at Josh's face close to him and suffused with anger.

He smiled at him.

"You know, Josh, I used to be as messed up as you right now, doing his shitty work and thinking I was somehow a hero, when I was only a trained thug at his beck and call. But you know there's hope for you. Believe me I was there. I actually believed the crap this psycho fed me. Now I'm free, totally free. Heck, Josh, I don't even hold it against you for beating me. There's hope for you too Josh. Stop listening to this maniac for starters."

Crawford nodded to Josh whose face flushed with anticipation as he lashed into Danny who just switched his mind off from the pain.

Finally, the beating stopped. Crawford chuckled again.

"That's what I liked about you Danny - always flexible. When captured just try to confuse the enemy. Nice try, but I don't believe you've been to a Pentecostal meeting or been visited by an angel, so just listen up. There's someone we want removed in the North. When I say removed, I mean killed - assassinated. With you're talents, that should be no problem Danny. Nothing you haven't done many times before."

Just stalling for time, Danny asked,

"Who is the person you want killed Crawford?"

"Gerry Adams," Crawford said casually, examining his face.

Danny gasped.

"Gerry Adams? That's lunacy, for crying out loud! The assembly is already up and running with both sides sitting at the same table amicably. That will blow things wide open! The Catholics will blame the Protestants and strike back and all the Prods, the UVF, the Red Hands of Ulster and the others, will be right back at it again. The province will explode man. You're crazy!"

There was silence in the room.

"Everyone's in agreement," Danny said thoughtfully. "Except you Crawford. You and your little clique, isn't that right? Your little empire here in the North taken from you. I see. They're onto you Crawford aren't they? They want to clip your wings, don't they, and hang you and your lot out to dry? And not before time. Not before time. I could see it in your last operations. You liked the power over people - the killings. Yes, playing God! Well, have I got news for you, for you and your pathetic bunch here. I don't kill people anymore. I couldn't even if I tried. I'm finished inflicting violence on others. Find someone else to do your dirty work!"

Colonel Crawford laughed again, but with little humor this time. Leaning forward, he spoke quietly in Danny's ear.

"Gerry Adams is in Strabane in a few days time, visiting his friend Martin McGuinness. You'll kill him then. He'll have relaxed security, so it shouldn't be difficult. Closer to the time, we'll brief you on the operation and the methodology. When you finish the killing we'll let the UK police know that we had you under 24 hour surveillance at the time of those thugs getting dispatched, so you can then go back to normal life. In the meantime, we have you under tight surveillance here. You are not to leave Ireland. Your wife and daughter are being watched in Bath as we speak and will be snatched if you try to avoid this mission or go to the authorities. We have ears all over the place believe me. You know our resources. The slightest sign that you're not going along with us on this and your little family disappears, permanently. Got it?"

Danny reared up, striving to reach for him.

"I'll kill you," he shouted.

Crawford smiled.

"That's my boy, Trooper. You're back in the killing mood. Good. Excellent! That didn't take long now, did it?" He patted him gently on his bruised face and stood up nodding to his team.

Later the van swung around the hotel, stopped briefly while Danny was thrown from it and took off. A shocked Courtney found a bloodied Danny leaning against his door when he heard the feeble knocking on it at 2am.

CHAPTER 44

Northern Ireland

Danny had no idea where the IRA were taking him. The trip lasted about an hour and the crew remained vigilant. Finally, the van slowed up and came to a halt. The occupants jumped and pulled Danny out, shoving him roughly towards a small farm house and other farm buildings. He was brought into a small room and one of his handcuffs was removed, passed around a pipe in the wall and fastened again. On the wall directly across from him was a rack with various restraining instruments including several sets of handcuffs and instruments of torture. In total, there were now four men in the room - Conlon, Paddy and two people whose faces he recognized from the pub.

Deciding that an innocent man would be protesting vehemently at that stage, he lifted his head and shouted at Conlon.

"Just what the bloody hell is going on here Conlon? We agreed to your little deal for Gods sake! Nothings changed. We're still happy to do it. Come on, this is crazy!"

Conlon strolled over and grasped the hair on the back of his head and thrust his face into Danny's.

"Just who the fuck are you me boyo? Tell me that. You're no common garden truck driver that's for sure!"

Danny playing the role of the innocent, and not knowing how much they knew of the operation, had no option but to portray a startled and shocked Danny Quigley, a simple truck driver caught up in something he had no knowledge about.

"Who am I? What sort of a question is that Conlon for Christ sake? I'm just a bloody truck driver that's who I am, plain and simple! Who the hell do you think I am?"

Conlon shrugged.

"If you want to carry on this façade, that's fine. Paddy loves his work when we have to make someone open up. A psychologist might say he's just getting some relief for all those morons he has to be nice to in the pub every night. He's all yours Paddy."

Paddy lumbered forward an eager look on his face, but it was what he was holding in his hands that made Danny shrink inside - a stun gun! With one hand he ripped off Danny's shirt and thrust the stun gun straight into his chest. Danny screamed. He couldn't help it. The shock and pain was excruciating. Sure, they were trained in the regiment to endure torture, deprivation and beatings, but nothing could prepare anyone for this.

Conlon nodded to Paddy, who stepped aside.

"We don't take any pleasure in this Danny, if that is your name, but we need this information or I just set Paddy loose on you, and he enjoys his work. Now again, who are you? Special branch? M15? That special detachment they have working out of Castlereagh? We're not stupid Danny. We've had 30 years to suss you Brits out. Make it easy on yourself lad."

Danny looked wildly around him.

"What do I have to do for Gods sake? I'm just a truck driver, who obviously made a mistake in offering to help you out, and you think I'm some sort of cop? That's absolute garbage, Conlon!"

Conlon stepped back, a resigned look on his face and nodded to Paddy. And so it went. After several jolts Danny was hanging by his arms, his jaws quivering, falling in and out of consciousness.

Conlon stepped forward again.

"Danny, here's the thing. Special Branch started following us around directly after our little meeting with you. Now that's too much of a coincidence for us to swallow. Make it easy on yourself and just say it - who are you and what group are you working with?"

Danny forced his mind back and lifted his head, just in time to catch a blur of a face peering round a crack in the door behind the men and unseen by them.

Theresa! Had he seen tears streaking down her face? He held to that thought and switched his gaze to Conlon.

"Tell me what to say and I'll say it if that's what you want Conlon. Just stop this … this pain. At this stage I'll confess to anything you want. I'm James Bond. I'm a CIA spy, if that's what you want for Christ sake! The truth is I'm none of those. Just a stupid truck driver, Danny Quigley, who wishes he'd never laid eyes on you to begin with. I haven't a clue what you're talking about. Look, just put me out of my misery and finish me off. I couldn't care less any more."

With that he slumped forward dangling on the cuffs.

Paddy lifted the stun gun again but Conlon shook his head and stepped back. The four men came together in the center of the room. Conlon looked back at Danny hanging there, spittle drooling from his lips, his face drained of color.

"There's no doubt he's just a fucking truck driver and nothing else. He would have spilled his guts before now." Looking at the others, "what do you think?"

They murmured assent. Paddy hefted the stun gun.

"I've interrogated some hard men and none of them lasted more than three blasts of this. This guys for real, unfortunately for him though, this is the end of the line. We can't risk letting him loose now."

Conlon turned a thoughtful face towards Danny.

"So, if he's for real then his mate Scotty must be too. The Special Branch attention must have been triggered by something else entirely," he suggested.

One of the other men cut in.

"So does this mean the deal is still a goer? Can we still ship that load safely to the UK?"

Conlon nodded.

"Why not. The shipment is sitting back there in Portadown, just waiting to be loaded onto their truck. It's a nice pay day for us, if we can get it across with no hassle. However, I think we need to clear out the rest of the cache in the barn and get it over the border into the Republic just in case the Special Branch are onto something."

They discussed the details together for a few moments then Conlon snapped his fingers,

"Okay, decision made."

Pointing to one of the men,

"Liam, you head back to that hotel where the Scotsman is staying. Whether he's there or at the pub, get him out and show him the picture that we took of Danny in the van. Tell him it's just insurance for the load getting across safely. Explain that you're now the second driver across to the UK until we unload, at which time we pay him and let Danny go free with a simple phone call back here. He was more into the money than his mate Danny. He'll go for it okay. Then load the stuff into his truck. They rarely check loads anymore, and Brennans are regulars, so I don't expect any trouble. Now Liam don't leave Scotty's side all the way across. I don't care if you have to cuff him in the cabin. The rest of us will start to clear the cache out of here using the farm truck. We can have it over the border by those back roads in an hour. Okay? Any questions?"

Scotty's newly appointed driver, Liam, had one.

"What about Scotty when we get to the UK?"

Conlon made a slicing motion across his throat.

"Finish him, once the load is transferred and burn the truck. Forensics would pick up the presence of explosives even after they're removed and Scotty could lead them back to us. He's a loose end as is Danny here. We don't need him anymore. We'll take his body across the border with the rest of the explosives and dump him there. The Gardai forensics aren't as clever as the Special Branch here and we don't want them sniffing around."

Paddy looked over at Danny.

"Do we finish him now or later?" he enquired.

Conlon yawned.

"Save your energy and let him walk to the truck by himself later, then finish him off. Liam, you take off and sort out the Portadown end. Paddy, keep watch at the front of the barn as we get the stuff up."

He pointed to one of the men

"Barry, you and I will start moving the rest of the stuff up out of the cellar and stack it on the floor of the barn. Let's do it."

Conlon took a cursory look at Danny hanging there, and they all left the cottage.

CHAPTER 45

Danny didn't move for a long time and when he did he groaned. He managed to stand up on his feet as he mentally went over his body. He didn't really know how bad he was hurt but his mind was completely out of kilter from the effect of the stun gun. He had never been on the receiving end of such torture before and the only thing that kept him from confessing in the end was the knowledge that if he did he was a dead man and so was Scotty.

Now having heard the conversation of Conlon and his crew, he realized that he had merely postponed his fate. He groaned again, more loudly this time as his injuries started to register on his body. On trying to move, he passed out again. He didn't know if it was for a minute or an hour but the sound of a van pulling away from the farm brought him back to alertness. He figured it was Liam going to surprise Scotty with the new plan. His mind seemed clearer somehow and he tested the cuffs. Not a chance there of getting free. His only opportunity of escape would be when they walked him out to the truck, but he probably would be cuffed and there would be three of them with weapons covering him. The odds on survival were very small. He froze suddenly, hearing the noise of the door opening. He slumped back pretending to be unconscious.

Next minute, he was aware of Theresa's perfume beside him. She reached up and touched his face.

"Danny I know you're not unconscious. I watched you through the door a minute ago, love. You probably thought it was them coming back again. God, I had no idea this was part of their plan. I heard them say after they'd tortured you that you weren't with the authorities at all, after all that. Can you believe it? I just got involved in all this, for the glamour of it. My life was so boring, but this ... this savagery! This isn't what I got involved for. Why, even the bloody Brits wouldn't do this to a man, bad as they are. And this so we'll have a united Ireland! Well, it's not worth it. Danny we had something going for us. At least I thought so. Did you feel that too?" she asked in a small voice as she caressed his face tenderly.

He nodded dumbly.

"Was looking forward to being with you tonight," he gasped.

He struggled for breath.

"Was going to ask you to meet me in London next weekend."

He sagged back, his voice faint.

"Oh Danny, Danny, what can I do?" she asked plaintively.

"Conlon said to kill me in the truck and dump me over the border. It's over for me and for us Theresa," he whispered weakly.

Her eyes went wild, darting around desperately.

"God, what can I do Danny?"

"Unlock me, Theresa. Get the key to the cuffs and you and I can slip away. Perhaps we can be together, somewhere else. Who knows?"

"But they'd kill me, Danny. My father is involved with them too. I don't know any more what they might do."

His voice hardened.

"Look at me, Theresa. I'm dead meat when they come back in here. It's as simple as that. Now does anything we did together mean anything to you at all? I know it did for me," he said, looking directly into her eyes.

She looked at him for a long time then dashed across to the table where the rack of restraining implements and cuffs were, along with some keys. "I've got one," she called out breathlessly.

"Quickly Theresa. Get these off," he urged turning his wrist as far sideways as possible.

She reached up as far as she could, struggling with the small key and finally managed to unlock one of the cuffs. He threaded the cuff through the pipe and slumped directly onto the floor amazed at his weakness and tried to rub his wrists, which bore deep marks from the cuffs.

"Here, let me do that," she said taking his wrists and rubbing them gently.

He knew he had to somehow get his act together before the men came back into the house. He remembered the many exercises in the Brecon Beacons in Wales during initial training when they just had to suck it in and keep going, even when their bodies and minds had stopped functioning. Remembering, he breathed in deeply, knowing his life depended on him focusing whatever strength he had left in order to survive. The success of the mission, and Scotty's safety, were equally important.

"Thanks, Theresa," he said reaching up and pulling himself to his feet.

He still felt off balance but his strength was returning. He still needed more information on the load going to the UK on Scotty's truck.

"Where's the load going to in the UK?" he asked casually.

She examined him closely.

"Don't tell me you're with the police after all. What makes you ask that?"

"For God's sake, Theresa, I'm probably ten minutes away from having a bullet in my head. I need to know what the situation is here and how we might somehow survive it, that's all," he burst out.

She rose to her feet facing him.

"Sorry, I guess I'm just paranoid. Okay, they plan to give the load to a bunch of militant Muslims in Bradford."

"My God!" he said shocked. "That would cause utter chaos over there."

She shrugged.

"As far as the lads are concerned, anything that hurts the Brits is just payback for the years of occupation they carried out over here."

He shook his head still reeling from the news he's just heard.

"You said *give them* Theresa. You mean sell them, surely? This could be a nice payday for them?"

"Well, they will be getting paid alright, but not in cash," she volunteered.

"How do you mean?" he asked curiously.

Sighing she looked away for a moment and then looked back at him.

"You might as well know the rest. I was trying to keep my father out of it. He was over in Iran two months ago, speaking with government officials. He has arranged for them to ship a load of improvised explosive devices over here in return for us sending the load of our C4 explosives from the barn, to their Muslim bretheren in the UK."

"Christ, you're talking about IED's! They inflicted massive casualties on the Americans in Iraq and the coalition troops in Afghanistan. This would bring the Brits and the police to their knees here in the north and if they smuggled explosives across to those radical Muslims in the UK. My God, that would create chaos!"

He thought for a minute before catching her by both hands,

"Just how on earth do the Iranians plan to get them delivered here?"

She pursed her lips.

"As I understand it, Conlon and his friends have just bought one of the fishing boats going out of commission in Glenties, in Donegal. It still has it's license, and they plan to meet up with an Iranian ship in international waters and load up the stuff. Then, the fishing boat slides back into port and our lads will unload it and away they go."

He thought quickly.

"It could work too. It's a simple plan and not too many people involved. When is it expected to happen?"

"As I understand it, the Iranian stuff is already on the high seas. Don't know the actual details. Why are you curious about this anyway? Shouldn't we be getting the hell out of here?"

"We should and we will Theresa, trust me. Now, just two more questions and we're out of here. Is there anyone else in the house right now and is there a landline telephone here?"

"There's no one else here. They're out at the barn and there's a phone in the next room. Why do you need to know that Danny?"

In answer, he reached up and squeezed some nerve centers on her neck and she collapsed into his arms without a murmur. He hated to do it but he couldn't go out and tackle her brother and the others at the barn without causing some opposition from her. He cuffed her quickly and lifting her up, he staggered out into the hall. Once there, he pushed open a door to another room, which turned out to be a bedroom, and flopped her onto the bed. He then covered her up with an old blanket and tied a scarf around her mouth to stop her from screaming when she came to. Using a second set of cuffs he re-positioned them so that each hand was attached to a bedpost . In that way she couldn't remove the gag and raise the alarm. Then he dashed through the house looking for weapons but was unable to find any. Going back into the room where he'd been tortured, he grabbed a wicked looking cosh and two sets of cuffs from the wall. Quickly, he checked out the window and after a moment spotted the large form of Paddy standing at the entrance to the barn. Some yard lights were on and it would be impossible to go directly across without being spotted. He carefully scrutinized the area around the barn for a moment, then dashed back to the room where the telephone was situated. He had a direct line for emergencies and immediately got through.

It was Patton on the other end of the phone.

"Where the hell have you been, Danny? Scotty's taken off with his load and a different driver. You just dropped off the face of the earth!"

Danny started speaking rapidly and there was deathly silence as he filled him in on what was happening, including the load going to the Muslims and the Iranian involvement.

Patton gasped.

"Danny, if this is for real we're talking an international incident here. This goes beyond MI5s brief. It's going to involve MI6 at this stage. I better get on to Crawford right away. Where are you by the way? You need to wait until we get reinforcement out to you, Danny."

"There isn't time. They're clearing out the cache and they'll be out of the barn in minutes, I suspect. Then they'll be back in here to finish me off. I have no weapon as such, so I have to take the battle to them. It's the only edge I've got. They think I'm still tied up. Listen, one last thing. Get me a chopper here a.s.a.p. I want to get in the back of Scotties truck, to even the odds when he hits the other side."

"How the hell do we do that?" Patton asked.

"When the truck's on board the ferry, and it's a good time for your people too to have a look at the stuff and switch it, so it can't be used by those bastards in Bradford."

Patton whistled.

"Good thinking, Danny. Now how do we get to you?"

Danny read him out the telephone number and left the instrument off the hook, which he knew would provide an immediate trace. He had no illusions as to how quickly they could locate a deserted farmhouse out in the country. Whatever was going to happen now was up to him.

He dashed back to the window for a quick look. Paddy was smoking by the barn looking bored. He held a shotgun in his free hand. Danny slipped out the back door of the farmhouse and carefully negotiated his way round the side of it. Some old farm machinery stood between him and the edge of the barn and he waited for his chance to scoot across, keeping low, when Paddy's attention was in the opposite direction. Once he managed to get there, he paused, taking stock. There was no way he could get up close to Paddy without being spotted so he eased along the side of the barn looking for a way inside. Like all old barns, the sheet metal had started losing nails and had got bent outwards over the years. He finally spotted a large gap in it, and lay down putting his head through. There was no sign of Conlon or his colleague, so he crawled inside. He knew the entrance was to his right and Paddy was on guard there. Looking left he spotted a glow coming from the floor down at the extreme end of the barn. He suspected that Conlon and his helper were down there clearing out the cache. He realized that time was getting very short, however he couldn't leave Paddy at his rear once he got involved with the other two. Quietly, he edged back towards the entrance, careful to watch for any objects that might make a noise and cause Paddy to check in the barn. With that shotgun, Danny would be history in seconds. Once at the entrance, he found the door slightly ajar. He couldn't take the risk of pushing the door open further in case it squeaked and Paddy's proximity to it was unknown to him. He tried his only option.

In his best Irish voice he called:

"Give us a hand here Paddy."

There was a moments silence. Then "right you are."

Paddy's large form started to loom around the door. He had only time for one look of astonishment before Danny smashed him savagely on the head with the cosh and then twice more on the back of his neck and kidneys as he fell. Quickly, Danny cuffed him and dragged him over behind some bales, before sticking a greasy rag in his mouth. Stealthily he crept back to the glow at the other end of the barn. All round the edge of the hole were stacks of weapons, blocks of C4 explosives, a box of hand grenades, and even a belt-fed M60 machine gun. Danny whistled under his breath. What a cache of weapons! They hadn't been turned in as required by the peace agreement and shortly would be across the border to be used for some other mayhem.

He was just trying to figure out how to handle the situation when he saw that the ladder that went down into the hole in the ground, had started to move with the weight of someone coming up. Quickly he assessed the material stacked around him but there wasn't time to locate the correct ammunition and arm a weapon. He hefted the wicked club again as a head came up through the opening facing away from him, with a load of rifles on his shoulder. It was Conlon. Danny brought his arm down and delivered a savage blow to the man's head and he disappeared down the tunnel, the rungs of the ladder splintering as he did so. Danny started throwing as much of the explosive devices as he could locate, down the hole, hearing them crash as they landed. After a few moments of silence some shots came flying up from below. He took another quick look around. A box of grenades was still lying there. He took three out of the box and threw the rest down the tunnel. Quickly he extracted the pins out of two and knelt on them, while he pulled the final pin in the third grenade. Then he tipped all three down the hole and turned and ran as fast as he had ever run in his life, not knowing how big the remaining cache down below or how far along under the barn it ran.

He didn't quite make the door before there was an immense explosion and both doors were flattened in front of him. He got thrown even further out into the barn yard, flattening a old wooden wheel barrow with his body in the process. Then he sat up, his ears ringing, trying to get his head, already shaken from the torture, to work.

It only seemed minutes before he heard the clatter of a chopper, which swooped down and landed in the farmyard, now brightly lit by a raging fire from the barn.

Patton was the first out and ran over to him, helping him to his feet.

"We were out there in the chopper trying to locate the farm and we saw the blast. Man you know how to send a distress signal. Fill me in on the situation Danny."

Some more men ran up wearing black balaclavas and stood in a tight circle looking alert and with deadly purpose. Danny quickly briefed Patton. Paddy might still be alive near the entrance. His sister was handcuffed inside. The cache was completely destroyed along with two men.

Patton scratched his head.

"God Danny, you've got to stop doing this to us. The boys were looking for some action tonight," he said nodding at the team.

He looked thoughtfully at him.

"Pardon me for asking, Danny, but the lady you mentioned who is handcuffed in the bed. Does that mean …?"

Danny took a swipe at him, then in earnest,

"No you nitwit! But speaking of her I don't want to be here when you take her out. Can you get me back to Belfast and onto that ferry? Scotty needs the back-up. Oh and by the way, the girl's father is a biggie too. He arranged the thing with the Iranians. Is he being attended to?"

"Already in hand. No worries. Let's get you out of here in the chopper. The boys will cover until the full reinforcements manage to get through, though what we need here is a forensics team."

Patton's voice had a touch of admiration, perhaps even envy.

A few moments later Danny found himself up in the air and heading swiftly towards Belfast.

CHAPTER 46

Sligo

"For God's sake, Danny, what's happened? Where have you been all this time? We looked all over for you earlier and eventually we went to bed."

Danny struggled to his feet, his eyes red-rimmed with fatigue.

"Fiona and Allison, they're being followed by this Colonel Crawford from MI5. They're in terrible danger C.C.," he said wearily.

Courtney caught him and steered him gently towards a chair and eased him down. Then he dashed inside the bathroom and came back with a damp towel and carefully started wiping Danny's face. After a few moments his breathing slowed down and the wild look went from his eyes. Without asking any further questions, Courtney put the kettle on and raided the mini bar, dumping a cognac into a hot cup of coffee. Danny's hands closed gratefully over the cup and he took two large swallows. Finally, he looked up into Courtney's anxious face and started to tell the story:

Fiona being followed; himself snatched from outside the hotel and taken over the border. Colonel Crawford's plan to get him to kill Gerry Adams and how he had initiated the situation back in London, that got Danny into trouble with the police and on the run; How Fiona and Allison's safety were being held over his head if he didn't carry through on the assassination. Finally he stopped.

There was silence in the room for at least a minute. Courtney's expression had gone from shock to disbelief and then to sheer horror as Danny outlined the MI5 group's plan to force him to kill Gerry Adams.

"You're here Danny so you must have agreed to carry out the job for them, otherwise you would have ended up in a bog hole out there somewhere, isn't that the situation?"

Danny looked back grimly at him.

"That was the choice. If I didn't agree to do the job, they threatened to do me in - Fiona and Allison as well. They meant it C.C. They're desperate right now to keep the game going in the North, and you know, it's just that - a bloody game to them but Box will use any tactic to keep it going."

"Box? What do you mean?"

"Oh, in the old days before they got that nice big building on the Thames, they just had a box number. That's what they were referred to and the name stuck."

Courtney looked at his watch.

"Perhaps in the morning this whole situation may not sound as totally unbelievable as it does right now; a maverick group in Her Majesty's Government's spy organization, who are engaged in torture, killing and the planning of an assassination, threatening to kill a civilian and his family. My God it's mind boggling!"

Danny finished the drink and placed it unsteadily on the floor.

"I need to lie down C.C. and get some sleep. I'm all in. Yeah, in the morning I'm going to have to make some serious decisions but I can't think right now."

Shortly, Courtney got him back to his room where he collapsed on the bed. He covered him with a heavy blanket and Danny was asleep in minutes. Courtney went back in his room and got out his telephone card.

It was late morning and they were back in Courtney's cottage overlooking the Garavogue River which ran into Lough Gill. They had just finished a large meal of bacon, sausage, eggs and toast. Danny had had a hot bath back at the hotel where they left Siobhan in charge of getting the group back to the facility on the shores of the lake.

Now Courtney sat back and observed Danny as he finished up.

"Danny, I'd hazard a guess that you haven't lost you're ability to analyze a situation and create a plan. That expensive training you received in Her Majesty's service has to count for something doesn't it, especially when you're up against an enemy like Crawford."

Danny sat up suddenly alert. He put his finger up to his lips and pointed to his ears. Startled for a moment, a dawning realization flashed across Courtney's craggy features. Danny got up and started methodically searching through the room in the usual places for listening devices. Finding none, he beckoned for C.C. to follow him into the bathroom, where he closed the door and started the shower. Leaning forward he spoke directly into C.C.'s ear.

"They're bound to have thought of installing something here to keep a monitor on my movements, but may have figured out that I'd find them. We'll check your car later, but they could just as easily be sitting across the river and bouncing a laser off one of the window panes. They may also have an intercept hooked into your telephone line along the road somewhere, so we have to be careful when we use it. Okay?"

Courtney's eyes widened. He'd never been on the receiving end of this type of intense professional surveillance and struggled to comprehend the scope of it. Undaunted, he leaned closer to Danny.

"Okay, we have a situation here where, as you see it, you have no option but to kill Gerry Adams. A lose-lose situation if I ever saw one. From what I hear about this group, they can't afford to let you, happily, go back to your normal life afterwards, carrying the sort of information with you that could destroy them. I'd be for the chop too for what you might have told me and probably Fiona and your child, so that option doesn't look so good does it?"

Danny listened intently.

"Go on." he prompted.

Courtney pointed a finger at him.

"What's obvious to me is that you've missed one key point. Just what lever are they using against you?" he asked.

"Fiona and Allison," Danny replied impatiently.

"Now hold on a moment, Danny. If they didn't have those two birds in the hand, as it were, where would that leave you?"

Danny's eyes brightened.

"They wouldn't have any pressure on me at all. It might give me the space to start unraveling Crawford's little scheme. It could be the edge I need." Then his face darkened. "But I can't make a move without them spotting me. The ferries and airlines. M15 have access to all their passenger lists and they'll be well covered if I tried to run. Believe me they invented this stuff. This is their forte."

C.C. smiled and patted his shoulder.

"I can get you out, Danny, and without your friends copping on, how about that? And back here again with your family in tow!"

Danny looked startled but a faint look of hope crept into his voice.

"I like the sound of it but Colonel Crawford would bag my family as soon as I ran. I'd probably get there too late even if your plan worked."

"Why haven't they bagged them already Danny, now that you mention it? Surely, this is the soft spot in their plan."

"That's easy. A family kidnapped in the UK would create a lot of police attention and publicity. Crawford would probably need to pull in an extra team to hold them, and that could be a problem. Some of those people might just start to question the whole operation and the word could get back to MI5 headquarters. I gather time is running out for him right now.

They'd much sooner the plan worked by keeping Fiona under wraps and me tied down here until the hit on Gerry Adams in a few days."

Courtney nodded musingly.

"I'm no military genius but let me lay out the plan I have in mind to get you out of the UK and back here with your family without being spotted. You pick holes in it and lets see if we can make it even better."

CHAPTER 47
The ferry at Belfast

Only a security organization like MI5 could get a ferry company to cordon off the truck deck and allow a truck to be broken into. Decks were off limits to drivers once they left port but it didn't stop the odd driver sneaking back down for something they had forgotten, if the doors were not locked. The MI5 cordon made sure this didn't happen. The bomb squad took over, examining the cache of weapons and explosives, which were stored in two separate containers. They had obtained a copy of the cargo manifest and quickly separated the legitimate load from the cache. MI5 had arranged with shipping to run a second truck on board, directly behind the one being driven by Scotty, with all the material and resources they would need for the operation. There was a long moment of tension when they opened the containers extremely carefully, fearing booby traps. Sighs of relief went up all round. No one fancied an explosion on a vehicle deck at sea. In fact, this was the one aspect of the operation that the ferry organization and especially the captain, had objected to. Now they had to replace the load with material from the MI5 truck that might fool the gang who would intercept it, long enough for it to lead to the Muslim militants. Switching the load was risky, but they couldn't risk the real explosives falling into the wrong hands. They also intended to plant a small surprise in the substituted material, for the militants

Finally, the job of the bomb experts was finished and Danny called Patton over.

"Will your mobile phone work on board with all this metal?" he asked.

"Perhaps. Might be better if I went on deck." he replied. "What did you have in mind, Danny?"

"I want you to put a call through to Scotty."

Patton did a double take.

"Are you kidding? That could screw up the whole operation and that's assuming they've left him with his cell phone."

Danny held up his hands.

"Hear me out for a moment. I grant you he may not have his phone still in his possession though he can be persuasive and may have given them a reason; you know, waiting for the information on which depots to drop the load off to, whatever. Here's the thing. Scotty's totally on his own as far as he's concerned. He'll suspect he's just a few hours away from being killed. He's going to be feeling pretty desperate right now. If possible, I'd like to drop a hint that I'm nearby and he'll be prepared for my play and not try to go it alone. Scotty won't go down without a fight, I can tell you."

Patton sighed. "Okay Danny, you've made the right calls on this so far and that Iranian information is way and beyond anything we hoped to get from this op, so what did you have in mind?" he said cocking his head.

Danny handed him a sheet of paper on which he'd written out a script for the phone call;

Is that Scotty? This is Doctor Patton at the intensive care unit in Carlyle hospital. Your brother survived the operation and thankfully has escaped the clutches of that nasty cancer. He sends his good wishes and only wishes he was tucked up in the back of your truck to keep you company. He'll be watching for you when you come back to visit him. That's it Scotty. Any message for him?

Patton grinned.

"Bloody ingenious Danny! I'll go up right now on deck before they lock you in. Get your stuff prepared in the meantime.

In fact, Scotty had convinced Liam, his guard, that the trucking depot would be concerned if he was not contactable. They might think that another hijacking had taken place and would alert the police. Liam reluctantly agreed but had insisted that he switch to speaker-phone if it rang. When it did, they both jumped. Scotty had one wrist handcuffed to the bed in the cabin and fumbled for the phone. He struggled to push the speaker- phone button, aware that Liam had jumped off his bed and taken out his pistol.

"Hello," he said. The message jumped out of the speaker at both of them. A Doctor Patton from Carlyle hospital. He listened without comment until the doctor asked if he had any message for his brother. Liam held the gun against his temple with a warning look.

"Ah yes. Tell him I'm delighted and would be even more delighted to have him on my truck. Even with his operation he'd be safe with me. After all I'm at the cutting edge of driving these damn trucks. Tell him I'll see him soon."

The phone went dead. Liam backed off putting the gun away. He looked at Scotty without much sympathy.

"Brother not well then?" he asked casually.

"Yeah bloody cancer … only found out a week ago. They whipped him straight in. Got a wife and two young kids as well, and the only family I got left. Thank God he's come through the operation okay," he said morosely.

Inside his mind was racing.

Danny was loose and right now in the back of his flaming truck! The operation was running on track. Now he could really start watching for the right opportunity. He hoped Danny had got his message. Just then Liam broke out his lunch box and Scotty looked longingly at the sandwiches but Liam ignored the look. Scotty was glad in a way because he was going to have to kill him soon.

CHAPTER 48

Danny and the team were sitting impatiently on the back of the truck waiting to shut the door when Patton raced back down. He pulled Danny to one side, excitedly.

"God it worked Danny! I got through to him and gave him the message. He just listened, as one would expect. He knows of course that the call is from us ... Dr Patton and so on."

Impatiently, Danny interrupted.

"What did he say? Anything?"

Patton repeated the message from Scotty. Danny smiled in relief.

"He got it. All of it. Great! You know what?"

"No, what?"

"The reference to the cutting edge. He's still got his knife Whoever's guarding him has not done a very good job."

Patton shuddered.

"God I'd hate to be in his shoes."

With that Danny jumped into the back of the truck and the door was slammed shut. In a few hours it would off-load in the UK.

Brennans trucking had booked Scotty on the shorter ferry trip to Scotland. Normally he sat up in the lounge with the other drivers for the few hours it took. Liam had insisted on booking a cabin where he had full control over Scotty.

It was still dark in the early hours of the morning when they got the announcement for drivers to go to their vehicles.

Liam removed the handcuff but stayed tight up close to Scotty as he proceeded to the truck with a gun pressed into his side. In actual fact, he could have disarmed Liam any number of times but that would have messed up the plan. Climbing up into the truck Scotty got a warm feeling knowing that Danny was ensconced in the rear and hoped that they would both survive the ordeal. He'd been in enough operations to know that anything could go wrong even with the best plans in place. At that stage, Scotty still didn't have a clue as to the cargo he was carrying, which he assumed to be illegal, nor it's ultimate destination. He understood though that MI5 would normally want to track the load and continue surveillance until they had netted as many as possible of those involved. Scotty guessed that the big Brennan's truck wouldn't be driven directly to it's final destination but that the load would be switched to another smaller vehicle, somewhere along the way. He assumed that they would finish him off at this time. The problem was that if they discovered Danny and he fought back at the changeover spot, it would blow the mission and the load would go no further. He was hoping that the gang's plan, once they had switched the load, was for Liam to take him and the truck to some out of the way location, before terminating him.

The truth was he didn't have a clue and was equally unaware of Danny's briefing and objective. Would he be detected when the gang opened up the back? If the truck was being moved to another location after unloading the cargo, would Danny be locked in the rear of the truck and unable to provide Scotty with any support when they attempted to kill him? If that was the gang's plan, a back up car would obviously have to follow the truck if they intended to dump it. That meant at least two people to deal with at the showdown, if he was reading it correctly. Scotty's grandfather had been a 'Carney', working on the carnival doing a knife throwing act and a bow and arrow display. He had introduced him to the skills and even used young Scotty as a target occasionally, unbeknownst to his father. Apart from his explosive head-butt and his SAS combat training, his knife throwing skills made

Scotty a formidable foe in any confrontation. He understood however that MI5 didn't want cleaning up bodies after him, especially in the UK, and he was expected to only use as much force as was deemed necessary. Scotty's new employer M15 would, over the years, tend to disagree on his personal interpretation of *limited force*. If it came to saving Danny and himself or the mission, there was no doubt in his mind, which way he would go. Crawford might not like it, but Scotty's loyalty was to his SAS mate Danny and to hell with MI5!

The truck was rolling now and heading in the Carlyle direction where they would pick up the M6 motorway, heading South. Scotty decided to see if Liam would divulge some information if he engaged him in conversation. "Tell me Liam, with this new switch and you here effectively holding me a prisoner, am I still getting paid for this run? Hell, that's the only reason I initially agreed to do this extra stuff."

"What do you think, Scotty?"

Liam's lip curled as he squinted across at him, tapping him on the shoulder with the gun.

"What the hell do you mean by that Liam? I mean what's changed? We could have had a long and profitable relationship together. Why suddenly stick a gun in my back and take Danny's place? Hell we were quite ready to work with you guys. That's what I don't understand."

Liam laughed cynically.

"Yeah sure. So how come Special Branch started following our people around, just after our little agreement back in Portadown? Answer me that then."

Scotty gave him an alarmed look.

"God, I haven't a clue, Liam! I don't even know what this is all about. Special Branch? Hell, I stay away from coppers as a rule. As for them following your people, perhaps they were already keeping an eye on them."

He glanced at Liam again.

"I gather this isn't just computers and DVD's you're bringing in right now, and you're not just some criminal gang making a few bob smuggling. Would I be right?"

Liam showed his teeth but the smile didn't reach his eyes.

"You ask too many questions Scotty. I don't myself when I'm working with Conlon. People end up in a cement foundation in Belfast or Birmingham when they get curious around him. He tells me to leave no loose ends, so whatever that takes, I do it. You with me Scotty?"

"Holy shit Liam, you surely can't mean ..."

That toothy grin again.

"I knew you were smart on the take-up Scotty. I don't have to draw you any pictures. Actually, I like what I do. I missed all the years of fighting the Brits in the streets. I was too young for it. Now I'm getting my end in as well and I have no problem shooting you fucking Brits at all."

"You call a good Scotsman a Brit? I wouldn't say that too loudly in any pub in Glasgow or Aberdeen, if I was you," he answered.

Liam sneered.

"I'm not stupid, Scotty. It's the Scots who have been the backbone of the British occupation forces in Ireland and elsewhere, over the centuries. Anyway, it's the Scots who came over and became landowners in Northern Ireland and stole our property, so knocking off a Scot is no problem to me."

Nice to know where you stand anyway, Scotty thought, and went back to concentrating on the road.

It was still dark, when some time later, the signs indicated that the M6 was ahead. Liam stuck the gun in his side and told him to slow down. He directed him into a large abandoned petrol station, with nothing but half a dozen wrecked cars at one end. A large van and BMW car were also parked there, with the motors running. Scotty eased the truck to a stop where Liam had indicated and turned off the engine.

"Out your side you Scottish bastard. No tricks, and get that back opened up. Then you and I go for another short ride."

When Scotty climbed down he found himself surrounded by three unmasked men with Irish accents, who hustled him around to the back of the truck, which he opened. He was then pushed to the side and grabbed by Liam, who held his weapon under his jacket, presumably, in case a curious passing motorist might spot it. Scotty figured that was why they were later going on a short ride, rather than finishing him off there in the rather public, but, disused petrol station. The lack of masks was probably to avoid attracting public attention, but it also told him they weren't worried about him being a witness to the hijacking. The doors of the truck were now wide open and the load was rapidly being transferred to the van. At the conclusion, one swarthy looking man gestured back at the truck.

"Worth checking out the rest of the load, Sean? Might be something worth nicking."

Scotty froze. Danny could be discovered if they started poking around back there. He turned his head towards the car and shouted

"Hey, its mostly containers of animal feed and some tractor parts. No skin off my nose if you take it."

Sean's eyes flicked towards him momentarily then he waved the swarthy man away.

"We're not here for anything but the load you've just switched over. There's very little room left in the van anyway, so just forget it. We haven't time to hang around here. Come on lets move out!"

Scotty breathed a sigh of relief. As Sean was turning away he had an afterthought.

"Might be an idea, Liam, to shove him in one of those feed containers later, before you torch the truck. Might slow the police up a bit."

Liam grinned.

"Hey, I like it! Give him some food for the long journey ahead."

The gang laughed uproariously with appreciation.

Scotty took the initiative right then, catching the truck tailgate and swung it around the back. When it slammed he went and got the other half of the door and closed it as well. Liam was watching him as he did this and as he meshed the two doors he pretended to close the metal catch by slamming his left hand on the door. "That's got it," he said and turned, stumbling as he did so onto his knees, hoping Liam had not spotted the fact that there was no brass lock on the hasp. Liam kicked him as he lay there on the ground and took obvious satisfaction from the shout of pain from him. He had, however, missed the unlocked doors completely. In effect the remaining load was no longer of any concern to the gang.

Scotty climbed awkwardly to his feet, holding his rib cage and pretending to be still in pain. Liam grinned in satisfaction and poked him in the ribs with the gun, pointing him towards the truck.

"I enjoyed putting the boot in, you fucking Brit bastard! Might do a little more later before I give you the chop."

Sean came over and had a brief conversation with Liam as he reached the cab of the truck. He explained to him that he was going in the large van, with the transferred cargo while the BMW driver was going to follow Liam and Scotty in the truck. Once they had reached their destination, which was a short distance away, they were to complete their business and head back to London. Scotty had no illusions that he was part of the 'completed business', to be taken care of.

Sean went over to the van, waved to Liam and watched as the truck and BMW eased out of the disused petrol station, turned left, and headed back along the road they had come in on. Sean then jumped in the van and turned in the opposite direction towards the M6 South.

After approximately twenty minutes driving, Scotty was instructed to slow down and make a right turn onto a side road. He was aware of the other car staying close behind and making the turn as well. Almost immediately, he was told to take a left turn up another even narrower road. He spotted a quarry sign as he swung the truck around. One hundred yards further along, Liam pointed at a right turn into a quarry where he instructed him to bring the vehicle to a halt. Still going at 10 miles an hour Scotty suddenly slammed on the brakes and Liam, who had stayed unbuckled so as to have more control over Scotty, shot forward two feet and slammed head first into the dashboard. Scotty felt the gun move from his stomach. Without further thought he hauled the wicked knife out swiftly from it's neck scabbard and slashed it across Liam's throat. At the same time he grabbed the weapon and thrust it down with his left hand to avoid any reflex action from the now dying man. Liam looked around dazedly at him, trying to mouth something and then slumped forward on the dash. Scotty slammed the butt of the gun back noisily against the metal portion of the truck cab behind them.

"Go, Danny, go," he screamed and still holding the gun, carefully opened the truck door, spotting the BMW pulling up behind them. The driver jumped out spotting Scotty, with a shotgun in his hand. At that moment the back doors of the truck exploded open and Danny emerged with a roar, jumping straight across the hood of the BMW and catching the driver, who was standing behind the open door in the chest and they both went flying onto the floor of the quarry. The shotgun flew off out of sight. The driver was incredibly powerful with a rugby players build, and he now rose and threw some solid blows at Danny who blocked the first three, before delivering a knife edge set of knuckles at the man's throat, a double edged chop to both sides of his neck and watched him collapse on the ground the life draining out of him. Danny bent and swiftly picked up the shotgun and turned to see Scotty, emerging from the cab.

"Everything under control up front Scotty?" he asked. When he nodded grinning, they threw their arms around each other and whooped, giving some high fives.

Finally, they stopped and brought each other up to date on events and where the mission was at that point in time. Scotty was amazed at the new twist to the mission with Muslim militants and Iranians supplying IEDs.

Danny had explained that he had tried the rear doors when they made their first right turn off the main road when the BMW lights were off the rear doors momentarily.

Scotty went back to the cab, got out the mobile phone and called their special number. He was surprised when he heard Crawford's frosty voice on the other end. He was shocked when he heard Crawford's first words.

"You didn't do a very good job of cleaning up the site back at the farm Quigley. I'm disappointed in you. Left us some loose ends."

Danny's voice grated as he gathered his thoughts.

"Can you please explain that sir? As I understand it, a cache of weapons have been destroyed, an Iranian involvement of IEDs uncovered and the IRA shipment still being tracked, with a possible Muslim involvement. Perhaps you'd enlighten me as to the so called loose ends."

Crawford's voice went shriller.

"Remember who you're talking to, Trooper. I am your superior officer and don't you forget it." he snapped.

Danny chuckled.

"Crawford, you're not my superior officer. You're just a bloody civilian that we humor by addressing you as Colonel. Now having said that, what loose ends are you talking about?"

There was silence for a moment and then Crawford continued his voice tight with anger.

"Yes, loose ends Quigley. Paddy was found alive but badly burned and his sister, as you know was tucked up in her bed."

"So, what did you want me to do?"

He was finished with calling the man Sir at that stage.

"You should have shoved them both down that tunnel in the barn and then thrown the grenades down. Save us all a lot of trouble. Now we have two IRA people going to prison who will be telling others how we operate, that our operatives can stand up to repeated stun gun treatment, that we use truck drivers to infiltrate them. We can't use that one again, Quigley."

Danny shook his head in disbelief. He had switched to speaker- phone and Scotty was making obscene signs at it.

He cut in abruptly.

"I can't believe what I'm hearing. I'm really sorry you weren't there to choreograph everything while I was hanging in handcuffs from a pipe in that farmhouse. Now you tell me I should have killed civilians so as to protect some of your operational secrets, and one of them a woman at that! Perhaps you'd like to give me that in writing! Anyway, you're always lecturing us on using appropriate force Crawford and that's precisely what we did."

Danny held the phone away from his ear as Crawford went into a long tirade about insubordination and made a face at Scotty who rolled his eyes. He then became aware that another voice was on the phone and realized that it was Patton.

"Hey Danny, take it easy man. Colonel Crawford just stormed out of here. Your career could be on the line right now. He's threatening to report you to the regiment and have you put on charge. You've both done a magnificent job here so why screw it up right now."

Danny spat the words out.

"Yeah sure. That bastard gets all the credit and probably gets another pay raise for unraveling this little mess, and he threatens me with a charge because I didn't kill civilians. Come on, he's the ego maniac who should be put on charge not me ... criminal charges at that!"

Danny took a moment to calm down and then updated Patton on events at the quarry. He'd known that MI5 were following the truck from the ferry in two vehicles. One to monitor the transfer of the cargo and follow it. The other to track Scotty and Danny, if were taken elsewhere, and render assistance. Because of a punctured tire they only had one car available at the transfer point so they decided to follow the IRA cargo on Crawford's instructions and leave Scotty and Danny, hopefully, to extricate themselves.

A good job we weren't relying on MI5 Danny thought.

Aloud he said.

"Crawford should be pleased. We left no loose ends here. Two dead."

They were instructed to clean up the truck and take it back to Brennan's and leave the BMW with the two dead men in it. Hopefully it wouldn't be discovered for some time and give MI5 a chance to roll up the Bradford Muslims. The local police were being left out of the loop for the moment on the incident but they would quietly be briefed at a later date

End of mission as far as they were concerned.

Their opposite numbers the SBS, the Special Boat Squadron stationed in Poole, Dorset, would be taking over the shadowing of the incoming Iranian boat and the fishing trawler.

Danny and Scotty cleaned up the site as instructed. The cab, where Liam had died, was a mess and took some time to sanitize. Within the hour they were speeding down the M6 and later the M1. A few hours later they pulled off at the Newport Pagnell service station and ordered a massive regiment style breakfast which restored their normal good mood before the run down to Brennans Trucking in Luton.

The following day they read in the national papers of a back street garage in Bradford that blew up killing six people - suspected terrorists, according to police. The MI5 surprise package had apparently been activated.

Ten days later, they read of an unfortunate incident on the high seas. An Iranian fishing boat in international waters had disappeared without trace. Cause of accident unknown. A message had been sent back to Iran.

They heard later that MI5 had arranged for the Irish special branch to scoop up a number of dissident IRA members returning to Glenties in the fishing boat

No charge was laid against Danny back at the regiment. It was either never lodged or the regiment just threw it in the waste basket which was more the style of the unit.

CHAPTER 49

Sligo

The bread van arrived promptly at 5am the following morning and backed up into the open garage as if readying to pull away again. The driver got out and went around the back of the van opening one of the doors and reached inside. He then re-emerged a moment later carrying two loaves and walked over and up onto the porch placing them carefully and quietly into the bread tin by the door. At that moment Danny slipped in the back door of the van, from the garage and the bread-man closed it behind him a second later. Danny discovered that the van was completely empty with no side windows, and he lay flat on an old mattress, which had been placed on the floor for that purpose. The van driver climbed in and slowly pulled back onto the road. Danny relaxed as much as possible, given the cramped conditions, and his military training kicked in. Waiting in cramped and difficult conditions was a byproduct of being in Special Forces. The van driver never spoke and drove steadily for nearly two hours. At last, the vehicle stopped and the rear door was thrown open. He emerged stiffly and nodded to the red headed, blocky driver, who grinned at him, jumped back into the van and took off. Danny glanced over at what obviously was a small airfield, with a half dozen small planes on the ground and a wind-stock fluttering in the early morning breeze.

He was expected.

A tall slim young man, with a distinctive drooping mustache walked over to him with a bright smile and an extended hand.

"Ah, Mr. Courtney? Steven Murray, your pilot. Great to see you and delighted that you want to look over our delivery operation to the UK. The plane is already loaded and I've got my flight plan sorted. Weather pattern looks good so it should prove a pleasant flight."

Danny found himself taking an instant liking to the pilot, who Courtney had informed him, was the owner of a flourishing mushroom business, that marketed into the UK on a twice-weekly trip from Knock airport. Today they were flying to Bournemouth on the south coast of the UK. As they later strolled out on to the tarmac, the pilot leaned forward and quietly said,

"You don't look remotely like Courtney without that distinctive pony tail, but just in case anyone is curious around here, I took off with a Mr. Courtney this morning." Danny grinned, feeling himself relaxing in the quiet confident demeanor of the man.

"Take more than a pony tail, Steven, to fill that man's shoes," he said fervently.

"Amen to that," he replied with equal fervor. "I may fill you in on our history, C.C. and myself, when we get off the ground."

A small twin-engine Cecina stood ready for them, and Danny was amazed when he looked inside and saw the number of mushroom cases stacked in the back. He whistled in appreciation.

"Are you sure this thing will get off the ground?" he asked, more by way of making conversation than any concern he might have.

The SAS had a good familiarization with small planes, their capacity for carrying loads, and their ability to take off and land on small pieces of real estate.

Steven flicked his gaze sideways at him, as if assessing his size and weight.

"Oh, getting off the ground isn't the problem. This baby can carry a thousand pounds and two passengers, no problem. It's the landing that might be the difficult bit. If it's a choice of getting my mushrooms down in good condition or yourself, be warned, I might just have to offload you to get the weight down," he teased.

Danny had previous experience with the craft and knew how tough a workhorse it could be. At one time he and a ten-man patrol had borrowed one from a drug lord and crammed into it, clinging to the sides like beetles, to get back over the border into Belize when their extraction plan had failed to materialize.

Danny dashed inside to use the toilet and on emerging, Steven went through his pre-flight plan, and shortly they were soaring over the Mayo countryside. Danny sat beside Steven in the two-man cockpit, enjoying the unique experience of being up in a small plane again. Reaching their pre-arranged height, Steven leveled off and sat back with a sigh of satisfaction. He glanced across at Danny.

"Do you have a name then? I can't keep calling you Mr. Courtney when I know darn well you're not."

"It's Danny," he replied, "and thanks for the helping hand by the way. Can I ask how you know our mutual friend?"

"I was fishing up the Moy river three years ago, during the mayfly season and bumped into him. We got to talking, as people do, but somehow at a deeper level. You know how he is."

"I certainly do. I know exactly what you mean," Danny responded.

"Well, the long and the short of it was that I unloaded on him. My Dad had died of a stroke and I had to take over the mushroom business at short notice. The problem was that every time I got some money together I gambled it away. I was only out fishing to clear my head before declaring bankruptcy, though a second option was looking more attractive - topping myself."

Danny's head jerked around.

"God, that was a pretty final solution, wasn't it?"

Steven shrugged.

"The whole thing was very messy. I'd borrowed from my mother to the extent that she had to get a job making up beds in a hotel, and her with her arthritis! My girl friend left me, and every time I went up in my plane I had to restrain myself from just flying straight into a mountain."

He lapsed into a lengthy silence, which Danny didn't attempt to break. Steven finally snapped his fingers.

"C.C. sorted it all out for me, just like that."

"How on earth did he do that?"

"How exactly? Well for starters, he came down and spent three days looking over the business. Pointed out a few things to me - well, many things really. I didn't have a business plan or specific personal life goals for starters. It was obvious how ridiculous that was for a pilot who has to file a flight plan before take off, and carry out certain specific checks along the way. I didn't really know what I wanted to achieve in life, so that's where we started. Then we linked it into measurable and achievable business goals. It made sense to my logical mindset. If you want to enjoy X in your personal life, then you have to achieve Y in your business goals to underpin it. C.C. worked out some personal development goals for me as well. I started doing an MBA course at Galway University two days a week."

He paused momentarily, as if reflecting on some of the details. Then Danny's curiosity got the better of him.

"What about the rest of it, the gambling and the near bankruptcy?" he asked.

"The rest of it? Yes, there was more, much more. C.C. financed me for a year, and part of the deal was that he spent one day a month on site, nailing me down on the written plan. It was all about focus he kept hammering at me - having clearly defined outcomes with specific tactics and steps to drive the business forward consistently. Oh, he was flexible enough to adjust the plan here and there where it wasn't being effective, but it reminded me of the moves you make when training a new pilot. Gradually letting the trainee take over. Building up their confidence and so on. I was raring to do a solo with the business but he insisted on coming down one day a month to monitor progress, and especially as I saw later, to get good habits embedded in me. I paid him back inside the first year, well, the money side of it. The rest is something I shall never be able to pay back." He looked at Danny, "though, in a small way, helping you may be a start," he finished thoughtfully.

"Yes, C.C. is quite a guy, that's for sure," said Danny.

"He sure is, which is why I'm flying you without question today, even though I suspect something is not quite kosher. Would I be right?"

Danny considered the invitation to share with Steven, and wondered how much to impart at this time.

"In one sense you might be right, but suffice it to say that my family are in extreme danger, and I have to slip into the UK unnoticed by the authorities and get them out. You'll hopefully be meeting them on the way back, Steven , if all goes well. Now, I'm still curious as to how C.C. helped you with the gambling and the rest of the mess you were in."

Steven made a voice check-in with Dublin flight control, and then pursed his lips thoughtfully, considering Danny's question.

"The gambling? Yes, he did help me. He used some techniques to change my behavior. Relaxed me down and talked me through a scenario where I discovered what triggered off the gambling. In my case it was always after I'd had a skinful of Guinness – at least six pints! C.C. installed in my unconscious, a built in alarm that sounded after four pints, and stopped me cold. He got me to visualize, hear and feel all the pain I'd caused to mother, myself and others who had placed their trust in me: my girl-friend, the bank manager and so on. At the end of the exercise when the pain of this was at its most intense, he had me anchor it or install it, as he called it. That means he had me squeeze my ear lobe with my fingers, and this embedded the trigger, as he called it. He made me run through it a few more times, visualize the pain, see it, feel it, relive the whole mess I'd made of my life and, when it was at its most intense, squeeze my ear lobe and anchor it. So Danny, here's how it worked. Sounds crazy, I know, talking quite objectively like this. When I was tempted to have a fifth pint, I hit the anchor point, in this case the ear lobe, and all that pain came flooding back in spades. You wouldn't believe it! As I said, it sounds off the wall but you know what? It worked!"

Danny nodded.

"Normally I'd be skeptical, but I've heard other incredible stories about CC and he did some work with me too. I'm a believer at this stage, Steven. By the way, did it work -stop the gambling I mean?"

"You better believe it Danny, and how! I've actually cut down on my drinking as well. Two pints is my maximum now, but that's just common sense, what with the tougher impaired drinking laws, and the fact that I need my drivers license to operate my business."

Danny looked suitably impressed.

"Look, could we just switch back to the business again? Did C.C. do any further work with you on this? I know he's a great systems man for example," he probed.

Steven nodded.

"Well spotted. In fact the internal changes he recommended, while fairly simple, actually revolutionized the business. First, he asked me what I liked doing, and what I was particularly good at. Well that was easy. I was good at dealing with people and promoting the business. I hated doing the admin, chasing up creditors, keeping the books straight for the tax man, and the actual day to day production of the mushroom crop."

He laughed. "You might be wondering why I'm in business at all, with all those deficiencies. Anyway, C.C. brought in two new people to take over those areas, and worked out a schedule that had me focusing on income-generating activities. It was a difficult time for me and the new staff, because I was used to sticking my nose into all aspects of the business, but C.C. was ruthless. He kept slapping my wrist and encouraged my staff to do the same, until we were all pulling in one direction. And you know what?"

He glanced across at Danny.

"No, what?"

"One day the business took off. Just like that!" He snapped his fingers. "I could almost put my finger on the time and date it happened. The only way I can explain is that it is as if we were clunking along on a bicycle where the wheels were misshaped and angled, and not a nice round circle, as they should be. Then one day a miracle happened and we were moving smoothly along like a beautifully well-oiled machine - having the time of our lives. Literally! I seemed to have lots of free time, and started making progress at my MBA and going to the gym three times a week, getting, what C.C. called, a balance, back into my life. And oh, the girl friend came back too."

A cheesy grin crept across his features.

"So, everything was rosy in the garden after that?" enquired Danny.

Steven groaned, throwing his hands in the air.

"If only! If only."

"So there's more to the story then," he prompted.

Steven nodded.

"As far as the day-to-day running of the business was concerned, all was hunky dory. I was learning more about business methodology through doing my MBA anyway, and that was great. C.C. stopped his monthly visits and everything was booming. I actually couldn't handle the volume in the end. I was approached by a business man from Hong Kong, an Englishman who had bailed out after the Chinese takeover, and set up a UK business in exporting. He was interested in starting a new company and expanding into Europe and some of the new EU countries with a viable product such as ours. He proposed floating the company on the stock market in two or three years, which would have made me an instant millionaire. I was made up, Danny. Imagine the sort of success I had never even dreamed of, right at my finger tips!"

"So what happened?" Danny asked, his interest piqued.

"Well, I had already paid off C.C., but out of curiosity, I asked him to meet the Hong Kong businessman in the UK, and I flew over for the meeting. At the end of it C.C. told me not to touch this guy with a barge pole!"

"He told you to turn down being a millionaire?" Danny exclaimed, surprised at the turn of events.

Steven made a face.

"Oh he told some gibberish about the man's words not being congruent with his body language, and also that he discerned something dark in the man. He didn't trust him and he didn't explain his reasons any more than that. Now Danny, that was as close as I ever got to telling C.C. to go fly a kite. People kept telling me how odd he was anyway, which didn't help. There I was, that close!"

He raised his two hands, holding them two inches apart.

"That close to becoming a bloody millionaire, and he didn't like his body language! Can you believe it?"

Danny's face reflected his amazement.

"So, what did you do?" he asked.

"Well, C.C.'s last words were to spend a few Euros checking the guy out before jumping into bed with him. So, just to prove him wrong, that's what I did."

"And?"

"Got an investigator to check with his former business partners, previous business dealings and tax history etc., and you know what? The guy turned out to be a real can of worms. He'd left a shell of bankrupt companies behind him. His landlord had him in court for non-payment of rent, and the taxman was preparing a major case against him. A check with the police suggested some murky Chinese criminal connection as well. All it cost me was buttons to check it out. I can't believe how stupid I'd nearly been. That guy would have torn the guts out of the company and finished me as a legitimate businessman in Ireland and the UK."

He paused, shaking his head in wonder.

Danny smiled in sympathy.

"Hey, I can understand your eagerness to get into that league. A millionaire at your tender age, heck, I'd be slavering over the chance too Steven. So anyway, what did you do after that discovery?"

"I took a few days off and went cruising on the Shannon. Took my accountant and my staff, which, by then, totaled six. We had a beautiful few days and spent one whole day discussing the future of the business. We made some major decisions right then. I brought in a bonus scheme that essentially made them all stakeholders in the company. We had been shipping mushrooms to the UK by truck and we decided to invest in a plane with a good haulage capability. I already had a pilot's license anyway. The new plan was to fly the crop over, essentially supplying a much fresher product. We contracted a distribution company, which took over deliveries, invoicing, and servicing the UK market, with myself still maintaining the contacts, promotion and expansion opportunities. My accountant had a brother-in-law who was a German national with European contacts, and we formed a new company to develop the European market."

"Wow," Danny breathed in awe. "What did C.C. say to all that?" he asked.

"He just smiled. Said everyone has the resources within them to get their life on track and work on purpose … the purpose we are all here for, which, he maintains, should be in harmony with ones fundamental beliefs and values. You know, every time I speak to C.C. I realize I'm a work in progress. Do you ever get that feeling, Danny?"

"All the time, Steven. All the time." Danny said with feeling.

They chatted together in that vein as the flight progressed across Eire and the Irish Sea. Reading between the lines, Danny saw that Steven was now an extremely successful businessman in his own right, who could have afforded his own flight crew, but who preferred to keep his finger on the pulse.

As Steven acknowledged UK flight control, he pulled out a map and spread it out before them.

"Now Danny. You need to listen carefully to what C.C. and I have laid on. It all hinges on you adhering to a specific time schedule, because I have absolutely no room to maneuver. Here's the plan then. Just past Bristol Airport, we still keep heading south towards Bournemouth, but I cut back north again, very quickly, staying low, and come into an old 2nd World War airport called Yatesbury. Small planes, microlights and gliders use it infrequently, but it opens at 8am daily and closes at 8pm. It's near a town called Avebury which has a bunch of ancient stones like Stonehenge, and I'm just mentioning this for map reference purposes. The reason I'm switching around the plane and coming in from the south is that RAF Lyneham is close by and I want to slip under their radar. If I keep under 500 feet I should be OK. I'm dropping you in now because it's only 7am and hopefully nobody is about yet. If there is and they quiz me, I can say I had concerns about a rough motor and decided to land and check it. The same applies when I pick you up at 9pm tonight. No one should be around. Now, when I drop you down this morning, you jump out and I take off immediately. I have to stress that this evening, you have to be here ready and waiting, and in plain view. If you're not, when I fly over at 9pm precisely, I'm afraid you're on your own Danny. Bear in mind that I fly into the UK quite frequently on business, and if they catch even a whiff of unusual landings, they will come down on me like a ton of bricks. That means that every cargo I fly in will be turned over, and any co-operation I have with British Customs will be suspended. You can imagine the effect that would have on my business," he emphasized.

Danny grimaced.

"I hear you, Steven, and I hate to think what you're putting at risk here. I really appreciate it. Thanks a lot."

Steven smiled softening his tone.

"I realize that you have a sensitive situation you're trying to deal with. As you know, I'm only doing this because I owe Courtney, otherwise I wouldn't touch it with a barge pole. The Brits are a decent lot and have treated me fair and square, and I don't want to screw that relationship up. I'm sure you can understand that."

He paused momentarily as he juggled with the map.

"Here's Avebury. It attracts a lot of tourists. Now, C.C. has arranged, as he's told you, for someone from the Swindon branch of his company, to leave a car at the gates of the airport, beside a memorial stone to the Royal Flying Corps and the Royal Air Force, with the keys under the mat. When you get back in the evening, just leave it as you found it."

He started to outline the area on the map, but Danny told him he was familiar with it. He was, because the SAS flew out of RAF Lyneham on a number of training assignments and missions. Courtney had also told him that the car had a disabled badge if he had to stop briefly in a no parking zone, because Bath was apparently bad for parking. Steven produced a mobile phone and handed it to him.

"I gather from C.C. that this is a dicey task for you. If you're not here this evening, obviously something's gone wrong. Now here's my UK mobile phone number and, as you can see, it's taped to the phone in case you need to contact me and advise me that the pick up is off. At least that will save me the detour. Call me anyway though if everything is on track for pick up. Destroy that number afterwards and also, if things go wrong for you in any way. I can't afford to have anything traced back to me. Okay with that?"

Before Danny could answer, Steven glanced downwards.

"Oops, almost missed with the talking. See those rings of stone down there? Those few buildings beside them are the center of Avebury, and the pub there is the Red Lion. It's worth a visit if you have time on your hands tonight, waiting for me to fly in. The pub has a deep well inside in the middle of the floor which goes down hundreds of feet. There's a story that someone fell or was thrown down it some hundred years ago. Just some useless information really."

He glanced at Danny.

"I'm sure you're in no mood for tourist points of interest right now, but anyway, for what it's worth. Get ready to jump out as soon as I've stopped, and Danny ..."

He looked directly at him.

"Good luck. See you at 9 pm."

CHAPTER 50

Danny was out on the grassy field even before the plane stopped and couldn't see anyone around the small huts, from where they obviously managed the recreational flights. He dashed across the field towards the gate as Steven winged back up into the sky. A tan, 3-year-old, Mazda was sitting outside the gates and he jumped inside. A hand clamped on his shoulder and he turned, looking into the grinning face of his mate Scotty who he had telephoned the night before. They hadn't been together since Danny got out of the Services over six months ago. Scotty brought him up to date on things in the regiment where he was now involved in the selection and training of new recruits. He was in superb condition with all the tough mountain work in the Welsh Brecon Beacons.

"Hell, we miss you Danny," he said quietly. "Mind you, switching me over to the new role was great for me. It helped me re-adjust from operating with the troop and having you in support."

Danny looked across at him as he drove the car along the A4 to Bath.

"No trouble getting time off today?" he enquired.

"Fortunately, we're in between groups right now, so it wasn't a problem. I would have come anyway, and so would some of the lads if it came right down to you being in trouble. Anyway, fill me in on the situation you're facing today."

Danny brought him up to date on the events that resulted in him heading off to Ireland, and his subsequent snatching from outside the hotel in Rosses Point. When it came to being run across the border, and the realization that Colonel Crawford was the instigator of all his problems, Scotty whistled.

"Oh man. Now there's a bad apple for you. What I can't believe is how the guy lasted so long, the way he weaves his dirty games. Next time I get him in my sights, he's a goner for what he's done to you and your family. Is he for real? Asking a civilian to assassinate Gerry Adams, and hoping to keep a lid on it. He's a right nut case for sure."

He shook his head in disbelief.

They drove along in silence until they came to the first open café where they went inside and ordered breakfast. Danny had bought a newspaper to see if there was any coverage of the London murders, but was pleased to see that there wasn't a mention. He had made an attempt to disguise his appearance with a pair of plain glasses and a peaked hat, to avoid any possible recognition. He needn't have worried. The few sleepy travelers were too buried in the newspaper headlines and the page three girls to notice.

Finishing their breakfast, they ordered a second pot of tea and waited until it had arrived and the waitress had cleared off the table.

"Okay. Let's have the plan Danny."

Danny had wondered if he should tell Scotty about his experiences in Sligo, and his new views on violence. He decided not to as it wouldn't exactly reassure Scotty at this stage, getting ready to go into action. He personally drew some confidence, however, from his reactions to Mullaghmore, when he was able, despite his reconditioning, to expedite the situation using his skills. Strangely, he felt that his detached clinical mind-set, his lack of hatred, had made him even more effective in combat situations. Almost as if evil itself had become the enemy and he was justified in opposing it with every fiber of his being and every tool at his disposal. Perhaps he was just rationalizing the expectation that he would shortly be called upon to inflict some physical damage on Crawford and his team.

Danny had activated his usual method of contacting Fiona the previous night, and he had outlined the plan to her on her proposed movements for the following day. Apparently, Fiona's mother was taking Allison and a neighbor's girl swimming around 11:00 am. Scotty was to follow Allison to the swimming pool, in the Mazda, keeping well back and trying to spot the surveillance team. He was to keep her under a loose watch, without giving his presence away. After swimming, her mother was taking the two girls to McDonalds.

Danny was going to lie low in town until Fiona took her car into town around 2:30 pm, with watchers in tow. She would park in an indoor parking lot, leaving the keys and parking ticket under the seat, and then go directly into the shopping plaza. As soon as Fiona departed from the parking lot, with her followers in tow, Danny was going to check out the car for bugs. Then he would drive the car out and go to the side entrance of a charity shop in the shopping plaza, and wait for Fiona.

She would take a casual ten minute stroll to relax her watchers, and enter the charity shop. She knew from experience, that the side door was always open during the day, for people to drop off donated items. Inside, and momentarily out of sight of the watchers, she would dash out the back door and join Danny at exactly 3:00 pm. They would just take off to a pre-arranged spot and wait for Scotty.

Scotty, meanwhile, in the borrowed Mazda, was to wait outside McDonalds for Allison just prior to 3:00 pm. Fiona's mother had been instructed to keep an eye on her time and exactly three minutes to three, instruct Allison to go to the washroom with her swimming bag. Once inside she had to change her appearance quickly with fresh clothes and a hat. Then she had to slip out the side door where Scotty who was known to her, would whip her away.

The previous evening, after Danny's phone call, Fiona's mother had been fully briefed and agreed to help. Once Allison was gone from McDonalds, Fiona's mother would wait for approximately ten minutes and then drive on home. If questioned by the followers, she would say that Allison had gone off to meet her mother somewhere, as pre-arranged, and plead ignorance if she was quizzed further. Scotty would then proceed to a pre-arranged spot on a specific exit road from Bath, where Danny and Fiona would meet up with them and swap cars.

The plan was for Danny and his family to head for the town of Swindon in the car, and spend a few hours there going to a movie and having a quiet meal before proceeding on a short trip south to Avebury for the pick up. They would leave the Mazda there. Scotty would abandon Fiona's car in some nearby estate and Fiona's mum would report it stolen the following day. He would then stroll back into Bath and take a bus to Bristol where a mate would come and collect him, the same one who had dropped him at the Yatesbury airport that very morning.

After outlining the plan, Scotty quizzed him at length on other possible obstacles that could arise. He didn't like following Allison in Danny's escape car, which might be spotted by the followers, and might even be bugged by the watchers if Scotty had to leave the vehicle for any reason. They discussed the pros and cons in typical SAS fashion, and finally agreed that Scotty would go straight to McDonalds around the time of the pick up, instead of taking the risk of being spotted at the swimming pool. Scotty also suggested another change.

"Why not keep her home and stop her from going swimming altogether?"

Danny disagreed suggesting that it split the watchers and made for looser coverage on them. Also the home address was a difficult place to shed her followers. Other aspects of the plan were discussed and dissected. Did MI5 have a big enough team to keep a watch on the main escape roads to avoid his family making a run for it? Would they use the local police to beef up their surveillance? They must know from Fiona's trips out to a public phone booth that Danny was in touch with her. Scotty wondered if they might have the resources to bug those public phone booths as well.

Danny shook his head at that.

"No, I used a new telephone booth last night, so it's unlikely they know of the plan."

They both realized that the timing of both Fiona and Allison was the weakest part of the plan. Both of them had to disappear at exactly 3:00 pm for it to work. If Fiona came out sooner than 3:00 pm and escaped, the watchers would immediately warn Allison's team to be on the alert. Equally if Allison made her run too early, Fiona's team would be alerted and they would close up on her. Allison's disguise might not hold up either when she tried to slip out of McDonalds. Scotty might have to run interference if she was accosted as she left the burger establishment.

"Just how much can I hurt those guys?" he asked. "After all I'm part of the establishment here in the UK, most of the time on their team, though like MI5 I have no powers of arrest. I don't want to crap on my own doorstep here. Know what I'm saying, Danny?"

"Look, these guys are mavericks working outside the loop. They've murdered people already. One as you know, was a woman that they burnt to death in her bed. Personally, I'd have no mercy on them, but then it's my family we're talking about here. Yes, this might just lead back to you if you're not careful. These guys are no slouches at this. They might just check back at the regiment to see who are missing today, and that could lead back to you. It's possible, but highly unlikely that some of them might even recognize you. Like me, you've worked for them before. So yes, there could be consequences, but I somehow feel that MI5 are trying to keep this whole thing under the establishment radar, and that means the local police too."

Scotty shrugged.

"So I hurt them but not kill them if I can help it. And if I can change my appearance, that could be a factor in not being recognized or traced back to the unit. Actually, I'm now going to call my sergeant at the regiment, and he'll swear that I never left the lines today."

They kicked the plan around further until satisfied that they had looked at all possible scenarios for the escape, and gave each other a high five. Then came the difficult part. Waiting for the action to start.

CHAPTER 51

Bath
The escape

It was Scotty who screwed up. Danny's part of the plan worked like clockwork. Fiona hustled out of the side entrance of the charity shop, jumped into her car driven by Danny. He tore off up the street and around the corner while the watcher inside was impatiently trying to catch glimpses of her inside the charity shop. It was a clean getaway and spot on 3:00 pm. Allison was on time too but when she walked hurriedly to Scotty's car, one man jumped out of a car parked three cars behind his and started moving fast up the sidewalk towards her. Then a second got out and stood there uncertainly.

"Excuse me miss," one shouted, hurrying faster.

Allison glanced back at them in fear and then opened the car door and froze.

"Get in Allison, quick!" Scotty shouted.

Allison knew Scotty from previous trips home with her Dad but the man sitting behind the wheel and shouting at her wasn't at all like him. That's because Scotty, at the last minute, in his effort to avoid being recognized, had purchased a chunky wig, and Allison hadn't been alerted to this. In the rear view mirror he saw the second man start to run towards them.

"It's me Allison, Scotty, I'm wearing a wig. Get in for God's sake."

Dawning awareness flitted across her face and she started to lift her right leg to get in but Scotty saw it was too late. The first of the two men had reached her and caught her by the arm. Scotty leapt out of the car, jumped up on the hood and leaped from there straight at the man holding Allison. Still in mid air, he directed a powerful kick at the man's face sending him sprawling. Scotty tumbled to the sidewalk with him. Rolling to his feet he was aware of two things simultaneously. The first man was lying dazed while the second man's footsteps were almost on top of him and his hand was withdrawing a pistol from a shoulder holster and shouting at him to stay down. Fortunately, for the gunman, when Scotty threw the knife, he threw it in such a way that the solid handle struck his forehead, instead of the eight inches of steel. He collapsed like a felled ox on the footpath, not six feet away. Scotty hadn't stopped moving since exploding from the car. Now in one continuous motion he thrust Allison in, slammed the door, casually kicked the groaning man in the head, knocking him cold, and just as quickly reached down and grabbed his knife and the second man's pistol, which was lying on the ground. Then, he leapt back in the car and streaked off, Allison sobbing beside him.

During the 20 seconds, while this action was going on, a number of pedestrians had stood mesmerized and now tentatively started to approach the fallen men.

Twenty minutes later after an impatient Scotty had bore his way through the typical slow Bath city traffic, he pulled into the pre-arranged meeting place, on the east side of the city, where Danny and Fiona were waiting anxiously. Both men and Fiona jumped out of the cars while Allison, still crying, rushed over to her mother.

Scotty threw his hands in the air.

"The Mazda is blown, Danny. They were watching the side entrance to McDonalds."

"How many?" he demanded anxiously.

"Two. I had to take them down."

"Dead?" Danny peered at him anxiously.

Scotty shook his head.

"No, but out cold when I took off. I took the gun one was going for with me just in case."

He passed the weapon to him. Danny breathed out in relief, his eyes alert as he measured the odds against them completing the plan.

"One good thing though," Scotty added.

"Christ we need something right now, Scotty. What is it?"

"I smeared some mud over the car number plates before I met with Allison, so they couldn't do a make on them - the civvies too, for that matter, who saw the incident. The tan Mazda would have registered with them for sure, though."

Danny breathed in deeply, his mind working.

"Okay, here's what we do. We put the Mazda plates on Fiona's car, which they know anyway, but there's a lot of this make on the road so the new plates might get us through. You take the Mazda without plates and abandon it in the nearest housing estate that you find off this road. Dump your wig and stroll back into town and get the first bus out in any direction. Also, if you have time, phone this number in Swindon. It belongs to the guy who loaned us the Mazda. Tell him to report it missing right away."

Scotty nodded.

"What about you lot, Danny. Can you still make your flight tonight? MI5 can cast a wide net as you know."

He thought about it for a moment, then nodded.

"I have to forget my side trip to Swindon. I'm now heading straight up the A4 to Chippenham and through Calne to Avebury and waiting it out there. When I get there, I'll take the plates off and that will keep that poor bugger in Swindon out of it. Then I'll stick the car out of sight somewhere. Who knows, when this all blows over, we may even get it back. You know, we may still have the jump on them and I still believe Crawford's people will keep the police out of it. Yeah we'll make it okay. Let's do it Scotty!"

Scotty fortunately had a small knife and tool set in his jacket. They removed the Mazda plates and placed them on

Fiona's car. Danny threw Fiona's old plates in the boot of her car, then embraced Scotty.

"Hey, thanks mate," he said looking steadily at him.

Scotty shrugged, saying nothing. Danny then gestured to Fiona and Allison and they all jumped in the car and took off.

Scotty coolly motored up the road a few hundred yards, then turned left into a poor housing estate, pulling the wig off as he drove. He proceeded further back into the estate and stopped on a road where other dilapidated looking cars were parked. He just left the Mazda there after wiping it down carefully for prints. He didn't think the car would last too long before it was nicked by joy riders and totally wrecked. Pulling on a peaked cap, he strolled back out on the main road again, dumping the wig in a garbage bin as he did so. Almost immediately, he actually managed to catch a local bus going into the bus center. There, having made a phone call to the Mazda owner in Swindon, and to his mate in Hereford, home of the SAS, he managed to catch a bus for Bristol. Within thirty minutes of arriving he was picked up by his SAS mate. He figured he'd got away with it. However, his thoughts were with Danny and his family as they sought to elude the wily Crawford, with his massive MI5 tentacles and resources at his disposal. It was going to be a long day for them.

CHAPTER 52

Avebury

Allison wouldn't stop sniffling on the run along the A4 towards their destination.

"It's all my fault Daddy," she wailed. "If I hadn't hesitated and just got in the car, Scotty wouldn't have had to fight those men back there."

Danny could see her tear streaked face in the rear view mirror. He reached back and took Allison's hand in his.

"Hey, it's okay sweetheart. It wasn't your fault that you didn't know Scotty was going to be wearing a wig. Hell, even I didn't know. Tell you the truth, Allison, I wouldn't have got in any car with a chap looking like him."

Fiona smiled at his attempt at humor.

"He's right Allison. It certainly wasn't your fault. You did everything according to the plan. You changed your clothes and made your way out to the car as arranged. Those guys were pros so they'd probably studied your walk since they started watching you. That's always a dead giveaway and something like that is hard to change without lots of rehearsal and practice. To be honest we didn't think the bad guys would be watching the other entrance at MacDonalds as well. Hey, we're proud of you, aren't we Danny?"

He squeezed Allison's hand as he negotiated the road carefully. "Absolutely. Chip off the old block, Allison."

He smiled at her in the mirror, seeing that she had stopped sniffling and was somewhat mollified.

"Did Scotty kill those men Daddy?" she asked.

He glanced at her again.

"No of course not. He only knocked them out. One of them was taking out a gun so he had to act pretty quickly. We three wouldn't be together right now if he hadn't done what he had to do. No, those two men will be awake already but with sore heads, I suspect, for the rest of the day."

Fiona looked across at him and he could see that she had many more questions to ask him but couldn't with Allison present, who then sat back then looking at the countryside. Danny let go of her hand and let his hand rest on Fiona's. She grabbed it and squeezed tight. He could feel the tension in it.

Once they got to Avebury, they followed a stream of tourist cars and parked on a gravel road among some trees. A sign stated that the gate onto the site closed at 9pm, so he would have to re-consider the parking situation later. The first thing they did was to go across to the Red Lion for a meal. The pub had been mentioned by Steven the pilot and Allison took a great interest in the hole going down through the floor. A waitress, with a gleam in her eye and probably a large tip in mind, told her of some fabled stories, of people who ended up down there over the centuries because of the landlord's displeasure.

The Lancashire hot pot was what she recommended, so Danny and Fiona went for that, while Allison settled for fish fingers and chips. He was dying for a beer but wanted to keep a clear head, as they were not out of the woods as yet. After a leisurely meal they strolled around Avebury and took time looking at and examining what it had to offer. The giant Stonehenge-like stones, were the main attraction for tourists. Allison liked standing with her back to the largest ones while Fiona took her picture. There was a fair on in the afternoon, where they watched falconry, archery and mediaeval jousting. They spent a long time in the museum and historical house, which seemed to pique Allison's curiosity. They had a chance to talk briefly when Allison went to the washroom but all he could do was re-assure Fiona that once safely in Ireland, he would start to fight back, clear his name and get their life back. Courtney had a few ideas on how he could get this started. She wanted to be convinced, but her face reflected her concern and doubts. Impulsively, he hugged her and she clung to him just as Allison came up to them grinning.

"Hey, you love birds. I leave you for two minutes and look at you," she teased.

They all dissolved into laughter and somehow the tension lightened.

Later Danny made some inquiries in a small shop on a side street, with lots of notices posted up on a notice board. He managed to hire a small garage for a month to store the car. Having the garage was a much better solution than abandoning it, where some locals would eventually report it to the police. He went and got the car, ran it into the garage and locked it up, slipping the key onto his key ring for safe keeping. It had taken only a few moments to switch the legal plates back on Fiona's car and he dumped the Mazda ones in the first rubbish bin he came across in the street.

Coming in from the airport that morning he'd realized that one could walk to Yatesbury in under half an hour, so they started out at 8 pm. Lots of other people were strolling along the road, where on both sides, various formations of the giant stones were standing. The walk was actually enjoyable for all of them and the beautiful evening weather helped. Once they turned the corner off the main road they saw the small airport entrance on the right up ahead. He noted that there were no vehicles parked at the buildings and no activity that he could see. He then took out the mobile phone and dialed the number Steven had taped on it. It was picked up immediately.

"Yes?" It was Steven's voice.

"On track here. The place is already deserted."

"Roger. On track here too. Out," and that was that.

Spot on 9pm the plane glided in, and as it stopped, Danny opened the doors and helped Fiona and Allison climb in and then jumped in beside Steven, who turned the plane around and took off. Not a word was said until he had gained his original height, all the time waiting anxiously for some curious official at flight control to query his unusual flight pattern. Steven breathed a sigh of relief and sat back.

"I think we pulled it off. I was worried someone might just be alert but probably Bristol airport keeps their attention anyway."

Looking around at the two in the back.

"Welcome on board you folks and enjoy your flight. Sorry no in-flight meals, though you both have bottles of water in front of you. Weather looks good, so you can look forward to a smooth flight. Small planes can be a trifle hairy when we have bad weather, so just settle in."

He turned to Danny.

"Well done, Danny. I must confess I was worried all day about you. Even watched the news, though you didn't tell me what's going on. I sensed something more than just slipping your family out. Anyway I still don't want to know. You're here, that's what's important, right?"

Danny nodded numbly, finding it hard to believe that they were actually in mid air and heading back towards the west of Ireland, after expecting the opposition to be hot on their heels. It reminded him of other operations, where he and his team, pumped up with adrenalin, were being extracted from danger zones after protracted action.

Unusual for him, he fell asleep and woke up coming into Knock Airport where an eight passenger van and driver, were waiting for them.

Two hours later they were being greeted by an effusive Siobhan back on the shores of Lough Gill, in Sligo, who had rooms ready for them and a pile of sandwiches. Later exhausted, they all fell asleep to the sounds of waves lapping outside. Danny was almost beginning to feel that he had come home.

CHAPTER 53

Belfast

Colonel Crawford glanced up as his special operatives phone rang and picked it up quickly.

"Yes?" he said briskly.

"Peterson in Bath sir. She's done a runner, both of them."

"How in hell … …?" he started.

"It was a planned extraction sir. Two cars involved - very professional. We nearly caught the girl but our guys got taken out."

Crawford sat back.

"Taken out, how for Christ's sake?"

Peterson sighed.

"I know sir. I don't understand it either - just a small guy too, but he used a knife."

"A knife! Were your people badly hurt?"

"No sir, nothing like that. He just threw the knife so that the handle slammed into one of my guy's forehead and polaxed him. The other got a kick in the face that put him down."

"Hmn …" Crawford mused. "He's got some help from his regiment mates Peterson. That's why they didn't have a chance. Got away light, I'd say, knowing the *sass*. Check with the regiment in Hereford to see who's missing from lines today."

"Yes, sir," said Peterson.

"And Peterson ..."

"Yes sir," he replied.

"Check on a trooper Scotty MacGregor. That knife thing rings a bell. Were the police involved at all?"

"No sir. There were some witnesses to the escape and fight, if you can call it that. My men recovered quite quickly and flashed some badges at the civvies who were fussing around them, and just said it was some criminals they'd try to arrest. Then the lads just bailed out of there. We set up checks on the main roads out of Bath but they were well away by then I suspect. We didn't try to involve the local police as per your instructions."

Crawford was silent for a while as he wrestled with the new set of circumstances. Finally, he stirred.

"Quigley always was formidable and extremely flexible, which is why I wanted him for this little job in Strabane. He's effectively destroyed any lever I had against him. He'll somehow get them out of the UK, probably to the Republic and his new friend there will help hide them away. Contact Josh and his team right away and tell them to ramp up surveillance on Courtney."

"Will do sir," ... he hesitated.

"Well man what is it, speak up."

"Well sir, what if Quigley now tries to contact MI5 direct and informs them of the plan? We'll all be up the creek, especially you sir. After all there's already a ground swell of opinion among the young Turks coming in, for technology to lead the way, not us soldiers on the ground."

Crawford laughed dismissively.

"The Director General knows damn well that it's our people out there gathering information that's protecting her butt in her nice office overlooking the Thames. An MBA from Cambridge won't have any answers to some crazy Muslim who gets on at Waterloo station with a rucksack full of semtex ... Anyway, back to Quigley. I don't underestimate him Peterson, but I doubt that he's ready to contact any authority as yet, what with the murders hanging over his head."

"What about the aftermath of the job in Strabane sir, if it's still on? Quigley could be a problem."

Crawford laughed cynically.

"All taken care of Peterson. I have his executioner all primed. All I have to do is point him in the right direction and Quigley is history - believe me. Now, get on to Hereford right away and call me straight back. Is that understood?"

Crawford hung up and sat there for some minutes. The phone rang again twenty minutes later.

"Peterson here again sir. I checked with Hereford and there were no men missing today."

"What about Quigley's mate Scotty?" Crawford demanded.

"Also there sir. Actually involved in the selection process of new recruits. That's pretty intense stuff, 24/7."

Crawford grunted.

"They're closing ranks Peterson. You'll get nothing further from Hereford. Don't worry, I have a long memory when someone tries to screw with me. We'll catch up with MacGregor at a later date. Now get on to Josh and alert him to the situation."

"Should we not put a watch on the airports and shipping sir? He's got to get his family out somehow. We still might catch them."

Crawford laughed.

"You don't know Quigley as I do Peterson, and as for catching him, just be sure you have more resources than you do right now or you'll be one sorry agent. He's something else. We never should have let him out of the service. I would have offered him something to keep him in. His discharge was done and dusted when I got back from that useless terrorism course I attended at Langley."

They discussed the logistics of moving the Bath team to Sligo if necessary and future reporting procedures. After the call Crawford sat there going over the mission that he'd set up to assassinate Gerry Adams. Ian Paisley's Democratic Unionist Party (DUP), and Gerry Adams were getting far too comfortable since their new power sharing agreement. The timing was now or it would be too late. The British army had already declared their campaign over in Northern Ireland, that they had initiated in 1969 as a short term exercise to contain *the troubles,* and which had lasted 38 years!

There was still time to recover the ball and get the leverage back that he needed in order for Quigley to do the job. Crawford had spent his earlier military career on the edge salvaging various precarious situations from disaster. He'd carried on in that vein when he joined MI5 and took over the Northern Ireland section. But Peterson was right. Quigley could well be the loose cannon that might destabilize the whole plot either before or after it's completion. He had no intention of letting that happen.

CHAPTER 54

Burton on the Water, UK

Patton grimaced as half way through lifting the shovel of cement, his telephone rang inside. At one time, when working for MI5, his life had been dominated by phone calls that came with frequency, either day or night. Usually with some sort of emergency to deal with and too little time. He dropped the shovel back in the wheelbarrow and picked up the outside extension.

"Hello. This better be good," he barked.

He heard a laugh on the other end.

"Still the same old Patton. Retirement hasn't changed you at all, has it?" Patton racked his brains knowing it was a voice from the past. Finally ... "Danny ... Danny Quigley ... well I'll be ... ... Hey, you didn't come to my retirement party. I sent you an invite care of the regiment."

"Well, you know the regiment Patton. They had me on an all expenses tour in Afghanistan climbing some mountains. You know the story."

"Yeah, I heard some of you were over there. How was it?"

"Apart from having to work with the Americans, okay. I didn't appreciate just how good we were until I had to put up with their methods of running operations. Half the time we were in danger of being strafed by their reserve flyers who couldn't differentiate between us and the Taliban. Their

Special Forces are good though. Learned a few tricks from them, and the resources at their beck and call were just mind blowing! Even thought about transferring over at one time but Fiona, my wife, put a stop to that. Anyway, that wasn't why I called."

"So why did you?" Patton asked, suddenly curious.

Normally there was no contact between the SAS and MI5 after operations, apart from the higher ranks who frequented similar circles and found it useful to stay in touch and maintain working relationships.

"It's a long story and I wish I was sitting down with you instead of using the phone, but here goes. Tell me, are you still in touch with the Director General?"

"We haven't talked since my retirement party over a year ago, but that's not unusual. You read the papers, Danny, you know what's going on out there. She has more important things to do than keeping in touch with those who bow out, but yes, I would have access to her if it proved necessary. It would have to be good though," he chuckled. "I wouldn't call her up to fix a parking ticket for me, for example."

Danny laughed too.

"From what I hear, she'd just tell you to hump off anyway. No it's not a parking ticket, you'll be pleased to hear."

Danny briefly filled him in on his getting out of the Forces and the events that followed his joining financial services. Patton was a good listener and let Danny talk, interrupting once or twice to clarify some point. Danny heard some sharp intakes of breath on the other end as he spelled out his present dilemma and the threat to his freedom and family. There was a silence on the other end, which seemed to go on forever. Then,

"I knew Crawford was prone to cutting corners and was capable of *in your face* aggression when he felt that the end justified the means. I remember you complained to me years ago on that work you did in Northern Ireland, when he wanted you to dispose of witnesses. I didn't agree with a lot of what he did either, but he gets results and that's what counts in this

9/11 world, Danny. The Americans have taken off the kid
gloves as well, as you know. Now that certainly doesn't excuse
him trying to sabotage the policy of the Government for his
own aims by having Gerry Adams killed. That's absolute
madness and if it's true he's gone off the rails completely!"

"Oh, it's true all right. You must have read of the murders
of those three thugs, surely. It was all over the papers and
television."

"Danny, I'm retired now. I thought I'd made a difference
with all my time in the Forces and then MI5. Reading the news
makes me realize that I didn't. It's worse out there now than
ever and hearing the daily deluge of bad news just depresses
me, just as hearing about Crawford and his team saddens me
too. More good men corrupted by the system. You see it in the
regiment too, Danny. How many of your guys top themselves
when the get out?"

"Yeah, I hear what you're saying and I am truly sorry to
trouble you with my problems, but I racked my brains as to
who I could approach on this, to get some advice and try to
regain my life. Crawford isn't finished with me yet. I know too
much. He may still have aspirations of me doing this job and
won't hesitate to grab my family to force me to do so. People
are dying, like poor Glenna, who previously worked in our
office and those thugs, but I'm running out of patience and I'm
getting increasingly frustrated. Hell, I worked on the same side
as these MI5 guys for years and it's hard for me to start
thinking of them like the enemy. I should also mention that
recently I have had occasion to examine my past life, and quite
frankly, I no longer regard violence as the solution to every
problem. Oh, I can still function in the old way when faced
with a dangerous situation, as I found out recently, but I'd
sooner sort this out than go on a vendetta against Crawford and
his team. Hell, I'd probably lose anyway with the scope of the
resources they have at their disposal."

Patton sighed again, gathering his thoughts.

"I think you've just ruined a wheel barrow of cement
Danny, but in a good cause, and I'm glad you came to me. I

have the utmost respect for you and the work you've done for your country, and I mean that. I'm not patronizing you. This should not be happening to good people like yourself and your family. As far as having some sort of change of heart about violence, Danny, that's probably not a bad thing anyway. Violence just feeds on itself. Though if Crawford confronts you with a choice of hanging on to your new sentiments or saving your family, you need to be absolutely clear as to which way you're going to go. He'll not give you a second chance and, as you well know, success or failure can be down to split seconds sometimes."

He paused, aware that Danny was hanging on to every word.

"Now leave it with me and I'll see if I can create a way out of this for you. Where can I contact you, Danny?"

"Why don't I call you back, say tomorrow? How would that be?"

Patton chuckled.

"Ever the cautious one, eh? We trained you well. Okay, you call me tomorrow, and promise me you won't do anything extreme in the meantime, Danny."

"I can't promise anything right now. If they threaten my family again, I won't hold back. I've learned that in the regiment. Give an enemy half a chance and they kill you. However, I won't go looking for trouble if that reassures you any."

"That's good enough for me Danny, and now you better let me go."

Patton hung up and after staring glumly at the load of cement he headed inside.

He sat down and booted up his computer, hit word and quickly typed out an account of the story he'd just heard. About to do an accompanying email and attach it, he hesitated and shaking his head, he switched off the computer and made some rapid phone calls. Eventually, he discovered that Colonel Crawford was at the MI5 office in Belfast. He gathered his thoughts, picked up the phone again and called him.

"Crawford here."

He heard the all too familiar voice at the other end and almost hung up. Crawford beat him to it.

"Patton, I see your number's come up on my screen. To what do I owe the pleasure of a call from a retired gentleman in the Cotswolds?"

Patton's resolve almost faded as all the old memories came back of the operations he'd been involved in and the victories they'd celebrated together. He steeled himself and sat up straighter.

"Colonel Crawford, I don't like having to make this telephone call. We worked successfully together for a number of years and I'm an admirer of your professionalism, or at least I was until I had a call from our now ex-trooper Quigley, who told me an interesting story."

"Ah, Quigley," he breathed. "Surely you didn't believe him?"

"How do you know what he told me Crawford, unless, there's some truth to it?"

"Well, Quigley has become somewhat paranoid since he left the regiment - attacked three men in London and put them in hospital. Then murdered them when the police didn't protect him and his family. Instead of cooperating with the police he upped and ran. Now he's spewing out all sort of claims just to get himself off the hook. Hell, he attacked two of my men in Bath who were merely keeping his family under observation for their own protection. Actually used a knife on one of my men. Lucky he wasn't killed. You know Quigley. He could eat Rambo for breakfast!"

Patton's voice lost it's steeliness and felt his resolve fading away.

"Used a knife? He never said anything about that."

"Why should he? He was pitching you a good story. Anyway what were you planning to do with this rather ridiculous tale if I may ask?"

"Well, I was going to inform the Director General of course. It's an extraordinary story and in my opinion warrants investigation Colonel."

"Hmm ... your call on that one my friend. Tell you what, to help you avoid some considerable embarrassment by crying wolf to the Director General, why don't I come down there and go through the whole thing with you. You know, in the process, perhaps we can help poor Quigley get this straightened out. Mind you, if he murdered those thugs in London, he'll have to face the consequences, but we have our contacts and can put in a good word for him. Smooth the way for him as it were. I could get a plane out of here to Bristol, pull rank to get a seat if I have to and be with you in a few hours. How does that sound? And, by the way, I appreciate your loyalty to young Quigley. Hell, I owe him too. He earned me some brownie points from that Iran incident and I won't forget it."

Patton hesitated. Now that he was finally retired he liked the quiet life and didn't like any hassle. The few hours would give him time to finish cementing the new floor in the greenhouse as well.

"That sounds good to me Colonel and I appreciate your offer to come down here at short notice. What you said about helping young Quigley, I like that. He deserves some help after his record, and the work he's done with us. Okay, I'll keep an eye out for you."

At his end, Crawford breathed a sigh of relief. The whole operation had been in danger of going up the spout and his reputation and career as well. He felt a rage building against Quigley and vowed to make him suffer. Perhaps kill his family in front of his eyes before terminating him. Already he felt better at the thought. He picked up the phone and called Peterson again.

"Where are you?" he asked abruptly.

"On the M4 coming up to Swindon," Peterson answered.

"Okay, here's the deal. Quigley has contacted Patton and told him the story. He was going to call the DG but thankfully decided to check with me first. Perhaps courtesy for times past and so on. Doesn't really matter why, but it saved our bacon. I convinced him to hold on and I would fly down via Bristol and go over the whole thing with him and that perhaps we could, between us help poor Quigley get out of this mess, which is of his own creation."

Peterson whistled.

"That's too close for comfort. Christ, all our careers would be on the scrap heap if that bitch of DG got hold of this. All she needs is an excuse right now and we're history!"

"Exactly. Now I want you to go up to where he's living at Burton on the Water, which I figure is about an hours drive from where you are right now, and take care of him. As you say, Peterson, all our careers are on the line here. Do I make myself clear? Here's the address and precise directions to find the place."

After jotting it down, Peterson tentatively voiced his concerns. "Are you saying what I think you are sir?" he asked.

"I'm not going to spell it out for you over the phone, but a convenient accident would be acceptable. I'm told that English gardens can be very dangerous places. Do I make myself clear?"

"Yes sir. Perfectly, sir. You want us to make sure he never contacts her again - ever."

Once Crawford finished the call Peterson looked at the driver. "Got the gist of that?" he asked.

The driver nodded and yawned.

"Nothing we haven't done before old chap. That's what I like about Crawford. He takes no prisoners."

Peterson reached for the map and started looking for the turn off. Patton was in for the surprise of his life, but then a lot of people died soon after taking retirement. It was almost an occupational hazard, he'd read somewhere. In Patton's case they would just be helping the system along a little.

Burton on the Water was probably one of the most attractive small towns in the Cotswolds and was busy with tourists throughout the year. It had a shallow river running through the center, crossed by many stone bridges. An interesting part of the river was that they played a certain type of football actually in the water, which was unique to the town. It had many other attractions too but all of this passed Peterson and his colleague completely by as they focused on finding Patton's address. It was on the edge of town, a small farm holding, according to Crawford. After a frustrating twenty minute search, they stopped to enquire at a roadside cottage which was against their better judgment. An ancient crone eventually came to the door and peered at them from rheumy eyes, and listened to their query before pointing up the road, they had just come from.

"Third right after the bridge. It's along there," she croaked, then turned and went back into the house.

"Friendly lot around here," he commented, getting back in the vehicle.

His colleague laughed.

"Women aren't your strong point, are they?"

"Just the sort of old bitch who remembers people," grumbled Peterson.

"We can always pay a visit on the way back," his colleague offered.

Peterson dismissed it.

"We don't want any more attention drawn to this area than necessary. If you had your way we'd be starting a fucking crime wave," he said, leaning forward and watching for the turn.

Within a few minutes they were at the cottage, where a highly polished BMW was parked in the driveway.

"Typical Patton," muttered Peterson enviously. "Everything top of the range and always ship shape."

They got no response at the front door and decided to go round the side. Once round the back they heard noises coming from a large greenhouse and eased up to the door. Patton was busy inside, shoveling cement into a new floor he was creating which was marked out with wooden slats.

Some instinct made him look up and it took him a moment for recognition to dawn on him.

"Peterson! What the heck are you doing here? I thought Crawford was coming over?"

"He is indeed, Patton. He is. Got some problem getting a flight out of Belfast and as we were in the area, he asked us to drop in and hold the fort until he gets here."

Patton cocked his head.

"Ah, of course, Bath. Were you the lads Quigley had a go at then?"

Peterson grimaced.

"Well not Quigley himself but one of his mates we suspect."

Patton examined him closely.

" I was told by Crawford that a knife was used. Was that you two?"

Peterson nodded.

"Yeah, Matthews here was on the receiving end."

Patton looked closely at him.

"I thought you were wounded somehow in that attack?" Peterson laughed.

"Silly bugger just got a blow from the knife handle on his forehead. Nothing in there to damage anyway. He was out of it all right. It pole-axed him!"

Patton pursed his lips thoughtfully.

"So it wasn't Quigley, and no one got cut down in Bath. Funny ... Crawford said ..."

Awareness flooded his features as he carefully put the shovel down and moved to go past them.

"Well, why don't we go inside and have a cup of tea while we're waiting," he said quietly as he started towards the door of the garden shed.

Both men glanced at each other, recognizing that something had aroused Patton's suspicions. Matthews bent over, picked up the shovel carefully and swung the flat metal head at the back of the unsuspecting Patton's head. He collapsed without a sound, knocking over some plants on a wooden stand. Peterson leaned forward and felt for a pulse.

"He's gone. All he's been through and a tap on the head and it's over. Makes you think, doesn't it? This retirement isn't all it's cracked up to be."

Matthews took out a packet of lemon drops and looked around.

"Old geezer twigged something there at the end didn't he?"

"Yeah Crawford must have spun him a crock about Quigley gutting some of us down in Bath."

He looked around the garden shed.

"Shame to waste the rest of this cement. Let's put it to good use. Dig that floor a bit deeper and dump him in there. That's what the mafia does isn't it? Puts them in the foundations of buildings and they're gone period. Nobody left around to complicate things. You go ahead and I'll look inside to see if he's left any notes of Quigley's phone call."

Matthews face showed displeasure.

"Don't take too long. This looks like bloody hard work and my flaming back isn't the best. You can do some of the shoveling after I start making a bigger hole."

Distaste flickered momentarily on Peterson's face. They'd killed before and it was no longer a big deal but Matthew's complaining about his bad back with a body lying there, somehow narked him.

Turning, he went inside and spent some time looking through any paper work he found lying on a desk and on the table. He scrutinized some notebooks that Patton had used for shopping lists and also his diary, which just contained the very occasional note for dentist, doctor and car service appointments. They didn't want to torch the cottage which would have created more police interest, on top of Patton's disappearance. He booted up the computer and examined the list of emails stacked up and was relieved to see that none referred to Quigley's current situation. He checked some yellow sticky notes on the fridge and did a search of some drawers and a metal filing cabinet. Nothing. Not knowing if

Patton was expecting any visitors that afternoon, Peterson was consumed with the desire to get away from the cottage as quickly as possible. He took a quick look in the two bedrooms and a utility room before hurrying outside to the greenhouse. Matthews had just finished deepening a hole in the floor and had dragged Patton's body across into it, cursing at the cement he got on his shoes. Breathless, he regarded Peterson balefully.

"Come on, let's see you expend some energy here. Christ, I'm knackered!" he exploded. Peterson said nothing and taking his coat off, started firing shovels of cement in on top of Patton's body. After a while he stopped.

"Hey, lend a hand here. Start smoothing that stuff out and make it look normal. Grab that trowel and forget your fucking back for a minute. We need to be making tracks."

Eventually they had the whole wheelbarrow of cement dumped across and Matthews made a reasonable effort at smoothing out the floor.

"What do you think?" Matthews asked.

Peterson nodded.

"It's a rough job but will have to do. Got rid of the old bugger anyway. By the time he's missed and someone comes looking, that cement will be rock hard. He'll never be found. It will end up just another Cotswold mystery for parents to frighten their kids with. Come on, let's go. I'll phone Crawford from the car. He's damn lucky we were in the area."

CHAPTER 55
Sligo

Danny hung the telephone up in frustration and looked at Courtney.

"This chap Patton should be there right now. He knows I'm calling him back to see if there is any joy with getting through to MI5 and having Crawford reined in."

Courtney nodded soberly.

"I can't believe my taxes are being used to support animals like your Colonel Crawford to kill UK citizens out of hand and to sabotage the government's foreign policy. This beggars belief."

Danny's eyes flicked towards him.

"Believe me, half the time you're better off not knowing C.C., and the truth is, most citizens don't really want to know what's going on to protect their lives. All they want is their little semi-detached houses, with football and beer on the weekends. They just want it to go on and couldn't really care about the dirty work carried out by some people to sustain their lifestyles."

Courtney was taken aback.

"That's a pretty cynical view, Danny. Surely you're not defending this man and his team? After all it's your family under threat here. You're the one they took across the border and beat up! Don't forget poor Glenna, burned to death in her bed!"

Danny raised his hands in the air.

"Far from it C.C., but at one time Crawford and his men did stand in the breech, as it were, defending freedom as it seemed then. I was right there with them and we did some good work. I can't say any more because of the official secrets act that I've signed but somewhere along the line. Since then, Crawford and his men have taken it upon themselves to create their own agenda. The scary thing is the resources they can tap into, which I've witnessed at first hand. I'd hoped Patton could contact the right people in MI5 and that they would stop Crawford cold. It's unlikely they'll have any public exposure because of the political fall out. They usually like to sanitize their own messes internally."

Courtney nodded grimly.

"Sanitize is the operative word. Apparently no problem for this group Danny. Have you some concerns about Patton's safety, since he promised to be a whistle blower?"

"Patton's a careful man, always has been, but that was the role he played when he was inside - thorough and methodical. I'm just wondering if he decided to check with Colonel Crawford before taking it further. If he did, I've no doubt that he would be silenced, one way or the other." he replied, his face creased with worry.

Courtney rubbed his face.

"My God, this gets worse and worse! The man is capable of anything it seems. I hate to say it but you have to start fighting back or he'll be on our doorstep before we know it. We've got some better security set up outside now, but nothing that would stop any serious invasion here. We don't want another Bonat type incident do we? So, what's your best solution for following up on your friend Patton at this stage? You've already called him several times."

Danny got up, walked across the room and looked out the window. He saw Allison and Fiona strolling down beside the water and heard Allison's shouts as she skimmed flat stones on the lake. Shrugging, he turned to Courtney.

"I could risk a trip over to the UK and look up Patton at his cottage. Perhaps cross over on the Rosslare ferry to Wales and hire a car from there."

Courtney interrupted.

"And risk being picked up by the UK police or Crawford? You just mentioned the resources they can draw on. Getting passenger lists should be no problem to them. Hey, remember, we only managed to get yourself and your family out by the skin of your teeth."

Danny sat down again nodding reluctantly.

"You're right of course C.C. It would be a long shot and it would take time to get to Rosslare from here and then across," he answered.

"What about your friend in Hereford? He was willing enough to bail you out in Bath. Would he take a run up to Burton-on-the-Water for you? It's not very far."

Danny nodded thoughtfully.

"Possibly, but he's now in a training role and may be out in the field with a new selection group, in which case it wouldn't be possible. Worth a call though."

Danny spent the next few minutes using the phone while Courtney left the room to freshen up the teapot. When he came back Danny was sitting there looking despondently down at his hands.

"No luck, Danny?" Courtney asked.

Danny shook his head.

"No, he's away out in the field with a group. Oh and by the way, MI5 did enquire if there were any people missing from the lines. They asked about Scotty by name so Crawford's made the connection. Of course the regiment covered for him but I wouldn't want to push my luck too far and risk Scotty's career."

"Okay, Danny. Then it's up to me. I'll get a Ryan Air out to Dublin this morning and a connecting flight to Bristol. I could be up at Patton's cottage by late this afternoon."

Danny started to object but Courtney cut him short.

"I'm the logical person to go. They probably haven't flagged me yet on the flights as a person of interest. Now tell me how to get to this Patton's cottage and what I'm supposed to look for. Remember I'm pretty good at financial planning, not working like an investigative journalist in some danger zone."

After expressing some more reservations he had about the whole idea of Courtney's involvement, Danny reluctantly agreed and started going over a suggested scenario for his trip to Patton's cottage in the Cotswolds.

CHAPTER 56

Sligo

After Courtney dashed off to catch the flight out of Strandhill, driving one of the center's cars, Fiona and Danny strolled along a narrow path that ran through some scrubland around the edge of the lake. Siobhan had taken Allison on a bird watching foray in the opposite direction.

"What's happening to us Danny?" Fiona pleaded. " I just don't understand how our whole life can be totally turned upside down like this, and basically, you're totally innocent. Where's that great British justice we hear about so much? Why can't you just go to the police - even the police here, for starters?" she asked, holding a branch so it didn't snap back on him.

He nodded, as he speeded up to come alongside her on a wider section of the pathway.

"I'm as frustrated as you are right now Fiona. Looking back I guess I started losing control when I fled London just to stay out of jail and somehow trying to establish my innocence, but I didn't know that was exactly what Crawford wanted. Not for me to run off to Ireland, but to disrupt my life and make me open to threats, especially against yourself and Allison. Then, I was grabbed by Crawford's thugs and whipped across the border only to be ordered to kill Gerry Adams, or yourself and Allison, would be killed. Not to mention that I would have been killed right there on the spot if I refused. That led to Courtney setting up a secret trip to Bath for me and getting you out from under Crawford's men. In effect getting rid of the lever he had over me. Then, I contacted Patton in the hope that he could get the word through to MI5 as to the criminal activities of Crawford's team and their plan for the assassination of Gerry Adams, all to protect their little autonomous fiefdom in Northern Ireland. Now Patton seems to have disappeared off the map and I'm seriously concerned that Crawford's somehow involved in this. Certainly, he wouldn't just sit back and let Patton blow a hole in his plans, if he knew about it. It's just possible that Patton, who always was a respecter of the chain of command, might have called him before contacting the Director General of MI5. If he did, he signed his own death warrant. I've also been thinking that Crawford's men, in pulling back from Bath, were pretty close to where Patton lives. Anyway, hopefully we'll soon know when Courtney goes up there and checks it out. He'll call me when he gets there and we have to then decide on the next step. As far as the Irish police are concerned, you, Allison and myself could turn ourselves in and ask for protective custody, pending any UK warrants for me to be processed. I agree it's a right mess and I don't feel that I have much control over events right now."

He stopped suddenly, impulsively putting his arms around her. She clung to him and he felt her muffled sobbing.

She stopped, struggling for breath.

"It's all gone, Danny, just like that. Our marriage, my career, the house, my car that I was so proud of stuck is in a scruffy garage somewhere. Allison and I being hunted by some ghost of yours from the past, and you in danger of being killed. It's almost as if I'm being punished. My mother told me I'd regret it when I gave her the news of our break up. Perhaps she's right."

Danny tightened his arms around her.

"Hey, it's not your fault at all. I don't blame you. More than half the guys in the regiment were divorced in the first three years of marriage. You hung in for a lot longer than that. Hell I know you had no life married to me, most of the time away and you never even knew where or when some officer would call with the Padre at the door. Even when I was on leave, my heart was still back at the regiment with my mates, missing the life, the action, the adrenalin fix. Despite this you were one heck of a mother to Allison and she's a beaut, thanks to you. Heck you even built a career for yourself, with absolutely no support from me, so you really do deserve a shot at some happiness and I don't blame you for starting divorce proceedings. It's time for you to move on Fiona, and you can tell your mother to put that in her pipe and smoke it!"

She stepped back out of his arms.

"You really mean that? About not blaming me and wanting the best for myself? Even if it means the possibility of someone else in my life and Allison's too?"

"Yeah, absolutely Fiona, and the sooner I can sort this out the sooner you can get on with your new life."

A hint of a smile now tugged at her lips.

"What about your new life Danny. I saw how Siobhan looked at you over breakfast. She couldn't keep her eyes off you."

His looked at her, startled.

"Siobhan? Me? You got to be kidding! Hell, I had a ride in a bus with her as a prisoner and that's about it. I doubt she'll have the time of day for me now that she's back with the real love of her life ... looking after that women's hostel."

Fiona shook her head.

"You men are so dense. You know, sometimes we have to hit you with a club to get noticed," she teased.

"I can't believe it. A minute ago you were in tears and now you're playing at being a match maker! You know what? With that spirit Fiona we can certainly beat Crawford and his evil brood at their own game."

She nodded pensively.

"What about my query about going direct to MI5, especially now that we are no longer under Crawford's control?"

"Good question and one I examined myself. A couple of problems with it though: one, it wouldn't be direct to the DG. You'd have to go through a series of filtering personnel first. They would make a decision as to whether you'd be allowed to contact her. It rarely happens. Can you imagine all the weirdos who phone up wanting to talk to her about some conspiracy or other? Crawford's been in the organization for a long time and has numerous contacts. Some people think he's what MI5 should be all about - taking down bad guys. So what's the odds on one of these people dropping the word to Crawford about some outlandish claim coming through from a member of the public?"

She looked up pensively at him.

"I've no idea. What could he do anyway if the cat's out of the bag about the stunts he's been pulling?"

"What could he do?" exclaimed Danny. "I'll tell you what he'd do! He'd start to clean house, and that means eliminate any or all witnesses so that there would be no substance to any charges being laid. That's why Patton was so important. He could have got through on a direct line on the basis of his past employment, and the charges would have been considered quite seriously, I suspect. Speaking of which, Courtney should be on the ground in Bristol by now."

CHAPTER 57

Burton on the Water

Courtney loved the Cotswolds and used to regularly visit there for short breaks prior to finding his second home in Ireland. He knew Burton on the Water quite well and used to take family visitors and some of the American life insurance industry speakers there.

He whipped down the M4 and cut left on the 419. Another right just before that Roman city of Cirencester and he was rapidly eating up the miles. He still had to enquire at two gas stations and a private house before he arrived at his destination. It was when he hauled his large frame out of the car that he realized how stiff and cramped he was from both the flights and the car trip. He stretched for a few moments then ambled up to the house and knocked on the door. No answer, so he knocked harder. Still nothing. Spotting the angle of the iron gate at the side of the house, he went through and around to the back, careful that there were no dogs lurking. He'd had some bad experiences early in his career with dogs which made him much more vigilant. Courtney breathed a sigh of relief. No dogs, so he went up to the back door and knocked on it.

"Anyone there?" he shouted.

He was greeted with silence and tried shouting louder. No reaction. He turned and looked down the garden and decided to check out the greenhouse. No one there either. He spotted what appeared to be some recent work on the floor, where new cement had been poured. A bit of a handyman himself he frowned when he noticed that the shovel and the wheelbarrow or the trowels hadn't been washed off after the job had been done. Looking closer he could see an obvious difference in the start of the job at the top of the greenhouse and the finish at the other end. It was expertly smoothed at the top end and just jaggedly finished at the bottom. He stared at the floor for a long time and his face clouded as he felt a heaviness in his spirit. Surely not, he whispered to himself.

Suddenly feeling a sense of urgency he exited the greenhouse and went up to the house again. Not bothering to knock or call he went straight inside and carried out a systematic search of the house. He wasn't surprised when he was unable to discover anything of interest. Finally he sat down at the computer and checked through emails but nothing that would indicate MI5 had been in recent touch with Patton. He decided to check word to see if any message had been set up for forwarding to them and struck it lucky. Patton's message was sitting there in a file headed *Quigley's story* with all the details of Danny's situation laid out in minute detail. Patton had obviously not sent it. He scrolled through his address book and came across a reference to a DG and an email address. Working rapidly now he typed out a quick email and fired it off.

It read: *I believe your ex employee Patton has been murdered and buried under some cement in his greenhouse. Check under word on his computer and you may find some answers.*

He didn't sign it. He figured that the intrigue in the message would get them down to the scene quite faster than attaching Patton's account. He fired off the e mail and then turned off the computer and sat back considering his options.

Almost immediately, he started feeling a sense of disquiet and tried to shake it off. He decided to call Danny back at the hostel and got straight through. He apprised him of the

situation and his suspicions. Danny was shocked at his
presumption that Patton was buried under some fresh cement.
Courtney was about to tell him about the email he'd sent when
he felt a hard object pressed into the back of his head. Looking
up he stared into the cold eyes of someone he would later on
come to know as Peterson.

Peterson casually reached across and took the phone out of
his hand.

"You won't be needing that any more."

Speaking into it he said

"I understand from what I just heard a minute ago that it's
young Danny on the end of the line. Would I be right?"

He heard a gasp at the other end.

"Who the hell's there? What have you done to Courtney?"
he demanded. Peterson laughed.

"That's two questions. Firstly, my name is Peterson and I
work for our mutual friend who suggested we come back and
see who comes a calling. We actually thought it might be you,
but not to worry, we will be seeing you soon. As to your friend
Courtney, he's going to be just fine as long as you do that little
job you agreed to do for us. We're disappointed you decided to
not honor your agreement. Now, here's the new deal. We will
obviously find out very quickly where you and your family are
from this telephone call. You know the resources we have
Danny don't you? Crawford will have Josh's team doing
surveillance on you within the hour. We wont make a move on
your family as long as you present yourself this evening after 9
pm, across the border in that little police station where we had
the distinct pleasure of meeting the great Danny Quigley not
too long ago. In truth, we were all somewhat disappointed in
you. It seems civvy street is responsible for blunting that
famous aggression Crawford was so fond of telling us about.
Josh was very disappointed, so he was. So to quote that TV
show I loved watching when I was over in the States recently,
- deal or no deal Quigley?"

"What happens over the border if I go there?" Danny asked
tersely.

"Fine tuning the little operation just as you lads do in the *saas* - logistics, weapons, back up, extraction. You know the script Danny."

"What about Courtney, and my family being watched?" Danny asked.

"Courtney will be released after the successful completion of the op and the surveillance on your family will be pulled. I give you my word."

Danny laughed cynically.

"Yeah, sure. Some guarantee! I know how Crawford feels about loose ends. What about my family? Are you still going after them?"

"We don't need to now that we have your friend Courtney, unless you force our hand."

Danny was silent for a moment, then.

"Okay Peterson, let me talk to Courtney," he demanded.

"Now wait a minute here, I'm the one giving the orders Danny boy!"

Danny's voice was hard and unrelenting.

"You want that job done? Then I talk to him right now. I can run with my family right now and all you've got is Courtney, a man I barely know. Now pass that phone over to him or explain to Crawford later, how you screwed up."

Peterson's face suffused with anger but he bit his lip and handed the phone to Courtney. Danny spoke rapidly.

"You heard the deal C.C. They haven't left me any room to maneuver ."

Courtney shouted into the phone

"Don't do it, Danny! You'll destroy your life for sure if you do. Don't worry about me."

Peterson started to tug the phone off him but Courtney's large hands refused to release it as he shouted

"I'm already dying. Ask Siobhan. Hang in there. Help is coming."

Peterson slammed him on the forehead with the weapon and snatched the phone away from him as Courtney crashed to the floor.

He heard Danny's anxious voice on the other end.

"Hey, what's going on there? What's happening? Talk to me C.C."

Peterson snarled into the mouthpiece.

"Nothing to what's going to happen if you don't make that little trip across the border tonight, Danny. If you don't we start to clean house and you know what that means. Now let's hear it," he demanded.

There was silence at the other end of the line.

Finally, Peterson heard a low voice reply.

"Yeah, I'll be there, and you better not lay another hand on Courtney or I'll personally take it out on your hide, you hear me?"

Peterson chuckled.

"I thought you just said you hardly know the man. Now you're threatening me. I don't like that."

He delivered a savage kick to Courtney's stomach, causing him to cry out. "Hear that Danny? That's how seriously I take your threats. I'm really sorry I won't be there tonight so I could deal with you personally, but you know we can carry on this little chat some other time."

He delivered another kick to Courtney and held the phone down so Danny could hear him cry out again.

"Be there Danny," he hissed "or he'll join your friend Patton in his retirement." Then he hung up.

360

CHAPTER 58

Sligo

Danny's face was creased with concern when he came back into the room where Fiona, Siobhan and Allison were seated for the evening meal. He nodded to Allison.

"Allison can you please go into the TV room for a few moments?"

She stamped her feet.

"Why do I always have to leave the room when it gets interesting?" she burst out.

Fiona turned a stern face to her and started to say something. Allison abruptly stood up, almost knocking the chair over, and stumped from the room muttering. Siobhan smiled at the whole exchange, perhaps remembering her own childhood. When the door closed Danny sat down and brought them up to date on what happened on Courtney's visit to the UK. Siobhan gasped when she heard of his capture, suddenly going pale. "Oh my God," she breathed. "He's fallen into the hands of those men! What'll happen to him? Will they let him go?" she asked.

Danny looked directly into her eyes.

"Hopefully, when this is all over Siobhan, though with these people, in all honesty, I wouldn't want to make any promises at this stage. By the way, C.C. said to ask you about his health - something about him dying. What did he mean by that?" he asked.

She looked down for a moment and then whispered.

"Yes he's got terminal cancer. One of the reasons he wanted you over here on the ground, so you could hopefully, take over some of the work he was involved in. Oh, he knew this wouldn't happen right away but hoped he had enough time to show you the ropes. He realized that it would take you a while to learn the business but somehow he felt that would come."

"How much time has he got left, Siobhan? Does he know?" Danny asked.

She shook her head.

"Six months was mentioned over a year ago but he's still around. I can't personally see anything killing that character."

She had tears in her eyes and Fiona impulsively reached across and held her hand.

"That accounts for him pulling out of the UK so suddenly then around that time. Now, he's more or less telling me to not to consider the threat to his life, because he's as good as dead anyway," mused Danny.

"But we can't just abandon him," Siobhan entreated.

"Don't worry, I've no intentions of doing so. I'm seeing those people tonight across the border to finalize the plan to kill Gerry Adams, but in a way it helps me to get close to Crawford and it may show me a way out. Remember I used to do this stuff for a living so the game is far from over yet. By the way C.C. shouted something about help being on the way. I've been running that through my mind since the call and I just don't know what to read into it."

Fiona sat forward.

"Could he have contacted someone before those men came? Got a message out somehow?" she hazarded.

Siobhan cut in.

"His mind is sharp, even with his illness. I'm sure you noticed that. If there was any way of sabotaging these

362

criminals, he'd do it in a flash, believe me, and he doesn't lack courage."

Danny looked at her shrewdly.

"Remember when Bonat had us in the bus and he somehow tuned into where you were? Does it work in reverse as well? I mean could you attempt to tune into where he is being held right now?"

She considered for a moment.

"Just to clarify one point, CC and I are not involved physically as I think you suspected from some things that were said. However on a spiritual plane we are somehow intertwined. It's hard to explain. I feel his pain when the cancer attacks him. I somehow feel his presence. Right now I know he's alive, but in some pain."

She looked at Danny.

"Did those men hurt him?"

He nodded reluctantly.

"I heard them kicking him, while we were on the phone. Sorry, I tried to spare you the details."

She looked at him calmly.

"Yes, he is hurt but not badly and better than that, he's madder than hell! Those thugs don't know what a bag of trouble they've got on their hands, given half a chance," she said, her eyes flashing.

Danny grinned, feeling his spirits lifting.

"Okay, keep trying to tune into where he's at. It could help us later on. Now, neither of you have asked me about my trip tonight and I can understand why. You probably wonder if you'll ever see me again. Well just remember that they need me for their dirty little scheme, which I intend to go along with for the moment. I can't assume that they'll let me come back here tonight after our meeting because the assassination is two days from now. I want you, Siobhan, if you don't mind, to take Fiona and Allison in to Mrs. McKeevers in town because MI5 now know about this place through tracing back my call from C.C. They probably already have people watching, both out on the lake and the front road."

Siobhan interrupted.

"I'm certainly more than happy to do that, but how can I get them away if these people are watching us?"

Danny smiled grimly.

"Leave that to me. I understand your boat has been replaced, so take Fiona and Allison in by the lake and phone ahead for a taxi to meet you at the dock. It'll be dark by the time I leave to cross the border so this will give me time to do what I have to do."

Seeing the concern on their faces he went on.

"Don't worry. This is what I'm trained to do, and Siobhan, I have come to terms with using my skills to combat evil. If it wasn't for the danger to C.C. and my family right now, I might even find something fulfilling in my battle with these people."

Concern creased Fiona's face.

"Danny, you know these people - the resources they have - their training as good as yours, perhaps even better in some areas. Don't underestimate them for one minute. They would have no compunction in destroying you or anyone else who has knowledge of their plans if things start to go wrong for them."

He was about to reply when a movement out on the lake caught his eye. "Right on time. That's Crawford's men just coming on site. I asked myself where they would set up to contain us and that was one position I chose, about 150 yards out. I'll bet the other team is at the gate to the road, probably in a car where they can view anyone leaving in either direction."

He caught Fiona and Siobhan throwing worried glances at each other.

"Look, I doubt if the actual hostel is in any danger. Their brief, I'll warrant, is strictly observation. Remember, this is the Republic of Ireland and M15 have no remit to operate here as such. The last thing they need is trying to take over a hostel with over a hundred people living in it, so relax ladies. In a way, it's reassuring to have them show their hand and I'll bet this really stretches their resources. It may make my meeting over the border a bit easier if they have a smaller team to play with."

Siobhan shuddered.

"Danny! I keep thinking of poor C.C. in the clutches of those monsters."

Both women came together again and hugged each other as Danny started to focus the set of binoculars that Siobhan used for bird watching. He kept well out of sight behind a curtain as he zeroed in on the boat and it's occupants. There were two men on board. Both looked familiar and he had seen them in the police station, across the border after he was snatched from outside the hotel in Rosses Point. He was sorry that Josh wasn't one of them and smiled grimly, his eyes hardening as he watched them. "That's right lads, just relax and settle in," he whispered.

"Just what are you up to, Danny Quigley?" Fiona demanded.

"It's time I started fighting back Fiona. Those people have wrecked our lives and I'm drawing a line right here and now. I'm going to reduce the odds somewhat and make those two out there disappear."

"Disappear? How?" both women interjected at the same time.

"That's a dangerous lake out there girls. Accidents happen all the time, I'm told, out on Lough Gill. Shortly, I predict, another two men unfortunately lost to the unpredictable weather and currents!"

Siobhan gasped. "You can't mean ...?"

Fiona said.

"He does, I'm afraid, Siobhan. I've know him a lot longer than you, and when he gets that look on his face ... ..."

Siobhan suddenly looked anxious.

"What happens when the people on the gate start to realize that the boat team are missing? Won't they come in here to check?"

"Possibly, but hopefully not when you are running Fiona and Allison up the lake and coming back. If they do come in just tell whoever you leave in charge to look concerned and offer to call out the local police to help. I'll bet they run a mile before taking your staff up on that offer. It's always possible that they won't have twigged that their lads have met with an accident and will tag along behind me when I leave for the border. A lot depends on how good their communication is with the boat team. Whatever they suspect about those two men disappearing later on, they won't be able to prove anything, especially if it looks like an accident."

Siobhan shuddered.

"Just talking about taking the lives of two people gives me the creeps, even if they are bad people, Danny."

"I don't enjoy it either Siobhan let me tell you, but just think of C.C. in their hands and what might happen to him eventually unless I start to unravel this."

They left it at that and agreed that Siobhan would start her run as soon as Danny had neutralized the two agents in the boat. Danny then went to prepare his plan and afterwards consumed a large sandwich in the kitchen with a cup of tea. He then went and read a story to Allison and played a game with her. Part of him accepted that it might be the last time he would ever do that.

Before he knew it, dusk had settled down around the hostel and then, complete darkness. Danny crept down through the bushes leading to the boat shed using it's bulk to conceal himself from any night vision glasses the MI5 team might have. Siobhan had mentioned that some wet suits occasionally used by C.C. and herself, were hanging up inside the boat shed. The suit used by C.C. was a bit large for him in the shoulders but he was counting on it keeping the chill of the water out. Unfortunately there were no air tanks available but he settled for a snorkeling mask and had already blackened his face from the fire-place inside the hostel.

He slipped into the water inside the boat shed and eased his way out into the lake, heading in the general direction of where the boat had been anchored. He figured that they would have put out an anchor to avoid the boat drifting rather than having to correct their position regularly. He judged that he swam about fifty yards, and started becoming more careful in his arms strokes, drifting forwards, eyes alert. Shortly afterwards, he spotted a vague shape further out and he slowed down again, creeping ever closer. He could actually hear the conversation of the two men clearly.

"I never knew the old man to get in such a stew over something. Why in hell's name didn't he get one of our team to do the job and keep it in-house? This could be a real can of worms if someone twigs we are operating south of the border." the first man grumbled.

Another voice answered.

"Yeah, it sure could. This Quigley could be a loose cannon and could blow us all out of the water. Christ, he's not even in the Forces any more."

The first man laughed.

"He won't be a loose cannon much longer. After the job's done Crawford has a nice little bog hole picked out for him. A few people may be joining him there. You know Crawford, when it comes to witnesses."

Those were the last words he spoke.

Danny reared out of the water encircled his neck and hauled him backwards, at the same time capsizing the boat. All three plunged into the water. Danny, still holding the agent around the neck with his forearm, broke it with a powerful twist. Letting him go he turned to locate the other agent and felt arms grabbing his shoulders from behind. He butted backwards feeling the grip loosen and spun in the water in order to turn and face his attacker. Fighting in water wasn't easy, as Danny had realized when attending training at the Special Boat Squadron school at Poole in Dorset. The SBS trainers recommended that a knife was the quickest and best way to take out an opponent in the water, but Danny wanted this to look like an accident, at least until the autopsy showed otherwise, as it would.

The man facing him was strong and fought with the desperation of someone who knew he was fighting for his life.

They were both getting tired as they gouged and wrestled for an advantage. Danny decided he had to try something different, otherwise the man might shortly be able to swim off in the darkness. He stuck his head above the surface and gulped in a lungful, then dived straight down and came up just as suddenly behind the man, slipping him into a strangle hold. The man spun and thrashed about, pulling them both below the water as he violently attempted to shake him off. Danny hung on grimly knowing this was make or break time. If the man broke loose now Danny knew he didn't have the reserves of strength to finish him off. He increased the strangle hold wrapping his legs around the man to stop him thrashing. Suddenly, he felt the man weaken and reduce his struggles. Danny was tempted to let him go but the SBS had warned him that a trained individual, with his wits still about him might fake it and hope to get you to loosen your grip, so he held on for grim life until there was no doubt that the man was dead. Then he let him go and felt him drift below the surface.

Danny held onto the upturned boat for several moments gasping for breath until he felt his strength return. Then he headed back to shore.

When he staggered back into the house both women were there waiting anxiously. Pulling himself together he assured them he was all right and hurried both of them out and down to the boat. They took off moments later after being warned to watch for the upturned boat. Then he went back inside and dried himself off thoroughly, even taking the time to use a hair dryer. He couldn't afford to go out the gate dripping of lake water in case the watchers stopped him, or to turn up across the border in even a slightly damp state.

He went outside and started the car Siobhan had made available and headed out the gate. He wasn't stopped, but a car that was parked down the road started up and followed him in to Sligo and down the Manorhamilton road. He smiled. That was a real break. It allowed Siobhan to get back to the hostel after delivering Fiona and Allison to the dock, where the pre-arranged taxi would whip them around to Mrs. McKeevers.

The weak part of the whole plan was if the watchers decided to get rough with Siobhan about what had happened to the two missing watchers out on the lake. The remaining agents would be genuinely puzzled and probably couldn't marshal any help locally, until daylight had come. They might even decide not to call in the locals for assistance.

The plans of mice and men! Danny thought. It was in the lap of the Gods right then and so was he. He put his foot to the floor and watched the car behind speed up. Before he knew it, they were at the border and with no customs hut open on either side, just sped across and pulled into the police station parking lot. Danny remembered the time when a visitor would have been checked over thoroughly before breezing in like he did.

He walked into the station and was confronted by a member of the Northern Ireland Police Service, who just nodded to him and pointed down the hall, saying nothing. He strode down the hall thinking of the last time he had been there, hooded and in cuffs. He hesitated at the door in front of him and then thrust it open and walked through.

Colonel Crawford, Josh and two other men were sitting there, obviously waiting for him.

"Running a bit late, aren't we, Danny?"

Crawford's black eyes peered accusingly at him.

"Well, I'm here now, let's get on with it," Danny answered briskly, grabbing a chair and swinging the back of it to face Crawford, started to straddle it.

Josh suddenly, sprang to his feet, his face dark with anger and came over to him. Danny decided to stay standing.

"What's the matter, Danny? No respect for rank any more? That's no way to address our Commander," snarled Josh, as he reached up and started to slap both sides of Danny's face.

Just then Danny became aware of the two men who had followed him, coming into the room, and they started chuckling at the spectacle. Danny moved suddenly and explosively. His hands flashed six times. It took almost but not quite five seconds. The six blows struck audibly at different parts of Josh's anatomy. Josh stood there completely paralyzed and unable to move a muscle, wheezing from his mouth, which started to dribble.

The room went completely quiet.

"Jesus Christ, did you see that?" Danny heard from a man at the door.

Suddenly, all the men sprang to their feet. Danny grabbed the chair and jumped over to the wall. The two men at the door withdrew handguns and Crawford's other two men reached behind them and grabbed some coshes from a table. Crawford never moved. He smiled and turning sideways roared.

"Sit down you morons. This is why I chose Quigley. He's an animal. Look at Josh, the hard man from Aussie land. How long did it take Danny to turn him into a vegetable, but then who was counting? Now we could put a beating on him but how could he pull a trigger with a smashed hand? Danny knew that when he came here. He knew just how far he could push me. That's what a professional does - a measured timely response. Forget Josh, he's expendable."

The men in the room looked at each other, then at Danny and very reluctantly and carefully started putting away their weapons.

Crawford nodded.

"Now can we get down to the business at hand. In two days Gerry Adams will be in Strabane visiting his old friend Martin McGuinness. A baptism at a catholic church apparently, and we want it to be Gerry's last visit. Hence Danny here. Now lets get down to business."

Behind them Josh crashed to the floor where he lay moaning. Crawford's team looked nervously at each other. Danny had a flash of insight. Turning to Crawford

"These guys aren't all MI5, are they? You've hired yourself some bloody mercs as well haven't you?"

"Mercs?" said Crawford.

"Mercenaries.. That's why you aren't worried about crossing borders. Completely deniable when you can account for the whereabouts of your establishment team," said Danny.

Crawford scowled.

"Too smart for your own good, Quigley. That could get you killed one of these days."

Some of his men stirred and looked bleakly at Danny. He had no doubt they would dispatch him in a minute if their boss didn't need him. As the plan unfolded it was made clear that he was being kept under tight control with Crawford's group until the job was done. He wouldn't be going back to Sligo. The plan itself was simple as most successful plans were.

Their sources had pinpointed the individual church where the baptism would take place, by special arrangement at 11 am on a Saturday morning. Gerry Adams was going to be the godfather for one of Martin McGuinness's grandchildren, and the group would be emerging from the ceremony at approximately 11.30.

A sympathizer, who lived in an estate house, approximately a hundred yards away, was allowing his house to be used for the hit but would be gone for the day and wanted it to look like a house invasion. One of Crawford's loose ends Danny thought, cynically.

"What about the weapon? I need to fire it and sight it in," Danny enquired.

"You'll have time on the way up through Donegal. The team will stop at a farm outside a small village called Ballybofey and you can do what you have to do. Mind you, a hundred yard shot doesn't need your usual sighting in time and we have a rifle I think you'll approve of."

"What about the ammunition?" Danny pressed.

Crawford waved his hands dismissively.

"Oh standard military stuff. At least we know it's reliable."

Danny showed his surprise.

"But won't this point to the military? Surely you want to avoid any hint of Her Majesty's Forces being involved."

"There's a ton of the military stuff out there pilfered over the years from the Forces. We're not concerned with that side of it," Crawford replied dismissively.

Danny shrugged. "If you say so. Now what about extraction after the hit?"

As he said it he noticed a smirk on the faces of some of the men and a warning bell went off. Obviously he wasn't included in the extraction plan. Crawford crinkled his face thoughtfully.

"It's simple really. When the job's done we get out by car across the bridge into Donegal and switch cars there. I don't see any problem Quigley."

Danny was puzzled.

"But you'll be very exposed going back down through Donegal on that one main road, if the Gardai get involved and set up road blocks. Surely you would be better staying in the North."

"We've looked at various options, Quigley. This is the one we like so just leave it at that, okay?"

The meeting broke up shortly afterwards and Danny was escorted out, back to a police cell and locked in for the night. He realized that he was not being kept fully apprised of the full details of the operation and also that he wasn't supposed to survive it.

CHAPTER 59

London

Thames House on Milbank was the official home of MI5, an imposing eight story building near the Palace of Westminster, housing a staff of approximately 2,000. The organizations main field of responsibilities covered counter subversion, counter espionage and counter terrorism, each with its own director. Since Stella Rimington was appointed Director General, in 1992, and the first DG to be publicly announced, her successful reign set a precept for another female to take over the helm some years later and finally, to Rebecca Fullerton-Smythe. Today she was not looking at all comfortable in her role as she waited impatiently for her direct line to ring. A tall, attractive, dark haired, early forties woman, with a fit tight figure that reflected her passion for hunting and shooting in her off time. But not a lot of that lately. Her hair was severely tied back as usual but her startling green eyes were now blazing with the imminence of battle. Earlier in the day she had contacted an agent at GCHQ, the government listening post in Cheltenham, Paul Sinclair, and briefed him on the peculiar tone of an email that had awaited her early arrival at Thames House. She had instructed him to proceed, post haste to Patton's residence and check out the veracity of the communication she found waiting on her computer when she arrived in her office.

He was also instructed, if Patton was indeed missing, to recover and take possession of any computer hardware on the premises and bring it personally up to Thames House. He was also to phone her from his car on leaving the residence and under no circumstances was he to involve the civilian authorities or draw attention to himself in any way. Having visited Patton's place at one time for a private retirement party, she was able to provide specific details as to how to locate the residence. Now she sat there on tenterhooks waiting for his call. If she had been a nail biter all her fingers would have been stubs by now. Still she jumped when it finally rang.

She pressed a button on the unit.

"Yes?" she demanded, wishing her voice hadn't sounded so shrill.

"Ma'am?" Sinclair's voice sounded breathless.

"Yes, yes, who else? Go on, what's the situation there?"

"As you suspected ma'am, it doesn't look good."

"Be more specific! Is he there or not for God's sake?"

"No ma'am, completely disappeared. There's freshly laid cement in the outside flower shed which was sinister enough but its what I discovered inside the house that alarmed me."

Rebecca's voice was getting more and more impatient.

"Get on with it man. Exactly what did you find?"

"The computer ma'am. It had been shot up. It was full of bullet holes."

"Bullet holes?"

"Yes ma'am. The tower mainly, but the screen had been hit a couple of times too."

"Good God Sinclair, so it's true! Something has happened to poor Patton. Is the computer equipment completely destroyed? I mean is it salvageable in any way?"

"Sorry ma'am. I'm not knowledgeable with computers in that capacity. However, I have all the pieces here in the vehicle with me and expect to be back at Thames House in under two hours. Expect your boys in the lab can help you there."

She was silent for a moment as she weighed her options.

"Okay Paul, well done. I'll have a crew ready to unload the cargo when you get here. I'm now going to involve the civilian police at Cheltenham. They keep a watching brief on our retired people in the Cotswolds and some of our people who have weekend cottages there. They'll know what our concerns are. Sure you were careful with footprints and fingerprints? It'll now be treated as a crime scene as you know."

Sinclair sounded aggrieved that she should even ask.

"As you advised me. I wore gloves and had some plastic bags over my boots. Didn't have any contact with locals either as your directions were spot on ma'am."

"Right Sinclair, I'll give you an hour to get back on the M4 and I'll then contact the police. In your case you were never there, understood?"

"Yes ma'am. Understood."

She hung up and sat there for some time, then stood up and strolled over to the window overlooking one of the Thames' bridges.

"Damn! Damn! Damn!" she shouted fiercely.

She hated surprises, especially when things were going so well. This weekend the Foreign Secretary was hosting a commonwealth conference and MI5 and the Metropolitan Police, with a consultative role for MI6, were responsible for the total security of the event. She had some evening dinner commitments as well and still had to do the shopping for clothes and get her hair done. A crisis was the last thing she needed on her hands right at that moment. But what was it about? she wondered. A retired MI5 field agent probably murdered. What were the implications? Did Patton keep any establishment information that put him at risk, or anything that would reflect adversely on MI5 operations? The media were like frenzied sharks these days if they got any inkling of unsavory incidents of the past.

She sighed, made her way back to her desk and picked up her inter-office phone. When it was answered she spoke briefly.

"Tim, DG here. I want you to dig out the files for one of our retired agents- Patton. Yes P-A-T-T-O-N. The cases he worked on for, say, the last 5 years. I may want you to go further back later but I'll start with those. a.s.a.p. if you please, and bring them up personally, there's a good chap."

Within 20 minutes she had a pile of files on her desk, which she started to go through. An hour after her call from Sinclair, she picked up the phone and dialed a particular number in Cheltenham.

"Hello Chief Constable Henson."

"Chief Constable, Director General Rebecca Fullerton-Smythe here," she answered, smiling as she envisaged him sitting up straighter in his chair.

"Yes ma'am. To what do I owe the honor for a call from MI5? Thought you'd be up to your eyes with that commonwealth thing that's going on."

"Well, I am actually and going under for the third time if you really want to know. I could use a few days down in the Cotswolds after this weekend, let me tell you. Now, we appear to have a possible problem here, which may just be a hoax. I'd normally have one of our people check it out before bringing you in but this damn conference has mopped up all the spare staff I've got. Let me just read off the email I received and I can fax a copy of it on completion of this call."

She pulled a copy of the email close to her and read it off to the Chief Constable. He whistled when she'd finished.

"God's truth ma'am, I can see why you might be alarmed. We do have this Patton's details on file as I recall, so we can shoot some of our people across there right away. It's probably about thirty minutes from here going at speed with the sirens on. Any special instructions ma'am from MI5's perspective?"

"Chief Constable, if it proves to be a crime scene then we're out of the loop. It's your show then. I would like to be apprised of the situation immediately after your people get there, and I'd also like you to have the computer confiscated until we can determine the information that it contains. It could possibly impact on national security, but we don't know yet."

She couldn't admit to him that they had already collected the computer.

"I get it. Okay. In the light of this I'll go up myself with my team and call you from there. Now here's my fax number to forward me that email." He read it out to her, then "by the way ma'am, what time did you get the email today?"

She thought quickly, sensing a trap.

"My computer shows that it was sent the previous evening but I only read it twenty minutes ago. This morning I went straight over to check security at the hotel where they're hosting the delegate lunch, rather than coming straight to Thames House. When I got the email I reacted by having records bring up the Patton's case files for the past five years and was just starting to read them when it occurred to me that I should call you to verify the message and possibly save myself some leg-work as well. Now could I trouble you to take down my mobile phone number, because I'm off out again on some more conference security details. I'll leave it switched on awaiting your call."

They hung up and she quickly faxed a copy of the email message to the Chief Constable. She hoped he had swallowed her story on the timings and didn't suspect that MI5 might have already sanitized the scene.

Before she dashed out of the office she instructed her PA Sophie, a pert, highly energized, 25 year old with closely cropped blonde hair, to go through the files on her desk and cull out the names of the people involved with Patton over the past five years. It was going to be a long day!

CHAPTER 60

Crawford dispatched the crew north the following morning and drove off. Danny, who had been hauled out of the cell, found himself squashed between two hard faced men in the back seat. One called Ray, was a middle-aged man with a crew cut and massive muscles and wore a constantly scowling face. He obviously had no liking for Danny as he shoved him into the car and deliberately crushed in against him a moment later. His companion in the back was an alert, thirtyish, thin-faced individual called Pete who had long hair pulled into a pony tail. Despite his scruffy appearance he had a look of an ex military type. He kept a watchful speculative eye on Danny and rode with his right hand inside a leather jacket. Danny had spotted a Glock pistol under his jacket as he crammed in on the other side of him. The driver was a young, pale-faced individual with scraggly blonde hair and a wolfish twist to his features. He kept glancing back at Danny with a look of almost anticipation on his face. He had a really broad Liverpool accent and the others referred to him as Yorkie, probably because of the amount of yorkie chocolate bars he consumed as he drove. Danny knew he was in dangerous company but he had the satisfaction of knowing that he had already reduced down their numbers.

He'd had time to reflect on the briefing of the previous night and was struck by the cleverness of the plan .The assassination of Gerry Adams followed by the discovery of a dead ex British SAS trooper with a sniper rifle and military ammunition, would set the province aflame, and all the splinter groups who still wanted an all Ireland solution, would re-emerge from the woodwork. Most of them didn't need much excuse anyway. A terrorist without a cause or a weapon to carry, was suddenly without any power when peace finally arrives. They weren't very welcome at the job center either. After the assassination, it could take years to get the genie back in the bottle and Crawford's little fiefdom would continue to thrive. It was a fiendish plot, Danny realized, and had every chance of success. He wondered where the other two of Crawford's men had gone and sensed an opportunity here. It was planned to stop the trip at some time, for Danny to try out the sniper rifle and sight it in. This could very well present an opportunity for him to take out the reduced crew and sabotage the mission before ever reaching the killing ground.

CHAPTER 61
London

The Director General was in the middle of a security briefing by an MI6 agent who was covering possible foreign terrorist intervention at the London conference when her cell phone rang. Making some apologetic grimaces she hurried from the room as she pressed the talk button.

"Yes, hello. The DG here," she answered.

"Chief Constable here ma'am. Bad news I'm afraid. We found a body buried in shallow cement in the garden shed as your email suggested. It's now a crime scene and I've just allocated responsibility to two of my best investigators. We haven't fully dug out the body but the coroner is on the way at this moment. Our investigators will obviously need access to any information you might have on Mr. Patton. I'm assuming it's him at the moment, pending identification by someone from your office."

Despite her foreknowledge of events and the expectation of Patton's demise, the DG felt herself shocked at the news. She finally managed to respond.

"God, that's terrible news Chief Constable! I was hoping somehow …" her voice trailed off.

"I know ma'am and I'm sorry to be the one to break it to you. Now our chief investigator would like someone from your office to come down tomorrow if possible to Cheltenham and

I.D. the remains. While they're doing that I'd like you to forward as much information as you can divulge on his past work and contacts so we can determine if someone had a grudge against him. Equally, it's unlikely that Patton would be a terrorist target now as a retired gentleman, wouldn't you agree?"

"Oh absolutely. Highly unlikely, however no stone unturned at this stage, no doubt. You have to start somewhere. Obviously we can't give you the raw files on his past work which have implications of national security and would require a higher security clearance than your people would have."

The chief constable sighed.

"With respect ma'am, this is now out of your hands and you, of all people, appreciate the need for speed in solving a crime. I don't want those files sanitized to such an extent that they are of no use whatsoever to our investigators."

"Point taken, Chief Constable and yes, I obviously do have some idea of what would be useful to your people and will co-operate fully in any enquiries you're making. Now what about the computer? Surely that should provide some clues if the email is anything to go by?"

"Gone ma'am. No sign of it."

"Gone?"

She hoped she sounded suitably surprised. At that particular moment the computer was probably being examined in the lab at Thames House.

"Yes ma'am. Nothing there at all. However it looks like some bullets were fired into the equipment before it was taken away. There's holes in the desk and the wall."

"Bullets!" she exclaimed.

"Yes, strange that. Why shoot holes in it and then remove it from the premises?" he added.

"Hmnn ..." she ventured, "Unless they had second thoughts about it after shooting at it. Perhaps called someone who wanted to be doubly sure and told them to take it with them. I'm just guessing here really."

"Well it's one theory ma'am. I have a feeling though that this is going to be a tough one to solve. No signs of a robbery or break in. No close neighbors who might have heard shots or spotted a strange vehicle. Still it's early days ma'am. We'll keep you in the loop, don't worry."

They talked for a few more minutes tying down identification of Patton and establishing his next of kin, which would be in his MI5 file, and the delivery of any relevant information. The chief constable also arranged for one of his investigators to come up to Thames House to interview her a.s.a.p.

After they finished she put a quick call through to the lab to see if they had gleaned any information as of yet but they were just in the process of opening up the computer tower. She snapped her mobile phone shut and stood there thinking for a moment. Then, shaking her head, she crept back into the security briefing.

CHAPTER 62

They stopped for a toilet break and some take-away in Donegal town. Ray and Pete crowded him closely as they went to the washroom and back out to the car. On the edge of town they pulled into a drive-through and ordered some junk food. When they collected their order, Yorkie drove away quickly and took the first opportunity to pull over to eat in a deserted lay-by. As the vehicle came to a halt Rays mobile phone rang. He jumped out and went off to one side as he took the call. Within a minute he rushed back and hauled Danny out of the vehicle and slammed him up against it. He drew a pistol and pressed it against his forehead.

"Okay, smart ass, what happened to my two men in Sligo?" he snarled, his eyes bulging with rage.

"What two men? What are you talking about?" Danny retorted trying to look puzzled.

"My two men on the lake. They've disappeared, missing when the team returned from the border last night. Now where the hell are they Quigley?" he demanded, thrusting the barrel painfully against Danny's forehead.

Danny threw his hands in the air.

"I haven't a clue what two men you're talking about. Hell, your people have been watching me ever since we left the hostel. The locals tell me it's a pretty dangerous lake. The weather changes like a shot. I was out fishing there a few days ago and was warned about that very thing. I had no idea your men were out there and have no idea what might have happened to them," he insisted, looking Ray directly in the eyes.

Ray measured him for a long moment before easing back on the weapon and shoving him back in the car where the team got stuck into the food. Pete picked through his food and threw most of it out the window. The wolfish faced Yorkie, matched Ray in the speed of stuffing it down his throat. Danny still went by the old army rule, eat and rest when you can, and had some chicken and fries followed by a coke. The squashed conditions in the back of the car made it difficult to eat but they finished the food up quickly and then the car sped north again.

A good hour later they were pulling into a small town called Ballybofey. Ray stirred and extracted a sheet of paper with obvious directions written down on it. They made a left turn in the middle of the town and followed the road for several miles through bleak deserted farmlands. Ray called out several more turns before they pulled into a vast disused quarry. They all wearily emerged from the vehicle and Danny was shoved to one side as both Pete and Yorkie produced hand guns, which they casually covered him with. Ray the muscle man opened the boot of the car and pulling some sacks back, uncovered a rifle lying there. He reached forward spun quickly around and hurled the weapon at Danny who caught it deftly without even appearing to notice the sudden move. Ray's eyes flashed dangerously.

"OK, Quigley, you're supposed to be the guru on these. Tell me about the weapon you're holding there."

Danny briefly glanced at it and then returned his gaze.

"It's a Lee Enfield L42A1 bolt action sniper rifle. 7.62 caliber, .46.5 inches in length. Weight empty 9.8 lbs barrel 27.5 inches with a ten round capacity."

He took a closer look at it, "and, oh yes, it's been modified for a silencer. That good enough for you?" he finished.

The men snickered and Ray's face flushed. He stepped forward and grabbed Danny by his sweater.

"Look smart ass, I could finish you right now and Pete there could do the shot in Strabane quite easily. Crawford said to finish you if you tried anything and I'd have no hesitation in inventing an excuse right now. So cool that superior attitude of yours or we'll leave you here in this quarry. Pete's pretty shit hot with a rifle. He's ex guards and supposed to be good with a weapon."

Ray suddenly remembered what had happened to Josh when he got close to Danny and quickly stepped back to the car. Danny smiled at him as if reading his thoughts.

"Pete may very well be an excellent shot but Crawford wants me here because I've done this in real live situations on a number of occasions and I'd hate to be in your shoes if Pete has to make the shot and screws up."

He paused for a moment before continuing.

"Now I'm sure the package there has a telescopic sight so I would appreciate it if you didn't hurl it at me, as it's a precision instrument and can be damaged easily."

Ray flushed again at Danny's patronizing tone and rooted around in the boot of the car before turning back to hand Danny the telescopic sight. He passed a box of ammunition to Pete, and whispered a few words in his ear.

Danny looked at the rifle again. The Lee Enfield was used by the Brits as a sniper rifle and, while it wasn't his favorite, it was more than adequate for the job at hand. As he hefted it he checked the chamber automatically, which was empty as he expected. He looked up at Ray and cast his eyes down the length of the quarry.

"Not a bad weapon. Now I need to step off a hundred yards and one hundred and twenty five yards points and stick up some targets."

He pointed to some tin cans scattered around.

"These will do."

"Why one hundred and twenty five yards?" Ray demanded suspiciously. "The target is one hundred."

Danny gritted his teeth impatiently.

"I've found that targets estimated by someone else can be way out when it comes to the actual shoot. Was it measured off accurately or just stepped off roughly by someone. A big person will take longer strides obviously than a smaller person and you can have a range that can vary by twenty to twenty five yards. I'm just trying to prepare for a possible longer shot."

Ray studied him before turning to Pete.

"Is he right Pete or this just some trick he's trying to pull, planning to miss Adams completely, for example?"

Pete nodded.

"No he's spot on there Ray. If there's any weakness in the plan it's that. Crawford didn't say how the distance was measured. He's usually a dead cert on the details so I guess we just accepted the hundred yard shot."

Danny intruded again.

"What about elevation?"

Rays eyes darted from Danny to Pete.

"What about elevation? What the fuck d'you mean?"

Danny sighed as if addressing an idiot.

"God spare me from the amateurs! Is the shot a level shot from a ground floor or from a second or third floor? It can make one hell of a difference."

Ray was about to step forward again but Pete intervened and turned to Danny.

"It's from a second floor, okay? But there's no elevation cos the church steps are high up anyway where the people come out. It'll be a level shot mate."

Danny nodded.

"At last someone who knows what they're talking about," he said rolling his eyes.

Ray grunted, still gimlet eyed as he watched Quigley. Then he looked at Yorkie.

"Pace off the hundred and twenty five yards and stick up some of those cans on the spots."

Danny cut in.

"Look, this is something I have to do myself. I'm not relying on some little short ass like him to determine something where I need to be as accurate as possible."

Yorkie's face flushed as he strode forward to confront Danny.

"Who are you calling a short ass, Quigley?"

Ray stepped forward and thrust his massive arm in front of Yorkie, stopping him dead.

"Hold it there Yorkie. We don't need any hassle. Quigley's the expert and we need him right now. He's right. We have to let him step off the measurements here and then he'll have no excuses."

Yorkie sneered.

"Okay Quigley, we need you now, but afterwards you're mine!"

Ray shoved Yorkie back a few steps and then nodded to Pete to go with Danny as he walked into the quarry to find the ideal spot to shoot from. Finally he stopped. Putting the rifle down Danny started stepping off down the quarry counting out loud as he did so. Pete walked behind him.

A separate part of his mind was working on how to extricate himself from the dangerous situation he found himself in. He had three killers to overcome and the rifle could make the difference. He would only get one shot however, before the others started using their weapons. Positioning would be everything. Just how close they were to him was the pivotal point. Even if one crossed the other's path during the range testing, and assuming he had a live round in the chamber, he might just go for it. Could he persuade them that he needed to rest the barrel on one of their shoulder's for accuracy? He doubted it but examining all the options, made one flexible and ready to capitalize on any piece of luck that might come your way. Just as he'd deliberately provoked Ray and Yorkie previously, he now decided, as they reached the hundred yard spot, to attempt to build some sort of relationship with the long-faced alert looking Pete. He started placing several tin cans up on a pile of rocks and sand and paused midway.

"In the guards, Pete? A good outfit. Had occasion to work with you guys on exercises."

Pete squinted up at the top of the quarry.

"Yeah, good lot. Officers were right bastards though."

Danny laughed.

"So I heard. Our lot are downright disrespectful to officers in general. On exercises, your guards *pippers* didn't like us at all. How much time were you in for Pete?"

Pete glowered, nudging some sand with his toes.

He looked up.

"Ten months. Got kicked out for assaulting one of the bastards. Little pip-squeak put our platoon at risk on an exercise. Couldn't read a map and we ended up in the middle of live fire. Two got killed, four injured. I marched up to him and cold cocked him right there in the field. Was out on the street in a week. Bastards! I liked being in too. Could have made a career of it," he finished morosely.

Danny whistled and made a face at Pete as he finished the last couple of cans.

"Should have tried our mob, Pete. We could have used someone like you, a dedicated soldier."

Pete shrugged.

"Maybe. That selection process in *sass* is tough I hear."

"Yeah it is but if you start preparing ahead of time for the fitness stuff, as some people do, and are committed, you can make it. It's not impossible."

He peered closely at Pete.

"You got the right cut about you. I wouldn't be surprised if you'd made it. As I say we don't have much use for rank in the regiment. We see too much action and rely on each other to cover our asses."

Pete stared closely at him.

"You're not bullshitting me, Quigley, are you?"

Just then Ray shouted at them.

"Get a move on you two."

That was the end of the chat but Danny hoped that it might just give him the edge when it came to taking them out. A moment's hesitation on Pete's part could make all the difference.

They finished the one hundred and twenty five yard target and started back. Danny wasn't finished with Pete yet. He decided to plant another seed. Quietly speaking out of the side of his mouth he said

"I've worked with Crawford before Pete, and he's very big on not leaving any loose ends - anyone, and I mean anyone, who could talk and be a witness against him at some time in the future. I have no illusions about what's going to happen to me. But you Pete, and Yorkie, would be loose ends as far as Crawford is concerned. Ray's probably got his instructions after the hit tomorrow. A word to the wise, mate."

Pete's eyes narrowed, as he looked sideways at him, saying nothing. Danny nodded meaningfully at him. They strode back up to the car and Danny lifted the rifle up and turned, looking back at the range he'd laid out.

Pete studied the rifle and the familiar way Danny held it. "Where did you learn your sniping Danny?" he asked with interest. "In the *sass*?"

Without moving his head he replied quietly.

"Actually, I was lucky. We were offered two slots on a US marine corps sniping course and I got one of them. We had some guest snipers as trainers on the course, who had chalked up nearly a hundred kills in Vietnam, and the tricks they taught us were just amazing! The American public have no idea of the magnificent effort the military did over there and the battles they fought with courage and honor."

Pete's jaw dropped.

"A hundred kills? That's hard to credit."

"Yeah, a hundred confirmed kills as well. Believe it, those guys were warriors!"

Pete nodded at the weapon.

"Is this the weapon you'd select given the choice?"

Danny shook his head.

"Well this is fine for the shooting I'm going to do tomorrow, but if I was doing some long range shooting, I'd go for a Winchester model 70, caliber 30-06, used by the marines and equipped with a variable-power telescope. The Russians have a decent weapon called the Mosin-nagant 7.62 x 55 mm sniper rifle with a stubby 3.5 power PU scope, which is good up to 1000 yards. It was the primary Viet Cong and NVA sniper rifle. The Winchester however could fire way beyond this range and gave the US marines the edge."

He reached his hand out sideways to Pete.

"Okay, lets do it. Where's the ammunition?"

Just then Ray strolled up to them grinning and gestured to Pete to stop him. He took out his mobile phone stepped to one side and spoke quickly into it. Snapping it shut he looked bleakly at Danny.

"Got a little surprise for you Danny, before we pass out the ammo."

They heard the sound of a car and in a moment it appeared and drove in beside them. It contained the other two members of Crawford's team who got out. Danny's heart dropped into his boots. There was one other passenger in the car – Siobhan.

CHAPTER 63

London

The Director General had just got back into her office and summoned a young technician wearing glasses, called Adrian from the lab. He had an apologetic expression on his face as he sat down in front of her.

"Tell me what you've got Adrian," she commanded.

Adrian blinked.

"Ah, not so much ma'am. You see the tower was hit in such a way that …" She cut him off.

"I don't understand computers and I don't want to. Just tell me what you've managed to salvage from it, if anything."

He passed a sheet of paper across to her. She glanced at the few words typed on it.

"This is it? Surely with all that expensive equipment you've got down there …" her voice trailed off as she saw him grimace and shake his head.

"Sorry ma'am, that's the lot. For the moment anyway. We're going to try a few more tests. No promises mind you, but we'll try our best."

She shook her head in frustration.

"I have a retired agent of the secret service murdered down the country and the chief constable is breathing down my neck for leads. This is not helpful. Anyway, back you go to your lab and let me know when you get anything else. Stay on after work if needs be. I'm authorizing overtime for this and keep it under wraps, whatever you know or suspect you know. Understood?"

He nodded and quickly left the office. She pulled the piece of paper closer and examined what was on it.

Quigley. Assassination. Crawford. Team operating. Republic. It was the last item listed that made her gasp. It was tomorrow's date. She sat down and clicked on her intercom and summoned Sophia to her office. When she popped her head around the door the D.G. queried

"Those files I asked you to go through, how far have you got, and more importantly, any relevant names coming up?"

"Making good progress ma'am. I'm back three years already and I've been jotting down the names of people that Patton worked with on more than one occasion."

She passed the list across to the D.G. who started running her eyes down it. She flinched at one time and highlighted a name. A few moments later she did the same again. At the end of the list she sat back in silence.

"The name Quigley comes up twice and I see you've written SAS beside it. Presumably he was part of a saber team we called in to support some operation and Patton was involved right?"

"Yes ma'am. Probably in the training end, but occasionally he was in the field acting as liaison. Oh, I took the liberty of checking with Hereford. Quigley was honorably discharged six months ago."

"Good work. Now who was in overall charge of those operations that involved Patton and Quigley?"

"Colonel Crawford, ma'am," she answered quickly.

"Crawford eh? One of the die-hards. They'll be prising his fingernails off the door jambs in his Belfast office when we stand him and his unit down soon. Gerry Adams and Ian Paisley's colleagues are practically bosom pals now and the Northern Ireland problem will soon be no more."

She was about to continue when Sophia interrupted her.

"I discreetly called the Belfast office. I know one of the admin girls there from a course we did together. Colonel Crawford came into the office briefly yesterday and left after making some phone calls. Apart from that he hasn't been in very much recently. No one seems to know where he is ma'am. I told her to keep my call to herself by the way."

"Well done Sophia. Now if I could only figure out what's going on here. There's a lot of loose ends but no hard intelligence. Grab a pen from that flip chart stand and start jotting down some points to see if they make any sense."

Sophia hurried across and turned over a fresh page on the flip chart and started writing as the D.G. called out the points:

Patton murdered and buried in garden shed.

Not a robbery.

Computer shot up.

Email from another party warning of his murder and pointing to a message on the word section of the computer.

Lab comes up with a few sparse words. Sophie listed those too.

Patton's files show a trooper, Quigley, was a participant in at least two operations in the past three years.

Quigley's name is on the list the lab boys brought out, so is Colonel Crawford's.

Colonel Crawford was in overall command of both those operations.

Colonel Crawford has only shown up briefly at his office in the last three days.

Tomorrows date listed above - was it the date when some assassination was taking place?

Where did Republic come in?

And teams operating there? M15 were only authorized to operate in the U.K. Was there some illegal, off the wall operation going down?

The D.G. sat back in frustration.

"It's not making any sense to me Sophia. Is there some assassination planned for the security conference? Should we warn them that some renegade, ex-SAS might be planning a hit? If so, knowing those lads as we do, we need to completely review our security arrangements. God how I hate washing my laundry in front of those MI6 people. We have to sort this out ourselves somehow."

She paused as something stirred in the back of her mind.

"Quigley, Quigley. Now where have we heard that name recently? Wait a minute, wasn't his name on the news not too long ago? His house burned down. Some thugs killed. That's it Sophia and I'm sure the Metropolitan Police were looking for him. Can you get on to someone and find out where they're at on this? It's Quigley's whereabouts I'm interested in, but don't reveal why you're calling. Understood?"

Sophia nodded and dashed out to her office. Within a few minutes she was back with a name and telephone number scribbled down. She pointed to it.

"D.I. White was in charge of the case and a warrant was issued for Quigley's arrest but he's evaded being picked up so far, apparently."

The D.G. stared at the details and picked up the phone. She put it on speaker so that Sophia could follow the call too. It took a few moments to get through to D.I. White.

"D.I. White, this is the Director General of MI5 I'm interested in the status of the ex soldier Quigley. Can you update me on the case? I know it was all over the papers but I don't tend to read them."

"The Director General! Honored by your interest ma'am. Does your call mean you have some information you can offer on Quigley's whereabouts?"

"My interests, as you know cover an extremely wide area D.I. White. There may be some connection but I can't divulge anything right now, but I promise to provide any or all information that we come across. Now can you briefly fill me in on the case?"

D.I. White sighed and then proceeded to go over the case: Quigley and an office girl in an attempted assault - Quigley's house burned and the office girls murdered in a fire - the three thugs killed in a fashion used by Special Forces - they go to interview him but he's fled.

"That's two weeks ago D.I White. What's been happening on the investigation since then?" the D.G. asked.

"Well, we eventually located his wife's mother in Bath and one of the locals interviewed her. Told a strange story about her daughter, Quigley's wife, being followed around in Bath by some men."

"Followed? Were these Special Branch from Bath or some of your people?"

"Absolutely not ma'am. That was my first thought, but they had apparently no interest in her whereabouts and we didn't know where she was until later. According to the mother, Quigley came back to Bath two days ago at which time her daughter and grandchild vanished completely. She's apparently quite worried about them."

"Came back from where D.C. White? You said Quigley came back."

"Oh the Republic of Ireland. We discovered that he'd flown out from Bristol the day after he fled London."

"The Republic of Ireland," she whispered. Louder she asked him, "did you discover if he flew out of the UK with his family?"

"We checked all airlines and ferries ma'am. No signs of them. Oh, and one other thing, on the day Quigley came back for them an assault was reported in Bath by two different citizens. Two men got knocked out on the street and one was reported to be trying to prevent a young girl from getting into a car. A small-statured man got out and flattened them. One report is that he threw a knife that struck one of the men on the forehead with the handle, then leaped across the car at the other man, and literally cold cocked him, if you'll pardon the language ma'am."

She was silent for a long moment.

"A small man, you say? You know of course that Quigley was nearly six feet in height. Sounds like he had some help, doesn't it?"

"We hadn't really given that assault any consideration as involving Quigley, but I see where you're coming from ma'am. We might look at that again."

"So where is Quigley now, have you any idea D.I. White?"

"No ma'am, not exactly, but the Irish Gardai were notified and there's been a possible sighting of him in a place called Sligo, on the north west coast. It's being followed up right now. As you know, we take murders very seriously and this case is still being actively pursued."

They talked for a while longer before closing the call. The two women looked at each other.

"Wow!" breathed Sophia. "This gets curiouser and curiouser doesn't it? Shouldn't you be involving one of your directors from the appropriate section at this stage ma'am?"

The D.G. leaned forward, her face intense.

"Probably Sophia but we don't know which section it falls under as yet – subversion, terrorism? In any event, I don't want to wash my dirty laundry all across the building. Wouldn't do my career any good that's for sure. But we do have a strong clue. Quigley, Quigley, Quigley! It's all about him. If we can find him we can probably crack this open. I don't like the idea of an ex SAS squaddy on the loose with possible sniping skills, and an assassination being mentioned. Get me a map of Bath and the Cotswolds areas will you please, Sophie."

Hot on the chase she dashed out and came back five minutes later with a map.

"Sorry ma'am, had to go downstairs for it," she said quietly as the D.G. laid the map out on a table at the side of the room.

She circled Bath with a highlighter and then moved to Burton-on- the-Water and circled that too.

Sophie gasped.

"That's close ma'am, very close. You don't think ... ...?"

"I really don't know what to think right now. People following Quigley's wife in Bath and they're not police. A mention on that lab. report of a team operating in the Republic, obviously the Republic of Ireland. Could it be one of ours? Impossible, we're not authorized. God if the media got hold of this! But who could be doing this?"

They both looked at each other their eyes widening.

"Crawford," the D.G. breathed in awe. "My God I should have axed him months ago but he has his mentors at the home office. What is he up to now?"

Sophie sat there saying nothing, hardly daring to breath. The D.G. finally looked at her directly.

"Okay, here's what we do Sophie. Get onto the right people who can trace all calls coming out of Crawford's office in Belfast for the past two weeks. Include his mobile phone in this too and come back to me. Organize all the help you need, overtime no problem, and keep this information between us two. We may have some really dirty laundry to wash here and hopefully it's not too late. We can only contain so much in the name of national security. Go to it girl!"

Sophia dashed out of the office while the D.G. sat there, her mind spinning. Finally through gritted teeth she muttered.

"Crawford you bastard, just exactly what are you up to?"

CHAPTER 64

The two new arrivals were grinning as they hustled Siobhan across and shoved her into Ray's grasp. He pulled out his glock and placed it on her head, as he positioned her between himself and Danny. There was a sneer in his voice as he spoke to Danny.

"Crawford thought we might need some extra insurance in Strabane, seeing as how your wife and kid have disappeared. He advised us to be especially watchful when you were sighting in the rifle."

Danny shrugged his shoulder's keeping his eyes away from Siobhan's stricken face.

"Hey, she means nothing to me," he chuckled. "Spent 30 minutes on a bus ride with her is all. I'm afraid Crawford's got his facts wrong – again," he emphasized.

Ray's face reflected momentary confusion as he looked uncertainly at the two men who had brought her. Then he pressed the weapon harder against Siobhan's forehead. Looking meaningfully at Danny, he growled

"Not much sense carrying spare baggage with us then. Might as well off her right here. The quarry's a good place to get rid of a body, Quigley."

Danny had to make a quick assessment but his instincts were strong that if Crawford had wanted Siobhan at the actual event in Strabane, the crew wouldn't top her sooner. Danny

THE QUIGLEY ALCHEMY

yawned and turned his back on Ray and the woman, speaking as he did so.

"Your call Ray. Right now my focus is on hitting Gerry Adams tomorrow and no weapon pointed at some woman is going to make any difference. Now where's the ammunition? I thought we came here to sight in this rifle."

Siobhan gasped.

"Danny, how could you?" her face stark with fear.

Ray seized on this.

"Ah, Danny is it? Now there's a thing isn't there? Sounds like she's sweet on him. Maybe there's something here after all. The Colonel doesn't get it wrong very often."

Turning, he shoved her back towards the two men who had brought her and she was hustled back into the car. Danny let the tense air out of his lungs. He had been one second away from a mad and useless charge at Ray, with the empty rifle, if he'd shown any real intent to shoot Siobhan. But his purpose had been to get the crew to discount the hold Siobhan might have on him. If they didn't believe she was that important they might not stay as close to her and give him an opportunity to spring a surprise attack.

Ray sprung another surprise on him.

"You only get one bullet tomorrow for the hit Quigley. Crawford's instructions. Kinda limits you if you get any ideas, doesn't it?"

Danny was genuinely shocked.

"But the target could move or bend down for something at the precise moment I fire. A photographer, if there's one there, could be ducking and weaving and just get in the way at the last moment. I might need a second shot and with a silencer I could because they might not have a clue that they were under attack. This is ludicrous! Crawford's knows this for Christ sake. What's he playing at?"

Ray chuckled.

"You're supposed to be the great hot shot, Quigley. One shot Quigley they called you in the regiment according to the Colonel. So now's your chance to show us all just how bloody

399

clever you are. One round is all you get tomorrow and Pete there is going to dole out one round at a time as you sight that rifle in. Go ahead Pete."

Pete coughed.

"You know Ray I hate to say it but he's right about that second shot. I was on the range a lot when I was in the guards and they taught you to be ready for that second shot, or a secondary target."

"I don't give a shit for what you think, Pete. You got tossed out of the Guards 'cos you couldn't hack it. Don't talk to me about strategy. We do it exactly as Crawford laid it out - one shot for Gerry Adams and there's no secondary target. Now get on with it or we'll be here all bloody day."

Watching Pete's expression, Danny noticed the anger clouding his face at being put down in front of the rest of the crew. Pete just ducked his head and started extracting a handful of ammunition to dole out. As Pete leaned forward he stumbled against Danny momentarily, but in that moment Danny felt his hand dip swiftly into his pocket. Turning the rifle casually in his left hand Danny reached in and took a tissue out of his pocket and blew his nose. In the process he discovered a single round that had obviously been transferred there by Pete whose expression never changed. With somewhat higher spirits Danny turned and started the important job of familiarizing himself with the rifle and setting it up for the kill the following day.

CHAPTER 65

London

Sophia came dashing into her boss's office without the usual knock and plumped herself breathlessly down in the chair opposite her. The Director raised her eyebrows, a slight smile creasing her features.

"You look like someone caught in the heat of the chase Sophia. I don't usually involve you in my work like this. Perhaps I should more often. Anyway what have you got?" she asked.

"Patton called Crawford at the Belfast office yesterday."

She laid the paper upside down on the desk and pointed to a date.

The D.G. whistled.

"My God, that's probably the same day he was murdered. If Crawford was in Belfast though, he couldn't have done it."

"There's more ma'am," Sophia burst out. "Crawford made a series of calls to Bath over the previous several days."

"Did you discover who those calls were to?"

"Yes ma'am, a cell phone registered to a Mr. Peterson. I checked with the employee section downstairs and we don't have an agent on staff by that name."

The D.G. pursed her lips.

"This gets more and more interesting. Crawford has been contacting this Peterson in Bath over several days and we know that Quigley's wife was being followed by a team, not the police. To properly follow someone 24/7, we know you need at least 24 people. Following a simple housewife could probably be done with a much smaller number, possibly two to three teams of two people each. What I can't figure out is where's Crawford getting them from? His people have been whittled down over the past year with the new stability in Northern Ireland. I'm obviously missing something here, Sophia."

"Yes ma'am. Oh I didn't mean that, but there's something else. Crawford called Peterson on the same day that Patton contacted him and the system picked Peterson up in the Swindon catchment area. Here, let me show you on the map."

She spread the map out and circled Bath, Swindon and Burton-on- the-Water. Awareness flooded into her eyes. She looked at Sophia.

"Quigley's friend zaps two people in Bath and Crawford's teams then leave the area because the target has disappeared. On the way they get a call from Crawford who just talked to Patton. They're practically on his doorstep at Swindon and they drop in on him."

"And he gets killed." Sophia finished for her.

"Yes, he gets killed, but who is this Peterson? Very unwise to use his own mobile phone for an illicit purpose. Surely he would know the scope of what we can do today tracing calls. He should have bought a disposable or a few of them and just dumped them."

"Well he's not with MI5, we've established that," said Sophia. "Perhaps he didn't know."

"No, but Crawford does and should have warned him," the D.G. said thoughtfully.

Sophia's faced shifted.

"Maybe the situation got so fluid that they had to cobble the whole thing together at short notice - Quigley and his wife making a run for it I mean ma'am."

Her boss looked at her, nodding thoughtfully.

"You could be right there, Sophia. Spot on in fact. Now this Peterson individual. We may just have our murderer and I'm sure he wasn't alone. Get our people doing a trace on this name right now. What I still can't figure out is how Crawford could mount such an operation with so few MI5 agents left on his staff?"

"Perhaps he hired his own ma'am." Sophia volunteered.

The Director General stared at her.

"Hired his own? How the hell would he fund it?"

Sophia made a face.

"He's been running that Belfast office for years. Who knows what he's been up to ma'am."

"His own slush fund," the D.G. exclaimed. "That could be it. But how the hell are we going to contain this now that Pandora's box has been opened?"

"Should you brief the Chief Constable on your findings and suspicion at this stage ma'am?" Sophia enquired.

"Absolutely not! We'd be pointing the finger at a senior MI5 employee, Colonel Crawford, and I don't want Special Branch people trampling around in our patch. No, leave that for the moment. I'll give him a call later because he'll be expecting that anyway. After all, it was one of our people who was murdered."

"You have one of their Special Branch coming up tomorrow ma'am for an interview and we have to send someone over to Cheltenham to identify poor old Patton," Sophia reminded her.

The D.G. nodded.

"Yes I know. Hopefully we may have more information by then. In any event you are still culling out some names from his past work. People whom he was instrumental in gathering intelligence on and who were put away as a result: terrorists, criminals, people smugglers and so on. Patton was a pretty useful chap from what I heard."

Sophia was rapidly making notes on her pad and after clarifying some areas she dashed out of the D.G.'s office.

The Director General's presence was required at the conference and she reluctantly left Thames House in the waiting car. She liked to focus on a case when it was starting to hum and the implications of the Quigley case were causing alarm bells to go off in her mind. Her biggest concern was that she suspected someone important was about to be assassinated and an MI5 operative was up to his ears in the organization of it.

CHAPTER 66

"You smell of death and death is coming for you Peterson," Courtney mouthed.

He saw the blow coming but he didn't try to avoid it. He crashed back against the wall of the room where he had been imprisoned since they returned from Burton-on-the-Water. Peterson had taunted him all the way back refusing even to stop at a washroom when Courtney requested it. He had received no food the first day. The following morning a cup of coffee and some toast were shoved in the door. This was obviously some sort of general holding cell with darkened windows covered with bars and a small washroom.

Peterson and another man came in during the day to interrogate him about his knowledge of the current situation and others who might have access to the information. They also wanted to know where the Quigley family were hiding, now that they had disappeared from the hostel at Lough Gill. His non-committal replies angered Peterson who shoved him into a chair and then proceeded to slap his face viciously. Peterson's eyes shone with malice and enjoyment as he punched Courtney several times in the stomach. Despite the pain, Courtney never made a sound, which seemed to anger Peterson further. After several minutes he stood there breathing heavily, perspiration popping out on his forehead. That was when Courtney had made his remark and it drove Peterson demented. He proceeded to beat Courtney unmercifully and, at one time, slammed him with an elbow to the side of the head which stunned him and he sagged forward.

"He's coming for you," Courtney whispered, "and death comes with him."

Peterson peered at him, his mouth twisting angrily.

"Who's coming? Speak up you bastard, I can't hear you."

Courtney lifted his head with great effort and looked straight into his eyes.

"Quigley's coming. Your time is almost up on this earth Peterson."

Fear flashed across Peterson's face and he lashed out catching Courtney on the point of the chin. He sagged forwards and his solid weight caused the chair to crash onto the floor. Courtney blacked out.

CHAPTER 67

Strabane

The two cars had crossed over the bridge into the North of Ireland at Strabane and eased through the late evening traffic. They stopped at the back of a detached house and all emerged wearily from the vehicle. Previously Siobhan, several miles back down the road and traveling in the same car as Danny, had cried out as if in pain, startling the group. She glanced at Danny and he could see tears in her eyes.

Ray grinned in the front seat.

"Slow reactor our girl here. Just think what will happen to her if Danny Boy doesn't deliver to morrow." He examined her lewdly. "Shame to off a nice piece of meat like her without some fun first. What d'you say Yorkie?"

The driver cackled as the car swerved on the road.

"My thought's exactly chief. Nice piece of stuff there," he drooled.

Ray leaned forward and whispered in Yorkies's ear and they chuckled together. Danny felt Siobhan's eyes on him again with an unspoken message. He could see fear in them. Once in the house they were hustled upstairs and led to a bedroom where the door was locked behind them. At the sound of the key Siobhan hurled herself into his arms.

"Oh Danny, he's being hurt, terribly!"

Danny lifted his head back looking searchingly into her tear-streaked face.

"Who's being hurt, Siobhan?" he asked, but he already suspected whom she was referring to.

"C.C.! I can feel it. He's been tortured. I felt it back there."

He tightened his arms around her.

"That's when you cried out. God, how do you do that? How does it happen? It's just hard for me to take in Siobhan," he ventured.

She pulled herself out of his arms and went over and sat on the edge of the bed her head in her hands, still weeping. Danny followed and sat down beside her, putting his arm around her.

"Sorry Siobhan. That was insensitive of me. I've seen this with you and C.C. before when we were being kidnapped by Bonat that time."

She nodded dumbly lifting her head.

"Oh, what's going to happen to him after tomorrow, and to us Danny? They wont need us any more will they?"

Danny looked around quickly wondering if the room was bugged. He stood up and quickly walked around examining areas where a listening device could be placed. He found none but he noticed that there was a cupboard-like room with a wash basin in the corner and he gestured to Siobhan to join him inside. She looked puzzled but came across and crammed in as he started running the water in the wash hand basin. Understanding flashed across her face. He leaned forward and started speaking quietly to her and when he'd finished he saw hope reflected in her face. Just to prop her hopes further he extracted the bullet that Pete had slipped and which he, during the car journey, had transferred to his sock.

"We get through tomorrow, then we go for C.C., that's a promise," he whispered feelingly.

"Do you know where he is, Danny?" she entreated.

He nodded.

"I've got an idea, but it could be useful if you were with me with that gift you have. You know, monitor where's he's at, his condition and so on."

"You mean if he's killed?" she said despairingly.

Danny stayed silent. He figured Ray's strategy in putting them together was the hope that they would bond together and she would be more of a hold on him on the morrow.

Back in the room a while later the door was shoved open and some sandwiches pushed inside. One of the men who had brought Siobhan up from the car stood in the doorway along with Yorkie, who looked lasciviously at Siobhan.

"Get her warmed up for me Quigley. I'll be back later for a sample of her goodies," he taunted, laughing as he pulled the door closed.

They weren't in much of a mood to eat after that but Danny forced himself, knowing that tomorrow he would need all his strength.

Her eyes pleaded with him.

"Danny, you heard him. Will he be back?"

He shrugged covering her hands with his.

"Don't worry. If he does I promise you I won't let him lay a hand on you. Okay?"

"But what can you do Danny? There's so many of them and with guns. They'll kill you?"

He shook his head.

"I don't think so. They need me for tomorrow. Let's wait and see what happens. He might not come back."

But he did. Two hours later he appeared in the doorway leering, and the grinning face of the second guard behind him.

Siobhan stood up fearfully, her face stricken. Danny eased himself forward between her and the door. Yorkie waved the pistol at him.

"Come on Quigley, you've had your chance. Now it's my turn. Move aside."

Danny looked bleakly at him.

"Go play with yourself. It's probably the only satisfaction you normally get anyway, you pervert."

Yorkie started to lunge forward, his face snarling with rage. Danny's first strategy had been to anger him to such a degree that he would come after him. That would have given him a chance to disarm him and use the weapon on the second guard. The second guard was smarter. He grabbed Yorkie and pulled him back.

"You stupid fool, you were warned not to get close to him. You see what he did to Josh back in the police station? He's just trying to provoke you into going for him."

Yorkie paused blinking, his eyes glaring with rage.

"Didn't fall for that little ruse did we? Now step back or I'll blow you apart. That little chick is going to have the ride of her life!"

Danny laughed with amusement.

"No, I'm not stepping back you moron. If you go after her you're going to have to come over the top of me. Oh yes, you can kill me, but be warned, I don't kill easily. If you do kill me I'd be interested in what you tell Colonel Crawford when Gerry Adams walks away, because you couldn't keep your pecker in your pants. Your call mate," he challenged softly as he slid his feet and hands into a fighting stance.

Yorkie looked uncertainly back at the second guard, whose face was no longer grinning.

"To hell with this. Crawford will have your balls for breakfast if you screw this up."

With that he grasped him by the collar and started to haul him out of the room. Yorkie resisted and thrust his now feral face forward.

"You're mine tomorrow, Quigley. You hear that?" He screamed.

Then they were gone and the door slammed. They heard the lock click on the door. Siobhan flew across the room into his arms. They stood like that for a long time.

Lifting her tear streaked face, she asked him

"Will he be back? I would die if that animal touched me," she gasped.

He shook his head.

"I don't believe so. They're more afraid of Crawford than they are of me," he said, as convincingly as he could.

Nevertheless he grabbed a chair and anchored it under the door-knob, to give them some warning, if he did return.

She looked up at him again starting to recover her composure.

"Yesterday you told those men that I meant nothing to you. Even suggested they kill me. I was so confused Danny. I thought you did care for me."

Ignoring any possible monitoring device, Danny led her back to the bed where he sat her down.

"Look sweetheart," he whispered "I like you an awful lot, but yesterday I was planting the idea in those people's minds that I didn't. They wanted to use you as a lever to make sure I go through with this killing tomorrow. If they thought you were important to me they would stay right close to you, probably with a gun shoved against your head. Oh they'll still use you as a hostage, but perhaps not with the same conviction as before. They might get sloppy, leave some space around you, which might give me an opportunity to take back control of the situation. Remember what I told you to do when the action starts? Be alert and ready because people's minds tend to freeze when bullets start to fly around them. I need you to react instantly. It's the only chance we have tomorrow, Siobhan. It's all down to split timing. You hear me?"

She nodded.

"But five men all armed, and you just with an empty rifle … …" she trailed off.

He grinned taking out the second bullet and holding it up.

"Not quite, not quite, Siobhan. This could be the great equalizer on the morrow."

Later Danny whispered,

"I need to get to sleep. So should you."

She nodded and avoiding his gaze went around the far side of the bed and carefully undressed down to her underwear. Then she slipped quickly under the covers. Danny did the same and crawled hesitantly under as well, keeping well over on his side. They lay like that for what seemed a long while. Then Siobhan rolled over against him. His whole body jumped

411

as if hit by an electric shock as he felt her bare skin against his. He rolled over quickly and put his arms around her. It was only then that he realized that she was weeping silently as he felt the wet tears on her face.

"Hey, it's okay Siobhan, it's going to be okay," he said tenderly.

He felt her head shake violently.

"No, it's not Danny. Our first and probably our last night together. I've dreamed of this since I met you, but not like this. Not like this," she said feelingly.

She clung to him desperately.

He held her for a while saying nothing. Then he started to kiss her wet eyelids and the side of her neck. Feeling aroused despite the situation he moved to her lips and gently explored their ripeness, aware of an excitement building inside him. He cupped his hand on her breast and felt her heart pounding reminding him of a small bird which got in the house, when he was a child, and he had to catch it and free it. He kissed the top of her breasts over her bra and felt a tremor run through her. He moved slowly down her body licking and nuzzling her stomach. It was when he was kissing the inside of her thighs that a moan escaped her lips. He was reminded of a motor car that his uncle had stored for years and allowed Danny and his mates to work on. The day it shuddered and burst into life was a memorable one for him. Now it felt like the motor in Siobhan's body was slowly coming to life under his touch as one nerve end after another was activated. He felt her thighs part and gently reached under and slid her panties off. She moaned again and sat up partly, and impatiently pulled her bra over her head. Danny's mouth eagerly sought out the new treasures and she gasped, reaching down and attempting to drag off his jockeys. His mind swirling he reached down and helped her and felt her hands, now eager, holding him. He shuddered at her touch and could only take it for a minute. Then he transferred his attention to the lower part, burying his face in her body, relishing the taste and the softness of her. She couldn't take it for very long either. He was amazed at her strength as she suddenly reached over and pulled him on top of her and guided him into her. Both could contain themselves no longer. Her nails drove into his back as she pulled him down thrusting almost desperately up at him. Danny didn't know how long it went on. They just lost themselves in each other, everything swept out of their minds. Danny had never encountered anything like it in his years as a married man and other liaisons that he'd had. They could have been both shot in the head right then and they wouldn't have noticed. Suddenly she cried out and gasped between her teeth as if trying to stop a scream. Danny exploded into her at the same time and they clung to each other for what seemed an eternity. Gradually, they came down from the pinnacle and murmured endearments to each other. Almost as one they drifted back lying beside each other, just holding hands, each in a land of wonderment of their own. They had snatched a prize beyond measure from the jaws of death that nothing could ever take from them. A short while later, as if by agreement, they rolled back to their own sides of the bed and were both almost instantly asleep.

CHAPTER 68

The Killing Ground

Danny woke suddenly, his mind alert as if some prearranged alarm clock had gone off. It reminded him of the many times in the regiment when they waited for dawn to get up and launch a pre-planned attack on the enemy. His mind felt clear and focused. He could see it was almost dawn from a shaft of light coming under the bottom of the door. Siobhan was still sleeping, her face partly buried in the pillow and a sheet covering one ear. He was tempted to kiss her but chose to slip out of bed, searching around for his jockeys and slipping them on. He then crept out into a square patch of the floor and started going through an intensive exercise program, which included hand strikes and kicks. Siobhan slept on through it. Finished at last and soaked in perspiration, he crept into the closet washroom and quickly and quietly washed his whole body with a washcloth and dried off. Then he carefully crept back into the room and dressed silently.

He sat there in a chair his eyes closed as he visualized the day ahead of him. The regiment used to have these preparation sessions where everything and anything was challenged and options were debated and considered or discarded. He felt the steel and expectation of battle start to course through his veins as he considered the enemy and their strengths and possible weaknesses. He felt his anger and resolve build as he thought of what Crawford and his team had done to him and his family over the past two weeks. He looked at Siobhan lying there and was astonished at the depth of his feelings. Was last night really their last intimate moment together? he wondered. He shook his head and felt his anger and resolve grow but also with a certain cold detachment.

He knew he would had to kill people today.

He heard Courtney's voice in his head warning him of the spirit of violence in him that could destroy him. He understood now that this was from his childhood when he learned to hate his stepfather. He'd let that go with Courtney's help. All that was left was a realization that he had a gift, that evil existed and that he had to fight it when and where he could. He took no satisfaction in this but accepted it as a truism for his life now. He lifted his head and tensed all his muscles, holding them for ten seconds and then letting them go. He nodded to himself. He was ready.

He reached forward and gently caressed Siobhan's cheek as she sighed and started to come awake. The day was here.

Siobhan was barely washed and dressed when the door crashed open and Ray stuck his head in and looked around suspiciously as if expecting an attack. Danny shrugged and spread his hands as if suggesting that resistance was useless.

"All right you two. Out," he snapped.

When they were outside he prodded Siobhan.

"Downstairs to the kitchen and get some breakfast organized for the team." He pointed to one of the crew.

"Go with her, and after we're all fed I want everyone back up here for the briefing. Look lively now!" he barked.

He turned to Danny.

"Quigley over here and take your first look at the target area."

He steered Danny across to a small bedroom window, which looked out on a squat church directly across from them. Danny opened the catch on the middle of the small window and carefully slid it down. It opened easily telling him that this had been previously prepared. The mesh curtains were still hanging down and Danny slid them apart about two inches on the wire. For Ray's sake, he nodded with satisfaction and turned to him slowly.

"This is ideal. I can rest the weapon on the lower frame for steadiness and these curtains will make me practically invisible. The distance looks more like a hundred and twenty five yards to me, so the weapon is sighted for that. The silencer will make it impossible to determine where the shot was fired from. By the way, will Adams have any security with him - squad cars or such?"

"Shouldn't think so. We've been shadowing him for six months and on personal trips he doesn't bother any more," he sneered. "That's the new deal now. Peace has come upon us Quigley, but not for long after today, eh?."

A few of the men loitering in the room laughed.

Danny looked around.

"Where's the owners of the house? I'm concerned about interference - a child coming upstairs or whatever," he suggested with a anxious look on his face.

Ray scowled.

"Not your problem, Quigley. Gone off on a shopping trip for the day by arrangement. We were going to tie him up but had a change of plan. Now any other concerns?"

Danny nodded.

"Just that one bullet you're giving me. I've no chance to recover the ball if the first shot doesn't connect."

Pete cut in from the other window where he was examining the terrain outside.

"He's got a point Ray. Most good riflemen don't just plan to make a hit on one shot. The chance for a second is always a useful option to have."

Ray narrowed his eyes and looked at him. Lifting the Glock up he pressed it directly on Danny's forehead.

"I'm a great believer in motivation, Quigley. If you miss that first shot you're dead meat. You hear me, and your little playmate with you."

Behind him, Yorkie cackled.

"He's dead meat anyway."

Ray turned on him savagely slapping him across the face with the barrel of the Glock, sending him sprawling.

"Shut up you fucking moron or you'll be preceding Gerry Adams. D'you get that?"

Yorkie crawled back onto his feet, blood trickling from a cut cheek. "Yeah, okay Ray. I get it."

His eyes blazed at Danny and he could see the pure malevolence on his face. Ray relaxed and directed half of the team to go down stairs for breakfast after which the second group would follow. Danny was escorted down with the first. It was a sullen breakfast with little conversation. Yorkie snickered, leering at Siobhain, and making lewd comments.

Danny felt proud of her stony demeanor, showing no reaction to the grim situation. Neither, by agreement, made eye contact and he treated her with studied indifference. Afterwards, they were replaced by the second breakfast shift, who ate quickly and came straight back upstairs. The impending action was getting to some of them, Danny observed.

Ray assembled them in the top room making sure that Danny and Siobhan were covered independently by the team. He knows his stuff, Danny thought, marking him down as a primary target if the opportunity presented itself.

"Now listen up. Some of you could end up behind bars if you don't follow the plan in exact detail. Danny is going to be positioned at the window obviously, with Yorkie standing directly behind him, weapon cocked and directed at his head. If he tries anything or misses the shot, you kill him. Understood?"

Yorkie, now recovered, grinned.

"No argument there boss."

"Pete and Claud."

He pointed to one of Siobhan's kidnappers.

"Stand directly behind the woman, with pistols at the ready, and blow her head off if Quigley screws up in any way. Understood?"

The two men nodded, glancing at each other.

"I'll be at the foot of the stairs making sure we have no unwanted visitors and watching the two cars which will be facing the road with the keys in them. I'll start both cars at approximately ten minutes before eleven. Harry," he pointed to Siobhan's other kidnapper, "will be at the top of the stairs in my view and I can warn him if anyone starts over to the house. This is, I should say, highly unlikely according to the owner, but just in case. I've seen the most detailed plans go tits up because of one tiny detail that wasn't covered. After the hit we disperse in two cars in accordance with the agreed plan and lie low when you get to your safe houses. Dump your weapons once you clear town in case you're stopped somewhere. Any questions?"

Pete shifted his feet.

"What about Quigley and the girl, and the rifle? What will the police find when they discover where the shot came from?"

Yorkie sniggered, glancing maliciously at Danny. Ray gave him a warning look, as he appeared to consider the question.

"We take both of them with us of course and just drop them off somewhere out in the country, where they'll have to walk a long way to get to any town. I'm not sure they'll be too anxious to go to the police and say; oh we just killed Gerry Adams. Sorry we didn't mean to. Those bad men made us do it."

Some of the men chuckled. Pete seemed unconvinced but said nothing. His gaze flicked across at Danny.

Ray continued.

"The rifle we leave here. It can't be traced back to any of us."

He coughed glancing at Danny.

"You'd better wipe it off before you clear out with us."

Danny reflected again on the brilliance of the plan. He wasn't going anywhere, and neither probably was Siobhan. What the police would find was a sniper rifle used by an ex Brit SAS squaddy, found dead at the scene, and Northern

Ireland would be set aflame. At least he knew where he stood, and it was on very thin ice! Ray handed Danny the rifle and he took it, snapping the breech open as all soldiers did on being handed a weapon. He attached the scope carefully and then slammed the empty magazine into the weapon.

Ray reached forward and held the rifle barrel with a gloved hand.

"Wait a minute, what do you need a magazine for anyway? It's empty."

Danny shook his head wearily.

"Do I have to do a training session with you lot. Some riflemen hold the magazine to steady the shot, instead of the stock. Okay?"

"He's right boss." Pete cut in, "I've seen it - used it myself."

Ray glanced in irritation at both of them.

" If you're so shit hot, Pete, how come the guards kicked your ass out?"

He nodded to Danny.

"Oh all right, get on with it, Quigley."

Pete flushed and glanced at Danny, who raised his eyebrows slightly.

Ray looked at his watch.

"Ten minutes to go. Lets get ready."

Danny held his hand up.

"Just a query, Ray. Who determined that Adams would be directly on the steps at 11 am? Is he arriving then or coming out after the baptism? These ceremonies can take awhile and each priest could take longer or less time?"

Rays voice was impatient.

"We timed this priest on two previous baptisms. It takes approximately thirty minutes and they always go in and out the church by the front door as the other doors are only opened up for the Masses. Satisfied?"

"So Adams is actually coming to the church at 10.30. What if I can take him out then?" Danny enquired.

Ray grabbed him by the shoulders in frustration.

"Because we found that people are rushing up the steps coming in, some running late. Afterwards they gather on the steps for some pictures or a chat. We determined that's you're best chance. Now hop to it and stop asking stupid questions!"

Danny made a face. This wasn't the SAS way of doing a mission. Too many loose ends. Hanging around during a church ceremony where a chance caller could sabotage the whole thing. Ray reached into his pocket and took out a rifle round and watched as Danny smoothly notched it into the breech and snapped it shut. He then nodded to Yorkie.

"Quigley doesn't take the safety off until the actual shot, understood? In the meantime keep your weapon trained on him."

Danny had a problem. Well, five really. Five people who would kill him in an instant and who intended to as soon as the hit was completed. His more immediate problem was that his hopes of inserting the second rifle round in the magazine had been thwarted which badly interfered with his plan of action. His visualization of what could happen had fortunately considered this possibility. However, it made the situation much more hairy and the timings were now too tight. He was going to need a lot of luck too. He didn't plan to wait for 11 am for two reasons: if shots were fired early by the crew from their hand guns, the noise would alert the group at the church and sabotage the assassination. Secondly, by moving sooner he hoped to catch the team by surprise with an unplanned move.

Pete and the other crew member were standing behind Siobhan who was sitting in a chair, untied, in front of them. Both their weapons were out and held at the level of Siobhan's head. At seven minutes to eleven Danny leaned forward, and in a shocked voice said,

"Christ, what the hell is that?"

Yorkie leaned forward too, and as he did so Danny chopped the butt of the rifle savagely back into the point of his nose, driving it back into his skull. He was dead as he flew backwards, his gun skittering off. Danny was already swinging round, deliberately staying low, and snicking the safety off as he did so, aware that Siobhan, as planned, hurled herself sideways onto the floor. As the rifle swung sideways he was aware of the crew member's weapon being extended towards him. A millisecond after Danny pulled the trigger, he was conscious of something hissing past his ear as the glass tinkled behind him. He had aimed the rifle for the chest and saw the man blown backwards with the shock of the big caliber bullet. Two dead. Still moving, Danny, ejected the empty shell. Pete stood there as if frozen. Danny's mind consciously tracked where the empty casing flew to. His left hand was extracting the round from his pocket. Time seemed to be frozen. He was aware of steps pounding along the corridor outside and a shout from downstairs as more steps sounded coming upwards. In that frozen moment Danny was aware that the second part of his plan had failed and that he was only moments from death. He had hoped to recover Yorkie's Glock and take out Pete with it, but it had flown off along the worn carpet. In that frozen moment as he coolly inserted the round, he was aware that Pete was still standing, shock and uncertainty written on his face.

Then the door crashed open and Danny fired his second and last round into the chest of Harry, the man who came barreling through, sending him crashing back onto the stairs. Three dead. There was a muffled sound of Ray's voice cursing and Danny leapt to his feet. He was preparing to make a desperate forward roll for Yorkie's discarded weapon. He was too late. Ray leapt into the room, his Glock extended out in front, directly aimed at Danny.

His eyes flashed wickedly.

"Crawford said you were a slippery one. You really have botched it now Quigley," as he squeezed the trigger.

Two shots rang out and Danny watched in amazement as Ray fell to the floor a look of astonishment on his face. His face turned momentarily towards Pete who had shot him.

"Why?" he gasped and died.

Four dead. Danny was already arching through the air and had his hand on the Glock when Pete's weapon swung round covering him. He froze taking his hand off the gun and carefully stood up. Pete looked at him.

"I want eight hours before you drop me in it Quigley. Deal?"

Danny expelled a long breath. "Shit yes Pete! Lets get the hell out of here. Those shots were probably heard by a number of people. He reached to help Siobhan to her feet, picking up the fallen glock as he did so. Pete suddenly fell to his knees throwing up on the carpet, his weapon sliding off. Danny moved forward and scooped it up, helping Pete to his feet as he did so.

Pete looked at his weapon now held by Danny who asked "First time you killed someone?"

Pete nodded. "Are you going to finish me off too?" he asked.

"No, it's okay Pete. We're on the same side now. But you'll have a better chance to make it without this. The shooting's over mate."

He looked closely into his face.

"Ray asked you a question, Pete. Why? Why did you turn on them?"

Danny was dashing round the room as he spoke picking up the spent shell casing and the rifle and hustling Siobhan to the door. He spotted Ray's cell phone attached to his belt and grabbed it. Pete was suddenly galvanized into action, aware that seconds could be vital. As they dashed down the stairs Pete answered him.

"You were right. They were going to top us anyway. Not here but out along the road somewhere. No loose ends," he said bitterly.

He tapped Danny on the shoulder as they emerged downstairs.

"Did you really mean it about the regiment? That I could have made it?"

"You sure as hell could mate." Danny lied.

Pete looked at him for a long moment and nodded.

"Thanks Danny."

He jumped into the first car and carefully steered out of the driveway. Danny threw the rifle in the boot of the second car, covering it with some sacks, then jumped in as Siobhan, without prompting, leapt into the passenger side. He pulled the automatic into drive and was only twenty seconds behind Pete, who had turned off towards the border. As he emerged from the driveway Danny was aware of two figures, a man and a woman, hurrying from the house next door.

CHAPTER 69

"Cover your face Siobhan," he shouted.

She ducked her head and he threw his elbow up across his face, as he flashed past the two people, who stopped and watched them drive off.

"Christ, we've just been lumbered," Danny exclaimed as he turned the opposite direction to Pete, through the center of Strabane.

"What will we do?" Siobhan gasped.

"Get rid of this car for starters," he replied, watching his rear view mirror and despite the urgency, kept sticking to the speed limits.

He was on the edge of the town in approximately ten minutes. Shortly after he spotted a sign for a golf course and swung the car onto the long driveway leading up to it. In a moment the club-house came into view, with a parking lot full of cars, from the early morning golfers. A few people were unloading their equipment, chatting easily to each other. Danny pulled in at the far end, where a few cars were parked just under some trees. This he judged was the spill-over parking for late comers as it was farthest from the club-house. He stopped the car and turned to her.

"Get out like a normal happy golfer coming for a game. No rush. Just walk casually, okay?"

She nodded and opening her door, stepped out. Danny marveled at her presence of mind after what she'd witnessed in the past few moments. He too swung out, already determined which car he was going to take. Opening the boot of the car, that he had been driving, he grabbed a cloth and spent a few minutes carefully wiping it down. He knew forensics would still pick up all sorts of evidence, fibers from their clothes, dust from their shoes, but he wanted the most obvious evidence obliterated.

He tried the Ford Escort next to him, and had his first break. It was open. Starting the car without a key was no problem to him and in a moment the vehicle purred into life. He transferred the rifle to the floor behind the driver's seat and in minutes he was driving carefully out of the parking lot.

Siobhan glanced at him.

"How long have we got Danny, before the man finds his car gone?" she asked.

He shrugged.

"An hour, two if we're lucky. Some of these golfers have a game and then retire to the club house for a jug of beer and sometimes some food. However we'll only keep the car for a short while anyway."

He looked at her.

"By the way, well done back there. You played your part brilliantly."

She looked at him, her lips quivering.

"I'm all churning inside. It's just starting to hit me. Seeing those men die like that. It was horrible!"

Danny nodded.

"I know what you mean, sweetheart. I didn't like having to do it either. Courtney warned me about violence but I can't seem to get away from it. You know Siobhan, it was either them or Gerry Adams back there, and this province would have exploded if I'd killed him. We wouldn't have been too far behind Gerry Adams either."

"I know, I know," she whispered. "It's just ..." her voice trailed off.

Danny reached across and held her hand as he drove with one hand. She clung to him desperately.

After twenty minutes he pulled off the road in a wooded area and drove several hundred yards until he found a place to his liking. Checking for any sign of life, he reached into the back seat and pulled the rifle through into the front. Siobhan shuddered again, looking at the weapon. He extracted the spent shell from the breech and stuck it in his pocket then carefully wiped the weapon over. Checking the road again in both directions, he leapt out and smashed the rifle butt on the stone wall that he'd pulled up beside. Then he hurled the broken stock off into some dense trees. He crossed to the other side and threw the rest of the rifle as far as he could, into some shrubbery. He then took out Rays mobile phone and scrolled down until he came to Crawford's number and hit the call button. It was picked up instantly.

"Yes, what's the news Ray?" A hoarse voice demanded.

Quigley laughed harshly. There was a startled explosive noise on the other end.

"Who the hell is this?"

"Gerry Adams is alive. That means you're finished Crawford."

"Quigley! That can't be!"

Danny could hear fear for the first time ever in Crawford's voice.

"Oh yes Crawford, it is I, and I'm now coming to get you, you pathetic excuse for an ex-officer."

He hung up hearing the intake of breath from the other end of the line. He then dismantled the mobile phone and smashed it into the ground with his heel before tossing the bits over the side of the road. Checking the road again he climbed into the car and turned it around heading back to the main road.

"I just called Crawford," he told a startled Siobhan, told him I was coming for him."

"But why warn him. He'll be ready for you now, won't he?"

Danny grinned.

"I want him to start running. I want him to feel what it's like; What he's been doing to me and my family. Anyway, I wouldn't go after him at the Belfast office. That would be like a fortress. No, I think I know where he'll run to and I'll catch up to him there," he said grimly.

Siobhan shuddered, looking at his face.

A mile further on, he fired both empty shells out the car window into a river, as they crossed a small bridge. He relaxed then and concentrated on his driving, making speed where he could and sticking to speed limits in the small villages. After about an hour they came to the town of Omagh, and Danny drove around until he found the bus station. Reaching across he opened her door.

"Siobhan, just slip in there and find out when the next bus is to Belfast. If it's in the next 30 minutes get two tickets."

He opened his wallet extracting some sterling and started handing it to her. She pushed it away.

"Oh I can use my credit card Danny. It's all right," she protested.

"It's not all right. Credit cards can be traced, sweetheart. We need to leave as few clues as possible right now. Remember, there's four dead bodies back there!"

She made a face.

"God, I'm so new at all this. I can't think clearly."

Danny watched as she made her way into the bus terminal and within five minutes emerged carrying two tickets, almost triumphantly it seemed to Danny. She came around his side and he opened the driver's window.

"We're in luck. There's one leaving in twenty minutes. It's already half full. I got two tickets."

He held her hand as he extracted one of the tickets, speaking quietly.

"You go on board now and sit by yourself halfway down the bus. Pretend you're dozing if anyone tries to engage you in conversation. You don't know me so don't even look at me when I come on board. Get off when I get off. Think up a story if the police stop the bus and come on board - going for a shopping trip in Belfast, whatever. Got that?"

She nodded and he patted her hand again and watched her head back inside.

He drove down the street a few hundred yards and left the car in the parking lot of a large busy food store after wiping it clean again. Then he walked casually up the street and handed his ticket to the driver as he climbed aboard the bus. He sat in the back several seats behind her with other passengers interspersed between them. He closed his eyes ignoring other passengers and newcomers as they came onboard. It seemed only minutes until the bus pulled out of the station, and groaned its way up the street, heading for Belfast. Fortunately, it was an express bus, and made very few brief stops, arriving in Belfast in the early afternoon. They encountered no police road-blocks on the way, and no police came on board at the regular stops. Weary after the trip, and the spiraling down of the adrenalin, he climbed off at the Belfast bus terminal, followed, not too closely, by Siobhan. There was a direct bus link to the airport and they both took this, still keeping their distance. The next challenge was getting across to the UK without any pre-arranged booking and trying to rescue Courtney.

CHAPTER 70

London

Back at Thames House the pace was picking up. Sophia dashed into the D.G.'s office again without knocking. Rebecca raised her eyebrows at her

"Just when I thought I'd trained you Sophia," she teased.

"Yes ma'am, sorry ma'am, but something's just come through. Shots fired in the vicinity of Gerry Adams who was down on a personal visit to Strabane," she burst out.

The DG dropped the file she was reading.

"Good heavens girl! Was Adams hurt?" she demanded.

"No ma'am, but four bodies were found shot in a nearby house. Two cars were seen driving away, one abandoned at a golf course where another car was stolen. That was off the main road to Belfast. I just checked my contact in Belfast. Colonel Crawford was in this morning but bolted from the office shortly after getting a phone call."

The D.G.'s face turned pale.

"My God, the penny just dropped! The assassination - it was Adams! Holy banana, that would have put Northern Ireland back ten years. So that was Crawford's plan. He would be back at the helm in Northern Ireland again."

She paused for a moment reflecting, then asked her another question.

"Was Quigley among those who were shot?"

"No ma'am. Apparently, the four had ID's on them which verified who they were. Quigley certainly wasn't one of them."

"Was there a man called Peterson among them?"

Sophia glanced down at some notes she'd written.

"No ma'am."

"So Quigley and Peterson are still in the game, Crawford too. Where is the man? No doubt he knows by now that his plan has failed. With four dead, will he still think he can button this up? But where is Quigley heading, that's the question Sophia?"

"You seem to put a lot of store in Quigley ma'am, just from your tone," said Sophia, a question in her voice and her eyebrows raised.

The D.G. picked up a file.

"Just got this faxed from Hereford as you know - Quigley's army record. It's something else. He sounds like Rambo and James Bond all wrapped into one. Listen to this:

He was dropped with a NATO Special Forces team in the mountains of Afghanistan on a mission. US choppers dropped them in but through some lack of communication, Quigley was left behind. It was then too dark to go back for him but they returned at daybreak looking for a signal. There was no sign of him. They returned to the area for three days running. No sign of Quigley at all. They were expecting a boastful message from the Taliban claiming to have captured him, but nothing came through. Now here's the kicker though. Who walks out of the mountains several days later but Quigley, dressed in Arab gear and the coalition forces very nearly shot him. His Arab caftan was crusted with dried blood as was the knife he carried."

Sophia gasped.

"Oh my God ma'am!"

The D.G. nodded.

"There's more. In the debrief, he hardly said anything. Just muttered something about running into some opposition up in the mountains. Then US intelligence who rescued him in a chopper, retraced his route and tells the whole story; Quigley had been instrumental in killing scores of Taliban and Al Quada, a hundred and sixty in all, in hand to hand fighting and setting up an air strike."

"Holy mother ..." Sophia breathed. "How did those men die?" she asked.

"You don't want to know, Sophia. Oh, and he had a seventeen year old Afghan girl with him, when he was rescued. Apparently, she helped him avoid the Taliban back in the mountains."

"A young girl! How did that happen?"

The D.G. grinned.

"Well, even his regiment picture shows him to be quite a good looking guy, and macho too. We may never know how, or why she agreed to help him."

She looked at the file again.

"He would be a useful resource to have on our side," she mused. Sophia stared at her.

"But you have the whole 22nd regiment there in Hereford if you need them. There's a sabre team on constant standby."

"Yes I know, but once I bring them in it's official. In an intelligence community that's not always a good thing is it?" she said smiling meaningfully.

Sophia backed out of the office, astonishment on her face. She was beginning to see another side to her boss. She wasn't sure if she liked it or not.

CHAPTER 71

Belfast Airport

Danny was fuming. All the airlines with flights to Stanfield in the U.K. were fully booked. Siobhan was gripped with an awful fear for Courtney, who she felt was in a worsening condition. Danny was back again at the British Midland booking counter waiting to talk to a petite lady who had turned him away before. Finally, his turn came and he leaned urgently over the counter. The lady looked at him and beat him to it

"Look, I told you before, the flight is fully booked sir. There's nothing we can do," she said, waving him off. He thrust his face closer across the counter.

"This is an emergency, Miss, a life and death situation here. My partner and I just have to get on that flight," he insisted.

The lady sighed.

"I've already turned away two other so-called emergencies," she said dismissively, obviously disbelieving him and his motive. Danny straightened up from the counter, conscious of people waiting impatiently in the queue behind him. He caught a glimpse of Siobhan's tight expression a few yards behind.

They were beaten.

As he turned to leave he had a flash of inspiration. Something he'd done some years before on a mission for MI5.

He'd had an identity card with him then of course. He leaned back across the counter lowering his voice and whispered,

"Look I'm with MI5 on an undercover mission and you just have to get us on that flight," he said tersely.

Her face creased with amusement.

"Well, that's the best excuse I've heard since I started here, and I thought I'd heard the lot. MI5 indeed."

She chuckled again and started to turn away. Danny grabbed her arm and her eyes widened. Danny knew she'd push an alarm in another second.

"You've got to listen to me. A man's been kidnapped and is being held prisoner near Stanstead. Look at the girl's face there. She's demented with fear." He pointed to Siobhan.

As if aware of their scrutiny, Siobhan hurried over and pressed against the counter.

"Oh please help us," she begged. Tears starting to trickle from her eyes. The Midland agent's eyes flicked across both of them and she seemed to make a decision.

"Okay, I'll go in and talk to my supervisor and it's up to him. Wait right here."

She waved to someone behind them and two large security personnel came across and stood beside them, their hands resting on their Heckler and Koch weapons. Danny sighed. It was the end of the line for them.

At Thames House the D.G.'s intercom rang and she picked it up immediately.

"Yes Sophia."

"Ma'am, there's a British Midland supervisor calling you from Belfast. He refuses to talk to anyone but the Director General. Shall I put him through or not?"

"Of course, go ahead Sophia." she instructed.

A man's voice came on the line.

"Is that the Director of MI5?"

"Yes it is. Tell me why you wanted to call me sir."

"It's like this. A man called Quigley and his partner are trying to get a flight to Stanstead, which is fully booked by the way. He claims to be working undercover for you people. Something about a kidnapping and a man in danger. I'm sorry to bother you ma'am. We get all sorts of stories from people here, you wouldn't believe it. There's something about this couple, that just concerned our girl out on the counter. I thought I'd check and make sure. I know this isn't the normal procedure for doing this, so please forgive me, if I've created a false alarm."

Surprise and shock moved in sequence across the D.G.'s face. She got many unusual calls at Thames House, though most of the weird ones were screened out before they got to her. She breathed in deeply and slowly and was silent for a few moments after the Midland supervisor finished. Her silence prompted him to cut in again.

"Ma'am, are you there? Did you catch all that?"

She nodded, realizing as she did that he couldn't see her. Then she said,

"Yes, Quigley and his partner are working for us right now on some national security issue and I'd appreciate it if you managed to get them on that flight by any means possible. What time does it get into Stanstead?" she enquired.

"Oh, seven thirty ma'am and yes, we will get them on board. We'll have to bounce some people but if this is a national security issue ..." he trailed off.

"Good man. It's vital and we'll remember your cooperation. Now while you're on the line, tell me if you had a Colonel Crawford, also one of our agents, on a previous flight earlier today. Unfortunately, I'm not sure of the destination at this stage?"

There was silence as she waited, tapping her foot impatiently. At last the man's voice came back on the line.

"Yes ma'am, he took an earlier flight out from here at 12.30 getting into Stanstead at approximately 2 pm."

The D.G. looked at her watch. It was now 3 pm. She asked the supervisor for the flight number of Quigley's flight, thanked him again and hung up. She then strode to the door and stormed into Sophia's office.

"Get that map out again," she commanded.

In a moment they were huddled around her table scrutinizing the map.

"Crawford's flying into Stanstead, and now Quigley's doing the same, but why Stanstead?" she muttered.

Sophia gasped.

"You said Quigley, ma'am?"

"Yes I did didn't I. He's trying to get on a plane from Belfast claiming to be one of our agents, at this moment in time."

"So he's in custody by now then?"

"No, in fact I told the British Midland supervisor that he did work for us and to get him on that flight at all costs."

Sophia's jaw dropped.

"You authorized it?"

"Yes, I rather like Quigley's style and he's the only game in town right now, to help sort this mess out."

She peered at the map closely again then tensed. She tapped the map. "That's where Crawford's bolted to; The MI5 training camp. Why it's almost a second home to him. He loves those training and briefing jaunts. I believe Quigley knows where he's heading for too and I intend to be there when he catches up with Crawford. Now lets get down to some planning," she barked assertively, her eyes gleaming at the prospect of some action.

Unfortunately, she wasn't able to raise what she'd hoped for, a Tactical Weapons Unit, from the Metropolitan Police. They were all posted on roof-tops around London, on duty for the conference. MI5 were not authorized to carry out offensive police work, where arrests were involved. Then an idea hit her. She dialed the number D.I. White had left with her and sat forward as his voice came on the line.

"D.I. White? Are you still interested in finding out who murdered those three thugs?"

There was a surprised moment of silence at the other end. Then.

"You better believe it ma'am. Have you some information for us?"

"I believe I will have but I need you to accompany me on a call I'm making this evening to the east of Stanstead airport. I think I can deliver your murderer then," she said briskly.

"Accompany you? This is most unusual ma'am. Normally … …"

"Yes, yes, I understand D.I.White. Well normal methods havn't helped you so far have they? Here's your chance Inspector; make a decision. Be at Thames House at 7.30. We'll go in my car, and by the way, bring one of those stocky detective constables with you if there's any left in the city with this damn conference and make sure you're both armed."

She hung up not waiting for a reply and shouted for Sophia again. When she had rushed back in she gave her some rapid instructions.

"Go downstairs and organize a car for me at 7.30 outside here. Go to weapons and have them cram in the back of the car anything they can put their hands on right now. Enough for three or four people. Oh and by the way, make sure a shotgun is included. One of those multi-shot automatic ones that are illegal in this country. Now hurry, this is coming to a head," she whooped.

An amazed Danny and Siobhan were escorted into a VIP lounge by a deferential supervisor who settled them in and arranged for a special escort to the plane prior to take off. He'd only asked for economy but they found themselves upgraded to business class, when they got on board. The word had got around and the red carpet was rolled out for them. The captain even came out at one time and chatted to them. Danny heard a whisper behind him from one of the stewards.

"MI5, national security!"

Neither understood what was going on but they were heading for Stanstead and that's all that mattered. Siobhan was going to cuddle up to him but he nodded to her meaningfully.

MI5 agents didn't normally act in that way. At least he assumed they didn't.

CHAPTER 72

Stanstead Airport, UK

When Danny and Siobhan walked out of the airport he spotted the flashing car lights straight away. In a moment the car had swung in beside him and he saw the grinning face of Scotty, peering out at him. He opened the back door for Siobhan and then jumped in the front seat. The two men threw their arms round each other, thumping each other. Danny introduced Siobhan and noticed the quizzical gaze of Scotty, as he looked sideways at him.

"Must be someone real special, Danny. Never known you to take a woman into battle before," he teased.

"I'll fill you in later. Lets go and have some food," Danny volunteered tersely. "By the way, did you bring your crossbow?"

Scottie grinned.

"In the back mate with a bunch of shafts as you suggested. A few other things too," he said offhandedly.

Suddenly, there was a yelping from the back portion of the car. Danny and Siobhan both swung around.

"What the hell have you back there?" Danny demanded.

Scottie reached out and touched his elbow.

"Easy does it old friend. It's only a dog."

"A dog, for Gods sake Scotty! We're going to take on a ... ..."

Scotty grinned again.

"You told me to expect at least four Doberman didn't you? Well," he nodded backwards, "that's part of my plan mate."

"But what exactly has a dog got to do with it?" Danny demanded.

Scotty cocked at eye back at Siobhan and then made a face at Danny.

"Tell you later," he said mysteriously.

Danny knew that was all he was going to get right then.

"Okay, lets find someplace to eat. That good with you Scotty?"

Scotty grinned. He was always hungry, even going into battle. "Hey I thought you were in a hurry Danny?" he queried.

Danny shook his head.

"I don't want to reach the training camp until it's getting dark. We have a better chance of slipping in then."

After a short time driving they found a roadside café and took a seat in a corner as far away as possible from the other patrons. They ordered and Danny slipped off to the washroom. When he was gone Scotty took a long appreciative look at Siobhan.

" Should see the ones we have to put up with in Hereford. So tell me. Are you two an item then?" he asked.

Siobhan blushed.

Scotty grinned .

"Hey, you don't have to answer that. I can see all the answers I need from your face. Danny'll kill me if he knows I was quizzing you."

Siobhan smiled.

"I won't tell him if you don't Scotty."

"Wow," he said again. "I can see why Danny would fall for you Siobhan."

Just then Danny came back and sat down, looking suspiciously at them. "What were you guys talking about? Scotty you look like a cat that's got all the cream."

Scotty looked innocently at him.

"Oh nothing really. Just chatting you know."

The food arrived and in typical military fashion, it became the focus for the next ten minutes, as they ate in silence. Danny wiped his hands and face with a tissue and sat back with his coffee cup.

He then covered all the events that had happened since Scotty had helped his daughter to evade the watchers in Bath. Scotty made the odd comment and asked occasional questions. The Strabane killings made him stare in astonishment at Danny.

"Holy shit!" he exclaimed. "You obviously haven't lost your touch, Danny. Just as well mate. This is serious opposition we're going to be up against tonight. Have we anyone else with us?"

Danny shook his head.

"I'm afraid not, but if we get the element of surprise, we can shorten the odds."

Scotty grinned again.

"Wouldn't be the first. Remember that time ..."

He stopped short, glancing at Siobhan. She took the hint and excused herself to go to the washroom. Scotty turned to him.

"Okay what's the plan? Fortunately, we both did our training at the camp there years ago so we know the layout and I'm hoping they haven't changed much in the interim."

"That's what I'm hoping too, but getting in might be a problem. Will there be a gate guard? They used to lock the gate in the evenings. Remember how we had to be sure to make it back from the pub in time?"

Scotty nodded, saying nothing but listening intently.

Suddenly Danny thought of something.

"What's with the dog?"

Scotty smiled broadly.

"You may have some Dobermans to deal with. I assume we haven't time for poisoned meat to do their job. My uncle breeds dogs. I stopped off and borrowed one of his bitches that's in heat right now. I figure that will draw them in and the crossbow will do the rest." He paused. "Well I hope so anyway."

"Bloody marvelous, Scotty!" Danny exclaimed. "Now I know why you didn't want to talk about it when Siobhan was listening."

He shook his head in amazement.

"A dog in heat! Who'd have thought of it?"

He paused, savoring the moment and then went back to the briefing.

"Now once inside, we don't know if they will have their ground sensors activated or if anyone is even watching the monitor screens. You know how lax people can get over the years. If they are expecting us then we're into a whole new ball game."

"Will they have guards out in the grounds?" Scotty asked.

"I wouldn't think so if the dogs are loose, as they can be temperamental at the best of times, and off course the guards can set of the sensors as well."

"Any idea how many bad guys we're up against Danny?"

"No idea. I've whittled down his team somewhat but he must have had at least six people in Bath watching my family. They're probably back here, and then there's Crawford of course."

"There's one slippery bastard, Danny. Don't take any chances if you get face to face with him. Remember how deadly he was on the firing range with that pistol of his?"

Danny's eyes narrowed thoughtfully.

"Yes, I'm looking forward to a face to face with Crawford, for all he's done to me and my family."

Scotty looked at his cold face and was glad he was not in Crawford's shoes.

"What about existing staff at the training center, Danny, will they be on Crawford's side or do we regard them as neutrals?"

"That's a bit tricky. A lot depends on what Crawford tells them. Are we terrorists attacking the camp? Will he say anything or just play the hand out? He's finished now anyway but he might still have an end game plan."

Scotty rubbed his hands with anticipation.

"Bastard won't know what hit him! Speaking of that, I'm afraid I only managed to get a SIG maremont p226 and a half dozen grenades. Oh and some stun grenades and a good chunk of rope, as you suggested.

"Not enough to take on an armed camp," he mused grimly, "unless we can rescue some from the enemy somehow. We've done that before. How come you couldn't bring more stuff, some assault rifles for example?" he queried.

Scotty made a face.

"They pulled a search on cars leaving the camp that morning. Some of the lads coming back from town mentioned it. Luckily I had the grenades and the pistol at my uncle's place. Sorry Danny."

Danny shook his head wearily.

"Can't be helped at this stage. It's great that you're here mate. Now lets talk strategy when we get inside. Don't forget Courtney. We have a possible hostage situation with him as well. Crawford won't go down easily."

They were still discussing it when Siobhan returned, and she sat there listening in amazement as they calmly went over a plan that would inevitably result in many deaths.

Some time later Scotty drifted the car slowly up to the gate at the training camp and sat they for a moment to see if a guard emerged to check them. Nothing moved in the small shack positioned on their side of the gate, which had a solid sheet of reinforced metal fastened to the front.

He extracted himself carefully from the car and froze as a vehicle they hadn't seen parked in the shadows, suddenly put it's lights on and leapt forward towards them. Scotty raised his pistol and Danny tensed, looking desperately around for some weapon, but with their back to the metal gate and standing exposed in the headlights, it was too late.

CHAPTER 73

The car ground to a halt directly in front of them. A large man and a lady jumped out. Neither were armed. Danny breathed a sigh of relief and Scotty lowered his weapon slowly. The lady smiled and nodded her head at them.

"I've been expecting you Quigley. What took you so long? This is DI.White, by the way. I believe you've met."

Both Danny and Scotty stared at her and then at each other. Danny, mystified, looked at them.

"I don't know how you expected me Miss ... ah. Who are you anyway?"

DI.White cut in.

"Just the Director General of MI5, Quigley, and, incidentally, it's illegal for citizens to carry guns in the U.K., so let's be having that right now," he said pointing to Scotty.

Danny and Scotty tensed. The D.G. held up her hand.

"Hold it there, D.I. White. I think we're going to be glad of these two before this is over, especially as you couldn't find a colleague to accompany you. They have the training and we don't, when we get inside this camp. Now," she continued "as to why I knew you'd be here, who do you think got you a flight out of Belfast as an MI5 agent? The nerve of you trying to pull a stunt like that!"

She smiled as a tug of admiration flickered momentarily across her features.

"Now, update myself and D.I.White as to what's been going on. I know Colonel Crawford is involved and I'm aware of the assassination plot on Gerry Adams, which I believe you probably sabotaged. So, let me have the full story and leave nothing out," she instructed.

Danny did so, starting with the events in London and his flight to Ireland. He covered his abduction from Sligo; how he was whipped across the border and held prisoner by Colonel Crawford until he agreed under threat to himself and his family, to carry out the assassination of Gerry Adams.

He verbalized his belief that Crawford wanted Northern Ireland to go up in flames so he would have his own little fiefdom back. The D.G. nodded thoughtfully at this, as if it confirmed something

He told about his spiriting away his family in Bath and his subsequent telephone call to Patton. How Courtney had gone to Patton's house to investigate and disappeared, followed by the threat from Crawford that they had kidnapped him and would kill him, if Danny didn't carry out the killing.

He re-iterated his belief that Courtney was a prisoner inside the camp and that Crawford had recruited his own team of mercenaries to carry out his dirty work. He didn't mention the two men he had killed and left in Lough Gill.

Briefly he went over Siobhan's kidnapping and the events of the day in Strabane, when he managed to turn the tables.

As eight hours had passed since he promised Pete not to drop his name to the police, he now told of the man's crucial part in the grim events of the morning. Both the Director General and Inspector White stood as if mesmerized by the story until he had finished.

The D.G. shook her head.

"This gets worse and worse - kidnappings, murders, torture, threats, attempted undermining of the state, the list is endless. You have a strange knack of leaving dead bodies around everywhere you go, Quigley."

She looked at D.I. White to see if he had any comment to make, but he was still staring at Danny in as if in shock.

Turning to Danny, she asked,

"Okay, what's your plan for taking this place?"

She peered at Scotty, "and I don't even want to know who your small friend is there. The way he held that weapon tells me all I need to know."

D.I. White suddenly stirred.

"Ma'am, we can't allow these two to start anything. Already they're breaking the law with possession of a deadly weapon. Let me call in some local back-up and take it from there."

The D.G. sighed.

"That's MI5 property in there Inspector, and I believe from what I've just been told that a kidnapped man is being held in there and his life is in imminent danger. From what Danny here has told me, Colonel Crawford doesn't like leaving loose ends around. While you're waiting for back up it may be too late. No, I'm authorizing these two to carry out the rescue as they planned and we're going in too. Now ..."

She hit the button on her key ring and the lid of the boot sprung open.

Danny, Scotty and White moved around so they had a view of the contents.

Danny gasped. It was crammed with an assortment of weapons, from a stubby Uzi pistol, shorter at nine inches than even the Uzi mini machine gun. Danny knew it fired a 9mm parabellum on semi-automatic, with a 20 round magazine. He immediately grabbed it and a wicked looking knife with a scabbard. There was also an American close assault 12 gauge automatic shotgun, which Danny knew had an effective range of 100 to 150 yards. The D.G. hauled it out and with a box of cartridges which she peered at.

"Ah flecettes," she remarked.

Danny knew the weapon could fire buckshot or 20 flecettes, small steel arrows. He'd seen what these did to a human target and grimaced.

There were two Austrian Glocks, a Browning high powered automatic and a heckler and Koch 12 gauge, close assault weapon, which carried ten shots. Scotty took this swiftly and started testing the mechanism.

Danny's eyes glinted when he spotted the revolutionary Hecklor and Koch G11 rifle, which he knew fired 3 shots with one pressure of the trigger and separated on the target by only a few inches at most. He'd heard that the shots were long gone by the time the firer even feels any recoil. He also knew it had taken 21 years to develop.

"Where the hell did you get this one?" Danny said in awe as he quickly reached in, adding it to his Stubby Uzi pistol.

She smiled.

"You'd be surprised what we pick up on some of our jaunts. We like to stay current on all weapons and their firepower," she offered.

D.I. White looked tentatively at the weapons and picked up the Browning 9 mm parabellum. Danny went and collected some grenades from Scotty's car and stuffed them in his pockets. The D.G. turned to him.

"Okay, what's your plan Danny?"

He explained it to her and she nodded in satisfaction.

"Right, lets get it started. Now when that gate opens the Inspector and I will drive through in our car with yourself and your small colleague walking alongside us. Your friend Siobhan will follow closely behind in your car."

Scotty cut in.

"Ma'am, this is going to be messy. Don't you think you should stay back and let us clear the camp first?"

She laughed dismissively.

"This is MI5 territory and I intend to be part of the solution to this mess. It seems I contributed to the problem in keeping that dinosaur Crawford on against my better judgment. Anyway, I spend many of my weekends shooting birds with this shotgun and I won the Shooting Trap contest two years running here in the U.K. I think I can hold my end up."

Scotty looked at Danny and shrugged. He was thinking that there was a big difference between shooting birds and people who were shooting back at you. Danny nodded to Scotty who spoke to Siobhan inside the car. She jumped into the drivers seat and eased it up to the wall beside the main gate.

They were ready to start the assault.

CHAPTER 74

Scotty clambered up onto the roof of the vehicle and from there onto the perimeter wall. He nodded to Danny who extracted the crossbow and supply of shafts and passed them up to him with the coil of rope. Scotty took a moment to set the equipment up and nodded to him again. Danny quickly got the bitch out of the cage in the back of their car, and attached a long leather leash to it and passed it up to him. The D.G. who was watching, shook her head. D.I. White's face reflected his scepticism. They lined the two cars up one behind the other with Siobhan prepared to drive one with the detective inspector in front. Danny waved to Scotty who then carefully lowered the bitch onto the ground inside the camp, and tied the lead to some wire on top of the wall. Two security lights inside the grounds made it almost as bright as day as the dog reached the ground and whined. Nothing happened for several minutes.

Suddenly there was a stirring in the foliage and a large Doberman darted out heading for the bitch. Scotty leaned forward and as the guard dog reached the bitch he launched his first shaft, catching it straight in the middle of the chest. It gave a yelp of pain and did a back flip, before it thumped to the ground dead. Two more guard dogs followed in quick unison and Scotty dispatched the second quickly. The third dog took longer to die and was howling with pain, as Scotty had to send a second shaft straight into its forehead.

Then there was silence.

A few moments passed. No more dogs appeared. Scotty looked back down at Danny and waved him forward to the front gate.

Danny shouted up to him.

"Be careful. There might be more out there," he cautioned.

Scotty nodded and disappeared over the wall. In a moment the main gate started to open with Scotty's help from inside. Danny grabbed it and finished the swing. The two cars moved inside and Danny refastened the gate, to slow down anyone trying to escape. Then he and Scotty moved up the driveway with Danny on the passenger side of the first vehicle and Scotty across from him. They had discussed shooting out the glaring gate lights but decided it would only warn the people inside.

Now they slowly started walking up the drive. Gradually they left the bright gate lights behind them until they were almost in complete darkness. Danny was thinking it was too easy when shots rang out catching the front car in the windshield. Danny dropped to the ground as more shots spiraled around the vehicle. The D.G. crawled out of the car, splatters of blood on her face, still holding the shotgun. Danny crawled over to her and grabbed her as she started to stand up.

"Stay down or you'll get your head blown off. Are you okay?" he whispered as the firing ceased.

She turned her head.

"Yes, I'm fine. I think though that they got D.I. White. He's slumped across the wheel," she whispered, still sounding totally calm.

Danny scuttled back on his knees to the second car and saw Siobhan's pale face reflected back at him. He indicated she should wind down her window not wanting to open the door and cause the indoor lights to come on and outline them. After some fumbling the window slid down.

"Are you okay?" he whispered.

"Yes," she replied, her voice shaky.

"Here's the thing. Stay here until we clear this driveway then follow up when the shooting has stopped. Go around the first car. I'm afraid the policeman's being hit - probably fatally. The shit has truly hit the fan. They know we're in the grounds. So much for surprise!"

"Be careful Danny," she entreated as he disappeared from view into the darkness.

He caught up with the D.G. again.

"Any idea where those shots came from?" he asked tersely.

"High up somewhere," she replied. "I saw the flashes. Perhaps they have a platform, but I was up here recently and there was nothing there. What's going on Danny?"

It suddenly dawned on him.

"They're up in the trees, I'll bet you. That way the dogs couldn't get them. Here, hang on a minute."

He crawled round the back of the car to the other side where he had last seen Scotty.

"Scotty," he hissed.

He jumped when he felt a hand touch his shoulder and was relieved to hear Scotty's voice.

"What's up mate?"

"They're up in the trees ahead Scotty. Try to take out the one that fired. He's on your side somewhere. The D.G. thinks the shots came from about fifty yards ahead. I'll continue on this side. Siobhan's car stays here for the moment. White has been hit bad we think. Watch yourself," he cautioned as he crawled back to the D.G.

"Okay, let's go ma'am," he whispered.

"Forget the ma'am Danny. If there's a chance we might die together I'd sooner you called me by my first name, Rebecca," she said lightly.

Despite the situation Danny couldn't help smiling and he tapped her arm in acknowledgment as they stood up. They started slowly up the driveway, their eyes now adjusted to the darkness after the gun flashes. Suddenly, Danny glimpsed two black shadows hurtling at them and cursed.

More dogs!

Automatically he let off a burst from his weapon without consciously aiming and watched with satisfaction as the first dog was hurled sideways. The second one was already launched and he heard the thud as it hit the D.G. square in the chest, and sent her flying. Danny knew he had only seconds to act. Grabbing his knife, he launched himself straight at the back of the massive dog, it's slavering jaws only inches from the D.G.'s throat. When he hit the back of the animal, he grabbed for one of its front legs, the momentum sending them both hurtling into the shrubbery. As his back hit the ground, Danny wrapped his legs around the animal and started stabbing into it's chest and stomach area, with all his strength. The animal gave an unearthly, almost human scream, and started snapping sideways at his face, attempting to dislodge him. He clung on desperately and kept stabbing. Then the animal's jaws fastened on his arm and Danny cried out with the pain. At that moment Rebecca loomed over them and delivered a massive blow with the butt of her weapon to the dogs head. Danny thrust the knife again into it's chest.

The dog quivered again and lay still.

Covered in the animal's blood, Danny staggered to his feet. Rebecca gazed at the dead dog.

"Christ, Danny, I was seconds from having my throat ripped out. That was a brave thing you did! Those screams that it made! How is that arm? He really fastened on you."

He grunted, "I won't feel it till later, but I've had my tetanus shots, so that's something."

She shuddered, seeing him covered in blood.

"I owe you one Danny and one day I intend to repay it," she whispered.

Suddenly, there was a burst of fire from Scotty's side, followed by a crash. Danny listened tensely until he heard a familiar bird sound floating in the air. He leaned forward and whispered.

"Scotty's got one."

Almost before he got the words out a gun fired from fifty yards ahead on their left whipping past them and slamming into the brush on Scotty's side. Almost simultaneously Danny fired the HK Gll at the flashes and felt the impact on his shoulder as the three shots kicked off. Seconds later the D.G. loosed off with her shotgun in the same general direction. A scream rang out and they heard thrashing around in the tree top. Danny loosed off a second burst but there was no return fire. It was followed by silence. He heard a whistle from Scotty and returned it.

He tapped her on the shoulder.

"Scotty is okay. By the way, ah, Rebecca, that was a fast reaction. Good shooting."

He couldn't see her expression but she smiled in the darkness, liking the way he'd said her name. She didn't hear it often at Thames House.

They continued cautiously on up the driveway but met no more opposition. Gradually they emerged at the edge of the large driveway in front of the house, which stood a good fifty yards away. The security lights threw everything into plain view. He wished he had his sniper rifle with him now to knock out those lights. They were both lying down in some long foliage and he whispered for a moment in her ear. She nodded and he turned and dashed across the driveway. Immediately, bullets whanged off the roadway, following his footsteps. He dived into the undergrowth keeping as low as possible as the shots followed him. Just then the D.G.'s shotgun boomed out and the gunman switched his concentration to the other side of the road where Danny had come from. He cursed. The D.G. had done it to distract the gunman from his location. Right then, Scotty crawled into view and slid up to him.

"Can you take out some of those lights with that G11?" he asked. "I haven't a hope of making it across to the house otherwise."

"I'll try," Danny replied, "but watch for that shooter. He's on the second floor over the entrance. Saw his flashes. Move away in case he targets me. Someone has to survive this."

Scotty slid away and Danny moved up to the bole of a large tree. He put down the UZI as the stubby barrel was sticking into his stomach.

Bullets lashed all around the shrubbery as Danny started calculating which light to go for first. After a few moments he started firing selective shots at the lights. One of the bulbs attached to the building exploded in glass and went out. Suddenly, a stream of bullets starting scything the shrubbery all around Danny and flailing a strip of bark off the tree he was crouched behind. He heard the boom of the D.G.'s shotgun again followed by tinkling glass from the house. Danny zeroed in on a second light in bursts of three. It flickered and died too. This time the gunman began firing again in both Scotty's and Danny's direction.

Scotty grunted in satisfaction as he spotted the man outlined against the window and squeezed off another six shots on full automatic. The gunman crashed out of the window and landed heavily on the steps of the house, his weapon still spitting rounds on the way down. Another two lights went out as Danny kept firing. Finally, just one weak light remained, which seemed impervious to his shots.

Silence fell.

Danny whistled softly and Scotty crawled up to him a moment later. They'd discussed this before and Danny gave him the thumbs up and watched him dash along the edge of the shrubbery and dive to the ground twenty yards from the building. Danny moved back rapidly across the road and dropped beside the D.G., who looked anxiously at him.

"You both okay?" she asked.

He nodded.

"Yeah fine. We've taken out three of them so we figure there's probably another three, plus Crawford. Thanks for the covering fire Rebecca. That was gutsy."

She glanced at him.

"Where do you reckon they are, Danny?"

He grimaced.

"I'd be guessing, but probably in the main house waiting for us. They may not have any more rifles after supplying the lads in the trees and the last gunman who fell out the window over there. Lucky for us," he added, feelingly.

She raised up slightly and pointed off to one side.

"I wondered if they would use the block house over there for your friend Courtney, where we debrief some of our reluctant visitors. It has it's own secure room. I don't know if you were ever in there when you trained here."

"Afraid not ma'am ... I mean Rebecca, but we have to take the house first. That blockhouse is within pistol range of the house and they would just cut us down if we try to go there first. Now, let's help Scotty carry out the next phase of the plan."

He nodded to the D.G. They both opened up on the front of the house concentrating on the windows. They caught a glimpse of Scotty sprinting along the edge of the trees, towards the side of the building. Some small arms fire started coming back at them and they both ducked just as they saw Scotty make the side of the building. The D.G. looked dubiously at the tall imposing building.

"Can he really get up there?" she asked.

"Just watch him. He's like fuc ... ah like Spiderman."

Scotty caught a corner water pipe and started climbing up it rapidly.

"He is like fucking Spiderman, isn't he Danny?" she said impishly.

Danny bit his lip. He couldn't figure out this woman at all - perhaps any woman for that matter, he reflected.

Just then Scotty reached the top of the building and disappeared from view. In a moment he reappeared, directly over one of the front windows and waved. Danny had handed over his more powerful weapon to the D.G. and now held the Uzi pistol in his hand. He rose to his feet and made a dash for the front door as the D.G. started providing covering fire at the windows.

Two weapons started up again, bullets whanging into the driveway around him. He gritted his teeth and kept running as the D.G.'s weapon stuttered behind him to the sound of more broken glass. He finally dashed up the steps and crashed against the solid door. Just to be sure he checked the door handle, but it was locked. He quickly rested a grenade on the handle, having extracted the pin carefully, dived sideways over the steps and huddled against the side of the cement foundations. The grenade exploded after about ten seconds and three things started happening simultaneously.

CHAPTER 75

Scotty came rappelling down the rope, hurling stun grenades into the top floor window and second floors as he went past, then continuing on down to the ground floor where he did the same. Danny dashed up the steps for the front door where he found it hanging on it's hinges. He kicked it down as he heard the D.G.'s footsteps approaching rapidly on the driveway behind him.

Scotty's top floor stun grenade went off followed in seconds by the two others. Scotty pushed himself off from the wall with his feet and swung back through the broken window, through which he'd tossed the last stun grenade. Danny nodded to the D.G. who had reached him and

noticed that she had her shotgun back in her hands. He sprang into the house doing a forward roll and coming back on his feet twelve feet into the hallway. As he did so a weapon opened up from under the stairway in front of him, ripping up the wall behind him but missing him. He crawled sideways behind a wooden cabinet and held the Uzi up over it directing a burst at the stairs.

Checking that the D.G. was under cover as well he lobbed a grenade over against the space where the fire was coming from. He heard a scream and started to get to his feet as he heard the shotgun boom deafeningly in his ear. Stunned for a moment, he could see a body sprawled out on the floor where the force of the grenade had hurled it. The D.G. reached forward and helped him to his feet as he dazedly shook his buzzing head.

"Sorry about the blast. We have to keep moving, Danny," she said,

He couldn't hear her but got the message and started for the stairs. Just then he heard shooting coming from the lounge that Scotty had rappelled into. She looked enquiringly at Danny. He shook his head and pointed towards the next floor.

She understood.

Scotty was well able to take care of himself. He started climbing the stairs followed closely by the D.G. On reaching the first floor without opposition, he saw wisps of smoke coming under the door, from the room where he estimated the second stun grenade had been thrown into. He kicked the door down and leapt inside, the adrenalin of battle now singing in his veins as his hearing started to return. He immediately saw a small group of four people sitting and lying on the ground, their hands to their ears. Some held their hands up as Danny crashed inside, his weapon ready to fire. The D.G. startled him by jumping in front of him and pushing the weapon down.

"They're staff, Danny! Take it easy."

He shuddered as he watched her move across and kneel in front of the most coherent of them. Looks of relief greeted her appearance. They obviously knew her from her previous visits. In a moment she was back again.

"It's okay, just some eardrums blasted." she said.

"What did they say? Who else is in the house? Where's Crawford?" he demanded, his eyes roving wildly with the action.

"Crawford's in the other wing across the way and he has one of the staff, Mrs. Brown with him. He dragged her out of here just a moment ago," she growled angrily.

He nodded.

"Doesn't surprise me. I knew he wouldn't go easily."

He looked bleakly at her.

"Want to leave this to me? He's screwed up my life and put my family in danger. You owe me this much."

She looked at him for a moment and sighed, lowering her shotgun.

"Okay Danny, he's yours, but take care he's an extremely dangerous man, well versed in weapons, as you probably know."

"Okay." he said and disappeared out the doorway onto the landing. He met Scotty who was slowly and carefully coming up the stairs. Scotty held up his thumb.

"One down below. I cleared the rest of the ground floor. No one else there. What's the situation?"

Danny told him and they looked at each other as they had many times before, prior to action. Nothing more needed to be said.

Danny moved to the door, carefully reached across, turned the handle gently and pushed it open. No burst of fire met them. Danny nodded and Scotty launched himself through the door in a forward roll with Danny immediately peering round the jam with his Uzi pistol at the ready. The room was empty. They crouched low and looked around fiercely, facing in different directions. Danny shrugged, straightening his legs.

"Where the fuck is he?" Scotty hissed.

Danny pointed.

"Must be in that small extension, that used to be the library. No window so we can't get him from behind. Good choice. Don't forget he's got a hostage."

They eased over to the library door and standing on each side they tried to hear if there was any noise inside. Nothing. Danny reached across and gently started to turn the handle. It was locked. There were a number of shots through the door and Danny cried out as a bullet ripped across his forearm. He snatched his arm back and gritted his teeth. The pain was unaccountably sharp and the open wound started dribbling blood. He pulled out a hand grenade and looked enquiringly at Scotty who nodded. There was risk in setting it off in terms of injuring the hostage but most of the force would be on their side. Scotty crawled behind a solid looking armchair. Danny then delicately pulled the pin and balanced the grenade on the handle as the metal strip whanged off. He dived for cover behind a second settee as the grenade exploded. The door flew off and they were still on their knees as Crawford leapt through the smoke holding a terrified woman by the neck. He pointed the pistol at them and screamed.

"Stay down, or I'll blow her fucking head off."

Danny cursed. They really had been caught with their pants down. Crawford had probably heard the metal part of the grenade whanging off and anticipated their plan. Crawford came further into the room pushing the woman ahead of him.

"Push them weapons away, you bastards. Now!" he screamed reading their hesitation. "Do it now!"

Reluctantly they did so as Crawford pushed further into the room, moving and shuffling towards the landing door. As he reached the middle of the room he spun around and started backing up. Crawford paused for a moment his face blackened with smoke and suffused with hatred as he looked at Danny.

"You had to screw it up, Quigley. I warned them to watch you. Now you've ruined everything. I'm finished. But you're finished too. I'd taken out insurance to make sure you got taken care of one way or the other today. I guess it's my lucky day. I get to do it myself."

He raised the weapon, pointing it at Danny and started squeezing the trigger. At that moment the woman he was holding slumped in a dead faint onto the ground and almost immediately a shotgun boomed out. Crawford was still standing there with his pistol as his midriff was almost cut in half. He fell over onto the floor, fountains of blood gushing out on the carpet. The D.G. stepped into the room, holding the shotgun.

She paused and looked closely at his dead body.

"Sorry Danny, but I'm glad it was me who killed him. I created the problem and now I solved it."

She dropped the shotgun on the carpet and collapsed onto a chair, waving Danny away as he started to approach her.

"Finish it now Danny. The blockhouse."

Danny and Scotty grabbed up their weapons and dashed onto the landing and out the front door, still alert to any further attacks. They sprinted across to the blockhouse as they saw Siobhan drive up cautiously and get out of the car. They reached the blockhouse and listened. Suddenly Danny felt his skin chill as he heard a keening sound coming from the hut. They looked at each other. They heard Siobhan's voice behind them.

"What's up? Is C.C. in there?"

With nothing but a glance between them, Danny and Scotty launched themselves at the front door and crashed through into the room. They stopped in astonishment. A big man was standing there looking down at a lifeless form on the ground. The keening sound was coming from him, tears running down his face as he gazed down on the dead man.

Suddenly there was a scream and Siobhan dashed past them and hurled herself at Courtney, who gazed dazedly at her.

"Oh Clive, what have they done to you?" she exclaimed, throwing her arms around him. His voice was broken as he answered her.

"Everything I've stood for, gentleness, love, caring for others. I was kidding myself. Something like this happens and it all falls away. I'm now a murderer," he whimpered.

He pushed her away gently and stumbled over towards the door, stopping beside Danny.

"That's Peterson lying there. He confessed to killing Patton and those three thugs in London … and other things. My God I've killed him! He still didn't deserve to die like this."

He looked up sadly at Danny, his face a mass of bruises and whispered. "Take care of her," nodding to Siobhan.

Then he stumbled out the door.

CHAPTER 76

Siobhan screamed and kept on screaming. Danny went over and held her.

The D.G. rushed into the room and looked around taking it all in. Scotty spoke quietly to her. She moved over to Danny and took over from him, hugging Siobhan. When at last she quietened down, the D.G. settled her into a chair. She looked at each of them directly for a long time. Then spoke quietly and authoritatively to them.

"Here's the deal. Terrorists attacked this place and we happened to be in the area discussing some possible initiatives for making the training camp more secure. Crawford was killed by the terrorists and we out-fought them. Scotty tells me Peterson, there, killed Patton and the three thugs in London. We give him to the police in London and Cheltenham. He wont be making any statements. If the real story blows up in my face I'm done for and I think you owe me at least that. What do you say?"

Danny and Scotty looked at each other and nodded. Danny asked.

"What about Strabane?"

She thought for moment.

"We place Peterson at the scene. An aborted assassination by terrorists hired by Peterson who subsequently got rid of them in case they were picked up and talked. How does that sound?"

They both nodded again.

Suddenly, Siobhan exploded with anger.

"It's not all right! What about poor Clive? Tortured and beaten and reduced to a shell of his previous self? What about justice for him?"

The D.G. stood up.

"Oh you mean the man who got in Scotty's car a moment ago and drove off? Certainly, if he'll give evidence we can lay charges. But against whom?"

She'd barely finished when Siobhan cried out and dashed out of the room followed by Scotty.

The D.G. walked over to Danny.

"Thanks Danny, for everything. We'll try to keep you and Scotty out of it, in the interests of national security, of course. I'll sort out the London side of things that D.C. White was investigating."

She hugged him then for a long moment, stepped back and handed him a card.

"What's that?" he asked, peering at it.

She smiled, a distant look in her eyes.

"I could have use for someone like you occasionally, Danny. Someone with your skills who could operate under the establishment radar so to speak, when I need them to."

He shook his head, starting to hand it back to her.

"No, this is it for me Rebecca. I'm sick of violence and the bodies that seem to stack up everywhere I go. I have a business to start up and make a success of."

She stepped back smiling faintly.

"Keep it. You'll be back Danny. We'll meet again, I promise you."

Outside Scotty was trying to calm Siobhan down and eventually got her to sit in a staff member's car that he had had requisitioned for her and Danny. The D.G. was calling in the local police as soon as they cleared the gates.

Scotty was given another staff car and he and Danny gave each other a hug. Scotty climbed into the vehicle ready to follow his car out of the grounds. As Danny went to follow suit the D.G. threw the Heckler and Koch Gll at him, which he caught smartly.

"You like this one Danny. Keep it as a souvenir. You never know," she finished, pursing her lips thoughtfully.

Danny smiled despite himself and said nothing. He turned the staff car round and drove carefully down the driveway past the car that D.C. White had been killed in. He was aware that Scotty would be behind him for a few miles before he cut off towards Wales.

He reached across and squeezed Siobhan's hand.

"You're going home," he whispered.

CHAPTER 77

It was about an hour later before Danny and Siobhan started down towards the M25. He had intended to stay at his fire-blackened house in London for the night, but when he glanced at her he could see that she was all in. Events of the past few days had finally caught up with her with a vengeance: The kidnapping, the assassination attempt, the killings, and the terrible events that happened at the training camp, especially where Courtney's disappearance was concerned. He spotted a new American style motel close to the M25 and swung over into the parking lot. She looked up in surprise.

"Why are we stopping?" she asked, as she looked up at the motel sign. Misinterpreting his motives, she raised her hands and went as if to push him away.

"Oh Danny, I'm sorry. I just couldn't ..."

He reached across and put his hand on her mouth gently.

"You're all in, kid. I think I better get you a comfortable bed for the night. Alone." he emphasized. "It'd be another hour before we got into the center of London at this stage. We really need to get you wrapped up in a warm bed for about ten hours. A cup of tea to start with, perhaps. Okay?"

She nodded, tears starting to show in her eyes. Danny went into the office and arranged for a ground floor room with two beds. It had tea and coffee facilities as well, so they were all set. Once inside they started to relax and Siobhan went for a quick shower and put the same clothes on again. She then jotted down a short list of items that Danny promised he'd slip out and pick up for her, and tossed it casually to him as he sat on his bed.

As she was walking back past the door they heard a knock and, without thinking she reached to open it. Danny jumped to his feet shouting, "no Siobhan!" but it was too late.

The door burst open and two men burst into the room. One was a large bulky man who jumped in past the startled girl, pushing her to one side, causing her to fall on the floor. The second was a thin, short, narrow-faced individual, who leapt over and placed a small pistol to Siobhan's head. The bulky man's face was horribly scarred and one of his eyes appeared to be without any eyelashes. Siobhan stared horrified at him. But it was what was in the man's hand that stopped Danny cold: an Austrian Glock, pointed right at him.

"Just what the hell are you after mate? We could barely afford the motel, if you're after money."

The man chuckled.

"No I'm not after money, Danny. Just sweet revenge. I brought along a wee friend, Tommy Doherty there, to make sure you don't get up to any of your tricks."

"Look I've never seen you in my life before. Just what in God's name is this all about? Who the hell are you? Just how do you know my name?"

The man chuckled again sending a chill up Danny's spine. There was something incredibly evil about him and his eyes pierced Danny like a snake about to devour its prey.

"Don't recognize me, Danny? I'm not surprised. I have changed a wee bit and that's down to you me boyo."

As he spoke Danny started to listen to the Irish accent as his mind struggled desperately to figure out what this was about. Something about the accent and the man's stature started bells of alarm off in his head. The man grinned, showing yellowed teeth and a gap in the front. It wasn't a smile of friendship. The man spoke again as Siobhan started sobbing and trying to crawl backwards away from her captor. Tommy grabbed her by the hair and his eyes lit up with satisfaction at her cry of pain. The big man grinned mirthlessly.

"I'll take you out of your agony, Danny. Remember Paddy from Portadown? You left me lying in a hayshed that caught fire. You left me there to burn, but those pigs you were with pulled me out from under a burning bale. You were long gone by then, Danny. Couldn't care less could you?"

CHAPTER 78

Danny stared at the man, his mind reeling. That incident was light years ago and here was this man standing in front of him talking about revenge.

"Wondering why I waited so long Danny? I was in prison. How about that? Seven years of it no less, and every day I thought of you and what I would do when I found you. I saw your picture in the paper about two weeks ago and then a Colonel Crawford called me and told me I might have a chance soon to get my hands on you. Then he contacted me today that you might be paying a call on him back there if I was interested. Told me I should wait outside for you. Unfortunately, I got here too late to catch you going in, but here we are nice and cozy."

He chuckled.

Danny's mind went back to Crawford's last remark.

"I'd taken out insurance to make sure you die today, one way or the other, but I guess it's my lucky day."

Crawford knew that Paddy was waiting for him outside the training camp with hate in his heart. Danny's heart was in his boots right then and his eyes flicked to Siobhan. Paddy caught his glance.

"Don't worry about her Danny. I have it all planned out. Tommy would like a little fun with her first. I might even join him when he's warmed her up for me. After we've finished with her she wont suffer for very long. We take no prisoners.

Isn't that what you SAS lads do sometimes when it suits you?" he taunted.

Danny lifted one of his hands and eased up off the bed .

"Look Paddy, what's done is done. Okay, I plead guilty if that's what you want but she's done nothing. She's a nurse for Christ sake! Just let her go and you and I can settle this. You've got the guns and you got me dead to rights. Okay?"

"No, it's not okay," he snarled. "Do you know what happened to my sister who you were screwing, just to get to us? I'll tell you, Danny. She went to prison and her life was hell when it was discovered that she'd been sleeping with one of the pigs. She was found in her cell one night hanged. How's that for justice? So no, your little missy won't be going anywhere."

Danny knew he and Siobhan were moments from death. He decided to change tactics and get Paddy mad enough to come closer to him and possibly get a chance to disarm him.

"She was just as big a loser as you Paddy. You were so dumb you couldn't see you were being set up. Sure I left you in the fire. That was fine with me. I'd have shoved her in there too, given half a chance."

Siobhan gasped.

Paddy smirked knowingly. He didn't move.

Danny knew the game was over but he tried one more time.

"Not stupid Paddy?" he taunted. "Remember that time we had a fight? I let you win, you big tub of lard. I could have taken you apart in seconds then."

This time he struck a nerve.

"You're fucking lying you bastard! I beat you fair and square! You were useless you Brit bastard. I would have crippled you for life if they hadn't pulled me off you!"

Danny chuckled, shaking his head.

"Afraid not Paddy. I let you win just to suck your IRA friends in and they bought me, didn't they? Thanks to you, you dumb Paddy!"

Something unhinged in Paddy's mind right then. He charged Danny, screaming at him as spittle came flying out of his mouth, and lashed out at his face with the weapon. Danny knew he had only one chance to survive the situation and he took it. He blocked the weapon and chopped it sideways sending it flying off into the floor. He followed it up with a double chop to Paddy's carotid arteries and even though he was probably already dead on his feet, followed it with a savage upward thrust to the throat with his elbow, crushing it. He couldn't have survived such a ferocious attack and his sudden slump to the floor caught Danny by surprise. He had planned to use Paddy's body as a barrier to launch an attack on Tommy, who had released Siobhain and leapt forward with his weapon ready.

Now he stood six feet from Danny, his lips parted in a sneer as he moved closer, his finger tightening on the trigger.

"Old Paddy must have had the gift of foresight," he chuckled.

"Practically insisted I come along. Imagine that. You'll be joining him in a moment and you wont be the first Brit I've sent to hell. Bye bye me boyo, as Paddy would say. Your girl friend wont be far behind you after I've had some fun with her."

Danny braced himself for the bullet.

Across the room Siobhain shouted "No!"

There was a tinkling of glass and a shaft was suddenly embedded in Tommy's head, sticking out the other side. An astonished look crossed his face as he tried to turn but failing, his legs suddenly went from under him and he fell.

Danny breathed

"Scotty,"

At the same moment the door crashed open and Scotty stood there, his eyes wide and alert as he scoured the room.

"Sorry it took so long Danny. I could hear his voice but I hadn't a chance until he stepped forward that last pace and I got a clear shot from the window."

He looked closely at Danny.

"Jesus, you almost got yourself terminated mate. Shows you what six months as a civvy street can do to one."

Siobhan rushed over and threw her arms around Danny, who was still looking disbelievingly at Scotty.

"I thought you were on the way to Hereford. How the hell did you end up here at this particular moment?" Scotty made a face.

"We pulled out behind you after you left the training camp and another car did too, ahead of us with what appeared to be two men in it. I didn't think much of it until it became obvious that they were following you. I didn't know if the D.G. had put a tail on you for your safety or what the score was, so I stuck on their tail." He waved his arms, "and a bloody good job I did, isn't it?"

He slapped Scotty on both shoulders and hugged him. Siobhan did so too and Scotty beamed all over. He backed off after a decent interval.

"You know," he said "I can't wait to get back to Hereford for some peace and quiet. This action is killing me."

He nodded to the two dead men.

"I'll take them with me and give them both a decent burial in Wales. After all they're both Celts so we can't leave them here on English soil, can we?"

Despite himself Danny grinned. Siobhan looked questioningly at him.

"By burial, Siobhan, he means some two hundred foot dry well in the Welsh mountains where Special Branch will never find them. Right Scotty?"

Scotty grinned.

"What are friends for after all, Danny?"

CHAPTER 79

12 months later

When Danny flew into Strandhill in Sligo he was nearly bowled over by Siobhan who dragged him out to the car, still chattering away. They hadn't met face to face for twelve months but had been in touch regularly during that time. In a way, Danny had been glad of the separation, as he worked on his business and saw his divorce finalized. It was Siobhan who had signaled that she was ready to meet him again. Now she was animated and laughing and her eyes were sparkling.

"We're booked into Mrs. McKeever's Bed and Breakfast and she has given us the prize suite, as she calls it, so no mercy tonight, Danny." she added.

Danny grinned.

"Hey, why so desperate sweetheart? I'm here and I'm taking Monday off as well, so we'll have loads of time for any naughtiness you might have in mind," he said hugging her.

There was something in her eyes that somehow disquieted him, despite her exuberance. She reached across holding his hand and looked briefly at him.

"There's somewhere I want to show you first Danny. A part of Sligo you haven't seen yet. I think you'll love it."

"Oh, surprises so soon? What is this place you're taking me to then?"

She looked teasingly at him.

"Wait and see," she said. "Oh by the way, how are Fiona and Allison?"

He took a deep breath.

" Both well thanks. As you know, Fiona has custody but we agreed on Allison seeing me regularly. It's working out thanks."

She nodded sympathetically glancing briefly across at his face. He shut up, taking in the beautiful green lush countryside and Ben Bulben in the distance. He remembered the day he climbed to the top with Courtney.

"Has C.C. surfaced at all?" he asked quietly.

She shook her head sadly.

"Not a sight nor sound since that night. I fear that he's probably dead from the cancer by now. I'd dearly love to know for sure. He only had a short time to live, as you know, and thank goodness he'd taken care of all the paper work for the transition of his business interests ."

He nodded, saying nothing. Even in the short time that C.C. had known him he had set up a legal arrangement for Danny to take over his business and all accruals coming in from existing clients. These had gone straight across to Siobhain for the Sligo businesses. He would never forget the amazing individual who had so transformed his life.

He was jolted out of his thought when the car came to a sudden stop and he saw that it was pulled off on the side of the road. The grass was flattened which suggested that lots of cars stopped there. He sighed, clambering out, determined not to spoil her mood of excitement. They started walking up a gravel track and met some people coming down. They walked for some twenty minutes and came out on a large grassy knoll on which stood a gigantic stone-covered monument. He turned and looked around, startled to see that, right then, he seemed to be standing right on top of the world. Around him in all directions stretched landscapes of the sea, mountains, rivers and lakes, with white wispy clouds scudding past. The sky was a deep cobalt blue and the sun poured through the gaps in the clouds as they sailed by. Ben Bulben loomed off in the distance.

He whistled.

"This is incredible!" he gasped. "What is this place?"

She pointed to the mound of stones.

"Queen Maeve's grave. It's stood there for over a thousand years. Isn't that something?"

He nodded moving closer and examined the grave.

"Impressive, I must say."

He turned and looked closely at her.

"Why do I feel that there is more to this than visiting a mound of rocks?" he asked.

Her face clouded.

"I just wanted you to realize that blips occur in life but that life goes on, sometimes for a thousand years Danny, so lots of time to make things right. To correct mistakes. To start again."

He turned her around facing him.

"What exactly is this about Siobhan?" he asked. "Go on tell me for Gods sake."

She was silent for a long moment.

"I know you hoped to take up the work that C.C. was doing over here but I understand you were just starting out learning the ropes. I know you're doing well as a new person coming into the business and I know you won an award for the top rookie of the year a month ago. You also passed on all C.C.'s accrual commission to us. That's great but our establishment out on the lake devours money, with over a hundred mouths to feed not to mention their travel and medical bills."

She paused suddenly in mid sentence.

"Go on." he urged.

"We have to close it at the end of this month and send all those women away," she burst out, tears now starting to gather on her eyelashes.

"God I didn't mean to collapse like this. I meant to be so calm, but just saying it out loud. It's so final."

He held her for a long time and then stood back, observing her closely.

"How much would it take to keep it open, Siobhan?"

She looked at him.

"Five hundred thousand would keep it open for twelve months," she replied, looking askance at him.

"Euros or sterling?"

"Euros of course."

He nodded looking off into the distance. Then his head snapped back as if he'd come to some decision.

"Stay here a moment. I need to make a call."

He moved around the side of the mound extracting his mobile phone as he did so. Her voice was on the phone immediately and she sounded as if she was right beside him.

"I got three phone messages on my voice mail this week from you," he said. "I wasn't going to call you back."

"I knew you would call, Danny," she answered.

"I need money," he said.

"How much money?" she asked.

"Five hundred thousand."

"What? How much?" Her voice went up several octaves, then a moment later, "Sterling or euros?"

He thought quickly.

"Sterling of course."

"OK. Where and when Danny?"

He took a slip of paper out and rattled off some bank numbers. He could hear her breath on the line.

"My office, 10 am next Tuesday, Danny. I have a job for you," she paused. "That will give you time to get back from Ireland."

How the hell did she know he was in Ireland, he wondered.

The D.G. hung up.

OTHER BOOKS
BY
RUSS MCDEVITT

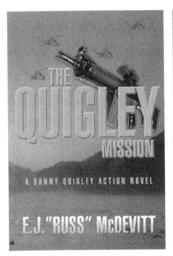

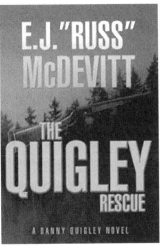

AVAILABLE THROUGH **RUSSMCDEVITT.COM**
AND OTHER LEADING BOOK SELLERS

ALSO AVAILABLE ON:

amazon kindle

Made in the USA
Charleston, SC
10 November 2016